The Eagle Has Fallen

The Eagle Has Fallen

To Andy,

Best Wishes

Brian Young (signature)

Brian Young

© Brian Young, 2012

Published by FirstFilm Production

A CIP catalogue record for this book is available from the British Library.

ISBN 978-0-9573004-0-8

Prepared and printed by:

York Publishing Services Ltd
64 Hallfield Road
Layerthorpe
York YO31 7ZQ

Tel: 01904 431213

Website: www.yps-publishing.co.uk

To Jacqui, Emma and Katie
with all my love

Contents

Acknowledgements

To Gary Sweeney, Brian Smith and Keiran Morley who all helped with ideas and versions of manuscripts.

In particular for the late David Vickery who set me on my way. Thank you.

Introduction – The Eagle Has Fallen

This book is written as a re collection of the events surrounding what happened in Northern Britain and the rest of the Roman Empire, when Hadrian came to power in 117AD. This was a turbulent period in Roman history. Of the three legions based in Britain, the Ninth occupied a permanent fort in York. This was the centre of the largest and most hostile British tribe: the Brigantes.

The Brigantes streched from Southern Scotland all the way down to north Derbyshire. The Romans believed the tribe to be 'pacified' and gave no thought of any warnings that had been given.

This is the story of Romes's most mysterious vanished Legion. Over 80% of this novel is based upon factual characters and events.

My story eschews international politics, military stability, global economics and, indeed, the day-to-day flashpoints of the Roman Empire. That empire was a sprawling institution, frequently consumed with bitter power struggles far removed from the diplomacy we take for granted in today's political climate. During the period of the First Century A.D., disputes tended to be settled at the point of a sword; or, if more tact was required, a wine goblet liberally laced with hemlock.

But it is the very rowdiness of ancient Rome, a paradoxical civilization where philosophy, chivalry and democratic ideals existed alongside slavery, corruption and brutal violence, where larger-than-life characters lived incredibly colourful – and often extremely short – lives, that drew me to such a richly inspirational setting in the first place.

Brian Young

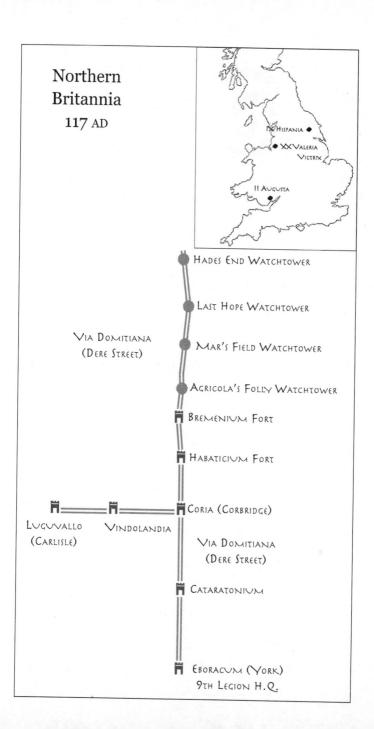

Northern Britannia

117 AD

IX HISPANIA

XX VALERIA VICTRIX

II AUGUSTA

HADES END WATCHTOWER

LAST HOPE WATCHTOWER

VIA DOMITIANA
(DERE STREET)

MAR'S FIELD WATCHTOWER

AGRICOLA'S FOLLY WATCHTOWER

BREMENIUM FORT

HABATICIUM FORT

CORIA (CORBRIDGE)

LUGUVALLO
(CARLISLE)

VINDOLANDIA

VIA DOMITIANA
(DERE STREET)

CATARATONIUM

EBORACUM (YORK)
9TH LEGION H.Q.

SPQR

War gives the right of the conquerors to impose
any conditions they please upon the vanquished.

Julius Caesar

I Adopted Son

3pm, 16 August, 117AD: the countryside outside Antioch, the Roman Province of Syria

Under the relentless Syrian sun, two bare-chested men crouched, spears at the ready. They peered into the undergrowth. Silent, motionless, barely daring to breathe.

One of them – Hadrian – stood like a statue, moving only his eyes as he searched the undergrowth beyond the line of trees. A trickle of sweat ran down his cheek and into his beard, already matted with perspiration. To the right of him, Turbo pointed one finger and Hadrian followed the direction with his eyes. Yes: almost invisible in the shadows, there they were – the rosette patterns of a leopard's hide!

This was the moment of greatest danger. Everyone knew that leopards were even more vicious than tigers, especially when being hunted. As usual, Hadrian wore no helmet, but today, neither did he have armour nor mail to protect him. Only his hunting spear. And his most trusted companion.

With infinite slowness, Hadrian eased back his spear-arm for the throw, held his aim steadily for a moment ...

Pounding hooves of a horse registered in their taut awareness. Hadrian started with surprise. The undergrowth quivered, and the great cat shot from cover, a colourful blur that vanished before either hunter could fully focus on it.

Turbo glanced anxiously at Hadrian. His passion for hunting was legendary; how would he react to this disturbance?

Hadrian lowered his spear and burst into a laugh, tension draining from his body.

"Ah well, my friend," he said. "Plenty more leopards in this country!"

"Yes, sir," smiled the general. It was a rare honour indeed to be called 'friend' by your commander, especially one who was *de facto* heir to the throne. But they were friends. And future emperors perhaps needed friends more than anyone else –especially those they could depend on, without question.

"I wonder who that fool of a rider is and what he's doing?" Hadrian turned his attention to the approaching horseman. "I left orders we were not to be disturbed."

Turbo was first to spot the plume of feathers on the rider's spear. Imperial business. They exchanged a questioning glance.

"Further expansions to the empire?" suggested Turbo, and they both laughed.

"After conquering the Parthians, I can't imagine where the Emperor would take his legions next," said Hadrian. "Unless he's following the footsteps of Alexander and has invaded India!"

The rider rode steadily nearer. There was no doubt for whom the despatch was intended. Who else would Trajan write to in Antioch but his adopted son Hadrian, the Commander of the Eastern Provinces?

Finally the rider arrived, jumped from his horse and saluted. He was grimy, dripping with sweat and smelled like his horse.

Hadrian returned the salute. He studied the rider. He must have come over the sea and arrived at the coast of Syria, riding inland and changing fresh horses at forts along the way. Using these means, and bearing the Imperial imprimatur to ensure quick passage, it was possible to travel from Italy to Antioch in seven days.

"From Rome?"

"From Selinus, Commander."

"*Where?*"

"I've heard of it," said Turbo. "A sleepy little seaside place in Cilicia."

Hadrian thought for a moment. What was Trajan doing in a place like that? He had left the Parthian battlefield several weeks ago, suffering from heatstroke and exhaustion, sending Hadrian back to Syria. His plan had been to sail back to Rome. So what had happened? Surely not a shipwreck? It was useless speculating.

"Give me the despatch."

The rider dug in his satchel, and passed over an ornate scroll. Hadrian broke open the seal, unrolled it and started to read:

My much beloved son.

It was from Plotina, then. Trajan's wife had always had a tender love for him. He read on:

It is with deep regret that I must tell you of our news. Your beloved father is dead.

A thousand memories and images flooded his mind: Trajan adopting him into the family at the age of ten, his endless campaigns, his triumphs, his new provinces, the way he had reshaped Rome with marvellous new buildings and public spaces. Trajan *was* Rome, and Rome had never been stronger. The Senate had given him the simple yet impressive honorific *Optimus*, the best. And now he was dust.

"*Sic transit gloria mundi*," he murmured. Thus passes the glory of the world.

But what happened next? And how would this affect Hadrian in his role as Commander of the Eastern Provinces?

His death comes as a great shock to us all and the only mercy was that it was swift. As you know, it was always our intention to formally transfer full power to you. No official document existed, but your father was able to dictate and sign a Will of Testament on his deathbed, adopting you as heir. Attianus as Head of the Praetorian Guard countersigned the document, and a priest witnessed it.

Hadrian paused again. Something didn't feel quite right about this. It was too formal and officious, as if Plotina was relating a version for another audience – going to great lengths to underline the document's authenticity. Was Trajan really able to dictate and sign the paper?

He thought back to the last time he had seen his revered adoptive father, Trajan's face pale, a palsy about his limbs, sweat running into his half-closed eyes. Of course, the extreme heat and the rigours of campaigning could do that to any man; but had he really recovered?

He pictured him, tossed about on the tiny boat on the Mediterranean, sailing back to Rome, slipping into a coma perhaps...but regardless of the truth, Plotina's version was clearly in his best interests, how ever it came to be. He bent over the scroll again, shading his eyes against the harsh Syrian summer sun, and read:

I have written to the Senate with a copy of the parchment showing your succession and confirming your status as the true heir. You know well, much beloved son, that there are those in the Senate who would be only too glad of any irregularities in the succession to exploit for their own ends. Until your confirmation is official, therefore, I urge you to remain at Antioch. Say nothing. Restrain your mourning for your honoured father until the news is known to all. It will be one week before the Senate knows what you now know. Remain calm and outwardly quiet, despite your inner turmoil. For I know you loved the Emperor as he loved you. I pray to the gods for you, and for your future. Your loving mother, Plotina.

Hadrian rolled up the scroll, and stood for a few moments in silence. Then he picked up his cloak and draped it over his shoulder.

"Rider."

"Sir!"

"How old is this message?"

"Five days, Commander."

"Five days!"

"Yes, sir," stammered the rider. "The first boat I boarded had to return to port when it was holed on a rock outside the harbour. I got here as soon as I could, sir."

Hadrian looked him in the eye and smiled reassuringly.

"I'm sure you did."

There was a silence while Hadrian considered.

"Very well," said Hadrian. "Ride to Antioch, get a bath and some rest. You've earned it."

"Thank you, Commander." The rider mounted and urged his horse inland.

Five days. So the news would be known to the Senate in three days or less. And from there, like a rock tossed into a pond the news would ripple on to the furthest outposts of the empire. And what disorder would those ripples cause?

"Turbo!" he called.

The general walked over to him.

"What news, Commander?"

"We're returning to the camp," he said. "We have plans to make."

*

Like the rest of the city, the fort at Antioch was imposing, monumental, glorious: an impressive signal to the rest of the world.

Hadrian and Turbo sat in the courtyard of the Principia in the fort. Although still hot, the sun was no longer blistering and it was pleasant in the garden. Lilies perfumed the evening air, caught on a light breeze. Guards stood at a discreet distance, out of earshot.

It felt good to have bathed and changed. Even better to have confided in Turbo. Hadrian poured vintage Falernian into two goblets, the wine still chilled from its subterranean cellarage. He raised his goblet in a timeless gesture. Turbo did likewise.

"To you," said Turbo, adding in a low voice, "Emperor of Rome."

Hadrian cast a glance at the guards but they betrayed no sign of having heard. He grinned.

"Not quite yet, friend," he said.

"Why not? The soldiers love you. Your appointment will be widely acclaimed."

Hadrian said nothing for a moment. He felt the security of the massive fort; of Antioch, the magnificent second city of the empire, capital of the East, a second Rome; of his five legions and thirty thousand regular soldiers at his command. Yet the East was not the West, Antioch was not Rome and five legions were not the Roman army.

"There are plenty of men who would disagree with you," he said. "Plenty of senators... and a number of Trajan's closest generals. The gods know I loved the man, yet at times like this..."

"We need to move quickly," agreed Turbo. "The Senate would appoint a politician as Emperor if they could."

Hadrian looked out across the camp.

"First things first," he said. "We need to appoint our own people to positions of power, especially across Rome. The next Consul of the Senate will be our choice. We must have a representative of the army there."

Turbo nodded, taking a sip from his goblet.

"Now is the time for us to act – to put strategies in place to make our position impregnable," added Hadrian.

He took a mouthful of wine and lost himself in contemplation for a moment. This was everything he had always wanted. And yet was not. He would be emperor but not by consensus – and not yet securely.

Hadrian looked up at Turbo. "After Trajan's cremation, Attianus will return back to Rome. He will watch the Senate for us and send reports on what is happening."

"Sensible, Caesar," whispered Turbo. "Very sensible."

"Commander," said Hadrian. "For now."

*

Three days after that evening, the great and good of the military were gathered in the splendid briefing room at Antioch. The Legates of the Fifth, Seventh, Tenth, Fifteenth and Twenty-fifth Legions, together with their advisers and secretaries, were discussing the orders for the week.

Turbo, as Legate of the Fifth, was in the thick of business. Hadrian heard that the Fifteenth Legion First Cohort was building a bridge, the Second Cohort of the Seventh was continuing its road-building project, and the Second and Third Century from the Twenty-fifth were supervising a tribal meeting: but the words flowed over his head. What did it matter? What did any of it matter? His plans were made. But the grief raging inside him cried out for release, while he had to smile and chat to generals as though nothing was amiss.

A guard entered the room, saluted, and approached Hadrian. He bent down and whispered in his ear.

"Sir, a rider has been sighted coming from the coast road. He bears a spear with a black cloth wrapped around its point."

Such a banner meant only one thing. The Emperor was dead.

Hadrian covered his face with his hands and let out a howl of pain. The generals and their advisers were shocked into silence. Turbo watched as tears ran through the Commander's fingers. He rose to his feet, and everyone in the room followed his example.

Publius Aelius Hadrianus continued to sob for his adoptive father.

*

Later that day the fort was bustling. The large briefing room was now almost empty of officers and instead filled with scribes.

"...and I promise to rule wisely and justly over Rome, its provinces and its possessions. Sign it *Imperator Caesar Divi Traiani Hadrianus Augustus*. Got that?"

"Yes, Caesar," said a secretary.

"Turbo, assemble the Fifth here at the fort. I need to make a public announcement."

"Yes, Caesar," replied Turbo, despatching his underlings in his turn.

"Send formal notices to all other legions throughout the Empire."

"At once, Caesar."

That evening, on the battlements of the colossal fort, pinnacle of the glorious city of Syrian Antioch, the new Emperor Hadrian proudly stood, framed by two enormous braziers. Sparks flew upwards and the flames bathed him in lurid, semi-divine luminescence and shadow. The shouts of approval from the mass of soldiers below were almost deafening.

"Hail, Caesar! Hail, Caesar! Hail, Caesar!"

Hadrian turned.

Turbo was at his side. "Glorious," he said.

"Yes," Hadrian agreed. "But we must ensure that it's more than a passing glory. Pack your kit – we're going to Rome."

*

The comfortable life of Marcus Valerius Quietus was about to change forever.

On a sunny morning, in the briefing room crowded with centurions, armour and helmets buffed and gleaming, Quietus stood with his four fellow tribunes, awaiting the commander of the First Cohort. He looked at his colleagues, each like himself a highborn young man, destined for importance – greatness, even. History beckoned. And for men of the right standing – with the right connections – it wasn't too hard to expect a bright future.

They were all *Tribuni Angusticlavii*, 'narrow band tribunes'. He fingered the fine-striped tunic under his body armour that gave the rank its name. Each had won in the lottery of birth: Roman citizenship, noble rank, influential family.

Take Vecentus, there. He was little more than a youth who still loved to play pranks on his comrades – but his father was a senator, therefore he was esteemed. And Parmenes – who was said to be distantly related to Trajan, whether it was true or not. To share a bloodline with an emperor, however remotely, was always useful.

Marcus himself was son of Lucius Quietus, provincial governor of Judea. And although only a junior tribune, hadn't he already caught the eye of the legate? To be put in charge of an *ala* of cavalry was an honour indeed at his age, even if it was only for a drill. It was opportunity enough to show them just what he could do. His head whirled for a second with some of the unorthodox yet brilliant tactics he'd been working on.

The door opened and Rufo entered, his face like well-tanned leather. He smiled at them: "Good morning, gentlemen."

"Good morning, Centurion," came a chorus of voices.

Here thought Marcus, was the real heart of the legion: the *Praefectus castrorum* or Camp Prefect. A career soldier from his centurion's helmet plume to his hob-nailed *caligae*.

Of the sixty centurions in the Twelfth Legion, Rufo was the foremost: a former chief centurion, he was third in command of the legion. He had that honour, not because of his birth or his familial status, but because he was better than anyone else at his job. His advice was valued by the legate himself, and rightly so: those twenty years of hard campaigning meant he knew every trick in the book – and plenty that weren't.

Marcus' fingers unconsciously touched his narrow-striped tunic once again. Although he was only a junior officer, he was technically fourth in command of the legion – with the rest of his colleagues. His mind galloped off on a momentary fantasy: the legate, the senior tribune, the camp prefect all wiped out by some swift and terrible uprising, and he, Marcus Valerius, in charge of over five thousand legionaries!

Leading the famous *XII Fulminata* forward, its thunderbolt emblem striking fear into the hearts of the barbarians, he'd crush that revolt and avenge the deaths of the legate and his general staff. The barbarian chieftain, bloodied, on his knees before him, bowed his head and surrendered his sword, held out on both hands; the legionaries calling out his name in triumphant praise! And what was this? A message from Trajan himself, confirming Marcus Valerius' appointment as *Legatus Legionis* ...

"Tribune Quietus, do you remember the order of action?"

Rufo's voice, always calm, always alert, dispelled Marcus's flight of fancy like a gust of wind. A twinkle in Rufo's eye told Marcus that he guessed where his mind had been.

"Yes, Centurion," he answered with alacrity. Here was reality. Marcus smiled to himself.

Rufo looked over the five young tribunes in the room.

"Gentlemen, as you know, today we are practising our siege techniques. Yes, it's a drill, but do not undervalue it on that account. Remember what Caesar said: 'It would not be wrong to call our drills bloodless battles, and our battles bloody drills.' And knowing the Thunderbolt Twelfth as I do, it may not be entirely bloodless either."

Laughter filled the room.

"Every unit will be involved," continued Rufo. "Since this is a live firing exercise, I expect you all to keep your positions until you receive your orders. Now, Tribune Quietus."

Quietus looked at the Praefectus castrorum. "Yes, Sir," he began. "First order is for the Scorpions. On the command, bolt firing to commence on fixed positions within the enemy fort."

Rufo nodded.

"Second order is for the Onagers. On the command, stone throwing will commence on fixed positions within the enemy fort. The Onager equipment should be set up a minimum of one hundred feet from our own units."

"Why so?" asked Rufo, his eyes keen.

"During one siege in Gallia, the Onager misfired, killing and maiming several crewmen."

"Very good," commended Rufo. "Yes, it's not called the Wild Ass for nothing!"

There was more laughter, and some rueful smiles from the centurions who'd had dealings with the unruly mechanical beast.

"We're going to try something different with the infantry and archers today," said Rufo. "We've heard from Dacia that the enemy cavalry charged headlong into our troops there. Total disregard for danger.

So today I want every cohort six lines deep when they go into battle. Behind them will be two lines of archers who will fire over their heads. So make sure they keep their heads down; we don't want to have to open the burial fund just yet!"

The officers chuckled.

"First, Third and Ninth Cohorts will advance on the main line. Cohorts Two, Six and Eight will be on the left, Four, Five and Seven on the right flank. Auxiliary Cavalry ala One will remain on the left flank and, on command, will ride round the side of the fort. The Auxiliary Cavalry *ala* Two will ride round the right flank on command."

Marcus's pulse quickened on hearing his unit named. Rufo smiled at him.

"I want to see nice tight wheels on the obstacle course we set up for your approach."

"Yes, Sir," said Marcus, and smiled back.

"Once the troops approach the walls I want ladders up smartly and men on the top battlements. First complete cohort up gets a generous measure of my best wine!"

The officers cheered and grinned.

"All right, Fortuna be with you, gentlemen." Rufo saluted and the centurions and the young tribunes returned the salute.

As they turned to leave, they heard the sound of hooves signalling a dispatch rider outside the walls. The rider dismounted and the door was flung open by a dusty and sweating soldier looked round the group who saluted Marcus.

"Excuse me, Tribune. Urgent message from the legate. He wants to see you."

"Now?" said Marcus. "Can't it wait until after the drill?"

"No sir, the legate said *'with immediate haste'*. I'm to escort you back."

Marcus grimaced at the other junior tribunes and several of them patted his shoulders in consolation. At the same time, his heart was pounding. Why did the legion commander want to see him so urgently? Could it be that promotion he'd prayed to the gods about?

"Let's go," he said, and the two soldiers left the room.

*

The two horses kicked up dust as they galloped along the sun-baked road. Marcus's mind was crowded with thoughts. Part of him was back with his comrades, who would be heading out to the training field shortly, and he wished he could be with them. The drill would go ahead as planned, but without his flashes of genius. He grinned to himself briefly.

But the interview with his commander drove the training field and his precision manoeuvres out of his head. Perhaps it *was* his promotion. He'd had a premonition something big was going to happen today. And the legate had already looked on him with favour. The promotion would be deeply satisfying in itself, of course; but it would also be the next step in his grander plan. He had it all laid out: civic life after the army, becoming a junior magistrate, working his way up to becoming a tribune in a province, then formal enrolment within the senate, a succession of magisterial posts, and back to the army as *Legatus Legionis:* head of his own legion. That role would mark him out as a deputy of the emperor, acting on his authority. As a result, such leaders were handpicked by the emperor himself. And was it foolish to think he could go even further? Other men had risen through the army to wear the imperial purple, including Trajan himself. He smiled again at his presumption.

Yes, there would be plenty of time for all of that, and other things besides. A family, children,...and that brought him on to Petronia.

"*Petronia pulcherrima*," he said, melodiously. Most beautiful Petronia. He loved to call her that.

He could see her before him now, her lustrous golden hair, her blue eyes and lips that often held a mocking smile, although he had known them look at him also with adoration. And something more than adoration... he grinned. It would be a busy life, but being married to him would certainly bring its share of compensations as his grand plan unfolded.

Lost in his thoughts, the five miles to the camp flew past. Now they were coming to the end of the open fields and approached the road leading into the fort. Marcus glanced at the series of steep defensive ditches on either side of the road. His military training had changed the way he looked at things. These ditches were no longer inconvenient holes in the ground, but tactical vantage points. Any attackers nudged off the road would have to make the near vertical climb out of the ditch to continue the assault on the fort, and even if they managed that, they would be out in the open and defenceless, a clear target for the weighted javelins and arrows raining down from the defenders above.

Marcus' eyes rose to take in the soldiers on the battlement fifty feet above him. Stone walls, thick and high, immune to the torch and the battering ram. He smiled with approval and pride. A pair of wooden towers stood above the gateway, staffed by lookouts constantly scanning the countryside. Two soldiers sat at a table next to the massive wooden gate, and one signalled for them to halt. Marcus and his escort dismounted.

"Password," said one of the guards.

"Heron," replied the escort.

One of the guards checked a papyrus sheet pinned to a board in front of him. They both stood, saluted Marcus and moved aside to admit them both. Marcus led his mount through the gateway and turned the horse's head towards the living quarters.

"This way, Tribune," said the soldier, directing him in the opposite direction.

"I need to get cleaned up first," said Marcus.

"Legate's orders, sir. I was to bring you directly."

Marcus looked at the young soldier, and saw in his face fearfulness that Marcus would ignore him and put him in an impossible position. The junior tribune looked down at his uniform at the mud and dust from the gallop that had obliterated the effects of its earlier polishing.

Marcus sighed, "So be it," and waited while the soldier mounted.

The horses walked on in single file, passing down the Praetoria. As with all Roman camps, large or small, the layout was identical. The Principia was always in the centre. They trotted down the stone road, avoiding the sunken drains on each side near the store rooms lining the route. Past the hospital, barracks, granaries: all plastered and whitewashed, all bearing identification signs. A little piece of Rome in a foreign land, structured, clean and in good order. The Roman way.

Both men dismounted before the single entrance archway of the Principia. Two guards saluted Marcus, and the escort explained their business. A guard left quickly and returned a minute later, gesturing to them to follow him inside.

Marcus had never entered this military holy of holies. He realised he was sweating slightly and wiped his brow. The centre of the courtyard was open to the sky, the surrounding roof dressed with immaculate terracotta, lush flowering shrubs fragranced the air. Marcus caught the distinctive smell of jasmine among the air of perfumes.

A shortly statured man came out into the courtyard, the legate's secretary, judging by his apparel and demeanour. He glanced at the escort.

"That will be all, thank you, Probus," he said. The escort saluted and walked away.

The secretary took a look at Marcus as if to make sure he really was the summoned guest, then ushered him into the building beyond the courtyard, with a summary "Wait here."

He left Marcus standing outside the entrance door for a few seconds, before returning, drawing back the thick red curtains, and standing aside to allow him entry, announcing, "Tribunus Angusticlavius Quietus."

Marcus entered and saw the legate. His expression was solemn. He didn't look too formidable but Marcus was not deceived by appearances. Aged around thirty years old, an ex-praetor and a senator, Legatus Legionis Gratialis was one of the emperor's right-hand men, his three-year appointment in command merely a stepping stone to even greater things.

Someone moved in the shadows behind the legate and stood up. Marcus started as he recognised the broad-striped tunic of the legion's second in command, Tribunus Laticlavius Flavius. The two most senior officers of the legion – and they had obviously been discussing him.

"Hail, Legate. Hail, Tribune," said Marcus.

"Tribune," said Flavius. His glance was subdued. This was no longer looking like promotion, Marcus feared. But if not, what was this about?

"I will leave you together," said Flavius. He saluted Gratialis and walked out through the curtained entrance.

The legate rose, came out from around the table and stood in front of Marcus. His blue-grey eyes looked searchingly into those of the younger man for a second.

"Please sit down, Tribune," he said. "I have grave news for you."

12.20pm, 4th September, 117AD: the Principia, Headquarters of the Twelfth Legion, Central Spain

Marcus sat in the quarters of his commanding officer, waiting for news he didn't want to hear. He seemed to wait a long time. Distant sounds, of soldiers and secretaries moving about in the building, died away to nothing. In the whole world there were only two men: Marcus Valerius Quietus, junior tribune of the Twelfth Legion, and his commanding officer Septimus Gnaeus Gratialis. The older man stood for a timeless interval, looking at the tribune with a troubled, sombre gaze, as though searching for something he couldn't define.

Finally he spoke, breaking the spell: "Our Emperor Trajan is dead."

"I'm sorry, Legate," said Marcus, automatically. At the same moment, his mind started racing. Sad news, but it didn't affect him personally – or did it? He didn't know the protocol in such a situation. Trajan had been emperor for a long time: for most of Marcus's life, in fact. Did the legate call each of his officers before him to tell him the news personally? That didn't seem like the army way...so what was it?

"Yes, he was a great Emperor." Gratialis's eyes were far away for a moment. He brought himself back to the present,

"I'm afraid it touches you more deeply, Tribune. I'm sorry to have to bring you this news," said Gratialis.

Marcus' eyes were locked onto those of his commander.

"Hadrian, the Commander of the Eastern Provinces, was announced as the new Emperor by the Senate. It was the will of Trajan, who had named Hadrian as his adopted son."

The legate paused again. Obviously this was painful for him; but it was even more painful to Marcus. *Get it out, man!* He wanted to shout. But junior tribunes do not shout at legates.

"Not long after Hadrian's succession was announced, a plot to kill him was discovered. Four senators were involved – they planned to strike the new emperor down. It is documented, apparently..." said Gratialis.

Another pause. Another moment while the world stopped turning. A line of cold sweat ran down Marcus's neck at the word 'senators'.

"The senators were hunted down and killed wherever they stood. Your father..."

... *Was named as one of the conspirators.* Marcus's mind signalled the next sentence, long before Gratialis actually spoke the words.

A chill flushed through the tribune's body. Shock slapped him into words, into protest against the monstrous jest of the gods.

"It cannot be! My father is a loyal subject of Rome! There's some mistake – my father loves Trajan, he would never..."

But it was true. He saw it in the reluctant eyes of his commander before he spoke: "Your father was struck down at his villa in Judea. And... " he sighed heavily.

"And?"

"And your family."

"My mother? My sister?"

Gratialis could not speak. But he didn't have to. Marcus prided himself on his Roman stoicism. No tear fell from his eye, nothing disturbed his military bearing. But he was thankful he was sitting down: his legs felt like grass in the rain. Vivid images of his father, of his family, lying twisted in the road like broken animals, their blood staining the dusty ground...

"Who could do such a thing? Who would dare?"

"The orders were in the name of the new Emperor," said Gratialis.

Another body blow. So, was this Hadrian his enemy? He had heard the name, of course – who hadn't? But it had been only a name – until now. Someone else writing his destiny in the wars a thousand miles from here. Had he condemned his whole family to death – just to make his throne a touch more secure? It was the kind of game they played in the palaces of Rome. Marcus bit his lip.

"One more thing, Tribune," said the legate.

Marcus looked up at him glassily. What more could there possibly be? What could be worse than this, when his whole life had been destroyed?

"The Emperor has promoted you to *Praefectus alae*."

He couldn't prevent the wryest of smiles at this ultimate irony. So he had his promotion after all. Prefect of a cavalry battalion. He'd dreamed of this. And now this and the rest of his ambitions were hollow mockeries.

"You're to be posted to the Ninth Legion. Britannia."

Marcus remained silent, looking up at the legate.

"Let's walk in the courtyard," said Gratialis, "My son."

He put his right hand on the shoulder of the army's newest cavalry commander.

*

The two men walked slowly in the immaculately tended garden. In a way it was a relief to be outside, exposed to the air and the sun, unconfined. In another way, everything looked wrong: the flowers seemed garish and out of place, the bouquet of their blooms an affront to the nostrils.

Gratialis was silent for a while, and a small part of Marcus's mind recognised this and was grateful. But most of his mind was on that well-known road that led to the villa in Judea, the white bodies of his mother and sister stretched out in their final agony, blood still pumping out onto the dust, the roadside plants stained and flecked with red. Perhaps his father had seen death coming and had tried to warn the family, to get them to run away. It would have been like him...

Marcus realised that his commander had been speaking, and he hadn't heard a word.

"I'm sorry, Legate," he said.

The legate smiled his understanding and sympathy.

"I was saying that my orders are to transfer you to the Ninth with immediate effect."

"Ah. Yes, Legate," Marcus said. The thought of the transfer, the travel, the new unit, his new command, acted as a tonic and brought his wandering mind to heel.

"But I don't want you to go alone. I thought of your cousin, Libo. He hasn't heard the news, but I feel sure that once he does he will want to be with you. I'll put through his transfer at the same time."

"Thank you, sir."

"No need to thank me. I knew your father well, served with him. He had a temper – dismissed for insubordination under Domitian, wasn't he?"

"Yes, Legate."

"Well, that fact alone would make Lucius Quietus a good man in most people's eyes."

Marcus managed a smile of gratitude.

The legate went on, "But I knew that well enough, in any case. He was a good and kind man – helped me get this position. When Trajan brought him back into the army there was no officer more loyal and hardworking. I served with him in Dacia, you know, where he was a cavalry commander. He was the best..." Gratialis paused. "I can hardly believe this news myself."

Marcus nodded.

"Anyway, I just wanted to say this: watch yourself. Whatever happens, stay on your guard. Particularly in Britannia. The likelihood is that you're being transferred there to get you out of the way. It's still half savage, especially where the Ninth is. And what do we really know about Hadrian? Not much, and anyway, many a man changes his character – or reveals it – when he dons the imperial purple. Some say he's another Domitian, another Nero."

A real bastard in other words, thought Marcus.

"That's not what I know, but I don't know for sure. Nobody does. This matter is too critical to put your faith in hearsay. You'll be alone where you're going, exposed to who knows what kind of dangers. From the enemy at the gates – and perhaps from the enemy within."

Marcus straightened up. "I'm grateful for your frankness, sir," he said. "Can you tell me anything about what I can expect?"

"A little. You'll join the Ninth at Eboracum – heard of it?"

"I'm afraid not, sir."

"It's on the northern frontier. To the south: order, civilisation, structure. To the north: unconquered tribes. We gave them a good beating a few years back, and there's been no trouble since. But you know what these savages are like – unpredictable. And the Ninth is undermanned, especially in infantry."

There was silence when the legate finished. Both men were thinking of the remotest outpost of the empire, far to the north and across the sea.

"Very well, Prefect," said Gratialis. "Go back to your quarters. I'll take you off the duty roster so that you can make your preparations, and I'll send your cousin to you. You'll have much to talk about."

"Yes, sir."

The legate reached out and clasped Marcus's forearm.

"My condolences, my son. Your father was a great man."

*

Muffled roars were the first thing that Turbo noticed as he approached the emperor's chambers. The two Praetorian Guards were looking at each other with uncertainty until they saw Turbo striding towards them. They stood to attention and saluted the legate, glad that the tumult within the room was now somebody else's responsibility. From inside the emperor's chambers, something very heavy was hurled against the wall. It shattered, and the three men outside felt the vibrations through their sandals as the floor shook.

Then came a deafening shriek: outraged and uncontrolled.

General Turbo's hand flew instinctively to his *gladius* and brought it half out of its scabbard before his head overruled his heart. That was not a cry of fear, of someone being defiled. It was an animal bellow of unadulterated rage from someone not used to being crossed. It was a shocked accusation flung at Jupiter himself – and at the whole pantheon of the gods. Turbo slid his short sword back into its sheath, knocked twice on the door and flung it open.

There was Hadrian standing in the middle of the room, surrounded by debris, his chest heaving. The floor was littered with broken statuary and the remains of costly ornaments, and the walls, floor, and even the ceiling of his chambers were scored and marked with the violence of his tantrum.

Hadrian's hair was wild, his expensive clothing torn by ungoverned hands. For a moment his livid eyes held no recognition of his trusted lieutenant: and Turbo's right hand inched down towards his sword handle.

"My lord ...?" said Turbo, aghast at the spectacle.

The rational voice in the midst of the chaos seemed to break through to Hadrian, to pull him back from the jaws of Hades.

"Turbo," he said. The murderous look faded from his eyes. He sank into a chair. Turbo saw that its costly pillows had been slashed by a dagger, spilling their luxurious guts.

Without warning the fury returned, raging against its impotence. Hadrian stamped on the marble floor, shook his fists in the air and leapt up, screaming obscenities, "In the names of all the gods! What has he done? He will not do this to me!"

Turbo rushed over to him and restrained the emperor's flailing arms.

"Caesar! Caesar!" he implored. He could feel himself trembling: he, the legate of a legion and a fell warrior who feared no man, was afraid of these unknowns.

Hadrian closed his eyes, relaxed, opened his eyes again. He relaxed, sighed and breathed deeply. Again. And once again. Finally, he spoke, "Forgive me, friend," he said.

Their eyes held each other. Turbo looked, concern and apprehension in his gaze. But then he too gave a sigh: what he had seen in Hadrian's face a moment ago was no longer there.

"There is nothing to forgive, Caesar," he said. "I see you have been sorely tried."

Hadrian threw himself down to a mutilated couch. He snorted, then clapped his hands. A fearful slave entered, almost cringing.

"Wine, two goblets."

"Yes, my lord," said the slave, glad to leave the chamber that had become a battlefield.

"Can I help? Can you share this with me?" said Turbo.

Hadrian took several more deep breaths, signaling with his hand to wait. The slave scurried in, and started to pour the wine. Hadrian took the jar out of his hands and waved him away. He filled the goblets to the brim, passed one to

Turbo and took the other. He drank, eyes closed, then set it empty back on the table.

"That's better," he said.

Turbo took a good mouthful of wine himself, and waited.

"Sorely tried, you say. Yes." Hadrian stood up, strode across the room to a small table, picked up a scroll and threw it across to his friend, "Read this."

Turbo unrolled the scroll with difficulty; there were deep rips in both sides of the parchment.

"From the Senate, Cornelius Palma, Publius Celsus, Avidis Nigrinus and Lucius Quietus have all been..."

He dropped the scroll, looking over to Hadrian for explanation.

"Yes," said Hadrian. "Have all been executed. Or should I say assassinated. Accused of treason against me. And murdered on my orders." He gave a sardonic laugh.

"What really happened?"

"Attianus. He gave the orders in my name as Head of the Praetorian Guard. And I had a message from him also. He talks about a whispering campaign against me in the Senate – rumours that my succession had been staged by Plotina."

"Did he think he was doing the right thing? Acting in your interests?"

"Acting in my interests? In his own, more likely," he shouted: "Scribe!"

A frightened little man entered, nearly dropping his writing instruments.

"Take down this despatch at once. To Attianus. You will *not* authorise any further executions of senators – or anyone else. *I* am the Emperor and *I* will make such decisions. Underline that."

"Yes, Caesar."

"It goes at once. *Now!*"

"Caesar!" the scribe hurried away and the door closed behind him.

The room was silent as the men pondered the future. Hadrian stood, walked over to the wine jar and poured himself another drink. He sat down again, sipping this time.

"No judge, no sentence. Summarily executed. The Senate is in uproar – not surprisingly. The Praetorian Guards are on the streets of Rome. Demands from the Senate – look at this!" he picked up the scroll, tried to unwind it, but its ravaged parchment was uncooperative. He threw it to the ground.

"Demands of me – the Emperor of Rome – no more executions, no more butchery! And then a lot of flowery diplomats' words; but underneath, the threat is clear."

"It's chaos," said Turbo. "And a chaotic situation can favour those who are prepared for it."

"Yes," agreed Hadrian. "Those – or the one."

There was silence for a moment.

"A thought strikes me," said Turbo.

Hadrian looked at him. His finger made a tiny gesture of permission.

"The Senate *should* fear you a little. They will get over their indignation. But in removing these loyal supporters of Trajan, Attianus has done everything that is necessary to ensure a smooth succession."

Hadrian's eyes rested on his friend's face, weighing his words. He stroked his beard.

"This is not the start I wanted," said Hadrian, in a quieter voice than he had yet used. "A great game has been set in motion."

"You were ever a player of skill," murmured Turbo.

"Well, one thing is clear," said Hadrian. "We're not going back to Rome for a while."

Turbo nodded.

Hadrian clapped his hands. A slave appeared. "Clear up this mess," said the emperor. "Bring us some meat, some bread and some more wine."

The slave bowed and walked quickly from the room.

"Our move," said Turbo.

*

There was a knock at his door, and Marcus called out an invitation to enter.

The door opened to reveal his cousin Libo, his ashen face telling Marcus that no explanation was necessary.

"I'm so sorry."

"I'm sorry too," said Marcus.

"I feel it as deeply as you. Or almost as deeply."

Marcus looked at his cousin, two years his junior; his face was young, yet hardened by action. Libo passed a hand through his nearly black hair, and Marcus noticed the slight tremor.

"The legate gave me some more details of the murders, recently received," he said. "Do you want me to..."

"No, no," said Marcus, hastily. His imagination had been graphic enough for him.

"The legate is a good man, Marcus," said his cousin.

Marcus reflected: Libo was just an ordinary infantryman, and to be granted a personal interview with his commander was an almost unheard-of honour. Marcus had no doubt that Gratialis had been courteous and gentle. It was his mark.

"Yes. He was very good to me. It was easy to see he took no pleasure in the news."

"This Hadrian, though…" said Libo. "The instant I heard what had happened, I wanted to desert from the army and seek him out. I didn't say that, of course, yet the legate seemed to understand. He's a magician, that one."

Not a magician, just a very good commander, thought Marcus absently.

"He told me he wouldn't blame me – or you – if we wanted to quit the corps. Astonishing frankness. I'm still thinking about it, about Hadrian. It's crazy, the idea of a madman, but…" Libo's voice trailed away, blood and revenge lying just below the surface of his words.

"Even emperors are not immune," said Marcus. They exchanged a glance.

Marcus's mind flew back in time, surveying the often visceral history of Rome. In the Year of the Four Emperors, two of the imperial line had been murdered and two more had committed suicide within twelve months. And that was less than fifty years ago. The tyrant Domitian had met his end at the hand of his own court officials within Marcus's own lifespan.

"It would be hugely satisfying," said Libo. "Blood calls out for blood."

"It would be, and it does," said Marcus: "but I've been thinking since I saw the legate. We must be revenged, and, the gods willing, we will be. But let us be sure of our target. *Festina lente*," he said, quoting the well-worn saying. Hasten slowly.

Libo nodded.

"People who kill emperors don't usually die of old age," said Marcus. Libo snorted in amusement, some of the tension leaching from his body. "An imperial succession is a time of confusion, of disorder. Is Hadrian really our enemy? Perhaps. But let's know that beyond all doubt before we strike."

"Agreed," said Libo.

"I'm still alive. Hadrian hasn't ordered the death of Lucius Quietus's only son. It would have been a logical move for an emperor bent on suppressing any possible opposition to his rule."

They looked each other in the eye.

"My instinct is to stay in the army," said Marcus. "I think it will be easier to take our revenge from within the ranks. But I will need help, a friend. Someone I can count on."

"I will stay with you, even to death," said Libo fervently.

"Let's hope it doesn't come to that. But if Pluto wants to haul us off to the Underworld, I can think of no better company."

They laughed together, and in the quarters of the newly promoted cavalry commander, the two cousins embraced.

*

It was a bright morning, and Hadrian rode in his imperial carriage through the glories of Syrian Antioch. Mount Silpius dominated the city, and the great temple to Jupiter Capitolinus dominated the mountain. Hadrian ordered the carriage to drive south, through the two long colonnades built by Tiberius. People were everywhere, well fed and of noble bearing – half a million of them, it was said.

As usual, Hadrian was bareheaded; even the highest rank could not change his lifelong habit. And also as usual, his friend and confidant accompanied him.

The sunlight burnished the granite pavings, making them gleam like precious metal.

"There is still damage from the earthquake of two years ago," said Hadrian suddenly. "Trajan did much to restore the city: and I shall make it even more magnificent."

Turbo smiled.

"You seem much restored yourself, Caesar," he said.

"Our long talk helped, my friend. And after all, courage is knowing what not to fear."

The epigram had a classical air about it.

"Greek?" hazarded Turbo.

"Plato," said Hadrian. And at that, Turbo's smile was even broader. Not for nothing was Hadrian known as *Graeculus*, the Greekling. But the fact that he could take solace in the sayings of a man who died hundreds of years ago spoke volumes for his reviving confidence. Hadrian saw the smile. He grinned back.

"I rose early this morning and worked my scribes' fingers off. I've appointed a whole gaggle of new governors – ones I can trust in place of others I can't. I've put an array of new quaestors in place across Rome, and new consuls abroad. I've written to every legion, declaring my legitimate claim to the throne."

"And reminded them of your army background?"

Hadrian grinned again. "Of course. Nothing carries more weight with military men – especially those one day hoping to follow in my footsteps." He paused. "I've also pulled out all the troops from Parthia."

Turbo whistled, "Galbanus will be livid. He wanted the honour of conquering the whole of the Parthian empire."

"The good general will learn to contain himself – or be demoted. I've also allowed the Parthians to elect their own king." Hadrian saw a flicker of doubt even in his closest friend's eyes. "It's too far away from the centre, my friend: the border is untenable, especially at a time like this. I've abandoned all of Trajan's conquests east of the Euphrates."

Turbo looked grave, but he bowed his head in acquiescence. "The army won't like it; nor the Senate. But I see your reasoning."

"They're not in charge of policy. I am. I want an Empire I can control, not one that is forever controlling its Emperor."

"Sounds like another epigram. Plato? Pliny the Elder?"

"No: Hadrian. Hadrian the Wise!"

And they laughed together as the carriage rolled on, bathed in golden light.

*

Marcus and Libo stood, side by side, in the prow of the warship. Behind them, a company of new recruits stood, sat or lay, bedraggled, soaked by the foam and the intermittent rain, depressed, and shivering. Some were sick, hanging over the side of the hull or groaning, clutching their faces in their hands.

Marcus was seemingly oblivious to the elements. Both he and his cousin kept their faces turned towards the north. Marcus' mind went over the recent events that had slipped by so quickly. Reporting to the legate, confirming their decision to stay in the army. The legate issuing them with passes and other documentation to travel overland, hundreds of miles to the coast. Waiting in a temporary camp. Standing while the ship was readied for them to board. And now being tossed up and down, from side to side, in a trireme, a fast and agile warship with three rows of oars – still struggling in the ungracious sea.

En route to Petuaria, wherever that was: some port in Britannia. And from there to head for Eboracum. Some town in Britannia. But these names faded away into mist. Everything Marcus had known, all the solid structure of his life, his family, his future – they'd all been cast away. Tossed into the air like the seaborne spume.

Ahead was the unknown. The whim of Fortuna. Was she to be a lady, to favour him with good luck and happy destiny? Would she be fickle? Would she bring evil luck that no man could stand against?

His father, his mother, his sister: all gone. His place in the Twelfth Legion: a part of history. His beloved Petronia, hundreds of miles away inland. And now he was sailing to a foreign shore, the farthest foothold of the empire. To be part of the Ninth Legion: a distinguished name, but full of uncertainty. All he had in the world was his cousin, Libo. He looked over to him: the rain ran down his youthful face, his hair slick and flattened against his head. Behind them, the moans of someone about to throw up mingled with the crash of the waves, the buffeting of the wind, the creak of the triple banks of oars.

Marcus smiled, reached out and put his arm around Libo, breaking his reverie. Libo smiled back.

They set their gaze once again to the north – and the future.

SPQR

*Courage may be taught as a child
is taught to speak.*

Euripides

III   Watchtowers

Although Carpex was fit, healthy and just thirty four years old, his last day on earth had already begun.

The day started like any other. He awoke in the dark, musty and cramped surroundings of the watchtower, breakfasted swiftly on cold meat and climbed the ladder onto the platform, leaving his comrades slumbering below. Outside, a livid crimson was slashed across the horizon. Pesus sprang to attention and saluted him, breath misting from his mouth.

"Cold enough, eh?" said Carpex.

Pesus gave him a wry smile, "Colder every day, Tesserarius."

"It'll get a lot colder."

"Makes you long for Gallia, doesn't it?"

"Gallia, Syria, anywhere in the Empire. Anywhere but this godforsaken place." Carpex looked down on the grasslands gradually emerging out of darkness, chilled from overnight dew. A stark contrast with the sunlit memories of his homeland.

"Still, only one more day and then back to Bremenium, Tesserarius."

Carpex nodded, and looked south. Three miles away was the next watchtower, "Last Hope", a squat black shape brooding against the greying horizon. Another handful of men would be waking up there too. Beyond it, but out of sight was "Mars' Field"; then another three miles and "Agricola's Folly": four tiny bastions of civilisation against barbarism.

After those – three more miles, and Castra Bremenium. It was only an army fort, but compared to "Hades' End" it was luxurious. There would be hot baths, fresh meat, space to stretch yourself – and to relax while some other unfortunate had the honour of manning the furthest outpost of the Roman Empire.

"One more day," said Carpex.

*

At about the same time, Tesserarius Gergovix of *Cohors I Gallorum* was taking the salute of Pedes Antonus on the "Mars' Field" watchtower, "Anything to report?"

Antonus was shivering despite his two cloaks, "When is there ever, Tesserarius?"

Gergovix looked down to the west of the platform. Despite the early hour, there was movement: a wisp of fire from a settlement, a figure gathering wood for fuel, a man riding an ox-cart along a rough track.

"*Brittunculi,*" he snorted in agreement. Pathetic little Britons. They'd got well and truly smashed north of here some twenty-odd years ago, and, apart from that brutal but short-lived rising, it had been quiet. Maybe they had accepted their fate.

It was the way of things. Four hundred years ago, the Gauls under Brennus had entered Rome itself, the proud leader uttering the famous phrase, "*Vae victis!*" Woe to the vanquished! And now Gallia was just another part of the Empire. Their warrior god Teutates, it seemed, was emasculated.

One day, probably, the same thing would happen to Caledonia. It too would give up the struggle and be absorbed, and its gods, whoever they were, would depart forever into the twilight, to be replaced by Mars and Mercury, Jupiter and Apollo.

But that was a matter for Gergovix's children, or his children's children. For now, in the present, he was responsible for five infantrymen until the relief squad rode up tomorrow morning.

"I'll send Arius up, and you can get some breakfast," said Gergovix. Antonus gave the tesserarius a smile of gratitude.

*

That afternoon, a thin sunshine washed briefly through the cloud-filled skies.

On the platform of "Hades' End", Carpex stood looking northwards towards the gently rolling hills. He pulled his *gladius* from its sheath and angled it to catch the light, blinding.

For an auxiliary of *Cohors I Gallorum*, he had seen surprisingly little action in the last eighteen years. Days, months and years of routine duty – reports, sentry work, building bridges and fortifications, parades for visiting dignitaries – interspersed with a few skirmishes. And since being posted to this armpit of the world five years ago: nothing.

Inevitably, he found himself living more in the past and the future than in the present. He simply wanted these days to pass as soon as possible. One more day, and his current shift in the watchtower would be over. Seven more years, and his twenty-five year term would be complete. He'd be free to leave the army with his prize: Roman citizenship. He'd even have the right to take a new Roman-style name. Not bad for a *Peregrinus*. A second-class citizen.

He hadn't seen Julia for three years, and he'd never seen the twins. They would likely be ten years old when he did see them, and he'd be a stranger to them. But at least he'd be bringing them the greatest reward a provincial family could hope for.

He watched Pedes Calix setting the daytime signal by adjusting the water level in the jar. In "Last Hope", another infantryman, trained and sharp-eyed, would be reading it and reporting to his tesserarius. The calibrated rod stood at the same level as always: *No enemy sighted*. Would it ever read otherwise, he wondered? Would signals of alarm fly from watchtower to watchtower one day, alerting the one hundred men in Castra Bremenium?

He pictured it: the staid, steady life of the fort suddenly transformed into urgent action. The *ala* of cavalry saddling up, grabbing their long swords or hefting their spears, organised turmoil as infantry units formed up, the north gate swinging open, the *ala* thundering across the grassland to the besieged watchtowers...

The sun disappeared from view again as a large drop of rain spattered on his *gladius*. He wiped the short sword dry with the edge of his cloak, sheathed it and walked past Calix to descend the ladder.

*

On the "Mars' Field" watchtower, Pedes Arius saluted his tesserarius.

Gergovix took the salute and clapped him on the shoulder, "Lovely weather!"

"And this is only the eighth month. What of the tenth, Tesserarius?"

"Ice, and hail – and snow and freezing wind. Just like last year, and the year before."

Arius grunted comically, shrugging his shoulders in a way that was definitely Gallic despite his long service in the empire.

The rain was now falling with vigour, and the clouds were one mass of grey. Water streamed down the helmets of the auxiliaries, down their faces, and waterlogged their cloaks. Gergovix wiped his hand over his eyes to clear his vision. It would be good to return to Gallia, to see his wife and his friends again; but that was so far off that he dismissed it from his mind. Unless they were posted back there, it would be ten years before he would see home. The wind drifted the sharp fragrance of wet leaves and mosses to his nose.

He looked down, at the long road below. The Via Domitiana, so called after the Emperor. As often, he felt a flush of pride. Soldiers like him had built that road forty years ago; it ran 150 miles all the way from Eboracum to Trimontium in the wilds of Caledonia. It was wide enough to allow two columns of soldiers to pass each other. That was Roman efficiency, if you liked! Straight as an arrow.

His gaze fell on two traders moving along the road. All travellers were under constant surveillance by the watchtowers here, and by other fortifications elsewhere along its distance. Imagine those *Brittunculi* ever building anything like that!

A clap of thunder came from above. Gergovix and Arius looked up instinctively.

"Taranis," murmured Arius almost inaudibly, but his tesserarius heard him, and understood. The Thunderer. When living with the trappings of civilisation, Gergovix had little time for Gallic gods, or any other denomination: but out here in the wilds, he wasn't quite so certain.

The thought of civilisation turned his gaze southwards. Three miles away stood the watchtower "Agricola's Folly". He could make out several men on the platform, and he wondered idly if his friend Hastus was among them. Another three miles after that, and anyone going south on the Via Domitiana would find himself at Bremenium, the place of the roaring stream. If this rain went on like this Bremenium would be aptly named indeed, Gergovix smiled sardonically. He saw in his mind's eye the familiar buildings, rain pouring from the roofs and cascading from the tiles as men looked out from their barracks at the sodden parade ground.

Pedes Oscans climbed the ladder, saluted, and relieved Arius, who was only too glad to scamper below and get a respite from the rain. Gergovix took the salute automatically, but part of him remained with his comrades at Castra Bremenium.

A flash of lightning lit up the drab countryside and a gigantic thunderclap shuddered the air. Oscans raised his eyebrows and whistled, and Gergovix grinned back at him.

*

At "Hades' End" watchtower several hours later, five men were warm and dry inside.

Tesserarius Carpex lay resting, his eyes closed, one hand over his face. Pesus was asleep, the oil lamps casting fluttering shadows over his body. Pretig, Calix and Tigar were engaged in a game of dice. Grimaces and muttered oaths mingled with soft grunts of triumph as the wooden cubes were rattled in a cup, thrown onto a cloth-covered board and then passed to the next player, coins changing hands at every throw. Pretig gnawed intermittently on an ancient piece of dried beef.

Outside on the platform, Pedes Novantes was chilled to the bone. He moved around as often as he could, chafing his arms with his hands in a vain attempt to create some heat. The rain had finally stopped, only to give way to a knife-cold wind undeterred by his two rain-sodden cloaks.

He was eighteen years old, and he was miserable. It was said that the Praefectus, the Cohort Commander, earned fifty times his pay. Fifty times! And yet the Praefectus was snug in a warm bed in Castra Bremenium, while Novantes froze to death this October night – on top of a platform exposed to the four winds north of the back of beyond, many miles from his native Gaul.

It was a strange sensation to be up on that platform at night. There was nothing to see, nothing to hear except the sound of the wind blowing; nothing to feel except the wind on his body. Floating above the ground like this, shivering, teeth chattering, bones aching, the mind could play tricks. Novantes was not so old to have entirely forgotten his childhood night terrors.

And there was one of the mind's tricks right now. He swore he could see a couple of tiny lights. He closed his eyes firmly, held them shut, opened them again. The lights were still there, slightly moving. Maybe it wasn't a trick of the mind, but glow-worms.

He watched. Several other glow-worms joined them. At least, they were probably glow-worms, but –

He wrenched open the hatchway, momentarily blinded even by the feeble light of the lamps. A comingled odour of unwashed bodies, hot oil and rancid meat wafted up to him. The rattle of dice continued.

"Tesserarius!"

"Wha – at?" groaned Carpex.

"Would you come up here and take a look? Something I'm not quite sure about."

The Tesserarius sighed, opened his eyes and stretched his arms. "All right, I'm coming."

Carpex threw on his chain-mail shirt, grabbed his cloak and started to climb the ladder, emerging onto the instantly chilling platform.

"What?"

"Over there, Tesserarius."

Carpex looked. Dozens of lights, growing slowly bigger.

"Everyone onto the platform! At the double!" he shouted. Dice, sleep and eating were forgotten in an instant as the four men swarmed up the ladder and stood to attention. Carpex stood watching for a second: "*Brigantes,*" he said.

"What are they doing, Tesserarius? Is it an attack?"

"I don't know, but send the signal. Now!"

Novantes scurried to grab a torch – and lit its moss and bracken tip at one of the lamps. At the same time, Calix and Pretig were working on the jar. The signal now said: *Under attack.*

Novantes raised his torch. The whole squad looked south. Across the darkness, light flared out, then rose higher. The watchtower "Last Hope" had responded. Novantes cast the light of his torch onto the jar so that the signal was plainly visible. The light from the south went out.

"Javelins," ordered Carpex. Tigar and Pesus sprang into action, portering armfuls of the weapons up from below and out onto the platform: less impressive than the *pilum* employed by the regular legionaries, but still formidable.

"Get the shields too," said Carpex. Pretig and Calix ran to bring up and distribute the round leather-and-wood shields. Small though the shield was, it was comforting to have its protection.

Something of the tension had drained from the troop with the acknowledgement of the signal by "Last Hope". They were not alone. Aid was on its way. They were still strung out but they were ready: trained for this. Even if it was an attack, even if they took casualties, help would come. And no amount of tribesmen could withstand an attack by Roman cavalry. Any who dared to stay would be cut down by the spears and the long swords pounding through the night like vengeful furies.

On the watchtower "Last Hope", trained men saw the signal from "Hades' End" and put the same drill into action. The signal was given, and the men of the squad waited for the answer. But the light from "Mars' Field" continued to shine.

"What's he playing at?" said "Last Hope's" signaller. "Why doesn't..."

"Signal again," said the tesserarius: but at that moment, every man on "Last Hope" realised that it wasn't a torch they had seen.

"The watchtower's on fire!" cried a man.

Infantrymen stood transfixed as massive orange flames licked up the watch tower.

"Put out our light, it's making us a target," barked the tesserarius. The light was doused, but there was fear and uncertainty now. Had the signal got through? What was happening? How big an attack was it? Would they be able to hold them off?

*

The lights were growing ever more numerous. Torches. In their shadowy gleam, Novantes could make out bare-chested warriors, their faces painted blue, their hair wild and matted.

"It's an attack all right," muttered Calix.

"They must be crazy," said Pretig.

"Esus," breathed Novantes.

Carpex heard the word, the name of the Gallic god. He smiled grimly, clapped his hand on the youth's chain-mail shirt, "Stand firm," he said.

A sudden hiss came from all around the tower. A horrible sound.

"Arrows! Shields up!" cried Carpex.

The soldiers reacted like lightning. Arrows bounced off the wood and leather canopy of their shields.

"Ready javelins!" shouted Carpex. Each of the six men grabbed a weapon and stood poised: "Throw!"

Death rained from the sky. Warriors fell apart under the metal thunderbolts. Agonised screams tore the air. The auxiliaries on the tower shouted exultantly, "Ha! Ha! That'll give them something to think about."

"Tigar! Calix! More javelins!" shouted Carpex.

The two infantrymen ran to comply, but before they could return, another flight of arrows flew screaming above them. Arrows with flaming heads. They struck, still alight, into the wood of the watchtower's upper levels.

"That's a Roman trick!" shouted Pesus, outraged, while war cries and cheers skirled up from below.

"Ready javelins!" called Carpex. The men jumped into position. Arrows flew up again. One bounced off Novantes' helmet. Another caught Calix, tearing through his chest. Searing pain. He fell off the platform, screaming.

"Throw!"

Five javelins shot downwards. There was a cacophony of anguished screams, war cries, and dancing flames. "Hades' End" was alight, orange flames flickering and sparks flying.

"Swords out!" called Carpex, drawing his *gladius* and raising his shield. An arrow hammered through his left eye socket. A soft grunt of shock escaped his lips. The sword fell from his lifeless hand and clattered onto the platform.

Novantes watched, spellbound in horror. The body of the tesserarius stayed upright for a moment, as though unharmed. Then he sank heavily to his knees and collapsed, sprawling against the watchtower wall. Cries of triumph redoubled from below.

The four infantrymen left standing stared at each other, aghast. Then crude ladders thudded against the walls from all sides.

"Jump! Every man for himself!" yelled Pesus.

*

On "Last Hope", the auxiliaries looked to north and south. Both of the neighbouring watchtowers were alight, "Mars' Field" now burning with a vengeance. Distant shouts and screams came to them.

"Get the ladder out, lads," quietly spoke the tesserarius. "They're done for, but we won't get caught like rats. Try and reach 'Agricola's Folly' and help out – or else head back to the fort, any way you can."

The ladder was eased down and through the hatch, over the platform and placed against the outer wall. Hearts pounding, eyes darting all around, sweat slicking brows; wordlessly, the six soldiers climbed swiftly and skilfully down the ladder and stood in a defensive group. The cries seemed louder on the ground.

"Wait, lads –" breathed the tesserarius, and at that, the long grass came alive, blue-painted warriors launching themselves at the squad. They were attacked from all sides. Long swords jabbed through Roman flesh with abrupt force. They fought to the end in the small circle they had made. A hellish melee of cries and moans were swiftly silenced, as the Brigantes finished off the wounded; knee to the chest, double-handed sword thrust. Down and in. Hot blood spurted into the darkness and steamed in the icy air.

Maddened by blood lust, one warrior pushed aside the helmet of a dying auxiliary, seized a handful of hair and severed the head completely, in an oblique slash. He lofted his dripping trophy and his comrades bellowed their victory to the heavens.

The tesserarius, his life draining from three deep wounds, still crawled feebly south, as though sheer determination could take him the six miles to "Agricola's Folly," to comrades, and help, and something to stem the pain.

A Brigiantian warrior, with a harsh laugh, ended the attempt with a sledgehammer sword blow, pinning his spurting jugular to the cold ground. The tesserarius died, his hand still reaching out for "Agricola's Folly".

But six miles south, the auxiliaries in "Agricola's Folly" watchtower were in no position to help anybody. The sentry on the platform had been disposed of in silence, and inside the tower, the four infantrymen and Tesserarius Hastus had had their throats cut while they slept.

*

"Mars' Field", its roof a roaring blaze, was under sustained attack. Waves of arrows crashed into the raised shields, the auxiliaries seizing the chance of momentary lulls to throw their javelins.

"Where are they all coming from?" panted Arius.

"Stand firm," said Tesserarius Gergovix. He looked down at the remaining metal javelins. Only seven left. Best kept for fending off attackers by hand.

"Javelins to the defensive position!" he called, and each man hefted a short metal lance in his right hand, the round shield on his left, covering the heart.

Without warning, warriors of the Brigantes emerged from the grasses, raising ladders from all angles. The men lifting the ladders worked together so precisely it was as if they had been professionally drilled.

A warrior clung to the top of each ladder and just a second before the ladders hit the parapet of the platform, the warriors jumped into the air, dagger in hand. Two of them were speared in flight by the hand-held javelins. One warrior caught an infantryman full on, clipping his chin with an elbow. They rolled on the platform, locked in combat. The fourth hurled himself at Pedes Oscans, his momentum carrying both of them through the parapet and into the tangled grasses below. A hoarse roar rose up from ground level as the warriors celebrated.

Fresh warriors appeared onto the platform from below, having scaled the watchtower. Antonus's javelin sprayed blood as rove one of them through, the momentum carrying the warrior over the parapet. Another warrior drove his sword through an auxiliary who fell to the platform, gasping and flailing. Arius finished off the Brigante with a single thrust.

Gergovix's eyes darted around the platform. Blood slicked the wooden floor and the groans of the dying assaulted his ears. The bonfire of the watchtower roof exploded with a roar, sparks flying up like a small volcano. There were three men left.

"Save yourself, lads!" cried the tesserarius. He moved quickly about the platform, choosing his position. In a split second, he'd found it. Drawing back his javelin, he launched it at a blue-daubed warrior below and flung himself from the parapet after it. The warrior threw up his hands instinctively as the javelin shot past him. The next instant Gergovix, gladius in hand, smashed into him like the missile from a ballista. They rolled over into the grass, and away from the conflict. Only one of them rose again.

*

Novantes was horribly winded. For a moment, it seemed he'd never catch his breath again. Then, slower than life itself, his lungs returned to normal. He raised himself on one elbow, peering through the grass, which was as high as his forehead. He was not in the thick of the fighting, but too near it for comfort. He crawled quickly away, head down, expecting a sword thrust through his shoulder blades at any second.

Outside the ambit of the hand-held torches it was as dark as Hades itself. Somehow, Novantes made it through the warriors, past bodies cold and prostrate on the ground, and beyond the tree line.

He looked back. Two watchtowers were lurid with flame. The field belonged to the Brigantes. There were no living auxiliaries in view, and self-evidently no roman cavalry riding in to destroy these presumptuous *Brittunculi*.

Novantes was bruised, shaking, cold and wet. His skull rang from where he landed in his headlong leap from the platform. But he was still alive. His mind dragged him back to the horror of his tesserarius, standing erect with a Brigantian arrow in his eye. But he shook his head and dispelled the image and crawled deeper into cover. Shouts and war-cries, laughter and jeers, surrounded him from all directions.

Now what? He wondered. Castra Bremenium was nearly seven miles to the south, half a day's march for even a fit Roman soldier. Anyway, there was nothing to do but wait, wait until the Brigantes had finished celebrating, plundering the dead, taking trophies.

"Save me, Esus," he whispered, surprising himself with a prayer to the warrior god of the Gauls. Life was full of surprises. He shivered and pulled his cloak over his head and closed his eyes.

*

Four hours later, in a large wooden feasting hall to the east of the battlefield, the celebrations were rowdy and tumultuous. Snatches of war songs, battle tales, tribal oaths and stories of heroes past and present vied for precedence. Ale flowed freely, cup clashing against cup. The chieftains were doughty warriors, many of them bearing the scars of the last great uprising twenty years ago. Yet compared to the leader who sat at the end of the table they seemed shrunken and old. He stood up, raising his hand to honour the chieftains and the tribe, and they in turn hailed him with a roar of approval: "Vordimus! Vordimus!"

He smiled, and beat his fist against the wooden long table until some semblance of order had been established. He began: "Chieftains and warriors of the Brigantes," but he got no further. Every man there felt the honour of the address. Every man there rose to howl his approval, his excitement, his recognition that all the givens had been overthrown. Vordimus beat the table again for silence.

"Chieftains and warriors," he said again: "Tonight you have won a great victory."

"The victory is yours!" cried a voice, and for a second time, turmoil interrupted him.

"Thank you," he smiled again, "I have had the honour to lead you, and instruct you in the ways of my former masters, the Romans. But the honour of victory is yours." He waited until the glad uproar had subsided, then continued: "I have yet more to teach you, ways that will take the overlords by surprise and throw them down to the dust. There will be more great battles, more great victories. But that is for tomorrow. For tonight, the watchtowers are destroyed. The road to the south lies open. They will come to fear you again and respect your land. No more shall they trample you underfoot!"

Amidst the tumult that greeted that phrase, a chieftain rose in his place at the long table. He was spattered with blood, his own and his enemies', but he disdained to wash off these badges of valour. All eyes turned to him with respect and deference. "Hail, Vordimus," he said.

"Hail to you, Ortagorus," answered the leader. "Your bravery tonight set you apart even amongst these heroes."

Cries of approval, fists thumping tables. Ortagorus bent down and lifted something from the floor beside him. He raised it high. It was the battered and bloody head of Pedes Tigar, once a Gallic auxiliary attached to the "Hades' End" watchtower and now no more than a trophy.

"It is fitting," said Ortagorus. "The head is the soul, the centre of life, the symbol of the powers of the Otherworld."

And Vordimus echoed, "It is fitting. And doubly powerful is the head of your enemy!"

The horde cried out its approval again. That night, everything was good and everything was right. The Brigantes were conquerors, as had been predestined.

"This will make a worthy standard for my home," said Ortagorus.

"You will get many more," said Vordimus. "Many more." But the roar of acclamation all but drowned out his last words.

IV   Prefect of Rome

6.30am, 30th October, 117AD: City of Rome

Publius Acilius Attianus, Prefect of the City of Rome and
Head of the Praetorian Guard, opened his eyes on a new
morning. He was fatigued, from his journey back from
that primitive backwater Selinus. He awoke to perfumed
air wafted by unseen slaves. The pine smell always relaxed
him every morning. He arose and clapped his hands. One of
the slaves became visible and a robe was wrapped around
his shoulders.

"Bring me breakfast in the courtyard," he said. The slave
bowed and departed.

Attianus walked over to the window. The sun had been
up a little while, the sky still retaining a hint of pearly pink
from the vestiges of dawn. Rome looked magnificent in the
gentle light, and the Regia was the perfect vantage point to
view it at its best. The Regia was originally the residence
of the Kings of Rome. He looked around the palace and
felt that he belonged there, that this was his rightful place.
Then he looked out at the Field of Mars, filled with temples
and public buildings, circuses, theatres, porticos, baths,
monuments, columns: the marks left by Caesars ancient
and modern.

He too was making his mark, Attianus reflected. He
had risen high for one born in the relative obscurity of
Hispania Baetica. He'd been guardian to a ten year old boy

now grown into the Emperor of Rome. He was the most powerful man in this most powerful of cities when the Emperor Hadrian was absent. And who knows, perhaps he would remain absent, he smiled briefly.

Then he thought of the day ahead of him and the smile was wiped from his face.

*

Almost reluctantly it seemed, a misty dawn broke over Northern Britannia. Behind the treeline, an eighteen year old auxiliary infantryman lay on his stomach in the grass, soaked to the skin from icy dew, watching light leach back into the world. He shivered, trying to still the chattering of his teeth. His body ached and his head rang like a bell whenever he moved it. Ahead lay the remains of the watchtower "Hades' End", still smouldering in the grey dawn. Novantes' mind kept slipping back to the horrors of the night. No wan, unearthly colours there, but stark vividness: crackling torches, spilled blood, shrieking demons with blue faces.

He looked out, through his opaque breath. As the light increased, two grey shapes resolved themselves as mounds lying on the grass. After long and careful glances around, he raised his protesting body onto its knees and then upright. All seemed still in the drifting mist, but he remembered the shapes that came and went from the darkness last night, and was wary. With a furtiveness Novantes crept over to the first mound. A soldier, lying face down. He turned the body over. It was Pesus, one of his closest friends. A deep gouge in his neck caused his head to loll unnaturally.

He walked over to the other body. It was Calix, an arrow through his chest. The moment of his friend's death returned to him with shocking intensity.

He spent some minutes warily searching, but found no more auxiliaries – and no bodies at all from the enemy. It seemed as though they had taken their own from the field for whatever rites they reserved for the dead. And his other comrades' bodies were gone too, unless they had survived like he had. But Carpex was certainly dead, and his body was nowhere to be found. As for Calix and Pesus, it was as though the savages had contemptuously left them, to return to the earth on which they had fallen. Novantes knelt for a while by the bodies of his two friends, whispering a few words of remembrance. But they were gone, and no words could bring them back. He felt ever more adrift in a sea of uncertainty.

Finally he rose to his feet, walked back to the treeline and began his journey. As he trudged wearily onward, a silent prayer squirrelled around in his mind: *Esus, get me out of this in one piece and I swear I'll dedicate a statue to you – even if I have to go back to Gallia to do so.*

He continued to walk, moving south, his eyes searching constantly for enemies. There was nowhere else to go. If there was any hope left, south was the only direction in which it could be found.

*

In Rome, the Head of the Praetorian Guard also looked south as he contemplated his day. The Forum met his gaze: the ancient heart of the city, still fresh-looking in the innocent morning light.

It sat between the Palatine and Capitoline Hills. The Palatine, where Romulus and Remus were found by the she-wolf, according to legend. And the Forum itself. Everyone of any importance in Rome's glorious history had added to it, enriched it, made it even more splendid. Caesar in particular had rearranged it on a major scale.

Now I'm the one making history, he thought. Would he be as famous as Caesar. The air of greatness hung about him, and he could command as well as any man. Without him, they might still have been living in the Republic; instead, the very name of Caesar was now synonymous with the word for emperor. His achievements would fill volumes, his name would live for all eternity. That made any price worth paying. Attianus smiled for a moment.

But Gaius Julius Caesar was also known for his leniency in dealing with political opponents. And there Attianus parted company with him. He preferred the iron fist. Strike first: that was the only way. Attianus had smoothed over Hadrian's succession and ensured there would be no protest from those senators most loyal to Trajan.

I did it. He flushed with pride.

But again his mood changed. Yes, there would be no protest from those four – but what of the three hundred and more senators still left alive? And especially Senate Consul Junius Aulus Cremonus. How dare he and that bunch of old women call Attianus to account! His furious eyes fell on the Curia Julia in the Forum, the seat of the Senate. Cremonus was going to be replaced by Hadrian, and it couldn't be soon enough for Attianus. But Cremonus was also intelligent and articulate. Besting him in open debate was no foregone conclusion. Maybe Attianus would be the one who would lose – and if so, who knew what would follow? There was much hanging on the day.

He headed down to the courtyard and his breakfast with a preoccupied air.

*

The day was sunny and bright as Attianus made his way to the Forum, just a hint of chill in the air reminding the citizens of autumn. Outside the Curia there were stalls and a market, business transactions being made.

A man stood on an improvised wooden platform, berating the name of Hadrian: "Our new Emperor, the imperial throne still warm from Trajan's body – and he kills four senators! Noble men, all of them!"

There were murmurs of agreement. Attianus stood for a few seconds.

"Who is this man, this Hadrian? A common soldier – and believe me, citizens, common is the word."

Some members of the crowd snickered. Attianus's eyes flickered from face to face.

"Wasn't even born in Italia, but in Hispania Baetica."

"Where's that?" someone shouted, to general laughter.

"Well you might ask! But here he is, five minutes in the imperial purple, and this outrage happens. What's next, I ask you? Where will it end?"

Attianus had heard enough. He knew how it would end for this rabble-rouser, in any case. His eyes sought out a familiar face on the fringes of the crowd. Contact. Attianus nodded almost imperceptibly, and received the same signal back. He turned to head into the Curia.

"Quite the orator," said the man next to him. "He has a point."

"He certainly has," replied the Head of the Praetorians, walking away.

The speaker continued his rant for twenty minutes or more, enjoying the crowd's obvious approval. Then he got down from his platform and headed into a street by the side of the Curia for something to slake his thirst. Attianus' man followed with several companions. Once away from the crowd, they surrounded him. Moving like lightning, one held a hand over his mouth, another pinned his arms to his sides; a third slit his throat with a dagger. It was as neat and efficient a job as Attianus could have wished for.

*

Attianus entered the Curia. His glance took in the beautiful ornate flooring, the statue of Victoria, goddess of victory, added to the hall by Augustus after Actium. All familiar. But the three levels contained over three hundred senators in rows of seats, and Attianus could see no empty places. An air of expectation buzzed like an angry fly – but was cut short the second he entered the hall.

Attianus looked around him. His eyes, seeking support, found almost total hostility. He bowed to several senators and took his seat. The rest of the senators did likewise, as though they had been awaiting this signal. The Augur entered.

"What news?" asked Cremonus, the Senate Consul. All heads turned to the Augur.

"The auspices are not good for this day's assembly," he said.

A general grumbling broke out.

A bad omen for you ditherers, perhaps, but not for me, Attianus thought. *As though the entrails of a bird could tell us anything about the future!* But he didn't voice any of that. The traditions of the Senate were sacrosanct.

Cremonus stood, thanked the Augur, and turned a baleful eye on Attianus – as though the bad auspices were his fault. Then he announced the name of someone to speak on behalf of the senators, and seated himself. Attianus scarcely listened to the name of the senator, nor to his diatribe. It was all as he expected. He felt a strange confidence growing in him. The senator finished his speech and sat down, a groundswell of support behind him. Attianus rose, to a hail of mutterings mixed with curses. He raised his right hand for silence and the voices died away. He looked around at the marble walls, at the crowded rows of seats. Everyone's eyes were on him.

"Senate of Rome," he began. "I have heard the words of my esteemed colleague. I can understand that these events have unsettled you. An imperial succession is often a difficult time."

Indignant voices were raised. He raised his hand a second time and waited for the silence that was his right, "But I must remind you that as Head of the Praetorian Guard and City Prefect, I have the right – no, the duty – to keep the Emperor safe. The accusations against these criminals were specific and serious. I sought them out quickly before they could do the harm they planned. You chastise me for my haste: but what would you have said if I had acted too late and your Emperor had been assassinated?"

A tumult broke out. Attianus took his seat with a feeling of satisfaction. But then he saw Cremonus rising. Typical of him to let an inferior speaker open the attack; keeping himself in reserve.

"Senators of Rome," said Cremonus, "these colleagues of ours were never given the chance to defend themselves. Even the humblest Roman citizen deserves that right: and these men were some of the noblest in the land!" Against roars of encouragement and anger, he continued, his voice intoning like a solemn bell the names of the dead: "Publius Celsus. Cornelius Palma. Avidis Nigrinus. Lucius Quietus." He paused, and let the baying die down.

"Men of such stature deserved a public trial in Rome. Deserved the chance to face their accusers. Instead, what happened? They were destroyed like rabid dogs!"

More shouts, angrier and longer than before. Cremonus let the fury run its course without trying to subdue it. "Hadrian knew each of these men personally."

Attianus rose, to jeers and catcalls he was quite unused to hearing, "I had no option but to have these men executed. The information I had gave me no alternative."

"What was the information? Where did it come from? Who ordered these killings?" shouted a senator.

"I reported the matter to the Emperor with immediate haste. It was decided these men had to be removed immediately– as the Senate Consul well knows. My duty is to act on such information as quickly as possible... " but the rest of his reply was drowned out. He gave up the unequal struggle and sat down.

Eyes turned to the Senate Consul again, "Is Hadrian to be another Nero?"

Attianus rose. "I protest!"

"Will the Senate be silenced by a tyrant?" Cremonus continued implacably. "Is Hadrian's name to be added to the *damnatio memoriae* and removed from history?"

"I protest!" cried Attianus again, "Hadrian is no traitor!"

"Had he not written to the Senate, promising to rule wisely and justly, only a month earlier? And now this! The killing must stop! And now!"

The volume of noise at this seemed to shake the ancient marble walls.

"Does the Prefect of the City agree – in open assembly – that there will be no further killings?" Sudden silence.

Attianus looked across the hall at the blazing eyes of the old man. Then he lowered his head. "I agree," he said.

And the roar at that statement was the loudest of all. Over the din, Attianus could hear Cremonus shouting that he would be brought before this house again if the need should arise; that the Senate would not accept being placed in a state of fear; that no hint of treachery would be tolerated... The speech went on a long time, but Attianus was no longer listening. He was planning his next moves.

*

Attianus, Prefect of Rome, slammed the door of his house behind him. It was quiet, but his ears were still ringing with the ugly noise of the crowd. He was master here and in the rest of the city, but the flush in his cheeks testified to his shame at being berated by the Senate like a disobedient child.

He sat down for a minute, collecting himself. Well, no matter. These were just more scores to settle, that was all; and the Prefect was a past master of that.

Then he was reminded of the most pressing score. He called for his secretary, and the man appeared. His nose and mouth were rodent-like, but he was efficient.

"Yes, Prefect?"

"Tell me about the recent promotion."

"Transferred to the Ninth Legion as you ordered, sir. At present, he is in transit to Eboracum, in Northern Britannia."

"and Metellus."

The rodent-like secretary smiled "At present, he is in transit to Eboracum, too."

"Excellent. And the contract was drafted as I asked?"

Yes, sir. For a killing: to look like an accident, or death in the line of duty."

Attianus recollected the huge centurion who dwarfed even an average legionary. *That should tie up that loose end,* he thought, and began to smile, but a frown took its place. After today, he wanted to make doubly sure of everything.

"Did you bring the visitor I requested?"

"Yes, Prefect. Waiting for you in your personal chamber."

"Very good. Write at my dictation."

Attianus waited while the secretary readied his writing materials and looked up.

"To Hadrian, Emperor. Use his full, official titles. There is disquiet among the generals at your decision to pull out of the areas most recently conquered by Trajan. There are similar voices among the Senate, saying that you are treating the provinces – and especially Parthia – too gently. Wild rumours have even reached me that your very adoption was manipulated. But all this is to be expected at such a time. I am of course keeping close watch on all events and will continue to report every happening or rumour. In reply to your recent letter, I confirm that there will be no more killings without your direct authorisation."

Well, maybe just one more, he thought, *but that hardly counts.*

"Signed Publius Acilius Attianus, Prefect, et cetera. At once."

"Yes, sir," the secretary bowed himself out of the room.

Attianus thought for a moment, and a different kind of smile appeared on his face. *Goodbye to the rat, hallo to the little fox.*

He rose and lifted a flagon, pouring wine into two goblets. He went to the door of his personal chamber, opening it softly and standing inside the doorway. He smelt her fragrance before he saw her. Then she came into his line of sight: her alabaster skin, her long brown hair, that slightly wistful expression that had beguiled so many...

"Greetings, Vulpecula!" he said with a laugh. He passed her a goblet and took a sip of his own.

"Must you call me that?"

"Little fox? It suits you. And I prefer it to 'little vixen'. How goes your assignment?"

"Concluded," she said, with the faintest of shadows crossing her face.

"Good. The wholesale business can do without him very well – even if it means hazelnuts, pinecones and apricots are raised a few sestertii!"

She lifted her wine to her lips, and he watched as she tasted it.

"He seemed a harmless enough man – not enough to warrant a contract."

"He had got under the skin of one too many people. But you don't want to know about that. Let me tell you about your next job."

She looked at him with horror, "I don't want to do this work any more. I'm too well known in Rome – and in Italia too. All I want is to be left alone." A tear brimmed in her eye, "A quiet life. That's all I ask."

"You will have it. But just one more assignment, Vulpecula."

"No! You can't make me!"

"Can't I?"

The softness of his words sent shivers down her spine, and she saw warning in his hard eyes, so she quickly back-tracked, "I'm sorry, Publius. I heard about your day in the Senate."

He laughed, "I'll get to them soon enough, and no -I won't need your services for that. But I need you to do one more job for me. Just one, but it will be the crowning achievement of your career. It's far enough away that no one will know you, and it's a princely sum. It'll set you up for life. And then you can say farewell to all this forever – my pretty little fox."

She chewed the inside of her lip, "Very well," she said after a pause. "Just one more job."

"Excellent," his hand momentarily brushed her perfect cheek.

"See my secretary as you go. He'll pay you what you earned for the last assignment. I'll arrange all the details and be in touch. And don't worry! After this mission, you can come and live with me in luxury."

"Live with you?" He had managed to surprise her.

"The right-hand of the emperor should have a consort, and the more powerful the man, the lovelier the lady." He let that sink in for a moment, "We'll have an extended holiday in my summer house in Neapolis. It's on the world's most beautiful bay, overlooking the magical island of Capri. You'll love it. The climate's always mild, it's rich in history and architecture, the food's a marvel, and it has all the empire's latest fashions. All you need to enjoy it, is the right man at your side."

She looked at him, eyes wide.

He smiled, "Think about it."

She left the chamber, her movement trailing a trace of perfume. Attianus watched her leave, sat down and sighed. Such beauty. And so fleeting.

*

A servant left the Regia, travelling down the main road leading up the Aventine Hill. Crowds bustled around him, taking no notice of a hired man about his master's business. He walked on, now paralleling the mighty Tiber River, heading towards Ostia, Port of Rome.

Walking along, he noted the familiar scenes: grain being unloaded, weighed, checked for quality, then loaded onto barges to feed the hordes of the world's greatest city. There was a mass of men, heaving, lowering, labouring, sweating, measuring but all were ordered, everyone knew his place. The Roman way.

Finally, he reached the office area. Two heavy bodyguards looked at him as he approached the stairs, and he moistened his lips with his tongue.

"Well?" said a thick-set man who looked as though he'd been diverting those grain barges for his own personal ends.

"I'm looking for Captain Paetus," said the servant.

"Stand still," the heavy approached, flanked by his comrade and patted the servant down, searching for weapons. "Well?" he said again, finding nothing.

"A message from the City Prefect " said the servant, lamely.

"Give me the note."

"Such messages are not written down. I have it memorised."

The burly man looked the servant in the eye, surprised, and then burst into a laugh, "Good," he said. "Come with me."

They walked up the stairs into the office area and over to a man with dark hair and weather-beaten skin, who stood watching a boat being loaded with wine and other goods for the provinces. He looked up quizzically at their approach.

"A message," said the heavy.

Captain Paetus took in the scene: the diminutive, timorous servant; the amused bodyguard. He dismissed the latter with a wave, and said, "Tell me."

The servant looked up fearfully.

"My dear Captain Paetus," he recited, "I regret to inform you that your main business rival, Captain Piso, has met with an unfortunate accident. As a result, we now have total control over all the imports into the Port of Rome. With the Imperial Fleet protecting your cargo vessels, we will soon both be rich men. I expect the price of all imported goods to rise a few sestertii from tomorrow. Meet me in the Aventine market tomorrow at noon and we will discuss details."

The captain's eyebrows rose, followed by the corners of his mouth, "Piso dead?

How on earth did that happen?"

"I don't know, my lord."

"Well, no doubt your master does."

The servant bowed his head "Do you wish to send a reply?"

The captain was silent for a moment.

"I have an excellent memory."

Paetus smiled. "I am sure of that. Just say that Captain Paetus will meet your master tomorrow at the time and place specified."

He stood watching as the servant bowed and began the long trudge back through the ancient harbour town, seabirds crying and wheeling in the sky above.

*

Seven miles to the south in Castra Bremenium, Cohort Commander Praefectus Severus was in conference with his second in command. Their faces were grave. They both knew the situation. An hour earlier, auxiliaries had been sent to relieve the forces occupying the watchtowers – only to find the towers were smoking ruins and their troops annihilated. The soldiers fled back to Bremenium, only too happy to hear the huge wooden gates bang shut behind them. Two squads had been sent to the south, for reinforcements. But the nearest fort was at Habitancum, ten miles distant.

"It's dangerous," said the Commander. "We've lost one fifth of our numbers with the watchtowers, and another ten men riding for help. Less than a hundred of us left – against who knows how many of those savages."

His second in command nodded, "Yes, sir. But we're in a fort. Well defended, well armed. Much better than a tiny, isolated watchtower. And help may arrive soon."

"It may never arrive," said Severus. "This was a well crafted plan, well executed. If I was their commander I'd have infiltrated warrior units between here and Habitancum. We're in their territory now." He moved over to the wall to consult the map, "We're too spaced out here, that's the problem," he said, tracing the line of forts south to Eboracum. Down there was the Ninth Legion, strong enough to slaughter any number of barbarians. But that was over one hundred miles away. "We're enough to keep order when times are normal," he said. "But if we have to re-conquer this godforsaken place..."

"All we can do is stay put," said his second in command. "Even in daylight, there just aren't enough of us to make it back. We'd be cut down."

"Agreed," said the Praefectus. "Let's take a walk outside."

They left the briefing room and went out into the rapidly chilling air. Severus returned the salutes of his officers as he walked along under the battle parapet, noting the doubled guards porting their weaponry.

"Let's have more braziers up there, more torches at the ready," he ordered and a soldier leapt into action, issuing orders of his own.

Castra Bremenium was in total readiness. Its walls were high, ending in sharpened stakes. Its defenders were well trained, well equipped, well armoured. But it was an outpost: a tiny bastion in enemy country. It seemed to

Severus that he could sense the hostility in the woods and grasslands all around.

*

And out there in the woods, out of sight and out of range, the worst fears of the Praefectus were realised.

"Are they expecting us?" asked Ortagorus, noting the men on the battlements, the flaming braziers lighting up the normally black sky.

"Yes they are," said Vordimus. "They know that their watchtowers have been destroyed. But that knowledge won't do them any good."

"You are confident," said the Brigantes chieftain. "Can you be sure that we can take the fort before help arrives?"

"If we had siege equipment, it would be easy. But we don't. Therefore we must depend on Fortuna."

"Fortuna?"

"Yes. Fate. Good luck," said Vordimus with a smile. "If a force of the watchtower defenders had survived and fought their way back here, for instance, the Romans would open the doors for them, would they not?"

Ortagorus looked at him strangely, "But no defenders did survive."

Vordimus laughed, and gestured behind him. A squad of Roman auxiliaries suddenly appeared in battle order. Ortagorus jumped to his feet with an oath, his sword half out of his belt...and looked more closely at the faces of the soldiers. And then he laughed too, loud and long, slapping Vordimus on the back.

SPQR

In war we must always leave room for strokes of
fortune and accidents that cannot be forseen.

Polybius

V   Bremenium

12.50am, 31st October, 117AD: territory of the Brigantes, Northern Britain

The Hallowed Eve of the Underworld

The night had seemed to last forever. Had there ever been a time when he hadn't been walking, left, right, left, even in his sleep it seemed? But finally, finally, the grey dawn had broken. It was chill and the wind was laden with rain, as so often in Britannia – but at least it was getting light. Novantes sank down against a tree, every limb throbbing with an immense fatigue; his head still pounding fiercely, as it had done since his encounter with the warrior of the Brigantes. That seemed like another lifetime ago.

He looked up as the last shreds of night faded away. There! Castra Bremenium! He'd made it! Against all odds! His spirit wanted his body to leap to its feet and run uphill the three hundred yards to the fort, but his body had other ideas. A few minutes' respite. After all, Bremenium wasn't going anywhere. His eyes sought out the sentries on the ramparts, patrolling, crossing, javelins at the ready, shields on their back. He saw the deep ditches protecting the walls. Order, safety, civilisation. All was as it should be. He breathed a sigh of relief. A sigh that was stifled almost before it was out of his throat. Some sort of movement in the trees behind him. He froze, hardly daring to breathe.

His hand strayed to the pommel of his sword, but it was useless. There was nothing to do but watch and wait. He didn't have to wait long. But what happened took him by surprise.

A group of ten or twelve men broke cover and ran into the open before the fort. Novantes' eyebrows shot up in astonishment. Roman auxiliaries, clearly: they wore chainmail shirts and metal cuirasses, but lacked the expensive body armour issued to legionaries. Also, their shields were round – the auxiliaries' *clipeus*, rather than the *scutum*, the curved, rectangular shield that legionaries carried.

They might have been his own comrades, the latest watchtower detail. But surely, most, if not all of them, were dead. These men looked like they'd been through it, though; they were bedraggled, their armour muddied, and some bore evident wounds. Who were they? Some detachment from another border fort, perhaps?

At the glad sight of Roman uniforms and armour, Novantes had almost jumped to his feet and ran over to join them. But something held him back. He continued to watch. The man leading the motley crew had more of a military air about him. He was uniformed as a tesserarius, but his demeanour suggested a centurion at least: a man who took it for granted that he would be obeyed. He saluted the men on the parapet. They called back with the request for passwords.

"I don't know your passwords, and I don't care. Let us in, can't you?" The wind carried the strong voice back to the tree line. Perfect colloquial Latin. Novantes couldn't quite place the accent, but that wasn't unusual; auxiliaries were drawn from all over the empire. Nevertheless the sudden appearance of these unidentifiable troops spread unease amongst the defenders.

"Come on lads, let us in. We fought our way through a force of *barbari* to get here. They can't be far behind us. And we're freezing our arses off in this godforsaken place!"

Novantes could see the guards chuckling. It was the perfect response for an officer of the watch or higher who had been through a bloody skirmish: slightly world-weary, yet still able to make the foot soldiers smile.

A second later, though, no one was smiling; a squad of Brigantes emerged into the open, running like the wind, weapons at the ready. The auxiliaries were now calling out for help, banging on the gates with their fists and swords.

Don't let them in! thought Novantes. Something wasn't right, something he couldn't quite put his finger on. He could see the confusion and apprehension in the guards' posture. He imagined the mayhem going on inside the fort, soldiers calling for their superiors, desperate for orders. There was a shout for the duty centurion.

"Let us in now!" bawled the tesserarius.

Someone in authority must have taken the decision, for the main gate started to swing slowly open. Guards on the parapets waved their comrades below into the safety of the fort. The trapped auxiliaries pushed on the huge gate to aid its opening and rushed inside.

Through the open gateway, Novantes saw an officer flanked by the men guarding the gate: foot soldiers carrying javelins. The fugitives paused, apparently out of breath as the officer approached. Novantes could see them bending over, breathing deeply, holding their sides. In a single moment, though, that exhaustion was gone. They moved as one, leaping into action, drawing their swords. An upward sweeping sword stroke flailed a parabola of blood into the air, almost decapitating one guard. In the next second, the officer and the guards lay dead.

The hairs on the back of Novantes' neck rose as he watched. The assault had happened so quickly that there was no reaction inside the fort. Time seemed to stand still. Two men whipped their shields from their backs and jammed them under the massive open gate, holding it fast. Someone from the parapets was shouting alarm. A trumpet from the battlements sounded three solid notes.

Novantes saw the fear and the frenzied reactions: the guards on the ramparts drawing swords, hefting javelins. *Wake up!* A voice shrilled inside his head.

The thirty Brigantes reached the open gate and stormed inside the fort, reinforcing their advance guard and formed a circle round the door. The strengthened formation was quickly under attack from auxiliaries, but they held their ground. Then a hoarse cry, filled with venom and deadly intent, broke from what seemed to be the whole tree line. Novantes shrank back in horror as the woods around him came alive with men. Brigantes, hundreds of them: blue-daubed, bare-chested, running into the now open and defenceless fort, screaming their war cries just as they had done when his watchtower had been attacked.

"Esus," Novantes breathed.

Inside the fort, the trumpet continued to sound. Novantes could hear orders being shouted from the ramparts. Archers had now appeared behind the battlements and launched a volley of arrows hissing into the air. A dozen or more Brigantes rolled screaming onto the grass, giving Novantes new heart for a moment. Everything depended on the defenders getting the gate shut before that horde closed in on them.

Novantes could imagine the scene inside the fort: men running, strapping on belts, pulling on mail shirts, arranging equipment as they hastened to get into position. He knew the centurions would be ordering men forward to retake the gate and repel the invaders. Groups of auxiliaries ran forward to attack the circle: but it was tightly formed and the invaders seemed well trained.

Indeed, at first they seemed to be invincible. The Brigantes reinforcements had mighty battleaxes which they swung high above their heads and scythed huge circles ahead of them. Everything in the way of those killing arcs – hand, arm, or head – was defenceless. Long swords clashed upon Roman armour, tearing shields in two, right down through the bone of the arms carrying them. The cries of anguish, screams of shock and pain, were horrible to hear.

Now, arrows from the parapets and javelins from the troops on the ground started to take their toll: the Romans were making some headway. The circle of invaders was slowly being pushed back. Some had now been forced back into the open, beyond the line of the walls. But the barbarian army was rushing ever closer, their numbers only thinned by the Roman arrows.

Cut them down! thought Novantes.

And then, confusion: the fort's defenders made a last desperate drive to push the circle out. At the same time, the tide of blue bodies swept into the gateway. There was an enormous clash and crush of bodies, swaying and shoving, slashing, spearing, dying. Then the defenders gave way under the sheer weight of numbers and the invaders won through, hoarse cries, oaths and screams mingling in the air.

The momentum of that triumphant, exultant surge of men broke over the still disorganised auxiliaries like a killing wave. As an auxiliary parried one sword thrust, another warrior would smash through from a different angle, breaking nose or severing arm, cleaving jawbone from face, hammering razor-sharp metal between ribs. Blood pooled on the ground and filled the air like hot mist, spattering the faces of victor and vanquished alike. Men scaled the ramparts and ran the archers through, or cast them down to be torn apart by the blood-crazed forces below.

And then it was all over.

The garrison of Castra Bremenium was wiped out, to a man. To one man: Praefectus Severus, backed up against a wall in his own commander's quarters, ashen-faced, cold sweat drenching him. He held his own *gladius* blade to his heart, both hands poised, white-knuckled, for the final lunge. He'd seen enough of the battle to know that defeat was upon him and dishonour – the worst fate that could befall a commander of the imperial army – waited implacably. The room darkened in his eyes and he stared towards eternity, but saw no glory there. The Roman pantheon seemed pale and colourless as marble, and his own Gallic gods looked on in contempt.

The door burst open and three warriors of the Brigantes surged into the room. Their eyes fell on Severus, and something about his dress, his uniform, told them that this was a man of great rank. One of them gave a huge cry and would have run at the Prefect; but another in authority restrained him, with an arm across his upper body.

The Brigantian and the Gaul looked each other in the eye. Nobody moved. The warrior took in the scenario: a proud officer, high-born, menacing himself with his own weapon. The fine workmanship of it gleamed bright in the light of the lamps. The warrior relaxed, and made a small gesture with his left hand, waving it towards the commander. They spoke very different languages, but there was no need for words. The meaning was obvious: *Go ahead, if you're man enough.*

But Severus was not, and the short sword clanged to the ground. The two other warriors leapt forward and pinioned Severus' arms to his sides, marching him out of the room. As he came alongside the Brigantian squad leader, they stopped, and again the two men looked into each other's souls. There was nothing in Severus's but despair. The squad leader smiled, gestured again and the former commander was hauled away.

Outside in the open, warriors stood looking around, panting: they realised that their victory was complete. The horde bellowed their invincibility to each other and to their gods.

The leader of the advance force, Vordimus, hurled the tesserarius' helmet from his head and looked around for the leader of the shock troops. He saw Ortagorus striding towards him, in delight. They slapped hand to forearm in a fierce, elated embrace. Wide-eyed with jubilation, the two men stood in the centre of what had been the Roman outpost fort, cheers and war cries resounding around them.

Vordimus took a deep breath of air: "Hail to you, Ortagorus," he said. "You could not have led your men with greater zeal."

Ortagorus laughed, his sword-blade running with blood and rain, "The ruse was yours, Vordimus. I was as impressed as the Romans were!"

Vordimus looked about him, "Your numbers have swelled, even in so short a time!"

"Yes. They are beginning to believe the unbelievable: that Brigantia may regain all its lost lands – and capture more territory."

"It can, and it will. Let the men get their breath and drink to the fallen. Then let the walls of this place be burnt to the ground."

Half an hour later, Novantes saw the first wisp of smoke curl from the undefended parapets. It was quickly followed by a lick of hungry flame and a huge roar of approval. He groaned, held his aching head in his hands for a moment, then raised his eyes. He had known almost every man within that fort. He had toiled side by side with them, digging the ditches, painting the Principia, building the road. Now the fort and its garrison were gone. And seemingly his journey southwards was far from over. Then he reflected on what had happened. If he hadn't been wounded in the attack on the watchtowers, he'd have arrived at the fort yesterday – and would now have been lying lifeless on the ground with the rest of Bremenium's complement. That was twice he'd cheated death in as many days. His misery lifted just a little. Maybe Esus had not forsaken him after all.

*

Marcus looked up, "Not bad for a provincial village," he said, and Libo grinned. Eboracum was finally before them. It was massive: a fort worthy of a proud Roman legion. It had been a longish journey from the port of Petuaria, even with the horse Marcus had commandeered. But this made it all worthwhile. Outside the walls were crowded with shops and stalls of merchants taking advantage of the proximity of so many troops. There were taverns aplenty, shops selling everything from soap to bread, fruit and jewellery. There were perfume sellers, *tabernae argentariae* handling currency exchange and other banking services, stone cutters and copyists. There were living areas for the wives, girlfriends and camp followers of the army. The noise, the smells, the bustle and sheer exuberance were tremendous. It was cold, though; colder than either of them had expected. A chill wind blew through the alleys between the shops. Marcus wrapped his cloak around his shoulders.

A street trader stood in their way. "What's the hurry, honoured sirs?" he spoke in just about recognisable Latin, although the accent was comically rustic. "Just off the boat? Quite so. Foul climate, ain't it? What you need is this here special linctus, guaranteed to cure your cough. Very popular with the soldiers. A marvel for the ague, too."

"As we don't have coughs, we don't need cough syrup," said Libo, and turned to go.

The trader steered him back with a gentle finger on his elbow, "No cough, sir? Why, you're the lucky one. I can see you take care of yourself – not like some of these layabouts! But a smart soldier needs to look smart. What about this polish? It'll clean the rust off your armour a real treat. Got to look just so for inspection, haven't you sir? All the legionaries have a bottle – swear by it."

Libo thought for a second, "How much?"

The trader looked at Libo, a pleasant expression on his whiskery face, "The usual price is four sestertii, sir."

"What! A day's wage?"

"Usually, yes," said the trader, smoothing Libo's cloak with his hand in a placatory way. "But I've taken a liking to you, sir. Don't want to think of you earning the wrath of your officer. You know what some of them officers is like! So to you, two sestertii." He looked him hopefully in the eye.

"Thanks, but I don't –"

"Ah, you're weakening, sir! Understandably so. Very well: one sestertius. Though I'm selling at a loss."

Libo pondered for a moment.

"It's wonderful stuff, sir. Just the smallest dab and the rust is gone. Beautiful it is. Makes it shine like silver. This bottle will last you four months – maybe longer."

"Oh, very well," said Libo. He dug in his purse and handed over a large brass coin.

"You won't regret it, sir," said the trader, passing over the bottle and pocketing the money, as Libo and Marcus turned to go. "And you're getting an even better bargain than you think."

"How so?"

"When you do get that cough, this'll soothe it away for you too!" and he darted into the crowd.

Libo and Marcus looked at each other: then burst out laughing.

"Well, come on," said Marcus. "I'm anxious to report for duty."

"Me too," said Libo. "But I always make it a habit to sample the local brew wherever I'm posted to a new place. Don't want to insult the natives."

"There's something in what you say," smiled Marcus. "We don't want to start by causing a diplomatic incident!"

They walked over to the nearest tavern and entered. It was dark inside but crowded. Men sat at tables, putting the world to rights in timeless fashion. The cousins went to the bar and asked for beer. They took their cups to a vacant table and sat down.

"Well," said Libo. He raised his cup. "To the future."

They sipped, and made wry faces at each other.

"That's going to take some getting used to," said Libo.

"A lot of things are, like the climate – as our opportunistic merchant pointed out."

Libo frowned, "Maybe we should stick to wine."

"Might not be any better after it's been tossed up and down on a stormy passage over the waters – I somehow doubt that there's any such thing as home-grown wine in Britannia!" laughed Marcus. "Besides, we should get used to the local fare. This place is our home now – for how long, the gods only know."

"I suppose so," said Libo. He took another mouthful, "Maybe it's not so bad."

A man built like the gatepost of a fort entered the *taberna*. Although not in uniform, he had the bearing of a centurion – and one who by the look of him had seen plenty of action. Marcus nudged Libo to look, as the man approached the bar, dropping his pack on the dusty floor and wiping his brow with a hand like a bear's paw.

"Beer," he said.

The barman jumped into action and set a beer in front of him. The man took a great quaff from his cup. His face darkened and he spat the mouthful onto the floor in an explosive spray: "What in Hades is that?"

"Beer, sir," said the barman nervously.

"Beer? Tastes like the water you do the washing up in!"

"I'm sorry, sir –"

A fist reached over the bar and lifted the barman up bodily by his shirt-front, "I don't want your apology, I want you to get me something fit to drink."

The barman scurried about and came back with a different coloured beer. He placed it tentatively before the hulking figure, "This is our very best beer, sir. We save it for the officers. Or there's wine, sir, if…" he trailed away, his eyes following the upward journey of the refilled cup with apprehension.

The soldier took a long draught and his eyes narrowed suspiciously as he absorbed the flavour: but no more violence followed, "I suppose it will have to do – if it's your best," he growled.

Muttering imprecations on the country, the weather and most of all, the beer, he sat down at a table, taking his cloak off and throwing it onto the chair beside him. Marcus noted the scorpion tattoo on his arm.

"Look at him," whispered Libo. "No neck – just a head and a body!"

"Yes," Marcus whispered back. "And something else. See that Scorpion tattoo on his arm? He's been in the Praetorian Guard – and maybe still is. That's their symbol. Better watch out. Anyway," he said in a normal voice, "Let's drink up. I want to report to the Commander – and even more, I want a bath."

Libo raised his cup again: "Hope you find what you're looking for."

"Yes," said Marcus, lowering his voice again: "But not a word about the past to anyone here. We'll just do our job and see what the Legate of the Twelfth can find out for us."

They rose to go. As they were passing the man, Libo tripped on the uneven surface and bumped into him.

"Oy, you brat!" he snarled. "Tavern's not big enough for you? You have to walk right up my nose? Watch where you're going."

"Sorry," said Libo.

Marcus looked directly at the man and got an equally direct brazen stare. Marcus was clearly dressed in his old tribune uniform, Libo clearly his companion, but neither fact seemed to impress the older man. They passed on outside, into the light and the chill wind.

"Goodbye, 'no-neck'! Hope we don't meet again!" laughed Libo, and Marcus rolled his eyes.

*

At the same moment, over 100 miles to the north, the wind was even more bracing: especially to fighters with the sweat of battle drying on their brows.

"My fellow warriors and I have spoken together, and it is our desire to honour you," said Ortagorus, gesturing for Vordimus to follow him outside through the open gateway. The wooden fort behind them was now ablaze with a vengeance, the flames competing with the icy winds for precedence.

"I thank you greatly, but I need no honour," said Vordimus.

Ortagorus smiled. "What we have in mind is not the empty Roman honour of laurel wreaths and awards. It is something from our heart."

Vordimus smiled too. "My apologies, my friend," he said. "I would be only too happy to please you – and your comrades."

Ortagorus looked about him, blinking from the smoke billowing into his eyes, "What did you say the Romans called this place?"

"Bremenium. The place of the roaring stream."

"Ah yes. I remember now. Well, let me take you to the stream itself."

They walked side by side through the long grasses blown around by the fierce winds on the exposed hilltop. Around them, warriors of the Brigantes were making an end to things: gathering up weapons, hauling off the bodies of their honoured dead, despatching those of their enemies who still moaned. Deferential, proud and worshipful glances followed them as the two chieftains passed by.

An oak tree, its glory already diminished by the depredations of autumn, guarded the approach to a scarcely discernable path. The two leaders reached the spot and looked down to a bubbling stream.

Ortagorus placed his hand in an almost fatherly way on the shoulder of Vordimus, "We call this force of water a *burn*, and the name of this one is *Sills*," he said. "It has been, for time out of mind. The Roman name for it is unimportant, and will be spoken no more."

Vordimus agreed. They walked down the incline to the Sills Burn, stubbly grass underfoot. They stood looking south. Both of them knew they were looking into their future, their destiny. Beyond those peaceful rolling hills were Roman garrisons, heavily defended, strong in depth – not like the watchtowers or this easily tricked outpost. But that was for tomorrow.

"Come," said Ortagorus. He bent down and cupped the clear water in his hands, wiping the blood of the living and the dead from his body and face. Vordimus did the same.

"We have cleansed ourselves," said Ortagorus. "Those stains were marks of honour; but we cannot enter the sacred grove without purifying ourselves. It is fitting."

"The sacred grove?"

"Yes, or so it was, before the legions desecrated it with their presence," he paused, sighed for a moment. "These Romans of yours: they have no reverence in them. They come trumpeting their false gods, but the real gods shrug and are untouched. Each place, each thing, has a spirit and a force of will: every rock, every tree, every river, every lake." He looked away again to the horizon line.

"They are not my Romans," said Vordimus gently.

It broke his companion's reverie and he smiled, "I know," he said. "But these Romans...they are mighty – yes. The world bows down before them. For now. They think they will last forever. But nothing of man is forever. We are here, then gone. Only the earth continues, unchanging, wondrous... The world is magical, and the Romans would snuff out the magic and render it commonplace."

Vordimus wiped the clean water from his brow. It felt good to be free of the reek of his foes. The peaceful setting and the soft words of his comrade calmed him, and took him years back, to when he was younger and the world was less complex.

"I am with you, for as long as we endure," he said.

Ortagorus smiled again. "It is fitting," he said again. "Come."

They walked back up the hill, past the blazing fortress to their right, and into a clearing of venerable oaks. Holy men, their heads and shoulders bedecked with mistletoe were scattering water from vessels onto the ground and chanting.

Ortagorus spoke: "This evening is the one most sacred in the whole year. Tonight, the everyday world of men and the Otherworld of the gods come together. On this hallowed eve, we will offer a sacrifice to the gods."

He moved back as two warriors of the Brigantes brought forward the sacrifice. Struggling and gagged, the cohort Commander of Bremenium protested against imminent death, yet the hopelessness in his eyes showed that it could not be averted. Vordimus looked at him; pity, contempt and the fitness of things in his eyes. A Druid stepped forward and passed a knife over the garrison commander's throat. A gush of blood spilled onto the sacred ground; the body convulsing, life quickly fading.

"The grove returns to its holiness, and the gods are appeased," said Oragorus.

They stood together while the cleansing was completed and then the holy men grouped together, facing the East, chanting with one voice.

"They salute our fallen and light a path for them to the Otherworld," said the chieftain. "Each man who died today will receive undying glory for his sacrifice."

As they watched, a hint of amber appeared in the sky, heralding the sunset, as though in tribute to the immortal dead. The chanting ceased.

Ortagorus moved around to face his comrade, and from all sides, the bravest and most distinguished in battle of the Brigantes moved into the sacred grove. They halted at a respectful distance and bowed their heads.

"Vordimus," said Ortagorus reverently. "I am proud to call you my brother." The warriors around them echoed his words.

"Say after me," and Voruminous repeated his comrade's words:

I bow my head
To the ageless ones
In the eye of the mother who bore me
In the eye of the gods who will receive me
In the eye of the maiden who loves me
In the eye of the Crone who guides me in wisdom:
Fill us with strength, with discernment, with valour
And let us walk always honouring our ancestors and
our gods."

Vordimus spoke the words, the sunset growing in the sky as though applauding him. Then Ortagorus bade him kneel on the grass and garlanded his head with mistletoe. He anointed his brow with water brought to him by an acolyte. He stood back, and one by one, the warriors bedecked his shoulders with ivy leaves and other sacred growths.

Finally, it was done. The solemnity was past. To the cheering of the warriors, Ortagorus said, "Stand, my friend! You are a Druid!".

Warriors ran in, plunging stakes bearing torches into the virgin ground. Others arrived, carrying wineskins; some, capering like animals and dressed in skins and fur, sported, lunged and cavorted. They caroused, laughing and exulted, welcoming their new brother.

Vordimus took a full wineskin, held it high above his head and squeezed. A stream of wine spattered his mouth, his face, his tesserarius's uniform. And there was a great cheer of approval.

As the sunset bathed the scene in scarlet, purple and gold, Novantes shivered. He heard the roar of laughter and rejoicing, though he couldn't see the object of the celebration. But he didn't need to. It was clear enough what was going on: barbarians shouting their victory over the fortress of Bremenium, now a burnt heap of charred wood.

Well, it was equally clear what he needed to do: head back south, to warn his comrades about the impending assault – or die in the attempt. He raised himself achingly to his feet, his head pounding like an insistent tolling, and recommenced his journey.

VI Eboracum

Marcus and Libo moved through the shops, past the traders, the hagglers and those importuning them for money. Marcus's mind was already on his first interview with his new commander.

At the gates of the fortress there was a delay while lengthy checks were carried out, passwords were verified, written orders examined. Finally, the soldiers were passed through the gates and asked to wait.

A centurion emerged from the office, "If you'll come with me, sir, I'll escort you," he said to Marcus.

The cousins faced each other. "I'll see you soon," said Marcus, slapping Libo on the back.

"Fortuna be with you."

The centurion led him on, past the usual buildings, on into the Principia. Here, he had to wait again while the centurion handed him over to a secretary. At last, he was escorted into the legate's quarters.

"*Praefectus alae* Valerius Quietus," he said, bowing and departing.

In front of him was a shortish man who didn't immediately look up, keeping Marcus standing at attention. Marcus looked down at the balding head and wispy hair. Eventually, the legate raised his head from his papers, fixing Marcus with a querulous glance, "Ah, Quietus," he said. "Let's see, you were transferred from the Tenth?"

"The Twelfth, sir."

"Ah yes. You're one of Gnaeus Gratialis's boys." Was it Marcus's imagination, or was there the slightest emphasis on that word "boys"? "He's a fine officer. Knew him well. Good voyage?"

Marcus smiled wanly, "A somewhat turbulent crossing –"

The legate snorted, "Not as turbulent as some I've had, I'll wager."

"No, sir."

The legate shuffled through some papers until he found what he was looking for, "A little young to be a cavalry battalion Prefect, aren't we?"

I wonder if "we" have ever commanded a cavalry unit? thought Marcus, but he said, "I'm told I showed promise..."

"Hmmm. Well, we'll see. The *Legio IX Hispana* is a proud legion, one of the oldest and most feared in the Imperial Army. My officers have to earn their rank. And if they're not up to the mark, they get demoted fast."

Marcus flushed, "Yes, sir."

"But cavalry is vital, especially against barbarians," said the legate. "My father was a cavalry commander in the Dacian wars. Singled out for especial merit by Trajan when he helped defeat Decebalus in the Second Battle of Tapae."

"Impressive, Legate," said Marcus.

"Oh yes, all my people are army," he said. "My grandfather served in Germania, you know. He won several distinctions too. Indeed," said the legate, "something of a hero, by all accounts." The heir of heroes stood up, revealing himself to be somewhat overweight, "Come over here and let me show you the map."

Marcus followed him to the beautifully executed chart.

"We're not quite at full strength presently," said the legate. "The Senior Tribune is in Belgica, supporting some legionary training there. But the *Primus Pilus* is a very able young man. You'll meet him soon. Fortunately, it's all quiet at the moment, has been for ages." A stubby finger stabbed at the map, "This tribe is the *Brigantes*, once a warlike bunch of savages, but we gave them a real thrashing some years back, and they're docile enough now. Of course, we need to maintain readiness at all times. Look here: this is the line of fortresses, forts and garrisons stretching right up into what was once Brigantian territory. This is Bremenium, the northern most outpost. The barbarians can't make a move without being observed. Man called Severus in charge there – excellent officer. I chose him myself for that assignment. You'll have the chance to be stationed at Bremenium, do some scouting. We have twenty cavalry posted there at all times. Very important, scouts; they're our eyes and ears. Nothing gets past them. Anyway, it's good to have some replacements, and you'll be valuable if you're as good as this report says." Again, the hint of doubt emphasising the word "if".

"Thank you, sir." Marcus tried to keep his look respectful.

"All right, that's enough; we'll go into details later." The legate seated himself at his desk again. "Get off to the officers' quarters and settle in, and draw your kit in the morning. Well, must get back to my paperwork – this fortress doesn't run itself."

Marcus saluted, but the eyes of his commander were already on the papers below him. He walked quickly from the room.

*

It was mid-day on the Aventine, one of the seven hills of Rome. Captain Paetus strode through the crowds in the famous Aventine market, slightly ill at ease as he always was on land. Even his legs didn't feel quite right without the pitch of the decks under him. A carriage, clumsily driven, knocked over the supports of one of the market stalls, and it collapsed with a tumultuous noise, sending fruit rolling everywhere. A roar of laughter went up. The sounds disturbed a flock of birds which rose with a clap of wings into the air, quarrelling and disputing. Part of an ancient memory came back to him at the sight of the circling flock of birds, *aves*: the Aventine was named after them. Bird Hill.

Then he saw ahead of him the nonchalant figure of the Head of the Praetorians, and he forgot about the birds in a second. Attianus stood, impeccably and expensively dressed, examining a pottery vase held in his hand. As he stood, a shaft of sunshine broke through the thick cloud cover, transforming the bustling scene. The seafarer approached the politician, a rare diffidence in his manner.

Attianus looked up as though surprised, "Why, Captain," he said. "This is well met." He clapped a hand on his shoulder and put the vase back on the stall. The two of them strolled away into the crowd.

Attianus waited until the buyers and sellers had thinned out, then spoke, his voice quiet, "So, Captain, I trust you are enjoying your more secure position." Although phrased as a question, it was a statement.

"Indeed yes."

"Then all that remains is to discuss how to divide the spoils. My thought was seven tenths to me, three to you."

The sun vanished again behind the banks of cloud: and a shadow passed over the face of the sailor, "That seems scarcely fair, Lord. I and my crews are the ones taking all the risks."

Attianus stopped to admire a display of sweetmeats. He smiled at the vendor and they passed on, "On the contrary, it's completely fair. And you are certainly not taking all the risks. How do you think you have come to this eminent position? Your vessels are safeguarded by the Imperial Fleet, and you even enjoy protection here in Rome."

Paetus was silent for a while, then "Six tenths to you, four to me," he suggested.

Attianus smiled again. "No doubt it's hard for you to keep up with current events, being at sea so much. But I hear that our new Emperor Hadrian is determined to stamp out corruption throughout the Empire," he said. "Quite right, don't you think?"

"Assuredly," said the Captain, although his tone was less committed.

"Yes. An iron fist is the best way to sort out those who seek to abuse the system for their own ends. For instance, tampering with the grain supply is a capital offence," he turned and looked into the eyes of Paetus. The captain was the first to drop his gaze.

"Perhaps your division is best after all," he said.

"We will agree to say so," said the Prefect of the City, urbanely. He smiled again and the mood lightened. He clapped Paetus's shoulder again, "I congratulate you," he said. "You will be a very rich man and more importantly, you have wisdom – which is worth even more than wealth. My duties call me away. As always, a pleasure to see you. I will send my man to you later to tie up the details. Farewell, Captain."

"Farewell..." there was an unfinished air about his valediction and he cleared his throat. Attianus raised his eyebrows and tilted his head in invitation. The sailor went on, "How did Captain Piso meet his end? He seemed so – well, it seemed as though nothing could touch him."

Attianus lowered his eyes piously, "So true. He was hale and virile. But none of us knows when Pluto will choose to pay us a visit."

Paetus looked uncomfortable, but the Prefect smiled warmly.

"Come, don't be glum, Captain. Wasn't it Hippocrates who said that life is short and opportunity fleeting? All the more reason to make the most of both!"

*

Roll call next morning, and the legion's newest officer slipped unobtrusively into his place. The room was crowded with centurions, officers and prefects. One or two fellow officers smiled a greeting. No doubt Marcus' transfer would have been announced to them, with the other business of the day. He looked around him. In the whirl of events – the numbing shock of his family being massacred, the hastily arranged posting, the wild voyage over the water and the headlong ride from the port of Petuaria – he'd had little time to think about his new unit. But now he did. This was the *Legio IX Hispana*, the Ninth Hispanic Legion, raised by Pompey, first commanded by Julius Caesar himself, which had served with distinction throughout the Gallic Wars.

Marcus took in the tattered standards adorning the walls, emblazoned with the legion's bull motif. Men of the Ninth had fought with Octavian against Mark Antony at Actium. There were many other honours: Dyrrhachium, Pharsalus, the African war, the campaign against the Cantabrians in Hispania from where the name of Hispana derived...Yes, this was a proud and mighty legion. Part of him, even after the turmoil of recent weeks, was delighted and humbled to be attached to it.

The roll call began and Marcus answered his name with pleasure. But then the sick list and the number of men unavailable for duty were announced by cohort. Pride gave way to astonishment, and even something like shock.

"...Second century, first cohort: five men sick, twenty posted to Luguvalium, fifty men fit. Third century, first cohort: ten men on cleaning duties, five on guard watch, two sick, sixty-three men fit..."

Marcus noted that a number of cohorts had only four or five centuries rather than the more usual eight. He did a quick calculation as the reports went on: instead of six thousand legionaries, the Ninth had around four thousand fit for duty. Undermanned by a third. The words of the pompous, pot-bellied legate came back to him: *Not quite at full strength*. He smiled wryly. The reports came to an end and the Camp Prefect addressed the assembly.

"Gentlemen, as you'll have noticed, we have two new faces on parade today. It is my pleasure to introduce *Praefectus alae* Valerius Quietus and Centurion Metellus. Both come highly recommended. I am sure you will extend the usual hospitality of the Ninth to them and help them settle in."

The men around him nodded and smiled. Marcus looked for his fellow officer. He was a hulk of a man with his back to him, and then he turned around. *Oh Jupiter,* thought Marcus. *'No-neck!' That's all I need!*

The assembly was dismissed. Marcus and Metellus found themselves heading in the same direction, to the stores. Metellus was walking ahead and Marcus caught up with him just before they entered the building.

"So you're Metellus?"

"That's me."

"Well, Centurion, don't you think I should enter first?"

The thick-set man stopped and gave him a bull-like look. *He's joined the right legion,* thought Marcus. *He could be the Ninth's mascot!*

"Listen, junior," said Metellus in a matter-of-fact way, "I can still see your schoolboy's purple-bordered toga sticking out of your fancy tunic. And you're not even in the infantry. So don't go trying to pull rank on me."

He walked on, leaving Marcus standing there for a moment. He didn't know whether to be angry or astonished. In the end he grinned and followed him in. Metellus was demanding attention from a bored-looking clerk.

"I'm doing a stock count. We're not open for two hours. Come back then," suggested the clerk without looking up.

After two encounters with the giant centurion, Marcus had a fairly good idea what was likely to happen next. He wasn't far wrong. A fist like a man's thigh reached out and grabbed the clerk by the neck of his shirt, dragging him halfway across the counter. Their eyes met. The clerk's boredom had vanished.

"Your stock count may be important to you, but I can't stand around here all day without a uniform, can I?"

"Yes, sir. I mean, no sir," stammered the clerk.

"I need a centurion's kit, if you'd get it. *Now*."

"Wait here, won't you. I will get it immediately," said the clerk, trying to get off the counter.

"I'll be right here," smiled the centurion.

Under the eye of Metellus, the clerk rounded up a centurion's helmet with its instantly recognisable horsehair crest, a shirt of mail armour, a leather arming-doublet, a cloak, a sword and a dagger. He beamed, for a moment.

Metellus picked up the items one by one, his thick hands fingering the weave of the cloak's cloth. He poked a finger into a hole and elongated it. Finally he ran his thumb along the edge of the sword. No blood. He held his thumb inches in front of the clerk's face, grabbed his puny body and dragged him straight across the counter in a one-handed move. Their eyes met again, their noses almost touching. The clerk's face twisted in fright.

"What kind of trash do you call this? This kit's all worn. The cloak's not fit for a knock-kneed Tesserarius. And I couldn't cut butter with this excuse for a sword! Get me the new stuff!" He deposited the unfortunate server back to earth with a bump.

"Sorry Centurion; you should have said," gasped the clerk. "As a matter of fact, you're in luck; we just got new kit in yesterday."

He was back even quicker than before, the difference in the two piles was plain even at a glance. The cloak was lustrous, the helmet gleamed and its crest stood proud. The sword was a work of art.

"That's better," said Metellus, sliding the sword in and out of the scabbard and listening to the familiar rasp of metal on leather. "I knew you kept the good stuff tucked away. Now listen. I've had some wine sent over from Gallia which will be arriving here soon. This consignment is for me only. If you – or anyone else – touch any of it, I will hit you so hard that your clothes will be out of fashion when you wake up!"

The clerk, now totally cowed, just nodded. Metellus strapped on the sword belt so that the scabbard hung to his left: the privilege of a centurion.

"Now, about the meat ration. I want the best cuts, every meal. I need to keep my strength up." The clerk looked as if he doubted that statement, but he said nothing, only nodded again. "Good. I know you lot in the quartermaster's office. It's the same in every legion: you keep all the best rations for yourselves. Well, from now on you include me in on the special rations. Metellus is the name. Think you can remember it?"

"I'm sure of it, Centurion."

Metellus laughed: a rich deep sound, the first time Marcus had heard it, "Good, because I am going to remember you. I'll be back to see you again soon." Metellus, his arms full of pristine kit, walked through the doorway.

The clerk breathed a sigh of relief. Marcus and the clerk looked at each other.

"Yes, sir: how may I help you?"

"I'm with him," said Marcus in a specially adopted gruff voice. "Fit me out as a cavalry Prefect."

"At once, sir," the clerk jumped into action.

When his pile arrived, Marcus examined it closely. The sword, the armour, the uniform – all of the highest quality.

"Anything else I can help you with, Prefect?"

"Actually, there is," said Marcus. "I like the prime cuts of beef too. My friend Metellus is most insistent that I get the best."

"Not a problem, sir. Could you sign here for it? Thank you, sir."

"Thank you," said Marcus, saving his smile until he was out in the courtyard again.

*

Marcus changed in his quarters and made his way to his direct superior's office, whose name had been on his official transfer scroll: Juventius. He fervently hoped that his commander was someone he could work with, not another superannuated fusspot like the legate.

After the usual security checks and delays, he found himself in the ante-chamber, occupied by a secretary who looked up enquiringly.

"*Praefectus alae* Valerius Quietus reporting to *Praefectus equitatus* Caelinus Juventius." He presented his scroll for inspection yet again.

The secretary nodded, went inside for a brief conference, and returned, waving Marcus in and closing the door behind him.

The man at the desk was young, fit and keen-eyed, a contrast in every way to the legate. He stood up with a smile.

"*Praefectus alae* Valerius Quietus, reporting for –"

"It's Marcus, isn't it?"

Marcus nodded, surprised.

"Hope you don't mind if I call you that. We'll be working closely together."

"Yes, sir. I mean, no, I don't mind."

"Good. So you're from the Twelfth? An excellent outfit. And I've been reading very good reports of you from your former Legate. He says you're a natural when it comes to tactics."

Marcus found himself blushing, "He's too kind."

"Well, I'm delighted to have you with me. Welcome to the 1st *Lingonum equitata*. It's particularly good to have a man who knows what he's doing and doesn't need wet-nursing," he grinned, and Marcus grinned back.

"Right, let me tell you how things stand with us. We've got quite a task, supporting all the duties here in northern Britannia, manning the forts and watchtowers and so on. We were already short of replacements last year, and when the provincial governor authorised the transfer of another thousand men to support the troops in Belgica, the situation got worse. The Parthian conflict seems to be a constant drain on the army's resources."

"Understandably," said Marcus.

"Yes. So with all this, we're spread pretty thin now. You know what staff officers are like: Londinium is the centre of their world – the Empire stops after the Thameses. They don't realize the commitments we have up here. Anyway, some replacements arrived with you, and we have been promised more. The cavalry are good men, but they need strong leadership. They're auxiliaries, of course. Most of them, including your battalion, are from Germania. But in a pinch – they're as brave as Romans."

"I'm sure they are, sir."

"So, let's look at your role. We have two hundred and forty cavalry here in Eboracum. Your battalion, the Second, comprises five *turmae*. Around one hundred and twenty men. Naturally you can appoint your own *decuriae*, but in my view all four of them in place at the moment are sound and can be depended upon. Obviously, you may need to command the whole *alae* in the field, depending on events, and I'm counting on you to help out with suggestions, insights, intelligence: anything that you think will make life easier," the cavalry commander smiled.

"Yes, sir. Thank you. I'll do my best to help," said Marcus.

"I'm sure you will. Now take a seat, and I'll explain the situation up here. Oh, and let me just say this," Juventius lowered his voice, "I've heard about what happened to your family. I just wanted to express my deep condolences. I didn't know your father, but I knew of him. And I also know that he could never betray his country – or his commission."

Marcus looked him in the eye with gratitude, "I –"

Juventius smiled. "There. We won't speak of it again. Now, pull up that chair and let me show you the disposition of the Ninth's secret weapon – its auxiliary cavalry!"

*

Novantes was tired, thirsty, hungry and footsore. His head was ringing. He looked left and saw the visible outline of the Via Domitiana running south. *Good,* he thought, *still heading in the right direction. But better keep off the road in case I meet any troops.* He continued to stumble southwards, half wondering what the point of it all was. And then a rumble came to his ears, and he realised that he was caught in the open. Horsemen – twenty or thirty – were galloping towards him, armed with spears and swords. He didn't bother to draw his weapon. They had seen him. All his fatigue seemed to overwhelm him and he sank to his knees, his eyes cast down in the dirt. The horsemen arrived and surrounded him. Horses pawed the ground, whinnied and snorted.

"You there! Get up, man!"

Novantes managed the ghost of a smile. Esus was still protecting him; the voice was speaking Latin. Latin with a foreign accent, but Latin nevertheless. He looked up, into the face of a proud and confident blond-haired cavalry unit leader.

"I am Decurio Drusus, commanding the seventh *turma* from Habitancum. Who are you?"

Novantes stood unsteadily, "Pedes Novantes, of the First Cohort Gallorum based at Bremenium. "

"What are you doing here?" asked Drusus, giving a curious look at Novantes' dishevelled appearance.

"I was on duty at 'Hades End' watch tower. We were attacked. They were too many for us. All of my comrades are dead."

"Dead? What happened?"

"*Brigantes*, Decurio. They fell on us in great numbers. All the watch towers were attacked."

"Hmmph." Drusus digested the news. "Some drunken raiding party, no doubt. Well, they're rue the day they got pissed!" Some of the horsemen laughed.

"No, Decurio. It's much more –" His mouth was suddenly dry as earth and he felt weak.

"What?" said Drusus. "Here, hold him up. Fulvio, Give him some water."

The draught revived him and the faintness passed. He looked around at the *eques alaris,* "Castra Bremenium has been destroyed too. I was making my way back to it, but it's gone..."

"Impossible!" said Drusus instinctively. The cavalrymen weren't laughing now, they were exchanging glances.

"It's true," said Novantes, and he poured out the story of everything he had witnessed. For a long moment, no one spoke. The autumn sun shone down, the sweating horses shifted position, blowing air through their nostrils, flicking their tails, tossing their heads.

"We need to verify this," said Drusus at last. "Novantes, you look all in. Fulvio, hoist him up into the saddle behind you and take him to Habitancum. Report all this to the Camp Prefect as soon as you arrive. We will ride north and investigate."

They stood watching while Novantes climbed gratefully onto the horse and Fulvio kicked his heels into its belly. They set off at a canter, the infantryman swaying in the saddle behind the experienced rider.

Drusus looked around his *turma.* They were now twenty-four. Expert cavalrymen, to be sure but a puny force compared to the numbers Novantes had described. But there was no alternative. "Swords at the ready. Let's go!"

The cavalry unit got into motion again, heading north – to an uncertain future.

SPQR

In the moment of action remember the value of silence and order.

Phormio of Athens

VII   Habitancum

3.50pm, 4th November, 117AD: Via Domitiana, Northern Britain

Novantes rose and fell with the canter of the horse – and wondered when anything in his life would be normal again. It was a relief to be off his feet, and reassuring to be escorted by an experienced cavalryman. His hands held on to Fulvio as they rode onward, and felt the confidence-giving touch of his mail armour shirt under his fingers. It was good to be covering the ground so rapidly compared to his recent snail's pace. But there were too many uncertainties for him to be content. How big was the uprising? What were the Brigantes doing? Drusus had told Fulvio to take him back to Habitancum; but would he be safe there, only ten miles from the ruins of Bremenium? Was there anywhere safe in this accursed province of Britannia?

And his head still hurt, making even thinking tortuous. So he gave up the effort for a while and looked about him at the open countryside. The sun was already sinking low into the west, tingeing the sky orange and purple and turning the clouds the colour of smoke. Fulvio pulled up his horse abruptly. He sat in the saddle listening, his head surveying the ground all about him.

"What –?" said the infantryman but he was silenced with a gesture from Fulvio. After a pause of many seconds,

Fulvio turned his horse and moved off the road. In a minute they were in the trees.

Fulvio turned, "Not sure; maybe nothing," he whispered. "But something didn't feel right. We'll circle round to the fort, through the forest. If it's nothing, there's no harm done. Just another half an hour or so".

The cavalryman turned around and looked Novantes in the eye; he saw his youth, his fear and his exhaustion. He gave a smile, "It'll be all right," he said. He put his head down and spoke to his horse, "We've been in worse situations than this, haven't we, boy?"

He patted its neck and gently kicked his heels into its side. They started again at a walk, heading into the forest.

*

Hundreds of miles to the east, sunlight turned the buildings of Syrian Antioch to gold. Those streets were full of crowds celebrating the public holiday that had been proclaimed throughout the empire. The avenues and walkways rang with cheering, shouts and acclamations. The citizens of Antioch loved a festival.

In a gilded chariot drawn by magnificently caparisoned white horses, Hadrian sat, resplendent, acknowledging the crowd's cries of approval. Before him, the smartest soldiers of the Fifth Legion marched in serried ranks, sunlight reflecting from burnished armour. The finest *corniceni* of the legion played martial music. It was undeniably impressive, even for a city as used to spectacle as Antioch, a scene of unsurpassed military splendour, never to be repeated. The crowd, kept back by auxiliaries, threw petals into the air as the parade passed, waved palm leaves, and shouted at the top of their voices.

The Praetorian Guard, dressed in immaculate white uniforms with specially decorated breastplates and ceremonial swords, followed the imperial chariot; then came more cohorts of the Fifth. An entire cohort of Roman cavalry deployed in the third body. Vivid hues, metallic flashes, the panoply of empire. On and on they came, men, horses and artillery as far as the eye could reach. The cheers drowned out the officer's words of command as the column wound through the main highway of the city; it took a very long time to pass a given point. Nobody in Antioch escaped its intoxication or observed it with detachment. The music, the splendour, the sheer power: all were hypnotic. All of it spoke of confidence, dignity, strength. But it did something else: it made every citizen there proud to be part of the Roman empire, and ready to believe that this was the dawn of an even greater age than those which had preceded it.

Finally, the chariot stopped at the foot of the great temple to Jupiter Capitolinus on Silpius. Hadrian stood up, the sunlight bouncing off his general's battle honours. The roar of the crowd intensified to fever pitch. He stood, turning from side to side, smiling and waving, bathing in the adulation of his people. Doubled legionaries lined the steps which Hadrian now turned to ascend. At the top stood his wife Sabina, and Turbo: with a great entourage of diplomats, princes, kings, and representatives of the Senate. Hadrian greeted the most distinguished guests, and then turned back to the crowd. He stilled the frenzy into silence with a slight gesture.

"Citizens of Antioch," he began in a ringing tone, "I speak to you today and to your fellow citizens throughout Roman territory. This is the greatest Empire the world has ever seen – and I pledge to make it even greater yet!"

The crowd erupted with applause and shouts of praise.

"But I also promise to govern wisely: to protect you, to stand firm against any threats to our sovereignty, to punish any who dare to raise a hand against you. Let it be said that we will battle the forces of our enemies wherever they may be by matching the might of our military with the power of our diplomacy and the strength of our alliances. And when we go to war, let our enemies know that each man stands firm in their belief in this Empire." He waited for quiet again as the crowd roared in exultation once more, "I will uphold the timeless traditions of Rome, reinforce the rights of citizenship, guarantee you food at a fair price and promise you awe-inspiring entertainments.

"Citizens, this is our time. Our time to make a mark on history. Our time to write a new chapter in the Roman Empire. And someday, when our children stand where we are and look back, they can say that this was the day when the Empire renewed its purpose. They can say that this was the day when the Empire found itself again. They can say that this was the day when all citizens learned to dream again. Citizens, I salute you!"

The volume of voices and applause redoubled as the whole city looked into the future, at the new golden age. A door opened inside the temple and three priests stepped forward into the light, leading an enormous bull, ceremonially washed, garlanded and shackled. The crowd looked on eagerly, knowing what was coming next. The bull was led to the top of the steps and the chief priest stood silently by the flanks of the animal. He raised its great head to the sky. The eyes rolled around the crowd in panic and it gave a mighty lowing – cut short by the knife of the priest razoring through its neck. The *tauroctony*. The ritual slaying of a bull. The carcass flopped heavily to the ground and the crowd bellowed excitedly.

The chief priest dipped his hands in the warm blood of the animal and anointed Hadrian's face and armour with it, chanting. No one but those nearest to the scene could hear those words, and few if any were listening. They were too busy shouting, stamping, clapping and cheering. The priest led the blooded Hadrian away and there was a pause, filled by more music played by the Legion's musicians. But there was no lessening in the volume of the crowd, nor any flagging of their attention. They knew the final, the greatest act, was about to come. They knew they were watching history being made.

Then at last the two returned, Hadrian now splendidly dressed in a toga of Tyrian purple, his face washed clean, a staff in his hand and a crown of delicately worked gold on his head – covered for once in his life. He emerged into the full sunlight from the shadows of the temple, and it seemed to the crowd that there were two suns shining down on them.

"Hail, Caesar!" cried the priest.

And from the temple, from the streets below, from every corner of the great city, the words echoed and re-echoed until the buildings seemed to shake: "Hail, Caesar! Hail, Caesar! Hail, Caesar!"

The fourteenth Emperor of Rome had been crowned.

*

Marcus tossed the scroll away from him, bitterness and
despair in his heart. How could she have done this to him?
Petronia, whom he loved. *Petronia Pulcherrima...* his pet
name for her now sounded hollow and mocking in his
mind. Petronia, whom he had already pictured so often
as his consort, as he rose through the ranks of the Twelfth
Legion, then back to Rome – different career moves,
but always upwards, ever nearer the centre... And now
the Twelfth was like a distant memory. As distant as his
settled, prescribed life. His family cruelly slain, his plans
disordered, his career diverted into this remote outpost of
empire, to an undermanned legion and an uncertain future.

And now this! When would Fortuna be done with him?
Not until he lay bleeding his life's blood out on some dusty
road like his father, perhaps. He sat down heavily on the
bed, and picked the scroll up again. Fragmentary phrases
caught his eye.

"Will always hold you in the highest esteem...but these
are difficult times...my family insists, and I agree..."

A thousand memories crowded into his head: the two
of them, strolling about arm in arm; idling beside the
shore; laughing together; chasing her and hearing her
infectious laughter; losing themselves as they looked into
each other's eyes.

How could she have done this to him? Perhaps it was
simple fear on her part: fear of being caught up in the
maelstrom that seemed to be engulfing him and his world.
He sighed deeply. Petronia had been the last link to a
happier time. And now that link too had been severed,
casting him adrift and rudderless.

He stood up, and ordered his uniform. No, not rudderless. He was still master of himself. The only thing to do was to take the challenge of adventure that the gods had thrown his way. Even undermanned, this was still a proud legion with a distinguished history. And he was a battalion cavalry prefect. As that pompous legate had said, he was young for such a role: perhaps the youngest the Ninth had ever had. There was still plenty of scope to carve out a great career for himself – and Britannia was not the whole world.

He chuckled, some of his old amusement at his grandiose plans coming back to him. Well, Britannia might not be the whole world but it was *his* whole world now. It was time to return to it.

*

Metellus pushed open the door of the barracks of the First Century of the Fourth Cohort. The first door inside on the right led directly to the *optio*'s room and he kicked it open, "Right, *Optio*! Get this bunch of horrible little men out here on the double! I am your new centurion!"

The *optio*, with a shocked look on his face, jumped up from the seat and shouted commands into the barrack-room next door. The men, taken by surprise, started pulling on their armour and dressing as fast as they could. After what seemed an age, the century were lined up at attention outside the barracks.

The *optio* approached the centurion and saluted: "All present and correct, sir."

The new centurion walked up and down the front line of troops, "If I'd known you were going to take this long, I'd have brought my mother with me?"

A snigger went up from somewhere behind. Metellus swung round to the next line and stopped in front of Libo.

"What's your excuse?"

"Excuse for what, sir?" asked Libo.

"I am asking the questions here, son. Can I be in charge?" asked Metellus.

"Yes, sir."

"Then keep your mouth shut!" said Metellus firmly. He looked them over.

"First Century of the Fifth Cohort. You're having a laugh. I've seen the seasons move quicker than you lot. Let me introduce myself. My name is Centurion Metellus. Normally it's understood that in order for us to get to know each other we should speak about sports, politics and other issues. Please do not do this. The only information I require from you is an indication that you have received and understood my orders.

"The only words I need to hear from you on this subject are YES CENTURION. I've had more time in the front line than you've had in the food line. I can run twenty miles with a hangover and I love deployments because there is less paperwork and more real work. I am the all-knowing, merciless god of your world. I have a sword, a shovel and one hundred square miles around the outside of this fort. Do not trifle with me. Do you understand? Well?!"

A loud chorus shouted: "YES, CENTURION!"

"I can't hear you...." Metellus said quietly.

"YES CENTURION!" screamed the century at high volume.

"Good! With my help we might be able to teach you some real soldiering. Back here in ten minutes and we will march out to the parade ground for the Sacramentum Oath. Now get dressed – properly. Dismissed."

Libo looked around his unit and smiled to himself. 'No-neck' as his centurion. This was going to be fun!

Today had been declared an official holiday across the empire as the new emperor was sworn in. The Sacramentum Oath would be taken at the parade ground just outside the fort. Every legionary and officer assembled in their centuries. Once all centuries were deployed, the cohort marched out in order.

The First Cohort, with the most experienced and able men, had the distinction of leading the column onto the parade ground. Here, just beyond the main gate, lay a massive flat area with a stone lectern at one end. Marcus joined at the back of the staff officers' group and was one of the last to march out.

At the head of the First Cohort stood the First Spear or Primus Pilus, recognisable from his position and also by his array of battle honours. Marcus looked at him. He seemed like a stalwart warrior, as one would have expected, but certainly no youth. In fact, with his grizzled hair, greying and thinning, he looked more like someone's grandfather. The words of the Legate came into his mind: *a very able young man.* He suppressed a smile. The *Praefectus castrorum* stood next to the stone lectern and called the Legion to attention. The legate walked out in front of the assembled masses of *Legio Hispana.* Marcus looked around the lines of men and felt a surge of pride. Undermanned it might be, but he wouldn't give much for the chances of any barbarian horde that came up against it.

The legate, bedecked in his finest uniform, looked rather more the part than he had done when Marcus had first met him. Maybe he had misjudged him. The legate saluted his men and they answered the salute as one. He unrolled an expensive-looking scroll, waited for a few seconds and then began reading.

"'To all Legions from *Imperator Caesar Divi Traiani filius Traianus Hadrianus Augustus.*'"

Marcus started at the full official name of his emperor – and perhaps his nemesis. Part of him was repelled. But another part was drawn to it, in the undeniable way that it spoke of the glory of Rome. Even the names within his name, Trajan, Augustus and Caesar himself, were three of the greatest Romans of them all: three Colossi who bestrode the world.

The legate was speaking again: "'My fellow soldiers, I send greetings from the Fort at Antioch. I will shortly be given a coronation in this city, formally recognising me as Emperor of Rome. It was you, my soldiers, who first acclaimed me as the rightful successor to the throne. This is something I shall never forget. You have my grateful thanks, and they will remain forever in my heart. To show that gratitude, I have passed laws that will ensure all veterans now receive greater benefits when they retire, and that those who are injured in battle will be given payment and the opportunity to continue to serve the legion in another capacity.

As a soldier myself, I know the heavy sacrifice the men of this Empire have made. You, and men like you, have made the Empire what it is today, and will help to make it even greater tomorrow. It is only right and proper that you receive a just reward.

On behalf of the Senate and the People of Rome, I salute you. May Jupiter and Mars, his son, pour down blessings and benedictions upon you all.'" The legate lowered the scroll, a placid smile upon his face. Spontaneous applause erupted from the soldiers.

When it finally died down, the legate raised a hand, "Men and officers of the Ninth Legion, the coronation spoken of has now taken place. As such, it is now time for everyone here to swear the oath of loyalty to our new Emperor, Hadrian."

Marcus stopped. He couldn't swear an oath of loyalty after what had happened to his family. His lips were silent as the legate spoke: "Repeat after me:

I swear to you, Imperator Caesar Divi Traiani filius Traianus Hadrianus Augustus, loyalty and bravery as Emperor and Divine Leader of Rome. I vow to you, and to those you will appoint, obedience unto death. In the name of Jupiter, Best and Greatest."

Marcus still didn't know if Hadrian had ordered the killing of his family. Instead Marcus took his own oath to his father: *"I swear to you my father, loyalty and bravery as your son. I vow to you and my family revenge and honour. In the name of Jupiter, Best and Greatest."*

The rumble of many voices resounded the last phrase: and fell silent again. Marcus had voiced those words in his heart and head.

The legate called forward the *Aquilifer* who carried the Standard of the Ninth. The man walked out and stood next to the legate, raising the eagle as high as possible for all to see. Marcus looked at the eagle bearer: this was a prestigious position. Typically, holders of this post moved up to centurion, and the young man occupying it in the Ninth looked well worthy of such promotion.

"Everyone in the Ninth Legion will recognise this Standard as our divine identification for all time." The golden eagle with wings outspread displayed the numeral IX: an honoured designation for one of the oldest and most revered legions.

"This eagle represents Rome. It represents our army. But most of all, it represents you: the Ninth Legion. This Standard will be our symbol forever. It is our honour to march behind it – and if it be, to die for it." He let that thought sink in, "But, the gods willing, it is our enemies who will fall – before this Standard, and before the might of Rome!"

"Remember our motto: Born by Caesar, baptised in blood and crowned in glory!"

It was glorious. Everyman on the parade ground joined in with the multitudinous chorus: "Hail, Caesar! Hail, Caesar! Hail, Caesar!".

Except one. Marcus looked around the parade ground of men. Each of them had travelled thousands of miles, fought dozens of skirmishes, endured hundreds of hardships all for their beloved Caesar. For them Caesar was their god – and more than a god, because he was a man, and a soldier, like they were. Marcus understood how they felt but could not feel it.

*

The Prefect of the City of Rome sat facing a plump and comfortable man, well attired, well set, at ease with the world.

"Thank you for taking the time to respond to my invitation, Magistrate," said Attianus.

"Not at all, my good sir," said the magistrate in an oleaginous voice, "All part of my civic responsibility."

"Yes," said Attianus absently. His forefinger flicked through some documents on his desk, "Let me understand the situation. You are responsible for the care of the city?"

The magistrate smiled pleasantly. "Quite right, my lord."

"For the repair of the roads, the upkeep of the public sewers, for maintaining the aqueducts, superintending the public baths and ensuring that the streets are properly cleaned?"

The magistrate inclined his head.

"Then perhaps I do not understand the situation," Attianus stood up, walked over to the window. The sounds of street bustle wafted up from below.

"Prefect?"

"Take the roads, for example. Beautiful and grandiose, I grant you: but not free."

"My lord?"

"Such feats of engineering are expensive – to say nothing of their constant need to be maintained in a fit state."

"Yes, of course –"

"The tolls have not been raising enough money. Not nearly enough."

"Well, that would be a matter for –"

"For *you*, Magistrate. I had one of my officials visit your men on the *Pons Aemilius*. Such a pity: the oldest stone bridge in the city, too."

The magistrate's face showed his confusion: and also his misgivings. The comfortable smile had vanished from his face, "What do you mean, Lord? What is a pity?"

"Your men told my official that they are allowed to pocket the odd coin – and that you yourself pocket considerably more than that."

The magistrate jumped angrily to his feet, tipping his chair over onto its back, "I protest! This is an outrage!"

The two Praetorian guards at the door moved forwards and to either side of the magistrate, prepared to deal with his outburst. Unmoved, Attianus picked idly at a stray thread on his toga. He lifted a small knife from his table and slowly and clinically severed the thread, restoring the pristine nature of the fabric. Something about his calmness, and his action, took the wind from the magistrate's sails. He stood, waiting, unsure.

"Sit down, Magistrate," said Attianus. He waited while the official picked up the chair, restored it to its position, and finally collapsed back down in it. He looked nervously at the two guards beside him. Attianus waved them back to their posts.

"That's better. Now, to continue. I am surprised that a Magistrate of Rome is unaware that diverting sums from the public purse is a serious offence – or of the penalty which that offence carries."

The magistrate started to bluster again, to accuse his men of lying, of trying to betray him but Attianus remained calm. Calm yet implacable. He began reading from a long list of names, mentioning precise sums, dates, times...

"Very well," said the magistrate more quietly, passing his hand over his sweating brow.

Attianus looked up at him, "So. From now on, the toll revenues will go directly to me. I will have to ensure that all sums are correct before distribution to the public purse. And they had better be, for your sake." Attianus stood again, signalling that the interview was over. The magistrate stood also.

"I'll have one of my men seconded to you for a time. He can make the transfer of funds for you."

The magistrate's face flushed purple again for a moment; but the flush faded as quickly as it had come.

"After all, I'm doing you a favour: relieving you of an onerous burden, leaving you time for more profitable endeavours."

The magistrate lowered his gaze, "Yes, Prefect."

"You have made a sensible decision," said the prefect. "I have no room for fools in my administration. But I do have room for men capable of exercising wisdom for the common good."

The magistrate bowed his head.

"Farewell," said the prefect. "I suggest you go and make the necessary arrangements."

The magistrate hurried from the room: and Attianus re-seated himself, the hint of a smile on his face.

*

As dusk fell, Drusus led his *turma* of cavalry onwards, trying to balance speed and caution.

He looked back briefly at his twenty-four men. Maybe most of them would be thinking of the ale, food, warmth and safety that their fort of Habitancum offered. He didn't blame them. Indeed, part of him envied them: all they had to do was follow orders, while he was the one who had to give them. The stress made his skin itch and crawl. Funny how the feeling of apprehension never quite vanished, even after all these campaigns.

Finally, they approached their destination. Drusus called a halt and gathered the troop together. Beyond the last line of trees lay the ditches and ramparts of Castra Bremenium. They cautiously approached the ruins of the once proud fort. The site was almost flattened to the ground. The men remained in a stunned silence.

Drusus looked over his squadron and picked out the strongest and ablest cavalryman, young but experienced. A future *Decurio* – Jupiter willing, "Pertinax!"

"*Decurio*."

"Go and see if there are any survivors."

The cavalryman saluted and galloped into the twilight, the sunset bathing his left side with purple and gold reflecting from his mail shirt and the point of his spear. The men of the *turma* waited and looked around. There was desultory conversation, and unease just below the surface. Unease was shading towards alarm when Pertinax galloped back and saluted.

"It is just as the infantryman said."

Drusus gasped, "Any survivors?"

Pertinax shook his head, "Nobody's alive, sir."

Drusus paused, his mind reeling at the enormity of the destruction of Bremenium and its portents. No time to dwell on that.

"Let's go," he said, turning his horse. "Back to base."

The steeds carried them on swiftly in the gathering gloom but not swiftly enough for Drusus, as the seventh *turma* galloped back to Habitancum.

Fulvio and Novantes were already there at Habitancum, behind the treeline, watching aghast. A horde of men ran forward carrying massive shields. Arrows, spears and other weapons flew down, despatching a few, quickly, the shields were raised like a roof, warding off most of the projectiles. The first rank knelt at the base of the wall, shields to their backs, dividing into groups of six.

"What's happening?" asked Novantes, unable to keep his voice completely steady.

"I don't know. I've never seen anything like it," whispered Fulvio.

They continued to watch. The many small groups were now clearly providing platforms with their shields, to be mounted by sets of three men, who adopted the same position. Finally, two more men climbed atop each platform and knelt in the same way. The platforms now resembled a series of steps which led straight up the walls of Habitancum. Novantes stared in disbelief. The twenty foot high wooden wall around the fort had looked impregnable. Now it was possible to negotiate it with relative ease by climbing the manmade steps which the Brigantes had made by sheltering under their shields. Shouts of alarm from within showed that the defenders realised their peril.

A cry sounded nearby as a squad of the attackers, bursting from cover to storm the fort, spotted the auxiliaries. Fulvio kicked his heels into his horse's belly and they spurred forward, clear of thrown spears.

"Where now?" gasped Novantes, bending low.

"South to Coria," said Fulvio, not turning around. All his energies were on survival. But Novantes looked back – to see hundreds of Brigantes scaling the manmade platforms and vaulting the walls of Habitancum. He shook his head in despair and faced southwards again.

Thirty minutes later, the *turma* of Drusus rode into the open before their home fort – and stopped in dismay. The ramparts were burning, cries of triumph echoed from within and the barbarians had clearly won the day.

A line of tribesmen sprang up to bar their progress, while a flight of arrows flew past Drusus's ear. Two of his men tumbled from their saddles, screaming in agony. Drusus looked around quickly but could see no other enemy cavalry. Only infantry, closing fast on them.

"Wedge formation! We are heading south," he called, lowering his spear as his comrades lowered theirs. They formed a killing wedge, flying through the air. Although barely more than twenty strong, his squadron formed an unassailable battery, sweeping all before it.

Drusus's spear shattered as it collided with a shadowy foe, and he hurled it away, drawing his sword in a lightning motion. A number of his *eques alaris* were now similarly armed. The sword felt good in his hand: a cavalry *spatha*, longer than the *gladius* of the infantry. The barbarians seemed defenceless before it, and the surviving cavalrymen surged on, slashing downward to left and right, flinging blood into the darkening air with every stroke.

The exhilaration of the charge felt like victory. And yet they were flying southward in headlong defeat.

VIII The Little Fox

9.20am, 5th November, 117AD: legionary fort at Eboracum, Northern Britain

The sign outside the workshops read "Armourer", and Marcus could feel the heat on his skin even before he opened the door. When he did, it was like entering an oven. Almost at once, perspiration beaded at his hairline. In front of him, a giant of a man clad in a leather apron was pounding on a long metal blade with a mighty hammer. His great arm rose and fell. Seemingly without effort, as though powered by something entirely different from muscle and sinew.

Others worked on similar items further back. The din was tremendous. Just as overpowering was the smell: burning charcoal, hot metal, human sweat. And apart from the intense brightness from the furnaces, it was shadowy. All of it like Marcus imagined Hades to be. But there were no cries of agony or pain, and indeed Vulcan's understudy in front of him hardly seemed aware of the harsh conditions. He was focused on his work to the exclusion of all else.

Around the benches lay piles of iron tools and weapons. In the centre of the room were several massive wooden tubs filled with water. On one side of the workshop lay finished weapons and armour, soon to be proudly worn by legionaries. A large stack of *pila* caught Marcus' eye, and he moved over to inspect them and picked one up. The missile weapon of the infantry. Four feet long, a thin iron shank ending in a pyramid-shaped iron point. The *pilum* was heavy, as he'd known it would be. When thrown, all its weight was concentrated behind its small head, giving it tremendous penetration power. Not even armour could stand against it, let alone flesh and blood. When it pierced a shield it was almost impossible to dislodge. Even better, because the shank bent on impact, it was useless as a weapon for the enemy to throw back. He smiled: typical Roman efficiency and design brilliance. He hefted the *pilum* with his right hand, automatically finding the balance point. It felt good. A confidence-giving weapon.

On the next bench lay a line of helmets with their distinctive cheek pieces which the legionaries wore. Next to them were the rectangular shields and short Spanish swords in more gleaming rows.

"Can I help you, sir?" said a voice. Marcus turned, to see a short but wiry man with wisdom and experience in his eyes.

"You are...?" said Marcus.

"Deiotarus, sir. Chief armourer."

Marcus considered for a moment, "I'd like a dagger."

"Certainly, sir. What size would you like? We have a selection over here, if you'd like to come this way."

Marcus strolled over to another bench indicated by the armourer. Various daggers lay on the wooden surface. He selected one and picked it up: a six-inch double-edged blade. It felt as light as a feather after holding the *pilum*. His thumb touched the edge.

"Not very sharp," he commented, taken by surprise. The workmanship of everything else was faultless.

Deiotarus smiled, his face creasing like leather, "These are just for display purposes, sir. The finished product will give you many years of satisfactory service. The steel I produce here has seen action all over Britannia. And our greatest metal-working secret has spilled the blood of thousands of barbarians. Are you familiar with the working of the iron, sir?"

"Only when it enters someone's body," grinned Marcus.

"If you have a moment, sir, let me show you," they moved over to where the giant man was still deep in concentration. "We heat the iron slowly with charcoal until it glows like a woman's blush," commented, Deiotarus pointing to the furnace. "The charcoal is the key: it mixes with the iron and hardens it to make steel – something far better than iron alone. A lot of barbarians would give everything they've got to know that secret. After the mixing, we hammer out the blade and temper it by plunging it into cold water."

Marcus's eyes followed ' Deiotarus's hand indicating the wooden tubs, "And then it's done?"

Deiotarus smiled again, "No, Commander. At this stage, the blade is hard – but brittle. Not much use in a battle. So we heat the blade again and let it cool once more, slowly this time. The brittleness disappears but the hardness remains." The armourer passed over a newly forged *gladius*, "Like to inspect it, sir?"

Marcus looked down admiringly at the fine edge and the sharp point. This time, he didn't allow his thumb to touch the edge, "You certainly know your job."

"Thank you, sir," the armourer reached across to a table and picked out a dagger which he handed to Marcus. "Worthy of a battalion cavalry commander, this one."

Marcus put down the sword and took the dagger. Everything about it, from the shining blade to the inlay of the handle, was exquisite, "Yes indeed. How much for it?"

"Two denarii," said Deiotarus. "Not cheap, but then you wouldn't expect the best dagger in Britannia to be."

Marcus grinned again and dug out the coins from his purse. The money changed hands.

"You won't regret the purchase, sir. That dagger could save your life one day."

"I believe you," said Marcus. Taking the dagger, he headed for the door and opened it, his eyes blinking in the light. He started the long walk back to the centre of the fort.

*

Libo was standing to attention on the parade ground just outside the fortress walls. He looked around him at the massed cohorts. A formidable assembly.

"Good morning, soldiers of the Ninth," said the *Praefectus castrorum*. All eyes turned to him, and he continued, "Yes, it's your honour to be part of a great legion. And like all our great legions, it represents order, efficiency, civilisation. We've brought the same things to Britannia. But if Rome left this country to its fate tomorrow, how long do you think it would stay that way?" The men recognised the rhetoric, and allowed him to continue, "It would revert to barbarism in a moment. Make no mistake: those forces of lawlessness are all around us. They would like nothing better than to drag Britannia back to its feuding savagery.

They're quiet now – but only because of Roman might. And the instrument of that might is the legions."

Without moving his head, Libo flicked his eyes around at the sight: rank upon rank standing straight as young trees, sunlight gleaming on burnished armour.

"A soldier in the Roman army requires not only bravery and strength but coordination, cunning and intelligence. It's a constant part of your life: and as long as there are barbarians inside and outside the Empire, it will remain so. With the exception of the First Cohort who trained yesterday, you are all going to start weapons training," said the *Praefectus castrorum*. "Carry on, Centurions."

The centurions leapt into action, issuing orders. The men in full marching packs stood ready, as carts rolled over to each cohort, distributing weapons and shields.

"One sword and one shield to each man!" shouted Metellus to his century.

When his turn came, Libo took a shield and nearly dropped it. The sword was also strangely heavy in his hand.

Metellus was in front of him in a second: "Sword too heavy for you, son? Want me carry it for you?"

"No, Centurion."

"Good," smiled Metellus. "All right, pick up the pace."

His men stood ready, fully equipped. "First Century, Fifth Cohort: column formation. Follow me!" cried Metellus. He headed off at the double towards the road around the fort.

A muttered groan chorused from all around Libo. He could hear some of the words.

"Look at him go!"

"Easy for him – no pack or training equipment."

But there was no time to stand around. The men were already in rapid motion, following as best they could. Libo looked around him as he ran, sweat already running down his cheeks under his face-armour and coursing in rivulets down his back. At the rear of his column he could see the *optio*, the centurion's second in command – personally chosen by him. He couldn't hear his threats above the rumble of the running men, the noise of segmented armour moving against itself, and his own breathing. But he could imagine them: *First man to fall behind is on a charge!*

For thirty minutes the legionaries ran, sweat dripping from their brows, into their eyes, flying from them as their heads moved; their arms tingling and aching from their heavy weights; the packs interfering with the circulation of blood to their backs. And always, threats ringing in their ears, the sound of dozens of leather boots rising and falling along the roman road. Libo wondered between his gasps for breath how long he could keep this up. All he cared about now was not being the one to fall behind. If he knew *Optiones*, the first man to do so would find himself on the end of a lot more than a charge.

As they came round onto the second circuit of Castra Eboracum, the men were slowing down despite themselves. Libo caught a glimpse of a signal from his centurion to his second. The optio smiled and commenced kicking the slowest men in the backside.

"Keep going! This century is going to finish before anybody else in the Cohort – or I'll know the reason why!" shouted the *optio*.

And on they ran, onwards and onwards like men demented with some strange sickness. And just when

Libo's eyesight was dimming and he could imagine himself sprawling unconscious in the dust, they were ordered back to the parade ground. He wasn't sure he'd heard the order to stop but everyone else was falling to the ground with sighs of relief. He flung himself down. It was wonderful to be relieved of the sword and shield which had become like lead weights on the end of his arms. It was wonderful to strip the pack from his back and chafe feeling back into his limbs. But perhaps most wonderful of all was to be able to wipe the torrents of sweat out of his eyes and to see again.

"Catch your breath quickly, battle drill next!" called Metellus, striding around his men who lay on the floor like bees expiring after stinging.

The break was short. "All right ladies, on your feet," said Metellus. "Put your packs back on, pick up your shields and swords. Gather round me."

The First Century of the Fifth Cohort obeyed: and out of the corner of his eye, Libo saw other cohorts behaving in similar fashion all across the parade ground. But there was no time to attend to them.

"Left foot points forward, right foot to the right side. Shield in your left hand, sword in your right." Metellus demonstrated and they copied. "Good! Form up the shield wall!" he barked out the order unexpectedly and the men jumped to it, the shields clashing together to form an impenetrable barrier, as close as the segments of armour protecting each legionary. Or at least, that was the idea.

Metellus signalled to his *optio*, and he ran along the shield wall, his *hastile* at the ready. Wherever he saw a gap between the shields he struck at the offending man with the staff which was almost as long as himself, "Close up that gap!" He didn't have to make the same request twice. The shields slammed shut, eliminating the smallest opening. Now not even a dagger could have been slid between any two shields anywhere along the wall.

Metellus stepped forward again, pride in his voice, "Good! That's the way to do it. Now remember this. That's how close the shields have to be. The next time it won't be a wooden staff trying to force its way in, it'll be a barbarian's spear." He relaxed for a moment, "I can still recall my training. My Centurion died a natural death. That's right – hit in the skull by a barbarian axe. And if you ladies don't obey my orders to the letter, you'll be hoping for the same fate! Follow me!"

He led them over to where a rank of dummies awaited them, "Where are the weak points in a man's body?" Nobody spoke. That note of pride in his men evaporated, "Come on, speak up! *Optio*, where do you do most of your taking from?"

"The throat, Centurion!"

Libo looked over at him, at the distinctive plumes of horsehair on his helmet. He had a deep voice for a relatively young man.

"Very good," said Metellus, his equanimity restored. He walked over to a couple of paintpots on the ground, picked up a brush and dabbed red paint on the throat area of the dummies, "Where else?"

A man stepped forward from the ranks, "The groin, Centurion!"

"Well done," said Metellus, sparing the soldier a glance of approval. More red paint was slapped over the groins of the dummies, "Where else?"

Something caught Libo's eyes, and he turned. Over in the corner of the field a *turma* of cavalry was being put through its paces by a decurion. Was Marcus there? Pain seared across his chest and his head jerked back to the front. Metellus stood in front of him, his centurion's staff in his huge right hand.

"Wishing we were in the cavalry, were we? No such luck! You're a proper soldier, not one of those arse-faced patricians. Or at least you're wearing the uniform of a soldier – and I'll turn you into one by the time I'm finished with you, even if it kills you."

Libo and the bull-necked centurion looked into each other's eyes.

Possibly Metellus saw something he didn't like: "How much do you like your face?"

Libo stood open-mouthed for a moment, "My face, Centurion?"

"That's right, boy. How much do you like it?"

"Quite a lot," said Libo.

"Then I suggest you pay attention to me before I change it permanently!"

"Yes, Centurion."

Metellus turned to the rest of the men, "Yes, lads, the face is a nice soft area to target, too." He daubed red paint a third time, "Take a good look. These red areas are where we want to strike. Don't want to waste our strokes, do we? We want to make every one count. Don't forget: the edge of a sword will rarely kill. The point will finish your man, more often than not."

Libo and his comrades looked on. There were no distractions now.

"When we stab with the sword, the arm and side are not exposed. But when the enemy attacks with a downward stroke his side and arm are open – making good targets." The *optio* demonstrated the thrusts to arm and side, and the centurion turned back to his men. "Remember: stab with the point. And then bring the shield back up. Your shield is your life saver. Now practice!"

While the foot soldiers went through their drill, Marcus rode over to join his mounted troops. Part of his mind was still in the quarters of his commanding officer, *Praefectus equitatus* Juventius. He smiled gently as he remembered his words – and perhaps even more, his manner.

The decurion who had been drilling the cavalry called them to attention. They lined up in a perfectly ordered row and gave the salute. Marcus smiled again and returned it.

"Good morning, men. My name is Valerius Quietus. Your new commander," he looked along the line. "Many of you are originally from the Germanic tribes. Caesar himself had an elite body guard of Germans – and wrote approvingly of their great spirit and ferocity in battle. So I have high expectations of you."

There were a few grins from the mounted men. Some of them seemed to sit even higher in the saddle.

"I want to see you go through your paces. Let's see what we have! decurions: form into double units. Straight line attack on the stalks in the centre of the field."

The decurions lined up the cavalry, divided into *turmae* of twenty each. The order came and the men drew their long swords with a swishing sound. Marcus leaned forward, keen expectation on his face. The charge was sounded. The leading men kicked their heels into the bellies of their steeds and burst forward in a wide spread, thundering down towards the stalks as though in a race. The commander waved his hand and the decurions ordered the recall to be sounded. The cavalry troops trotted back, looking a little crestfallen.

"Good speed," said Marcus as they came level with him, "but the impact of a horse charge is far greater if you stay in formation. Slow down and look at the riders on either side of you. Keep a line."

He ordered the first group to the rear and had the second readied. They maintained perfect formation – until the moment the charge was sounded. Then the result was just the same. *Typical Germans*, thought Marcus. *Too eager for a fight!* He ordered the whole troop back into a line.

"Every man will place his *spatha* across the man to the right," Marcus entered the middle of the line next to the decurion and laid his long sword across his chest. "Ride too fast now and you could kill the man next to you! So pay attention! Unit Slow trot. That's better. Keep that line straight."

More cautious and steadier now, the auxiliaries advanced more or less in line abreast.

"Excellent!" cried Marcus. "Much more control! Speed will come later. Watch the line."

Hours passed as the German units learned the value of restraint.

Finally, Marcus gathered the decurions around him, "Well done, men! The most difficult of exercises is to stay in one line with fixed spaces while accelerating to maximum speed for impact into the enemy. Typically, we'll attack in waves. If an enemy is hit in full gallop by a line of horses, we'll ride right over him!" Marcus clapped his subordinates on the back. "Take a break. This afternoon we'll go through the wedge formation with the same ideas in mind."

*

The evening was painting bands of red, purple and gold with slow brushstrokes across the blue canvas of the sky. Inside the *taberna* just outside the fortress walls, however, the barman had eyes for only two things – and the sunset was not one of them. The bag of coins was satisfyingly heavy in his hand. And the serving girls were even more satisfying as they crossed into his line of vision. His eyes followed them both for a while: the blonde, and especially the brunette. He felt the weight of money once more. A patron called his attention, a sarcastic smile playing on his lips. The bar owner smiled back and turned to his business.

Marcus and Libo pushed open the door and walked in. Marcus winced for a moment as he lowered his arm. They both laughed.

"I know what you mean," said Libo. "Quite a day."

"Yes, easy to see that the Ninth doesn't cut any corners when it comes to training. We'll be glad of it one day – no doubt."

"No doubt. But this day, I'm glad that it's over – and that we're in here, not out in that arena of a training ground."

They looked around them. The place was crowded, but there were a couple of tables free.

"Grab those two chairs before anyone else does," said Libo. "I'll get the beers."

Marcus smiled wryly, "Part of me definitely doesn't want to sit down right now. But I suppose I have to start sometime." He walked stiffly over to the table and eased down in the chair with a sound somewhere between a sigh and a groan. He glanced up, but his cousin had been swallowed up in the throng at the bar. His eyes defocussed and he sat, staring at nothing.

Libo returned and set the goblets down, startling Marcus out of his reverie: "Hey, none of that," said Libo.

Marcus smiled. "Sorry. It's fine during the day; so much going on, so much to think about. But afterwards –"

Libo patted him on the shoulder, "I know, Marcus. But we did come in here to enjoy ourselves. And I think I've definitely started."

"Really?" said Marcus, sipping his beer, "What about your aching muscles, your strained back?"

"Completely forgotten. Say, what was that poem you told me about once – about the heart pierced by arrows of love?"

Marcus grinned, "Sounds like lots of poems." He thought for a moment. "Might be Cupid talking to Psyche. He was pierced by his own arrow and fell in love with her."

"That's it!" said Libo. "Just the verse for a soldier – or for this soldier, anyway!"

Marcus looked up quizzically, and Libo nodded towards the bar. The crowd cleared away momentarily.

"Ah yes," said Marcus, "The serving girl."

"You must admit that her beauty is as sharp as any sword."

"It's a pretty fine edge, for sure."

"Pretty fine? It's got straight through my shield wall and pierced my heart!"

Marcus laughed.

"Watch out," he said. "Here comes the goddess of love to claim her victim!"

The girl came over to their table and gathered up the empty cups left by the previous users of the table. She felt their eyes on her, "Can I get you anything?" Her voice was low and sultry.

Libo smiled. "Yes: just ask Cupid to pull his golden arrow from my heart!"

She smiled, "You're with the Ninth Legion?"

"Just arrived. Here to help make this country safe for civilisation."

"I'm sure Britannia will sleep more easily now."

She looked up at Libo's silent partner, a question in her gaze.

"Valerius Quietus, *Praefectus alae*. Pleased to meet you."

"And you, Prefect."

"Oh, you know about Roman military ranks then?"

A faint blush coloured her cheeks, "I'm trying to learn. It's so complicated. So many titles, different roles for the same title... But I'm doing my best."

"I think you'll do very well," said Marcus.

She smiled again, "Sure I can't get you anything? I'm afraid Cupid's unavailable at the moment," she added to Libo.

"Yes, bring us two more beers," said the infantryman. She looked down at the two almost full drinks, and he followed her gaze, "Don't worry about those; we'll have downed them by the time you get back!"

"We've earned it," said Marcus.

"Then it will be my pleasure to see that you get it," she said demurely. "It won't take long, gentlemen."

The gaze of both cousins followed her until she disappeared into the heaving mass of bodies near the bar.

"Britannia is full of surprises," said Libo happily. "I wonder if she'll get back before we finish these!" And he picked up his cup again. "You know, it doesn't taste so bad this time."

"After today, brackish water would probably taste like Faustian *Falernian*," grinned Marcus.

At the bar, the girl bustled about, taking orders, giving change. Then in a brief lull she dug into her pocket. She took out a folded cloth and opened it carefully to reveal the delicate and dry feathery flower leaves. She crushed the dozen small leaves in her hand to a brown powder. A disagreeable smell, reminiscent of mouse urine arose, momentarily overpowering all other smells. Only one plant smelt like that when its leaves were broken – and that was hemlock.

Taking two clean cups, she filled one cup with half of the powder. She looked up then, over the hordes of carousing soldiers and citizens, and caught sight of Marcus relaxing at his table. Her eyes creasing as though suffering a flicker of pain, she picked up the remainder of the dust and sprinkled all of it into the cup. She added dark beer into them and swirled them around, placing them on a wooden platter. The barman touched her shoulder, and her hands trembled for a second.

"You startled me," she smiled, looking down at the spillage.

"That's all right," he said. "Fabia says she's not well. Can you go to her?" he nodded in the direction of the woman.

"Of course," said the girl. "These beers are special orders for those two." She indicated the table of Marcus and Libo.

"I'll take care of it. Now off you go," he said.

When she returned, the beers had gone from the bar and the place was busier than ever. She looked over to Marcus: two cups in front of him and two more before his companion. Part of her was smiling, but the rest refused to join in. She sighed and turned back to her duties.

"Fabia?" queried the barman as he bustled past.

"Just a headache. She's fine." Her eyes returned to Marcus and lingered there.

A few minutes later, her duties took her close to their table. She gave a mock salute, glancing down at their hardly touched beers, "Don't you like it?"

"I want to savour this one," said Libo. "I didn't even taste the first!"

Her eyes found Marcus's, almost reluctantly.

"What's your name?" he asked, unexpectedly.

"Cornelia."

"You speak excellent Latin. You're used to Rome. What brings you to this far-flung outpost of the empire?"

"It's a long story. But now I'm here, I might try to offer my services to the medical corps. I have some skill with healing, so it's been said."

"Good! You can heal me," said Libo.

She looked at him, a hint of an upward curve to her lips, "Where does it hurt?"

"Right here!" Libo slapped his hand to his heart.

She laughed. The barman called her, and she walked back to the bar with a wave over her shoulder.

As the hour passed, Libo and Marcus glanced often in her direction as she moved gracefully about the crowded *taberna*. She glanced at them also, surreptitiously – and with increasing perplexity. In the middle of one of those looks, her attention was diverted. Two regulars who had been in the bar for hours were getting louder and more garrulous.

"You know what?" said one, slamming his cup onto the wooden table. "I'm so drunk, I can' feel my feet any more!"

The other man laughed, "Who needs feet, anyway? They're overrated."

"Overrr –" slurred his friend.

"What bothers me is that I can' feel my head. Know I had't with me earlier."

"Don' worry," said his companion. "You've got two of 'em. I see 'em, clear's the moon..."

"Clear's the moon!" cried the other, delighted by this for some reason. He stood up, swayed like a tree pole-axed at its base, and collapsed over the table, dragging it and its contents to the floor.

His companion stood unsteadily, roaring with laughter. The barman and one of his male helpers appeared on the scene. They picked up the unconscious man like a baby.

"Come on, you," said the barman, prodding the still hysterical local, "Out. You've had enough."

"Not much as he had! Leasht can walk," he said, although it was clear he needed assistance to do even that, his legs apparently being of varying lengths. As he passed

Cornelia, he cried out, "Look't! Drunk! Can' 'old's liquor. Dead to th' world..."

She watched the procession as it was escorted from the premises, gales of laughter following its progress. She frowned. He's dead to the world alright, she *knew*. How did he end up with the wrong beer? Then her eyes wandered back to Marcus and Libo, who were relaxed, but certainly not in that sort of state. She would have another opportunity to kill the cavalry prefect.

She sighed again, but there was a kind of happiness even in her despair.

*

The sun had dropped below the horizon and the last vestiges of the day remained. But it was fading fast and already the light was tenebrous, full of shadows and foreboding. Although nothing had happened, no foe had risen up to bar their progress, Novantes was fearful, expecting every second to be his last. What Fulvio thought he never knew – there was no time for conversation. The cavalryman was using all his guile and experience to get them through to the next fort. Their journey was roundabout and cautious, even timid. It didn't seem right or proper for a Roman military unit, even one as basic as a cavalryman, an infantryman and a horse. But then all the givens had been suspended with the attack on the watchtowers and what had followed. Eventually they emerged from a thicket and Fulvio reined in his mount.

There it was, darker than the descending night. Castra Corsopitum: but everyone called it Coria. They could see sentries moving about on the ramparts, their armour reflecting the light from recently-lit braziers. For all the world as though everything was normal and Britannia's civilised peace had never been troubled.

Fulvio kicked his heels into his horse's belly and they emerged into the open apron before the fort, entering the killing ground of ditches and rampart cover. Novantes was impressed by the size and the scale of the place: much bigger than Habitancum. It was also built of sturdy timber. And yet, and yet... Before all this turmoil, Habitancum had looked impressive enough the first time he had seen it. And now where was it? Its glory and its defiance were at one with the earth. Just as Bremenium was. Just as the watchtowers were. Just as were his comrades at "Hades' End"...

A challenge from the fortress wall interrupted his brooding. Fulvio obediently brought his horse to a stand and awaited the opening of the gates. Fifteen minutes later, they stood together in the quarters of the camp centurion. He listened to their story, his face growing longer by the minute. At first his inclination had been to disregard the wild-eyed, dirty-faced youth. He looked half-crazed, his eyes creasing sporadically with some intense spasm of pain, real or imagined. And it was too incredible, too monstrous...but such things happened. That was why one of the greatest legions of the empire was based one hundred miles to the south of Coria: for just such an eventuality.

As the story unfolded, his gaze fell more often on the youth's companion. This was no raw recruit, his nerves stretched to breaking point: it was the face of a sober, experienced trooper. His papers were in order. Everything about it rang true. The centurion sat down as the report came to an end. He considered for a while, his hands cradling his face. This would explain why two of their own units had not returned today and yesterday. He stood up, called for his *optio*, his second in command, and crisply relayed the facts.

"There's only one thing to do," he said. Eboracum must be warned. We must get word to the Ninth so that these northern outposts can be reinforced and the barbarians engaged. Give them a fresh horse, and see that it's well supplied with provisions."

"At once, sir."

The centurion turned to the young men, "Whatever happens, you have to get your message back to the Ninth Legion. I will give you a scout to lead you directly back to Eboracum," he said. "And one other thing...." He sat down at his desk and wrote briskly on a piece of parchment, "Give that to the Prefect at Eboracum – just in case he doesn't believe you."

They stood to attention, and he smiled approval. "May the gods be with you!"

An orderly led the dusty and begrimed soldiers away.

The two experienced campaigners looked at each other, "Can it really be true? The Brigantes have risen and are moving south in numbers? It's what we have always dreaded would happen: a civil uprising," the *optio* said quietly.

"All the indications point that way. We need to quell this quickly before the flame becomes a fire. I'll send out a few more scouts north," the centurion got up and walked over to his map, "of all the postings I've had... and a fight breaks out when I am Legion Supply. Typical bloody timing. Here I am, surrounded by clerks and book keepers and up to my

eyes in orders for socks and uniforms and this happens...
There may be thousands of them out there -and we have
two hundred men."

The *optio* nodded. They sat, thinking, for long seconds.
The centurion jumped up, began issuing the usual orders:
doubling the guard, having *pila* placed in readiness, posting
more lookouts. The *optio* saluted and hastened away to put
the orders into practice. That was all he needed to think
about, and there was only decisiveness and certainty in
his face. But the centurion sat down again, his expression
far less confident.

SPQR

Men grow tired of sleep, love, singing and dancing sooner than war.

Homer

IX   Coria

9.05pm, 7th November, 117AD: Castra Corsopitum, Northern Britain

Decurio Drusus, commander of the seventh *turma* of a now non-existent fort, stood before the camp centurion of Coria and his *optio*. The two senior officers looked at him for some time without speaking, taking in his dusty and bedraggled appearance. The centurion noted the spear wound on his right arm and sighed.

"No need for those scouts now," said the *optio*.

"So it would seem," said the centurion wryly, "How many of you are left?"

"I still have most of my *turma*, Sir," said Drusus proudly. "Two were killed outside Habitancum, and I sent one on ahead with a survivor from the attack on the northern watchtowers."

"Yes, one Novantes. He and your man Fulvio arrived here, not long ago."

"Thank the gods!" breathed Drusus.

"I sent them with a scout to warn Eboracum, and alert the legion," said the centurion.

"And it's really true about Habitancum?" said the *optio*, incredulity written across his face, "You're absolutely sure?"

"I saw it with my own eyes," said Drusus, "Bremenium too. Completely destroyed."

The centurion stood fuming for a second, "Are your men still able to fight?"

"They're all in good heart, sir and all eager to avenge their comrades."

A smile interrupted the centurion's brooding momentarily. He clapped the Decurio on the back, "I have no doubt of that," he said. "And, Mars willing, they'll get the chance. Well, your men will be a welcome addition. The question is what to do next. We could send some of you on to Eboracum, in case your trooper doesn't make it."

"Perhaps a sortie with the cavalry," suggested the *optio*. "Barbarians are always afraid of well-trained horsemen."

"Excuse me sir," asked Drusus, "but what kind of camp is this? I saw no praetorium as I entered."

"This is Legion Supply," said the centurion. "We supply all northern forts with food, weapons, horses – and anything else they need."

Drusus was digesting this information as the sound of a trumpet echoed and re-echoed through the fort. The door was flung open by a soldier who hastily saluted, "*Brigantes*, Centurion. All around the fort."

The centurion strode from the room, the *optio* and Drusus close at his heels. Quickly they made their way to the ramparts. In the flickering shadowy light from the braziers, a vast mass of men was plainly to be seen, in all directions around the fort. Well armed and equipped, their faces painted for battle, and balefully silent – for now.

The centurion turned to Drusus, "It seems you and your men won't be leaving just yet," he said with a ghost of a smile.

"No, sir."

"Well, we'll try to make you at home here. Have your men ready once more. Coria won't fall without a fight."

Drusus saluted and made his way down from the ramparts to rejoin his troop. The centurion heard his *optio* barking orders, bringing more units to readiness, calling for men to stand ready to attack. But the words hardly registered. His eyes had turned back to the sea of hostile men out there. It looked very much as though they wouldn't fall without a fight, either.

*

Several hours later, a tiny Roman detachment was picking its way through clearings, in and out of trees, with frequent and prolonged pauses of seeming inactivity. To Novantes, the terrain seemed featureless and indistinct, dark shapes and darker shadows. Perhaps it was so to Fulvio too; at any rate, although he looked frequently about him, he was content to follow directions.

The scout spent a long time checking the position of the stars, gauging the height of trees that might or might not have been landmarks. Occasionally the moon emerged from behind thick coverings of cloud, casting an unearthly light on the trees and the grass, the outbreaks of rock. It was quiet, but not silent: and as Novantes grew more accustomed to interpreting the sounds, they seemed richer every minute. A stream was flowing some way to the left, and gentle babbling came to his ears. An owl hooted. Some small animal moved in the undergrowth and away to the left in the distance he heard a soft crash as a deer or other game broke a branch. He raised his left hand to his temple. For once the insistent throb of pain had abated, and he felt almost human again, his every sense heightened by the journey through the night. The scout had signalled yet another halt.

"Sure of the way?" asked Fulvio in a whisper.

"No doubt of it," said the scout in a voice even Novantes, sitting just behind the trooper, could scarcely hear.

"How far?"

"Thirty miles maybe. The Roman road's over there beyond that hill and those trees. Of course, this way is less direct, but we'll make it."

They waited a while longer: three servants of the empire, two horses. A breeze rattled the trees and Novantes pulled his cloak tighter around his neck. The moon came clear of the clouds once more, lighting up the tableau. Fulvio's face looked dirty and unkempt, and Novantes guessed that his own face mirrored it. Fulvio reached out swiftly and held the scout's sleeve. The detachment was motionless again. Frozen. Hardly breathing. Novantes glanced at the cavalryman, unknown to him a few days ago, who now seemed closer than a friend. The infantryman strained his ears, but all he heard were the same indefinable rustlings he'd grown used to.

"Ride!" yelled Fulvio, kicking their mount into abrupt action. The scout did the same.

Then full-throated battle cries seemed to come from all directions: flashes of faces, shields, arms; weapons glinting in the treacherous light; warriors, coming at them swiftly with murderous intent. "Swords out " shouted Fluvio as they charged through the ambush, the long cavalry swords seemed to outdistance the attackers' weapons: or perhaps it was their horse speed that made them a hard target. As their horses galloped for their lives, heads down, ears back, Fulvio's sword flailed and slashed through flesh and bone; blood spurting, voices screaming.

A battle-axe scythed past the scout's shoulder and through his neck, tumbling him from his horse without a sound. A glancing blow caught Novantes around the head, and as the sword stroke carried through, the blade turned, opening a wound that poured warm blood into his eyes. But now the attackers were thinning.

"I think we're through," gasped Fulvio over his shoulder, and received a spear-point straight to his under-arm. The force of the thrust skewered him and wrenched him out of the saddle, leaving him writhing in the grass. Novantes's legs gripped the horse's belly, just allowing him to keep his balance. He slumped forward, over the neck of the still plunging and rearing horse, blood staining his face and matting the steed's mane, and then fell into welcome oblivion.

*

Over two thousand miles away, four men sat in silence in a sumptuously apportioned room, the light from lamps reflecting in burnished brass. No one spoke. The sense of expectancy was palpable. The door opened and Hadrian walked in. The four men stood.

"Forgive my summoning you to Antioch and assembling you in this way, gentlemen," the Emperor said with a smile, "As I think all of you know, I could never resist a dramatic moment! Please, be seated." They sat down, as did their emperor, "I believe I'm right in saying that none of you knows each other," said Hadrian. "Quite surprising, for I know and esteem each of you – and in your own spheres, you are without peer."

The four men bowed their heads at the compliment.

"Let me introduce you to each other," He held out an arm, inviting each to stand in turn, "Quintus Marcius Turbo, Legate of the Fifth Legion and commander of the Misenum Fleet until last year. He led the elite naval unit with distinction during Trajan's Parthian campaign."

He signalled Turbo to sit down and the next man to stand: "Lucius Ceionius Commodus Verus, Consul ten years ago and the descendant of almost royal Etruscan stock. A true friend.

"Apollodorus of Damascus, a Greek highly skilled, even among his people, as an engineer and an architect. His name will no doubt be familiar to you as the designer of Trajan's Bridge over the Danube which he built during the Dacian campaign.

"Lucius Neratius Priscus, the foremost jurist of our age and a member of Trajan's Imperial Councils."

The men looked at each other with respect and recognition of each other's fame.

"Gentlemen, you all have two things in common. You were important supporters of Trajan. And I trust all of you implicitly. These are difficult times, and decisive action is needed. I am now about to take that action."

Again, the expectation in the room intensified. All eyes were on the emperor as he continued: "Turbo, I now promote you to my Chief of Staff. Your loyalty and service to me have always been exceptional. And I need men that I can depend on without question at this time."

"I will do my best to justify this honour, Caesar," said Turbo.

"Priscus, many of your law reforms have been passed by the Senate. You have helped to make the Empire a safer – and a saner – place. I now promote you to be my chief legislator."

The ascetic face of the jurist reddened with delight for a moment, "Thank you, Caesar," he said.

"Apollodorus, you have helped transform Rome into an even more splendid city. You will be my principal architect: and I have no doubt that you can yet excel even the triumphs you achieved under Trajan."

"I shall, for you," promised the man from Syria, stroking his beard.

"And Commodus: you know men better than you know wine! You will watch and advise the Senate for me."

He looked around him again, at his newly appointed inner circle of advisers, "Rome is no longer confined to a city or even our homeland. The true ramparts are now thousands of miles away. Henceforth she must identify herself with half the world – or perish. Our city has become a state, and for that state to endure, it must adapt. Rome must replicate herself, so that even in the smallest towns in our farthest outposts of the Empire, magistrates will keep the peace, clean and light the streets, stop public disorder and ensure that Roman values are upheld." A flush crept into his cheeks. "In one stroke of a pen I erased all conquests that would endanger our state: in Mesopotamia, for instance. In Armenia also, I forced a peace with the Parthians. My adversaries in the Senate said this was a backward step. They said that it was a reversal of Trajan's policies! And no doubt some of them used the word 'betrayal', at least to themselves."

No one moved. The four men waited for their Emperor to continue.

"I let them know that Trajan himself had told me to do so before he died. Peace was my aim but not my idol. Now months later, where are we? The Empire is stable and prosperous. Instead of fighting costly wars with us, the Parthians send us merchants wishing to trade again, bearing numerous gifts to Rome. With this action I have succeeded in bringing in greatness and honour to Rome!"

He looked around the room again. The four men whose shadows were mirrored in brass might have been statues.

"How fickle are the Senate!" Hadrian laughed dismissively, "They have asked me to bestow upon my beloved Father a fitting tribute to Rome and offered me an honorary title. I have refused all worldly honours. History shall judge me, and my prestige shall be my own. To this end, we shall embark upon a sequence of reforms for Rome. Reforms that all of you will be involved in. And after our work, perhaps I shall bestow some titles myself," he smiled, "The cynics supposed the worst of me: I will prove them wrong – and I will do so through each of you. Gentlemen, your names, like mine, shall be given the credit for the marvellous reforms that we shall make."

He looked at his oldest and most trusted friend: "Turbo, I will abolish special privileges forbidding too frequent leave for army officers and order the camps to be cleared of costly gardens and banquet halls. These useless buildings shall be turned into infirmaries and homes for veterans. We are recruiting our soldiers at too tender an age and keeping them too many years: a practice that is uneconomical and cruel."

Turbo nodded his approval, "Excellent idea, Caesar. I shall have it changed."

"To build is to collaborate with the earth and put our human mark upon it. You, Apollodorus: you will design for me libraries, store houses, a magnificent system of aqueducts throughout Asia: works to astonish the citizens and help them realise that the Empire is greater than ever before! But even more important, I want you to build a fitting monument to our great father; something that trumpets his greatness and achievements."

The Syrian's eyes gleamed. "What have you in mind, my lord?"

Hadrian looked up, a smile wreathing his face as he followed his thoughts, "I was thinking of a column. A column of the finest Luna marble from Etruria, one hundred feet tall. With stairs rising up the inside. In the very centre of Rome itself!"

Apollodorus beamed his delight. "Truly magnificent, Sire! I can see it already. With a frieze of Trajan's exploits around the outside, to show off his glories?"

"The Senate would love it," smiled Hadrian, "Have some drawings prepared so that I can see it as clearly as you!"

Apollodorus bowed his assent.

"Yes, these reforms will make a clear statement to Rome," The smile faded from Hadrian's face. He clapped his hands and a servant walked in, placing a sack of scrolls on the table. The Emperor unrolled several and read out extracts.

"Look here. Grapes, peaches, other fruit – their price is soaring in the capital. Why is this? There are no major wars, no material droughts or other physical problems. And listen to these: complaints from senators and even beseeching notes from common men – all grumbling about corruption in Rome! Commodus, this is part of your new role. Find out what exactly is going on there."

"I will start my investigations this very night, Caesar," said Commodus grimly.

He turned to the jurist. "Priscus, we will cancel all public debt immediately, and introduce reforms for senatorial families who have fallen on hard times."

"A clever move, my lord," said the lawmaker.

"From this moment, any fields which have not been tilled for two years can be used by any man to grow his own produce -and similarly, mines that have lain unused for the same period can be used by any who wish to do so."

Priscus nodded in approval, "You seek to make Rome less reliant on imports."

"The Imperial Fleet must be reinforced. Rome no longer supplies itself. We depend totally upon the grain dealers for our subsistence. I seek to make it self-sufficient again!" smiled Hadrian.

Plans were discussed and made, notes were scribbled down by servants as ideas and suggestions were thrown around the inner circle. At last the Emperor rose to his feet, joined by the other four. Wine glasses were handed out and servants poured a large measure into each cup.

Hadrian called a toast, his goblet raised, "We have come together to celebrate the greatness of Rome."

They drank deep, pledging their city and their Empire.

As Priscus and the Syrian pored over the plans, Hadrian motioned Commodus and Turbo aside.

"Turbo, some months ago I told you that Attianus would watch the Senate for us after Trajan's death, and send us back reports on what was happening," he paused, and included both men in his next remark, "I regret that I must now have the watcher himself watched. The murder of four consular men was ill-received by the Senate, and there are those who will not forget it. I cannot afford any further scandal or loss. I have anonymous letters, some, by their style, from senators, who claim that the corruption is at the very heart of Rome. No one is named; however, it seems likely to me that Attianus is no longer my faithful servant. Commodus, I want you to set up a secret network of men: men who can be trusted. Report back to me as soon as possible."

"Caesar, you suspect your guardian?" breathed Commodous.

Hadrian sat silent for a moment: then his mood lightened again, "My suspicions are unreliable. I prefer to promote them to hard facts! Gentlemen, Rome shall become a safe and secure place once again. I will not tolerate corruption within my own Government – even if the highest man in the land is the perpetrator. Together we will stamp out any troubles – and any troublemakers – before they arise."

And the two loyal confidants bowed their heads and went back to the table, strewn with papers, plans – and dreams.

*

The reveille had just sounded. Marcus looked along the line of cavalrymen, which seemed to go on forever. He couldn't restrain an excited smile. All two hundred and forty men of the Ninth Legion's cavalry lined up in front of the barracks, waiting for his orders. He watched as the roll call was taken with typical Roman efficiency, even though most of the cavalrymen were from Germany. But that made no difference: the empire was the empire, wherever you found it. That was its great strength. The decurio of each *turma* reported his numbers smartly and rapidly. Not a single man sick or injured after last week's punishing training schedule. Marcus looked over the men and nodded approvingly.

He raised his voice so that it would carry down the line, "Cavalry of the Ninth! Today we are going on the assault course with the legions. I expect each one of you to pay close attention to what the legionaries do. We are going to show them we can complete the course just as well as they can – if not better!" he looked along the line of troopers, holding themselves more erect, hanging on his next words. "Mounted troops don't always have the luxury of being able to fight from horseback. If you get knocked from your mount or it's killed under you, you have to be able to fight like regular soldiers. This means you need to run, climb, keep your balance and even swim!" A portly German caught his eye, "I was surprised to hear that you've never taken the assault course. So I spoke to the Legate. From now on, we do it twice a week."

The German troopers seemed pleased. There was a general nod of agreement, although the fat one in front of Marcus looked rather less enthusiastic.

"I also know that some of you don't swim. Well, you need to start. As you know, bridges in this country can quickly become useless, when rivers flood due to heavy rains. They might even be washed away entirely in the torrents. Is the Ninth Legion going to hang around waiting for the rain to stop before it crosses the river? Could take a long time in Britannia!" There was some rueful laughter. "We will practise swimming, both in and under the water. Follow my instructions or those of the Legion officers. Cavalry, dismissed."

Marcus turned to the senior decurio, "Can you swim?"

"Yes, sir. I was taught by my father."

"Good," said Marcus. "I'll take the first four *turmae* round, you take the next four."

Marcus led out his men at a steady jog, past the main gates and out past the parade ground. He noticed his cousin Libo, just about to start the course and waved over to him. Once his troop was lined up, he led them onto the ground, the earth churned up by many feet. Behind him he heard the senior decurio barking out orders.

The day was cool, cloudy and sunless: but Marcus quickly found himself sweating as he heaved himself quickly over the high and low obstacles. The men's sandaled feet pounding the course sounded and felt like thunder. As he reached the top of a tall frame, he looked forward. Libo was just ahead of him and he doubled his pace to try and catch him up. He felt rather than saw his men trying to respond to his spurt of speed. He clambered up ropes and swung on them to cross streams. This was tough enough but he couldn't help imagining how it would be if this was for real and there was an enemy force harrying their every move. The men were crawling under wooden posts hammered low in the ground. Between the puddles and the sweat running down his body, Marcus's clothes were wet through. His legs were aching. He looked back, and grinned to see an outsize German trying to squeeze his frame under the wooden posts.

Finally they had come through all the obstacles. The ground was open now. Marcus reached a river, swollen with recent autumn rains and with several huge tree trunks half submerged in it. There was a chill in the air as the breeze came across the surface of the water. The cavalry prefect's chest heaved as he caught his breath.

An *optio* from the Legion stood to attention, "Right, sir," he said. "Just swim up to the logs, head under the water for thirty seconds and kick with your legs. The current will take you through – and if not, I will."

Marcus smiled back, "Very good, *Optio*," he said. Tiredness was coursing through his whole body and he felt that he was more than ready to recline on a couch rather than continue the punishment. But he was the leader and he had to set the example. He grimaced and jumped into the turbid water. The cold knifed through him, holding every inch of his body in a freezing vice and he gasped with the shock. But he got into motion, his arms arcing out of the water as he swam, his movements hampered by his clinging, waterlogged clothes. Swimming took his mind away from the freezing conditions. He put his head below water and opened his eyes. As his vision cleared, he looked up the manmade tunnel. He swam a few strokes up it. Through the cloudy and congested water, he could see the light on the other side. He turned, swam back, surfaced and filled his lungs to capacity. Then he dived back under the gloomy river. The current tugged at him like hands, pulling him along. He opened his eyes again and the water seemed even more opaque than the last time; but there was the light up ahead of him. Just a few more strokes…

And then something heavy and implacable was pushing down on his head. He kicked furiously, flailing mud into the already brown water, unable to move forward or back. He desperately needed to take a breath but forced himself to keep his mouth closed. He felt upwards with his hands; he touched something solid that wouldn't move. Some obstacle? Part of the tree trunk? He pushed again with all his fading strength but he had no leverage. He kicked his legs as hard as he could but nothing moved. The panic faded away and he composed himself for death; but all he could think about was the monstrous injustice of dying senselessly with his father's murder unavenged. Now everything was receding, become more remote. And now nothing mattered in the muddy blackness…

And then the pressure on his head was gone and he felt arms about him, as if from a long distance, dragging him up and out of the water. He lay on the shore, coughing uncontrollably, all his strength gone. Dimly, voices came to him. The first voice was swearing coarsely. He opened his eyes to see indistinct, wavering shapes grappling with each other.

"How dare you! Striking an officer? I'll have you on a charge, you piece of dung!" That roar was Centurion Metellus's bull-like voice.

"You just tried to drown him! You're the one that'll be on a charge – or worse!" came Libo's voice, shaking with anger.

"It was a bit of fun, that's all," said Metellus, his voice dropping to a normal level, "Just a little initiation for the cavalry: see if he could take it like a real man. I'd have let him go in a second."

"No! You were holding him under!" screamed Libo, "I saw it for myself!"

The *optio* appeared on the scene, "It's our word against yours," he said with his insincere smile, "Who are they going to believe, you new boys or us veterans?"

Metellus pulled Libo over and whispered in his face, "Anyway, it was a joke. No harm done, nobody hurt. You're already in trouble for raising your hand to me, you filth. Keep your mouth shut or you'll be in a lot worse." He released him with a shove and walked away with the *optio*. A laugh floated back over their shoulders.

Libo clenched his fists, his body tensing. Marcus was still gasping for breath but raised himself up on his elbow. His head felt like lead but he grabbed Libo's sodden tunic. His vision was sharp again, and he could see the bulky figure of the centurion and the lesser shape of the *optio* as they crested a ridge.

"Leave them," he panted. "Our time will come. Just leave them." He felt some of the tension drain from Libo's body.

"That was no joke," muttered Libo, "He nearly killed you."

Marcus nodded, "And without you, he would have. I owe you a life debt, cousin." He grasped Libo's arm with his hand, "But at least we've been warned. Those two won't catch us unawares again."

"Yes," breathed Libo, "Maybe next time we'll be the hunters, not the hunted."

Marcus panted, "Meet me at the baths afterwards. Watch yourself. Now go!"

Libo frowned but nodded and ran off to finish the obstacle course. Marcus lay on the bank, relishing his returning strength, rejoicing that he was still among the living. But that was no thanks to Metellus.

A big German burst out of the water, spluttering and looking bewildered but relieved. Even to the exhausted Marcus there was something comical about the sight. He smiled and waved him on to complete the course. He raised himself into a sitting position and sat, leaning forward, drawing in precious air. He reflected. Coming out from under that submerged obstacle, out from the freezing muddy water into the air and the light was like coming from death to life. And in his case, that was exactly what it had been.

*

Marcus was waiting outside the barracks for Libo. His cousin was late, but the young cavalry prefect didn't mind. Weakness still coursed through his body as though his blood had soured in his veins. Finally Libo showed up. Marcus waved a weary hand.

"Sorry," said the infantryman. "It's Metellus. I'm on latrine duty for the week. I really need that bath now."

"Me too," said Marcus. They smiled wanly at each other.

"That Metellus..." began Libo.

"We said we wouldn't talk of him," said his cousin. "I think he's ruined enough of our day!"

Libo nodded and they entered the bath. Greeting their entrance was an expansive blue mosaic floor. Neptune sat on a stool with a large trident in his hand, winking suggestively. The cousins went into the first room. They used the latrines located in a side chamber and left their clothes hanging on pegs. They picked up robes, thrust their feet into wooden sandals and moved on into the next room. The heat hit them both like a bake-house, even though they had been expecting it. The very floor was warm to the touch, something both men were grateful for.

A few soldiers sat playing dice and talking, "Want to join our game?" one called to them.

"No thanks, haven't got any money to lose" Libo said.

Marcus and Libo sat down and doused themselves with oil. It felt smooth and satisfying, a rare moment of indulgence. The sensuous aroma of olives wafted into the air. Marcus picked up a strigil and gently scraped the oil from his shoulder. It was cleansing and invigorating at the same time.

"Ahhh," he said. "That's more like it!"

Libo grinned. Even the heavy smell of ordure was fading from his nostrils as the scented oil rose in the heat. He too took one of the small, curved, metal tools and began pulling it up his skin with a sigh of satisfaction.

After a while, they entered the hot room. More mosaics: two young ladies, wantonly clad and a Roman galley at sea, sailing into a glorious sunset. The floor would have burned unshod feet. The cousins lay down and called for a massage.

The masseur's fingers dug powerfully but skilfully into Marcus's back, shoulders and neck, soothing away the stress of the day. He closed his eyes and surrendered to the blissful sensation. Later, in the relaxation room, Libo lifted weights with his right hand. Even Marcus felt equal to hefting a small one. Finally they moved to the changing room, feeling relaxed and vibrantly alive.

"I feel like a new man," said Marcus.

"And I feel like a new woman!" said Libo.

Marcus laughed. "The serving girl?"

"Well, if we don't deserve a beer after a day like today, when do we?"

"You win," said Marcus. "Let's go!"

Half an hour later, the door to the *taberna* opened and two young men entered. Everyone was engrossed in his own affairs and no one looked up. But one pair of eyes surreptitiously noticed their arrival.

The Little Fox's heart quickened as she recognised her prey. Her sharp eyes noted what many would have missed: the weariness that hung about him like a cloak. Weariness was good. It took prey off their guard. Her glances, seemingly disinterested, followed the pair as they found a table and sat down heavily in a couple of chairs. They seemed reluctant to move a muscle but eventually the younger, more impetuous one rose to his feet and walked to the bar.

"Evening, Cornelia," said the infantryman. "Remember me?"

"Yes, I remember."

"Libo's the name. Beer for the infantry and the cavalry, please!"

She reached for two cups and started to fill them from a barrel. He passed his hands over his face and leaned against the bar, "Hard day?"

"Was it!" he grinned. He took the beers and walked back to their table.

She could almost hear Attianus's voice in her ears at that moment, softly insidious in that way of his: *The day was nothing compared to the evening they're about to have.* Her hand moved down to her apron pocket. But it stayed there as she looked over to their table again. That cavalry commander was good looking, for sure... Well, so had many other of her prey. Or rather, victims. That word removed the varnish of grim humour and left the situation stark and unadorned.

Her fingers crushed some leaves in her pocket, and again that faintly repulsive odour drifted to her nose. But her hand remained. She looked at the array of clean cups in front of her. Clearly the two men would be having at least one more round of drinks, and probably a lot more than that. It would be easy... Perhaps that was it. It was all too easy. And it was even easier for Publius Attianus, pulling the strings from faraway Rome, like some fat spider at the centre of its web. All he had to do was to give the orders, not do the killing himself. Part of her realised with a shock that she was disobeying Attianus even by delaying. Men and women had died for such acts of rebellion. Is that what she really wanted? To flout the orders of someone so powerful that his mere word meant death? But he was hundreds of miles away. He was also a puppet-master who cared about people only so long as he could use them. He had spoken about her being his consort, about retiring to Neapolis together. Just one more job, he had said. She was more than ready to retire from this foul and degrading career. And even if they came to an end, he would discard her like an orange peel when he found someone younger or more beautiful.

She sighed, and looked over to the handsome youths. They were tired, yes; but there was life and sparkle in their eyes, unlike the hard, calculating stare of Publius Attianus. And she remembered her sense of surprised relief when her previous attempt had failed the other night. True, she didn't really know anything about this young commander, apart from a few facts she'd been briefed, and his name. Yet he seemed reliable and straightforward. Could she trust him? Would he protect her? Or would he brush her aside – as so many others had done? She flushed at the thought. She thought long and hard, while the sounds of laughter and bantering conversation seemed to die away to nothing. Finally, she lifted her hand from her pocket and brushed her fingers against her apron to clear them of the lingering powder.

She emerged from behind the bar and walked over to their table, "Good evening," she said.

"Good timing!" said Libo, indicating their cups. She gathered them up.

"Very good, Libo – and Valerius, isn't it?"

"Call me Marcus," he smiled, and she smiled back, her face softened and transformed.

When she returned from the bar, she put down the beers, then paused.

"Yes?" said Marcus.

"You won't remember, Commander, but I mentioned to you last time you were here that I was thinking of offering my services to the medical corps."

"Yes, I recall."

She looked into his steady gaze and smiled, "Thank you. I was wondering whether you could ask if I could help as a nurse at the infirmary? I know that all you've seen of my work is here, but I really do have the gift of healing. I'd make a good nurse," she produced a letter from her apron.

Marcus held out his hand, "Leave it with me," he said. "I'll look into it and pass it on to the doctor of the Ninth Legion. He's a Greek. Very good man."

"Thank you, Commander," she moved away with lissom grace, watched by the two cousins.

Finally, Marcus picked up his fresh cup, breaking the spell, "You're very quiet," he said.

"Only thinking," said Libo.

"What about?"

"How I could get myself transferred to the doctors's office!" smiled Libo.

X   Vordimus

7.15am, 19th November, 117AD: Castra Corsopitum, Northern Britain

The sun had risen in a grey dawn but there was no gladness in the sky. A cold and cheerless wind blew strongly across the open ground. For the second morning in succession, Brigantian warriors stood just clear of the killing line and taunted the Romans imprisoned in their own fortress with jeers of derision, rude gestures, mocking laughter. *Come and get us*, the whole tableau said. But the Romans just looked down on the scene and made no move.

Behind the screen of trees, Vordimus stood, surveying the fortress. A noise behind him made him turn and he looked back at the ever-swelling numbers of barbarian troops. He also saw Ortagorus approaching him and it was clear that there was little gladness in his face either.

"Hail, Ortagorus," said Vordimus. "Your army grows stronger, I see."

"Yes," said the chieftain. "Word is spreading about your great victories over the accursed oppressors. Tribesmen and clan chiefs who held back before think they can see the way the leaf will fall, and are eager to be part of the revolt."

"And win part of the spoils!" laughed Vordimus, while Ortagorus nodded half-heartedly. "Come, my friend," said Vordimus, "Let us meet our chiefs of the tribes".

Arthmael, the son of my father's brother: is a mighty prince of our people, and his men are eager for blood."

"They are ready to listen now. Arthmael and his clan chiefs seek an audience with you."

Vordimus looked at his friend, trying to read his expression "Very well."

In a small clearing, six men sat around a campfire. They looked up as Vordimus strode into their midst. His military brain at once sized up the leader: his fair hair was tied back behind his head, a beard straggled over his chin. He was powerful and stocky, a fell warrior in the noonday of life.

"You are Arthmael," said Vordimus.

"I am."

"I salute the Bear Prince," The remark provoked surprise on the face of the warriors.

"You know our tongue, then?" said Arthmael, "That is unusual for an outlander."

"A little. I always try to gather knowledge."

The warriors exchanged glances. Ortagorus stepped into the circle. His eye fell on Arthmael.

"Well met, cousin. This is Vordimus."

"So I surmised," said Arthmael.

"He is the planner and builder of all we have achieved. Or have you not heard? The watchtowers and two forts have been razed to the ground. If any defenders escaped, they fled and scattered like children. All the rest are as one with the earth. The Romans' hold on our country is weakening, and soon it will be loosed forever. We shall retake all that was ours – and more besides."

There was silence as Ortagorus finished. A log collapsed in the fire and sparks shot into the air, the crackling of the burning wood the loudest sound in the clearing.

"I am aware of what this man has achieved – up till now," said Arthmael, "But that is the past."

"And you are concerned with what is still to come," said Ortagorus. "That is understandable: you want your share of the glory. But be patient just a little longer, cousin. It only remains to make the decision to attack this fort and it will be done!"

"Then let the decision be given."

"Let us be sure that it is the right decision," said Vordimus. "This is a well-equipped fort, with many men."

"Many Romans. But I am not afraid of Romans."

"It is not fear to respect your opponent and to gauge his strength correctly. If this and other forts fall, the Romans will send out the Ninth Legion to meet us. They will make slaves or kill all those men they catch."

"They will have to catch us first. Or perhaps we will do the catching. But in any case, I am not afraid to die in battle gloriously." He stood up proudly, and his chiefs followed suit.

Vordimus moved over to him and looked him in the eye. "Neither am I afraid. But a battle is even more glorious when your enemy dies instead of you. And that's what I'm trying to bring about."

There was a pause in the conversation as both men weighed each other up, broken by a growled comment from one of the chiefs, "Let us attack the fort this hour and have done with it! We are all brave men; braver than these foreign invaders who hide behind their wooden ramparts."

"This is Tobar, greatest of my chiefs. He speaks for us all," Arthmael explained.

"Your bravery is not in doubt. Indeed, it is renowned," Vordimus acknowledged, "Two generations of your forefathers were no less brave. And they died on a Roman spear without victory."

There was an angry murmuring.

"I am not insulting you. But is it not so?"

"They were not united as we are today. Men continue to rally to us, even since this morning. Our forces are superior!" Tobar frowned.

"Yes, numbers are important – one reason why I have delayed until now. But they are not everything. The field of battle is the key to beating the Romans. We must fight them one unit at a time on our chosen ground; not in an open field where they can use all their units at the same time."

"What do you mean, our chosen ground?" asked Tobar.

"The Roman legions are made to fight in one way and one way only, in a battle line where they slaughter our war bands from behind their shields. They will never fight us man to man, because they know they can lose – unless, of course, they have no choice."

Arthmael smiled, relieving the tension, "That is good. Yes, why should we fight them in the way they want to fight!"

Vordimus clapped him on the back, "You have understood! To beat the Romans, we need to think as they do – and then out-think them. We will wait for this mighty force to arrive here. We will draw them up to this area and make sure they know the way we retreat north. And then we will strike when they are weak. We avoid their strength in the open field until we are ready to lead them into a trap of our making."

The late autumn wind blew cool through the trees and all the men seated themselves around the fire again, drawing up to its warmth. An old tribal leader spoke, "What happens if they refuse to fight us?"

"I do not look for their refusal," said Vordimus. "They will surely be eager for vengeance and to put down the rebellion before it grows any stronger. But if they need persuading, Tobar here can take an army of men west and attack Vindolanda, the most important fort close by."

Tobar's eyes gleamed, "I pray that the Romans need our persuasion!"

Vordimus smiled, "And when the Ninth Legion arrives, you, my friend Arthmael, will lead your men north with me and lie in wait at our chosen point. When we have them strung out and marching through our ground, then we attack – and you will lead the charge of these men. It will be a triumphant charge, killing many legionaries and turning the battle."

Arthmael nodded, as did his people.

"Convincingly spoken," said the old man.

"Yes," said Ortagorus, "Vordimus's judgement is entirely right. Trust him."

"Why should we trust him?" said one of the other chieftains, whose look suggested he still needed convincing.

"Because he is a Druid. Because he has saved my life. Because he has brought us our victories. Because he hates Romans!"

"Why do you hate Romans?" asked Arthmael.

It was a story they had heard many times, since some of them could have told him similar tales of their own. His people had had no defence against the Roman invaders.

They had taken their lands, violated their women, enslaved their leaders. Yes, it was a familiar story.

He paused, then spoke again, a different tone in his voice, "But the Roman people themselves are no stronger than we are; maybe less so, with their decadent and corrupt practices. The difference is their Legions. The only thing between us and those oppressors is the Ninth Legion. And once it is destroyed, the nation of the Brigantes will rise again, stronger than ever!"

They greeted his words with gusto. Even the doubting chief now seemed convinced.

"I swear to you, my friends, that my life began anew when I met Ortagorus. It is forged in fire and our blood is mingled. When the time comes to die, I shall do so gladly for the sake of our brotherhood in arms. But that time is not yet!"

All the leaders nodded in agreement.

"Break out the drink – let's toast each other as heroes!" called Vordimus.

It was quickly arranged, and the eight men stood, their drinking horns touching at their rims, "I give you: victory over Rome!"

"Victory!" responded Arthmael and his men.

Ortagorus laughed, "Brigantia herself is smiling on us now!"

*

In the infirmary, the chief doctor stood looking over the ward. There was tiredness in his face and in his very gesture as he pushed back a straggling lock of hair with his hand.

Marcus looked in at the infirmary door and waved to him, "Diocles!"

The doctors's leathery face broke into a weary grin, "*Prefectus alae!*"

"How are you enjoying life in Britannia?" smiled Marcus, "Quiet enough for you after serving under Trajan in Germania?"

"It's quiet enough, yes. Didn't realise how bad the weather would be, though. Winters too long, summers too short – or non-existent. I've applied for a transfer back to Germania with the Legate," his Latin, though perfect, still held a touch of accent: a hint of Greek sunshine in this weather-lashed north.

"Well, who knows how long that will take to go through," said Marcus. "In the meantime, you mentioned that you'd like someone to help you. Still interested?"

"Deeply interested," said Diocles wryly. "Have you found someone?"

"Yes, a girl who wants to join the legion as a nurse."

Diocles looked at the cavalry prefect and nodded several times in his thoughtful way, "Interesting. And what qualifications does she possess?"

"Great figure, long dark hair, big blue eyes..."

Diocles smiled, "Last time I enquired, those qualifications did not exactly meet the legionary medical corps requirements."

"She claims to have some knowledge of healing. She's also keen to learn. I think she'd make a great student for you."

"I appreciate your gesture; however I can't just employ someone just because you think she's the next Venus!"

"Give her a chance. Ask her some questions."

Diocles looked at him, "Perhaps I will, at that. Even we doctors are not averse to good-looking nurses. But I have to check on all these patients. Bring her here next week."

"She's standing outside now," nodded Marcus.

Diocles sighed, "Well, I can't fault her punctuality," adding, with an air of resignation to the inevitable, "You owe me a favour. All right."

Both men stepped back towards the corridor. Cornelia stood demurely, clad in a long dress. Diocles looked her critically up and down.

"My name is –"

The Greek raised a hand, "You are just in time to accompany me around the infirmary."

Cornelia nodded obediently and followed the doctor. Marcus added himself to the end of medical inspection.

A dozen beds were laid out on either side of the central room. In each one was a soldier suffering from some ailment or other. Diocles stopped at the first bed. A portly German lay in it, his ankle twice the normal size. He smiled up at Marcus, who nodded at him.

"This man was brought to us today from the assault course. What's your opinion, miss?"

Cornelia examined the foot and turned it around gently in a circular motion. The German grunted in pain.

"Just badly swollen. It should be strapped tightly with bandages and lifted high so that the fluid drains. Within a week he should be fine."

Diocles turned towards Marcus and shot a look in his direction, "Very good. Orderly, make sure this man is treated as you heard," and they moved on.

A young soldier's left leg was heavily bandaged. Blood was seeping through the linen strips.

"Your opinion?" said Diocles.

Cornelia unrolled the bandage. Despite her lightness of touch, the young man squirmed in pain. The last of the bandage exposed a large gash down the calf of the leg. Maggots had been applied to eat away the dead flesh. Marcus turned his head from the sight in disgust: fat maggots engorging themselves on human flesh were more suited to a corpse on the battlefield than a hospital.

Cornelia didn't wince, scrutinising the maggots, "The treatment is sound. But look how fat they are. These maggots need replacing with fresh ones."

Diocles looked at her.

"It would be better to get maggots from the north, they are smaller and eat more, so they last longer on the leg. They are available in the market. Once the flesh is clean a poultice can be applied with lime: an excellent purifier, also on sale in the market." She returned the surgeon's glance.

Diocles was silent for a moment, "I was not aware there were different types of maggots here in Eboracum. Or that you have a lime-based purifier available. We will try both, as you suggest, and see what difference they make."

Finally Diocles stopped in front of another bed, "What's wrong with you?" he asked of the soldier.

"My arm, doctor. Can't move without pain."

"Interesting," said Diocles, and turned to Cornelia. "Any ideas?"

Cornelia took the soldier's hand, "Tell me when it hurts," she said. She gently moved the arm all the way over his head and back down beside his waist without stopping. She let go his hand when it reached the bottom. The soldier's eyes never left hers.

"I find nothing wrong with this man," said Cornelia. "Full movement is normal."

Diocles smiled, "Let me introduce you to Hetorix, our professional malingerer. He is in here every week, always complaining of some new problem. The orderlies don't know how to deal with him," he looked down. "Looks like you've met your match now, my man."

Hetorix frowned and then smiled, "It does seem a lot better, suddenly. Thanks doc, I'm cured. Quick work! Thank you so much, miss!"

Diocles thought for a second, "Do you speak fluent Latin, Miss –?"

"Yes, I do." Added Cornelia.

"Then you are now on my staff," smiled the Greek. "I will see the Legate about you this afternoon. You have a two-month trial. If you pass this trial period I will enrol you as a full-time nurse within the Ninth Legion. And having some help will allow me to check on the progress of my transfer instead of slaving away in here all the time," he spoke the last sentence more to himself.

"Thank you," she said. "Two months is perfect," she turned and smiled at Marcus, who gave her an even bigger smile back.

A small cheer from the last bed caused the doctor to turn.

"All right, Hetorix," said Diocles gruffly. "Back to duty! This hospital is for wounded heroes, not bystanders!"

*

The Prefect of Rome poured wine into two goblets. He walked over to his beautiful consort and held a hank of her hair in one hand as though weighing it. She answered his challenging look with something that hinted at impudence.

"Perhaps I should go," she said, making no attempt to leave.

"What's the hurry?" he said, walking over and opening the shutters. Bright autumn sunlight poured into his chambers. "Let's make the most of the sunshine; winter's on its way, you know."

She sighed deliciously. He passed her a goblet and they sipped together.

"If my husband knew I was here..."

Attianus waved his hand, "Don't trouble yourself," he said. "If he meant anything to you, you would not have come. And what can he do for you? Just more of the same indolent life, more little luxuries..."

"I like luxuries," she pouted.

He smiled, "Why then, make sure they are genuine luxuries, real rarities – the kind of indulgences that most men can only dream of. And most women too."

He looked at her perfect figure, held her auburn hair again and let it cascade through his fingers, "You're quite lovely, Livia. You're a luxury yourself."

"Thank you, Acilius Attianus."

"Call me Publius."

Her eyes widened and she nodded imperceptibly.

"I can be good to you, Livia. I can be very good. If you are willing to be good to me."

She said nothing but took in his immaculate dress, his finery. She glanced fleetingly around the room and its sumptuous fittings. He smiled again but as always, his eyes didn't quite participate in the levity, afraid to be caught off guard, even for a moment.

"I'm not exactly without prospects, you know," he murmured.

"Everyone in Rome knows that," she said.

There was a flush of genuine pleasure in his face for a second, "How would you like to spend a week with me in my summer house in Neapolis?"

"Neapolis!" she breathed.

"Yes – it's still summer there, you know – or so it feels. The magical island of Capri is in view of my villa. We could sit on the veranda, enjoying the warm breeze. The climate's always mild there. And it has all the Empire's latest fashions" repeated Attianus with his practised line.

"I love Neapolis."

"All you need to enjoy it to properly is to have the right man at your side."

"But my husband," she said.

Attianus shrugged, "I am sure he can be induced to release you."

"For a week?"

"To start with... And now, my lovely Livia, I am expecting a guest. You run along. I will send a man with the details in due course."

"A guest?"

He laughed at her expression, "Yes. But much older than you – and considerably your inferior when it comes to looks and personal charm. A senator, in fact."

He held her hand and maintained the touch a fraction longer than etiquette demanded.

"Farewell, Livia."

"Farewell, Acilius – I'm sorry. Publius," she glided to the door, opened it, looked back and met his gaze. Then she was gone.

Attianus picked up his goblet again and drank deeply. He set it down.

"*Uxor formosa et vinum sunt dulcia venena,*" he said to himself, quoting the Roman proverb. Beautiful women and wine are sweet venom. A minute later there was a knock on the door, and his ratty secretary ushered in his guest, who wore a *toga praetexta* with a vertical broad purple stripe down the centre.

"Senator Secundus Blandinus," said the secretary.

The visitor was indeed far less prepossessing than Livia, in terms of physical beauty. But he made up for the lack with his shrewd eyes that seemed to weigh everything – and find everything wanting.

"Please, take a seat, Senator," said the head of the Praetorian Guard, "How goes the campaign?"

"I think well, my lord. There are some waverers, but they can always be bought," Blandinus stroked his wispy beard absently.

Attianus laughed, clapped his hands, and a servant entered with a strongbox. The Prefect waited until they were alone again, then threw open the lid, "Is this enough?"

The senator rose to peer inside the box. His eyes dilated with greedy joy, "Assuredly, Prefect."

"Disperse it as you see fit. You know these men. Oh, and make sure you take a sufficiency for your own trouble."

"Thank you, my lord. From your own purse?" he ventured.

"Well, we may call it so. Although there are some contributions from various magistrates and other supporters," he put his hand into the box and picked up a handful of gold and silver coins, jingling them back down like a metallic waterfall, "Do not fear to pour this out where it will do most good," he said. "This is a well that will not run dry."

Blandinus nodded. "I understand, Prefect. It shall be done as you say."

"Farewell then, Senator. I will have this box brought round to your villa discreetly this afternoon."

"Farewell, my lord," the senator departed, in obvious high spirits.

The Prefect of the City of Rome sat down and poured himself another goblet of wine. In his own undemonstrative way, he was even more elated than the senator. He raised the goblet in front of him, and the autumn sun glinted off its burnished surface, "To the fifteenth Emperor!" he laughed.

SPQR

Few men are born brave: many become so
through training and force of discipline.

Publius Flavius Vegetius Renatus

XI   To be a Soldier

**3.40pm, 20th November, 117AD: Castra
Corsopitum, Northern Britain**

With livid crimson streaks raking the sky, birds of prey
fluttered to their roosts in the treeline, waiting attentively
as though sensing death. And indeed the tension was
palpable. The sentries of Coria patrolled its ramparts,
uncertainty in their gaze. Seasoned men as well as raw
recruits felt fear grip their hearts, colder than the late
autumn wind that buffeted across the open ground in front
of the fortress.

Then it came, a mass of men carrying the trunk of a
mighty oak between them. Stripped of its branches, the tree
was even more formidable than when it been a living thing
swaying in the breeze. The sentries looked on; the fact that
the Brigantian warriors made no attempt at concealment
added to their consternation. The warriors below threw
down the oak ram, its impact shaking the ground, and
stood mutely looking up at the fort, waiting for the signal
to spur them into action.

A soldier clattered down the steps of the rampart,
heading for the command centre. Minutes later, Drusus
stood with the camp centurion. The young blond-haired
cavalry squad leader looked rested and eager, almost
completely recovered from his fatigue, "It's true then,
Centurion," he said.

"Yes. The barbarians are waiting with a battering ram just outside arrow range.

No doubt they prefer to knock at our gates rather than burn them down. It's as if they know there's enough food here to feed them for several months, not to mention weapons that they can use. Although how they can know about all of this..."

"They seem well informed," said Drusus, and then there was a pause.

"Decurio," said the centurion at length, "I had hoped to spare you this. I had hoped that our riders would have got through to Eboracum. Perhaps they have. But it is clear that no relief can arrive this evening. We are on our own."

The centurion paused, looking briefly at his map, "Their intentions are clear enough: knock down our gates with that ram, wait for nightfall and then attack our walls on all sides. Slaughter, just like at Bremenium and Habitancum. They would gain the camp and all the goods within it."

Drusus nodded, "I agree. It's a foregone conclusion." He grinned suddenly, "In that case, I would propose taking as many of those bastards with us as possible. My men are eager for revenge and even experienced barbarians will fall apart under a proper cavalry charge. They have none of their own, so I can ride unopposed and cut down the enemy while they're still disorganised."

The camp centurion nodded, taking in the plan. His mind was made up, "I will bring out the other two centuries and get them in line formation with the shield wall up," said the commander of Coria. "Let them taste some Roman steel before we fall."

"And if I might suggest, Centurion: send a dozen men to set fire to the stores of food, weapons, maps and all buildings. You have plenty of parchments, don't you?"

The centurion laughed. "We do – and they will make good kindling!"

Drusus looked knowingly into the centurion's eyes, "May the gods be with you," he saluted and left the room.

"And with you". The camp centurion picked up the flagon and tilted it over his cup. He watched the wine glisten in the lamplight as it poured. In just the same way, his life was seeping out.

Five minutes later, the great wooden gates of the fortress creaked open. The soldiers inside felt the wind rush in as though taunting them, rejoicing at its release from captivity. The turma of Drusus, almost at full strength, filed through the gate and drew up in battle formation. For a seemingly unending moment, there was virtually no movement. The only sound was the harsh cawing of a bird. The lightly armed Brigantes clustered around the ram stood like statues, watching the Roman cavalry. The turma was now immobile but for the swish of a tail, the shake of a horse's neck.

In the first line of twenty or so mounted men there was an indefinable air of pride, of military training but also of freedom. They were cavalrymen, and in a moment they would fulfil their destiny as cavalrymen. No longer confined behind walls, skulking like fugitives. And still there was nothing. The soldiers on both sides might have been carvings on a battle frieze.

A large mass of blue-painted Brigantian infantry ran forward to join the men around the ram: archers and fighters armed with swords, which they swirled through the air in grim invitation.

As if that movement were itself a signal, Drusus raised his right hand and shouted, "Seventh Turma, forward: slow trot."

At his command the line of cavalry moved smoothly forward. It was a parade-ground manoeuvre, executed with easy style.

Drusus shouted again. "Seventh Turma, charge!"

The small party of horsemen jabbed their feet into their mounts and urged their horses at maximum speed. Drusus smiled at the exhilaration of the onrush. He glanced to either side of him: a perfect straight line with spears pointed out. It was the moment any cavalryman lived for: the horses' pounding hooves, the wind flying in their faces. There was a magnificence about them, twenty young men in the prime of their lives, the last rays of the sun glinting from their helmets and armour as their horses pounded on. They were fit, thirsting for revenge, spears fixed in the attack position. The cavalrymen leaned forward, putting all their weight behind their spears.

Inside the fort, the cohorts had rapidly assembled and were marching in column formation through the front gate. The camp centurion leading the front line raised a cheer at the charging cavalry.

Ahead of the turma, a few barbarians had fled, but most stood their ground, hefting sword or spear. Now Drusus could see fear and apprehension on their faces. The line crashed into the lightly armed warriors around the ram. The cavalry tore the first line asunder, bodies and parts of bodies flying, hurled away by spear points that were already homing on the next target.

Drusus fixed his aim on a huge warrior with a long sword. At the last moment the man realised that his sword was shorter than the Roman spear but he was transfixed like an animal. Drusus felt the force as his spear lanced through the warrior's neck, blood spurting crazily into the air. Another man raising his weapon to strike was picked out by the *decurio* quickly drawing his sword with his left hand. His long spatha swished through the air and the warrior's arm was gone. The man fell back, eyes wide, screaming in terror.

Another enemy: a young man with a long dagger leapt at him, in front. Drusus shot out his foot and pushed him off. A swift strike of the long sword and the barbarian tumbled backwards, a large diagonal cut across his chest. Drusus snatched a glimpse around the turma and saw the enemy breaking. The Brigantes fell back quickly.

"Leave them!" shouted Drusus, "Form a line."

The threat from the ram was over – for now, at least – and the shock of the cavalry charge had stunned the remaining Brigantian infantry. New hope flowed through the cavalrymen's veins and they breathed more freely. Drusus wiped his sword over his tunic and sheathed it.

The charge had clearly surprised the barbarians. They screamed war cries in defiance but made no immediate attempt to engage. The turma, still virtually intact, wheeled round back into a line formation once again. New Brigantian infantry approached: a mixed mass of both heavy and light infantry. They moved with great speed to engage the small party of horsemen which they greatly outnumbered.

But then came something unexpected, something shocking in its immediacy: a line of chariots thundered down the road. Two leading chariots, one to the left and one to the right, formed the battle-line's two horns.

Drusus knew he could do nothing about the chariots. If they got to the gates of the fort before the two centuries had formed up, they would mow them down. His men alone stood a chance of killing them in greater numbers and delaying them. He looked back at the centurion deploying the men out of the fort.

Drusus wheeled his horse round and faced the road, "Seventh *Turma*! Form line on me."

His men looked at him in surprise.

"Form line!" he repeated, pointing his sword at the chariots. His men promptly fanned out either side of him. Scarcely had they formed up before they were charging again.

"I shall see you in the after life," shouted Drusus to his men, the blood pounding in his ears, "Kill as many as you can!"

At either side, the lead chariots were drawn by yoked ponies and moved with furious speed. Barely noticeable, the man driving the chariot crouched on the front of the platform. Behind him, a nobleman screamed oaths.

On his left, Drusus felt, rather than saw, Pertinax disappear in a scything blow that flecked hot blood across his face but he never flinched. He lowered his sword again and charged straight for one of the lead chariots. A heavy blow from the side sent waves of shock coursing through his arm. An arrow spanked off his chain mail shirt, and then he was up to the lead chariot. A sword swung at his head, he ducked and slashed with his own blade.

It connected with the arm of the Brigantian leader, slicing away flesh and sinew, pouring blood. The barbarian cried out in pain and anger, shaking his head to clear his vision as Drusus surged past him.

Vordimus turned in his chariot, his left arm running with blood from Drusus's last sword blow. Looking behind him, he saw the turma commander overwhelmed by numbers and dragged from his horse as he ploughed into the remaining chariots. He was moved by the valour of the charge, against overwhelming odds. Death and glory. That was the way for a man to die. He looked ahead again. The lines had hit each other with speed and power but the momentum and force of the chariots had been greater. A Roman horseman, unseated, was run over by the chariot in front. The man's body was torn into two halves by the flying wheels, yet he continued to scream in agony.

Vordimus' eyes took in the rest of the battle. A series of single combats between the Roman cavalrymen and the charioteers was largely concluded, mostly in his army's favour, thanks to the speed, bulk and momentum of the chariots and their stable platform for warriors to use their swords. However, the Roman cavalry had taken its toll: a third of the chariots were missing men or drivers.

"Halt!" cried Vordimus, rallying his troops, "Halt!" he cried again, this time answered by a roar from the remaining chariots.

Ahead of him, came the Roman infantry, forming rapidly into line formation. The barbarian infantry screamed oaths for revenge but did not advance. Vordimus kept his hand raised high to the front for all to see, a gesture mirrored by Ortagorus on the other flank. The infantry remained stationary.

The Roman troops started to advance, their disciplined silence a stark contrast to the screams and skirls of the Brigantes. In tight formation, with shields interlocking. They may have been storemen and clerks, but they were still trained, professional Roman soldiers, armed with their short swords for close fighting, protected by their helmets, mail shirts and large shields. They were taking part in something that had been seen many times before throughout the empire: Roman discipline and training overcoming a larger force of courageous but uncoordinated rabble.

Only this time, it was different. Sighs of dismay arose from the Roman legionaries as another force appeared on the field. A horde of barbarian cavalry thudded towards them, eating up the distance. They were rough and ready, without armour, without the precision manoeuvring that Drusus's men had displayed – but they had surprise on their side, for no one in the enemy ranks had even guessed at their existence. As well as surprise, they had axes and swords, and those weapons were flying towards the Roman troops at twenty-five miles an hour.

The camp centurion in the front row of the infantry looked back at the fort and saw the first clouds of smoke billowing up. He gave a grim smile, then turned back to face his enemy.

Vordimus dropped his hand forward and unleashed the forces of Hades.

*

Cornelia entered the hospital and began her duties, checking every patient and reassuring them they would soon feel better. The work was congenial to her, and she took a simple almost childlike pleasure in helping others.

An orderly called her from her routine tasks, "This man was under a wagon when the axle collapsed. It came down fully loaded onto his chest, breaking several ribs and crushing some internal organs." The orderly shook his head.

One glance from her took in the wounded soldier's pallor, the trickles of sweat running down the sides of his face and his stertorous breathing. She sat down beside him, picked up a wet cloth and held it to his brow. His eyes opened and he tried to form words. His speech was fragmentary and confused but she thought she heard the word, "mother". She took his hand in hers as she continued to anoint his forehead with coolness. She also made sounds in no worldly language but soothing, comforting, reassuring the soldier. A wan smile flickered over the soldier's face. The sweat was drying on his face and his contorted posture relaxed. He laid his head back, carrying the angelic image of her with him on his long journey.

Unbeknownst to her, someone had been watching her every movement for over half an hour. He moved forward from the shadows and put his hand on her shoulder.

She looked up, to see the doctor's face looking down at her, "You are now a full-time nurse in the Ninth Legion," he said. He reached down to the soldier's head and closed his eyes for the last time with gentle efficiency.

"But my trial period?" she said, surprised.

"Is over."

*

~193~

On a bright autumn morning, the Prefect of the City of Rome walked from the Regia in the direction of the Flavian Amphitheatre. As usual, his six bodyguards marched in a square formation around and ahead of him, clearing a route.

At the sight of the Praetorian uniform, people moved quickly out the way. These hardest and most brutal of soldiers were instantly recognisable from their distinctive black cloaks: an appropriate colour for their reputation. Most had been recruited from the ranks of other legions and promoted for their prowess as fighters.

Attianus watched the precision of their movement. The Praetorians were the better of any unit in the entire Roman army when campaigning: and he was their chief. His mind's eye took him swiftly back over the last twenty years, selecting highlights. There was no doubt that he had done well for himself, as his two exalted ranks testified; but he had also done well for those he had served: in particular, Trajan and Hadrian.

The Praetorians were a formidable force but a force for stability. Attianus liked that. While they had wielded enormous power, they had helped strengthen the empire by removing weak or unpopular emperors – and supporting strong and virile ones.

The shrewd-eyed senator came into Attianus' view as though by chance, interrupting his reverie: "Secundus Blandinus! Join me!" he called, and the two men strolled onward together, behind the marching men. Heads turned at the martial splendour of the escort but neither Attianus nor Blandinus minded that.

"Is all proceeding as planned?" said the City Prefect in a lower voice.

"I believe so," said the senator in equally subdued tones, "All is in readiness for you."

"Excellent."

The conversation died away and the two continued to walk. All about them was the bustle, the order, the contentment of the world's most powerful race of people. As they approached the great amphitheatre, the enormous statue of Nero, the Colossus Neronis, caught their eyes. At thirty metres tall, it was impossible to miss. Its proximity to the amphitheatre was no doubt the reason for its increasingly popular name – the Colosseum.

They walked under the shade of the towering walls. Crowds milled around, excitement and expectation in the air. Smells of meat cooking, bread, herbs and spices came from stalls selling refreshment, mingled with the fruity bouquet of wine. There were puppet shows of gladiators, the wooden toys artfully fashioned to resemble the favourites of the crowd. There were other entertainments designed to lure and ensnare passers-by into leaving some of their money behind as they made their way inside the amphitheatre. Men with worldly wise expressions offered odds on the outcome of the forthcoming bouts. The babble of voices, shouts and cries of the stallholders, friends and relatives calling to each other, was deafening.

The soldiers from the escort marched to a grand double door at the main entrance. Normally the emperor would enter the Colosseum through this route. Today Attianus smiled at the crowd like an emperor, as he approached the doors. The guard turned and saluted as their Prefect passed through them. More Praetorians guarding either side of the door saluted, as Attianus and the senator went inside.

Blandinus followed the Prefect through an underground passageway lit by torches in sconces on the walls. Although he had been to the Colosseum many times, this procedure was all new to him and he was slightly apprehensive. Suddenly they emerged into the bright sunlight again, and he recognised where he was: in the emperor's box at the north end of the stadium, reserved only for the man wearing the imperial purple and his family. The senator stole a sidelong glance at Attianus, but he showed no sign of anything being unusual, and nor did the crowd.

A servant bowed and retired. Blandinus blinked in surprise at the long table, piled high with enough food and wine for a banquet, immaculately and temptingly laid out. Enticing aromas from the hot dishes wafted his way. The Prefect waved him to a seat, and the senator sat down in the sumptuous trappings of royalty. He looked around him. The Colosseum could seat fifty thousand people and today it looked more crowded than ever. There had been a scramble to get tickets when the Senate had announced free games in honour of the deification of the old emperor Trajan. People had queued for hours outside in the blistering heat just to get a seat. However, it was worth the wait. The magnificent tiered rows gave everyone a handsome view of the spectacle below.

A roar from the crowd distracted Blandinus, and he peered down. The view from this box was the best in the whole stadium. The gladiators had been wheeling around warily, sizing each other up, but at that moment the one with the trident had seized his moment and struck. His opponent fell, blood pouring from his side onto the sand of the arena. The crowd bellowed its appreciation of the gladiator's skill. Then Attianus nudged Blandinus, and he remembered why they were here.

"Have them come up one at a time," Attianus said, indicating the twenty or thirty senators clustered in the private row immediately below the royal box, "I want you to smooth things along."

"That will be my pleasure, my lord," said Blandinus, with an oily smile. Attianus smiled also. He could imagine the senator picturing another strong box stuffed with gold coins.

The Prefect sat back in his seat, perhaps the only man there uninterested in the spectacle below. Already the victor had bowed to the imperial box, slaves had run to pull the body of the defeated gladiator, and two new contestants were striding out, both fit, young and in their prime. They bowed in Attianus' direction and raised their weapons in the traditional salute.

Blandinus led in the first of his colleagues, and Attianus held out his hand in invitation. The visitor seated himself and looked down the table at the array of delicacies: there was Setine wine, said to be the favourite drink of Caesar Augustus, and Mammertine from Messina. There was shoulder of hare, peacock, roasted chicken and other luxury items, set off by bread, fruits and fine cheese. The senator's eyebrows went up at the display set before him.

A horn blew in the arena. The gladiators sprang back facing each other, and the crowd erupted with fierce joy once more.

Attianus bent his head down and put his mouth to the senator's ear to make himself heard above the tumult, "I am planning some very special games here in the amphitheatre later in the month," he said. "If you could make yourself free to join me, I am sure you would find it worthwhile."

Attianus talked for some time, and then his audience was at an end and the senator rose, his body language indicating his decision.

He was replaced by another, skilfully steered along by Blandinus, as Attianus's go-between. The procession of senators went on for many minutes. One or two left abruptly, uninterested in the offer; but most stayed to talk. They had, after all, been hand-selected.

As it happened, there was one other spectator in the Colosseum with no interest in the sport. Commodus had seen many shows in that stadium, many lives ended, many reputations made. But he had never seen such a display as he witnessed now, his eyes like eagle's fixed on the imperial box.

*

Marcus strode through the streets of Eboracum, the afternoon light already giving way to shades of evening. All around him were passers-by, people milling about, shopkeepers, soldiers, camp followers and all the crowds that hung around a legionary fortress. But he had eyes for none of them. His orders had come from his commander, Juventius. A rumour had reached his ear: almost certainly an idle one, but still, he would be obliged if Marcus would investigate its truth or otherwise personally. The servant who brought the message carried a note with details of where to go. The message seemed to indicate that the Ninth's head of cavalry put store in Marcus' judgement – and his discretion.

An auxiliary soldier had returned from the outposts of the north, alone. That much was fact, the rest hearsay. Was he a deserter? Had he lost his mind? Was he feigning, for some purpose of his own – or someone else's? Speculation dried up for lack of information.

Marcus quickened his pace. Lamps were being lit on some of the street stalls, casting shadows ahead of him. He entered the small, cramped room and stood there in the door frame, transfixed by the scene. In the flickering light of an oil lamp lay a soldier dressed in the uniform of an auxiliary. He lay on a large pile of straw, and kneeling before him was Cornelia, dipping a cloth in a bowl of water and wringing it out. The simplicity and the gentle peacefulness of the tableau struck him. She looked up at that moment and smiled at him.

"Greetings, Valerius Quietus," she said softly.

He smiled at her and walked further into the room, bending down to look at the soldier. He was little more than a boy of seventeen or so. His eyes were closed, he was muddied, blooded and there was an ugly looking wound on the left side of his head. He smelt strongly of horse and human sweat.

"Why is he not at the infirmary?" asked Marcus, in a whisper.

"He fell from his horse in the street outside this house and they brought him in. I can do as much for him in here, as they can."

Marcus sat down in a chair by the bedside.

"He hasn't regained consciousness"; she whispered, "Yet the wound isn't that deep – it looks worse than it is."

He watched her silently as she opened a bag that lay beside her. She lit pungent-smelling roots, treated with something to make them burn. They filled the air with an earthy, rousing aroma that made Marcus breathe more quickly. She prepared a concoction in a cup that looked foul, murmuring words over it. The stench of it assaulted Marcus's nostrils and he reached out a hand, touching her shoulder in warning and alarm. She turned to him.

"Trust me," she said.

He withdrew his hand. She reached over and opened the soldier's mouth, pouring some of the witches brew into it. The soldier coughed violently and began to moan. She reached out and touched the temples of the soldier. As she did so, she remembered many times that she wanted so much to forget; when those hands had been the instruments of death.

Well, now, the gods willing, they would restore life rather than take it.

The soldier reacted to her touch, jerking his head from side to side and groaning before lying still again.

"Ah," she said, "Such pain. A wound, not long ago; but it is as though the tip of the blade entered his mind, freezing it to pain and darkness."

The soldier began to sweat and shiver, and she applied the wet cloth to his forehead again. Marcus was struck by her gentleness. The soldier's body jerked more violently.

"The crisis approaches," she said. "Jupiter and Pluto battle for his soul."

Marcus touched her arm, "Make him live," he said.

She continued to minister to him, to murmur invocations, to apply poultices. Then there came a moment when the fever stilled, and a coldness struck her, as though he was slipping away. And she remembered the nameless soldier who had died in her hands in the sanatorium, and redoubled her efforts, her gentle yet strong fingers moulding the young soldier's temples as though pleading for his life. She leant back, exhausted.

"It's in the hands of the gods now," she said, "But I think he will live."

Marcus leaned forward, and she smiled a little at the compassion in his face. The soldier opened his eyes. His surroundings and his companions were unknown to him, but the pain that had dogged him for so long was gone. He reached out his hand and Cornelia gave him a drink of water.

"What is your name? Where are you from?" asked Marcus.

The soldier sipped, spluttered a little, sipped again, "Pedes Novantes," he said, weakly, "Hades' End."

Marcus remembered the name from the map in the legate's office, "The watchtowers? What happened to you?"

"Brigantes," said the young man.

"An attack? But the forts – Bremenium and the rest?"

"Bremenium...Habitancum...destroyed. Saw them. All my comrades, killed." Novantes lay his head back as though this long speech had drained his strength. Marcus sat for a moment, looking at the youth. His head rebelled against the enormity, the impossibility, of what all this implied. But his heart felt that it was true. Novantes opened his eyes again.

"Well done, infantryman," he said. "You are very brave."

Novantes' mouth creased into a smile as though the muscles of his face had almost forgotten that position, and a tear glistened in his eye. Suddenly remembering, he reached inside his tunic and pulled out a blood-spattered piece of parchment. He passed it over to Marcus, who read it slowly through. Now his head and his heart were in agreement, and the time for thinking was over. Marcus stood up.

"Cornelia, you're a miracle worker," he said, "but you need to work another, and quickly. This young man needs to be ready to ride tomorrow."

"Impossible!" she cried.

"Essential," he said with a smile that held sadness, "That's what it means to be a soldier." He turned for the door.

"Where are you going?" she asked.

"To see the Legate of the Ninth."

XII Commodus

4.10pm, 21st November, 117AD: chambers of the Legate of the Ninth Legion, Eboracum, Northern Britain

Marcus stood before his commanding officer, increasing puzzlement on his face. He had concluded his brief report half a minute ago, and had expected the legate to jump to his feet, calling subordinates to him, issuing orders, throwing the whole camp into vigorous action. But instead, the legate just sat, gazing into the distance, passing an occasional hand through his wispy hair. Marcus had expected him to be animated, as excited as himself at the prospect of a real fight. But instead he seemed thoughtful – and even a little annoyed.

The legate looked up at last, his mind apparently made up, "I'm not convinced," he said.

Marcus stood in disbelief, "Sir, I saw him myself, saw his wounds, heard his tale from his own mouth."

"I have no doubt that there is a wounded auxiliary foot soldier lying in a hovel outside the camp. But what does that prove? He may be lying – a deserter who has made up some story to avoid punishment. Perhaps he is mad. Perhaps even an imposter."

"But this parchment, Legate – signed by the commander of Castra Corsopitum himself," said Marcus, pointing down to the table.

The legate waved its existence away, "Not even a prefect. He's just a centurion."

"What does that matter? ...Sir."

"It matters a great deal. The man's not a patrician, he's just a common person."

An angry retort rose in Marcus's throat, but he controlled himself, "He is the officer in charge of Legion Supply, sir."

"Yes, but that doesn't qualify him to make tactical and strategic evaluations. He is a pen-pusher, a recorder of numbers and totals – like most of the men at Coria." The legate looked down at the dispatch again, "And what does he really know about it? 'The watchtowers and the forts of Bremenium and Habitancum overwhelmed and destroyed by Brigantes.' How does he know that? Habitancum is twenty miles north of where he is, Bremenium nearly another ten miles further, and the watchtowers even more remote from him. Has he been there? Has he sent scouts? No, or he would have said so. This whole alarm is the cause of that auxiliary, who's even now enjoying sweet dreams in a hut in Eboracum. He arrived at Coria – probably on a stolen horse – and spun some tale to that fool in charge, who promptly panicked."

Marcus forced himself to breathe deeply, "This parchment speaks of a cavalry escort named Fulvio, from a turma stationed in Habitancum."

"Well, where is he? Did you see him? Did this infantryman of yours mention him?"

"No, sir."

The legate looked at him, "No, sir. I'll tell you what happened. This man of yours – who in your own words is a stripling and a raw recruit – encountered some barbarians out on a drunken spree. Maybe they killed an auxiliary or two, maybe they wounded him. He got away, but in his cowardly fear he magnified the threat a hundredfold. And no doubt made up the cavalry escort to give his story more credence."

"In my judgement, Legate, the infantryman was speaking the truth when he said he had seen –"

"Your judgement!" barked the legate with a snort of derision, "What action have you been in?" Marcus flushed and was silent. "Besides, the whole story is preposterous. Bremenium is commanded by Severus, a nobleman and an experienced campaigner. I appointed him myself! Do you really expect me to believe that he and his entire force of men, secure behind wooden ramparts, have been wiped out by a rabble of *Brittunculi*? Nonsense!" he slammed the palm of his hand on his wooden table. He glared at Marcus as though expecting him to bow and leave his office, but he caught him unawares.

"Such things have been known, Legate," muttered the young man.

The legate looked up at him with a blend of anger and surprise – which in turn gave way to more complex emotions. Such things had indeed been known, throughout the empire, and even here in Britannia. Perhaps there was something in this – some small rising of the barbarians to the north. And perhaps he could win himself a rare honour in this outpost of empire that the gods had surely forgotten.

"Don't think I'm not appreciative of your action, Quietus," he said. "You reported promptly to me, as was your duty. But I need to weigh up all the aspects of such incidents. I will send two turmae tomorrow morning."

"Tomorrow morning?" asked Marcus.

"Yes" nodded the legate. "I assure you, forty-eight fully trained Roman cavalry will be more than a match for any number of drunken savages! As to the commander of the scouting force, it will be led by Caelinus Juventius. I need an *experienced* officer whose judgement I can *trust*," he looked at Marcus' flushed face and noted his silence with satisfaction. "You will go and visit our local clan chief. Enquire in town for a man called Tobar. Ask him what's happening locally and report back to me. You will find he's as docile as an aged dog – and perfectly happy with Roman rule."

Marcus stood numbly, forgetting to acknowledge the order.

"Dismissed, *Praefectus Alae*."

Marcus saluted, turned and left the room.

The legate sat looking after him for a while; then called his secretary: "Write this. **To Quintus Pompeius Falco, Praetor, et cetera, Governor of Britannia, Londinium. Most revered Governor: I write to advise that by means of the intelligence network I have diligently put in place, I have become aware of a rising of some *Brigantes* which reside some one hundred miles to the north of here. Thanks to the excellence of my information, and the alacrity of my response, I have no doubt that the rising will have been quelled by the time this report reaches you. I will send a full dispatch complete with trophies, captives and the like in due course…"**

*

Under grey and minatory clouds, Tobar sat astride a horse on a hill overlooking the Roman fort of Vindolanda, marshalling his troops and organising the attack according to their strict training. At that moment, he certainly didn't resemble the docile aged dog of the legate of the Ninth's fantasy: he looked more like a slavering wolf, with his necklace of animal teeth. As he watched, one of his friends fell under a Roman spear, and he bellowed in rage and anger.

The Brigantian cavalry galloped around the fort, always on the move, firing arrows over the ramparts. They ventured inside the killing zone occasionally but stayed mainly outside it, taunting, inviting the gates to be flung open and the enemy to accept the challenge. But the great gates stayed firmly shut. Tobar looked at those gates, and allowed himself a smile of satisfaction. *Now*, he thought, *now we will surprise these invaders*. Yes, they thought themselves the greatest race the world had ever seen. They thought themselves immeasurably superior to the people they ruled over – *even though this is our country and our race had existed long before Rome had been even a city state*. And they thought themselves secure, behind their fortresses and palaces, their opulent buildings and their villas. Now they were about to discover that they were mistaken. Tobar raised his hand and let it fall, and the cavalry withdrew. He could almost feel the intensity of the gaze from the watchers on the fortress walls.

Then it came: a huge battering ram, suspended on a frame of wood with hurdles made of wicker on the sides. It was slung on ropes from a beam, under a great canopy of uncured hides, doused in water to resist fire. The canopy sheltered the men carrying the ram from arrows and also protected the greater number of warriors huddled under its cover. Well behind the ram, the heavy infantry of the Brigantes started to form an immense line and began to move, step by step, ominous in its slow but relentless tread. Brigante archers, behind a wall of shields, fired from around the sides of the structure as it moved forward. Romans fell from the ramparts, or hung over the wooden parapets, and the screams of the wounded and dying rent the air. The Romans fired back and some archers fell but the shelter remained effective.

Tobar thought he could feel the astonishment and dismay of the troops penned inside the fort, watching in disbelief as one of their own classic formations, combined with their siege weapon, 'the tortoise', was used against them. The clan chieftain looked around him. All the faces were familiar to him. He knew all of them by name. All were eager for the new dawn that was coming. They, like he, had grown up under Roman subjugation, aliens in their own country. But thanks to their bravery – and the sapience of their leaders – all that was about to change.

The enormous ram, a massive and weighty tree trunk, reached the gates. The ram swung back inside its cover and was pushed with full force to shudder against the portals like a maddened demand that would not be denied. Tobar imagined the panic and the fear of those inside. The Roman soldiers redoubled their attempts, hurling spears, rocks and burning torches down onto the hide covering.

Still the ram was pulled back and thundered forward, to beat implacably against the gates, now starting to buckle at the centre. And still the infantry line advanced, slowly, inexorably. At the very next strike of the ram, the gates burst asunder: the signal to the cavalry to charge, for the infantry to run, and to pour into the breach that the Roman-inspired siege engine had wrought.

Tobar laughed exultantly and rode onwards and downwards, buoyed along by the tide of his warriors. The main body of cavalry was riding through the open doorway while others stayed back to harass soldiers on the ramparts with arrows. Soon, the infantry would be up at the fort, funnelling into the narrow entrance and then widening out as they rushed inside. There was much still to do, much fighting, much killing, much dying. But Tobar had no doubt that the once mighty fortress of Vindolanda was as good as destroyed.

*

At the same time, Commodus was walking through the streets of Rome – contemplating a busy morning. The sun was high and instead of being hidden under wads of grey-black cloud, it blazed in a clear Roman sky. In place of his senatorial toga, Commodus wore common grey woollen garb which rubbed against his skin and made him itch. Just behind him, a single bodyguard in similarly unremarkable dress blended into the crowd. The hub of the civilised world was abuzz with activity as always: shoppers, stallholders, people idling away the morning, people on urgent business like Commodus. But he ignored all the sights, sounds and smells around him as he walked onwards, thinking about his first meeting.

He entered the Palatine, one of the most ancient areas of all Rome, and made his way by a circuitous route to the

Temple of Cybele. But there was no avoiding the flight of steps at the front of the temple leading to the entranceway. He quickened his pace, lowering his head and keeping his eyes averted from every citizen.

He passed quickly through the throng in front of the statue and the temple stalls selling souvenirs and curios, and made his way to a little-used side chamber. A man was lounging against the door but at Commodus' approach, he nodded almost imperceptibly and moved aside.

Commodus and his bodyguard slipped past him and inside the chamber. The door closed softly behind them. He looked intently in turn at each of the four senators, who stood, upon his entrance, and greeted each one by name.

"Hail, Ceionius Commodus," they answered in turn.

"Who is this man?" asked the nearest senator, nodding at Commodus' companion.

"He is a personal bodyguard given to me by Hadrian himself. A sad necessity, gentlemen. I will procure one for each of you also," he motioned to the bodyguard to return to the door.

The senators resumed their seats and Commodus drew up a chair for himself, breathing a sigh of relief, "So, we may speak freely here?"

"You are among friends" said one.

"Good. The reputation of this temple for assignations is well deserved, then. Let me come straight to the point. As you know, doubtless better than I, there are difficulties here in the capital: unsettling problems that, rather than resolving themselves, seem to be growing.

Each of you senators is implicitly trusted by the Emperor. Hadrian has asked me to enlist you into a secret network of men," he passed out a scroll bearing his orders, "And this is to be our sign," he distributed four purple-blue star-shaped flowers. "Borage. From time immemorial, it has stood for courage. I fear we may need it in abundance."

"What is the purpose of this network?" asked one senator, his head balding but his eyes full of wisdom.

"What purpose, Quintus Gario? To gather knowledge. The Emperor bids you be his eyes and his ears. He remains in Antioch – for now. Not out of fear, as his enemies suppose, but to glean and sift information, and to bide his time until it is ready. You noblemen can advance his coming. Do you agree?"

All nodded without hesitation.

"Gentlemen, do you remember when the order for the execution of the four senators was given out? The Senate believed it to be from Hadrian."

"I remember," said one senator, in a voice more like a growl.

"The order was not from Hadrian. It was from Acilius Attianus. *He* ordered those executions – on his own initiative."

"Attianus stood before us and made out they came from Hadrian," said Gario, "I couldn't believe it."

"It was not like Hadrian to order the deaths of four men he knew," added another, "Hadrian would never resort to alarming the whole Senate and city in such a way."

"You did right to trust your instincts," Commodus said.

"Then let the Senate know that the order came from Attianus. Whose word will they believe when they know the truth?" cried Gario.

"Gentlemen, this is politics – and in time, Hadrian will prove his innocence beyond all doubt. But let us not underestimate Attianus. *He* is the City Prefect and head of the Praetorian Guard: the most powerful man in this city. And who knows what other allies he is cleaving to him even as we speak?" He told them what he had seen at the Colosseum the previous day, and their faces looked grave.

"Attianus has put a great game in motion," suggested one of them.

"Yes, Sextus Scaevola," said Commodus, "That is how I read it. A great game. And Attianus is a skilful player – who plays for great stakes. The winner claims the title Emperor of Rome." He paused, his glance taking in each of them in turn, "And as we know, there are no prizes for second place. Be careful what you speak, in your private and public lives." He departed with those words, the senators reflecting on what he had said.

His next call was to a villa in the Esquiline Hill area. His rank, his bearing and even more his name gained him access to the owner of the home. He left his bodyguard in an inner room. Servants ushered Commodus out of the morning sunshine, into the coolness of a delightful walled garden open to the sky. Wine was served, as etiquette demanded.

"The General will be with you shortly," announced the servant, and gracefully departed.

Commodus poured out a small measure of wine into a goblet, raised it to his lips, and as he looked up, the head of the household arrived: a grizzled yet still powerful man in his fifties who seemed to fill the substantial space of the open room.

"Hail, Ratho Livianus," said Commodus.

"Senator, hail," said his host. "You do me an honour visiting my humble home"

"We've never met," Commodous said, "but you come highly recommended. Do you remember Marcius Turbo?"

The veteran gave an explosive laugh of approval, "Turbo? That son of a bull! He's leading the Fifth Legion these days, isn't he?"

"He is."

"I always knew he'd get on – thanks to my advice, of course!"

"Nice place," Commodus looked about at the white stone walls decorated with scenes of Roman history: the conquests of Germany, the victories of Trajan, "General, do you not miss the old days?"

The throwaway question provoked a vehement response "Not miss them, you ask? I'm going mad! When you're a military man, it's in your blood. And when you retire from the military, it stays in you like fever. I'm as restless as a fly in the height of summer."

"How would you like to be of service again?" said Commodus, looking at him shrewdly. The general looked back at him, his eyes twinkling, waiting for the next step in the dance. Commodus dug in his satchel and pulled out a scroll which he handed across.

The general unrolled it and read aloud: "Senator Lucius Ceionius Commodus Verus, is acting on my direct authority on a matter of the utmost importance for the Empire. He is answerable only to me. All Citizens of Rome, military or civilian, without distinction of rank, will assist him in any way he deems necessary. I will reimburse any expense

from Imperial funds. Signed Hadrian, et cetera, et cetera..."
He looked up, "Your credentials are impeccable, Senator."

"As is your record," nodded Commodous.

The general smiled, "I'm not one for changing horses," he said.

"Your reputation precedes you. And when that reputation is attested to personally, by Hadrian's closest confidante, there is nothing else needed." He leaned forward, speaking passionately, "Things are not going to order here in Rome," he said.

"I know it," muttered Livianus.

"Hadrian himself has asked me to charge you, General, to set up a secret network of men: a new *frumentarii*."

"What do you mean?..." said the general, sitting forward.

"I mean knowledge. Secrets of what is behind the machinations. Rome is being manipulated – to what end, we're not entirely sure. We need more information, and you can give it to us. Are you still in touch with your men?"

"Of course," smiled the general. "What's more natural than old comrades meeting for a drink and a talk about old times?"

"Can you get fifty men, whom you trust with your life?"

"I could have ten times that number here in a week," smiled Livianus.

"This is not armed rebellion, General," said Commodus, "At least, not yet. It's more subtle than that – and we have to move quietly, inconspicuously."

The general was silent, thinking for a moment.

"General, of all the missions you have undertaken, none is more important to Rome than this one. The Emperor will not forget those who assist him in this matter."

The general looked up, his eyes shining. "Senator, I have never refused an order from any Emperor – and I'm not about to start now."

SPQR

Let him who desires peace prepare for war.

Vegetius

XIII Rumours of War

It did indeed feel colder in Eboracum and not entirely due to the chill winds. The legate had promised to send his scouting force out in the morning and he had succeeded – just. The preparations had been intense and many of those who now watched the formation hold position had assisted in them. Everyone stood, deep in his own thoughts.

Marcus noted the precision of the men with pleasure. Two turmae of cavalry, motionless, only the heads and tails of the horses occasionally flicking; otherwise they might have been cast from lifeless metal. They would be animated enough when the time came, which would be soon. His thoughts changed, to a bitterness that he was not leading those staunch cavalrymen. It was his place but that mood changed too. If his instincts were right, it would be his turn before long.

He looked over to the legate, who stood watching the preparations, his uniform and accoutrements more martial and more splendid than anyone there, even though he was going nowhere, leading nobody into battle. But tradition dictated that he give the order. And finally, he did. The *corniceni* sounded their horns, and the soldiers and even the observers seemed to stiffen momentarily as the blasts sounded over the parade ground.

Caelinus Juventius, looking every inch a warrior, called his horsemen to advance. Again, a flash of envy flared in Marcus, quickly dissolved by his respect for his commander. The line of forty-eight cavalry moved forward at walking pace, as though welded together. Another order was given and the line of horsemen effortlessly became a column.

Cornelia's eyes were distracted by the pomp and spectacle of the serried ranks of soldiers, as were everyone else's but she caught sight of Marcus, and paid no more attention to the bright warriors. There stood a young man, who, if she had followed the orders of her master, would now be dead. She watched his changing emotions move across his face like shadows and felt she could read some of them. Not for the first time, an involuntary shudder gripped her as she thought of what might befall her, for betraying her master. But her mind dwelt on the young cavalry officer's sincerity, his tenderness, his compassion, as he had sat at the bed of that youth. After all, what had he done to her, or to anyone, that she should wipe his life out like an insect's? He had shown her only kindness.

And Attianus? Attianus smiled too much. He was not her master, he was her puppet master, and she was no more to him than a piece of wood in a game, to be moved around at his whim. If she lost her life, he would shrug, knock the piece from the board, reach out and push forward one of his many other pieces. No, her mind was made up and her conscience was easier than it had been for many a day.

The doctor, Diocles, noticed her out on the fringes of the parade ground and smiled at her zeal, her youthful enthusiasm...her beauty. He sighed and turned away.

He had been young once also. But there was no time to stand around watching those warlike fools march off; they would be marching, or more likely hobbling, back soon enough, and then his infirmary would be crowded to bursting point and he would be rushed off his feet. And all these administrative tasks to handle already! He gave an impatient grunt and hurried back to the hospital, to kick out any remaining idlers and return them to duty.

The second *turma* passed in column formation through the gates of the legionary fortress and bringing up the rear was Novantes, eighteen years old, a foot soldier who had inexplicably joined the cavalry, or so it seemed. Part of him wanted to sigh with despair but he surprised himself with a smile. He had come through the needle's eye of seemingly certain death, not once but several times. And his head was free of that torment, which once had looked everlasting. Esus was with him. So, who could stand against him?

The young man sat up straighter in his saddle and gripped the belly of his horse more firmly with his knees, as his lost friend and teacher Fulvio had taught him to do. As he and his new comrades rode at walking pace through the gate, the cloud cover parted and wands of sunlight broke through, transforming the scene and polishing their armour with its brightness. Everybody's mood lifted. And for the first time in his young life, Pedes Novantes looked like a soldier.

*

At the same moment, the Emperor of Rome was in Syrian Antioch, that jewel in the crown of empire second only to Rome itself – and he was happy. Apollodorus' infectious enthusiasm had transported Hadrian far away from the cares of state and the machinations of high office. And the designs were magnificent: as magnificent as the architect had promised. Hadrian spent ten minutes examining the plans for Trajan's Column, following the explanations and descriptions of the architect from Damascus. He could see the column in his mind's eye, as clearly as if it stood before him as a finished structure. And he could hear the adulation and awe from the people as they saw it for the first time.

"Well done!" he said benignly, and the architect rolled his plans up and departed, beaming.

Hadrian stood looking after him for a moment, his pleasure already fading. That lovely vision had vanished from his inner eye as the plans had disappeared from view. And all that was left was reality. He turned with a sigh back to his desk, covered with parchment and scrolls. He picked up the top one and began reading it, although he knew its contents well enough.

The morning drew on. Visitors came and went at their appointed hour. Every one of them was of consequence to Hadrian's plans, to a greater or lesser extent and he wanted to communicate the importance he attached to each of them. When Neratius Priscus was announced, Hadrian looked up with an impatient air.

"Neratius," he said. "Why have my reforms not been presented to the Senate for approval?"

The jurist looked at him in mild surprise, "The Senate is in recess, Emperor."

"Recess?"

"For the *Ludi Plebeii*, Caesar."

"Ah, yes. The Games. They had slipped my mind."

"All your reforms are fully drafted and will be laid before the Senate when the house is in session again. I gave the matter my fullest attention."

Hadrian smiled. "I'm sure you did, Neratius. Thank you. I'm eager to see them implemented, that's all."

Hadrian was glad when the time came for his oldest friend to join him. Turbo entered, preceded by a servant and Hadrian greeted him like a brother. He leaned back in his chair, stretched his arms out and relaxed. They went through many matters, discussed promotions and demotions, startling dismissals and daring appointments. It was far more detailed than any of the other discussions that morning. But to Hadrian it didn't seem like work. Everything they decided was furthering his reign, or removing hindrances to it. And he knew that here was a man whose experience, honesty and loyalty he could trust implicitly.

"These revolts in Judea are becoming troublesome," said Turbo.

"Yes, I've been watching them carefully. It might be my imagination but it seems as though they're gathering momentum."

"As revolts will do, unless they're nipped in the bud," said Turbo. "I would suggest sending a new general. Sometimes, a fresh pair of eyes is needed."

"Yes, Judea," said Hadrian, stroking his beard absently, glancing at parchments, dispositions, reports. He looked up and his eye caught that of his friend. Neither of them spoke the name *Lucius Quietus* aloud, but both were thinking it. Now there was a man who would have made a difference here, who knew these Jewish zealots, knew their religious mania, knew the terrain. He would have slapped them down with an iron hand...

"Galbanus will sort the situation out," said Turbo, "A wise appointment."

"Thank you. But there's more going on. The newly crowned Parthian king..."

"Yes," said Turbo, "and reports of a revolt by the Syrians. The region is a hotbed of intrigue and insurrection, of local leaders watching which way the wind blows and seeking to exploit any opportunities."

"Hmmm," mused Hadrian. "You're right. Intensify our efforts here. Put more spies in the field. I need better intelligence. I need to know what is going to happen."

"It shall be done."

Hadrian let his eyes rest on the map for a while. Then he cleared his throat, dismissed the region and its ferment from his mind, and turned to the next item. Quickly, that situation became the only one that mattered, both men marshalling details, offering views and suggestions. And so it went on. After several hours, Turbo stood up to excuse himself.

Hadrian smiled, "Yes, let's stop for a while. We've achieved a great deal."

Turbo left the chamber with a mock-weary nod. Hadrian sat for a moment, then called a servant into the room. He ordered, "Meat and freshly baked bread. We're hungry – or I am, anyway."

The servant bowed again and left. Hadrian stood up to stretch his legs, walking on the beautifully laid mosaic floor. The room was large but in his mind he strode through his whole empire, thinking of appointments, of rivals, of threats; of commerce and treaties, trade and conquest. All that would come, once he was truly secure and could give it all the attention it deserved.

From the corner of his eye he saw the door opening. Without turning his head, he gestured to the side table, "Put it down there," he said.

"Put what down?" said a voice. It was Vibia Sabina, graceful as ever; some would call her beautiful perhaps but after seventeen years of marriage, her charms seemed jaded to Hadrian. What he did notice was her too prominent nose, and her unchanging expression that spoke of always being in the right. A crease returned to his brow.

"Well, wife?" he said.

"I thought we might share lunch. It's been an age," she looked around her at the lavish apartments crowded with reports, dispatches, work in progress.

"I'd like to," he said. "But just at present..." he lifted some of the parchments from his desk and let them fall back. "Also, I'm in a meeting with Turbo. It may go on some time."

"You've changed," she said softly.

"Yes. I became Emperor."

"No. Earlier. Much earlier. It's always the next step in the path, the next move upwards. Sometimes I think you forget that you're married at all."

"And sometimes I think that you've never known you're my wife!" he cried in irritation. He waved her away like a junior officer who had overstepped the mark. But Sabina was not to be dismissed so lightly.

"What do you mean by that? I've accompanied you on your endless campaigns, I've rallied people to your cause.

I've done everything for you!"

"Everything except give me a child!"

"That's no fault of mine," she said.

"Isn't it? That's not what I've heard."

"How dare you!"

They spent the next minute or so exchanging increasingly unprofitable remarks. Then she was gone like a whirlwind, the door slamming behind her.

Hadrian was left alone but not for long. Turbo re-entered the room unobtrusively.

"You heard all that?" said the Emperor irritably.

"I heard some of it," said Turbo. "I thought it best to leave you alone."

Hadrian nodded grimly, then he caught the eye of his trusted confidant. His frown faded. And a moment later they were laughing together. Hadrian ran his hands over his face, gestured Turbo towards a pitcher of wine and filled a goblet for himself. The servant entered again, set down a tray loaded with food that smelled enticingly of herbs, meat and fresh bread, and departed.

"Women!" said the Emperor. "What do they know of affairs of state?"

"That ignorance has never stopped them dabbling in them," observed Turbo.

"No indeed!" laughed Hadrian, taking a pull at his drink. "That's what happens when you marry for political reasons. She was only thirteen when we were wed. Not even a woman. And now she's too much of one. Moody, difficult, always... Women!" He laughed again. "It's the old story. They're either too young or too old, too married or too single, too docile or too dominant. But we can't do without them," he picked up some meat, still warm from the pan and chewed absently on it.

He turned to his desk again and his frown returned, "So much to consider, so much to do – but we cannot afford to make a false move."

"Attianus," said Turbo.

"Attianus – probably. And others like him – almost certainly."

Hadrian looked down at his toga, splendidly lined with purple, "You know, sometimes I envy our ordinary soldiers," he said. "What have they to worry about? And no doubt they think the same of me. But no one is Emperor by right – and Emperors have been deposed before." They were silent, reflecting on Rome's turbulent history.

"You are sure that Attianus is at the back of what's happening?"

"No. That's my concern. Everything points in his direction – but he is an able man. I don't want to jeopardise our relationship if all this is wrong. Nor do I want to act prematurely if it is true. I need facts. Facts!" he thumped the table.

"Commodus will find them, have no fear."

"I know it. But I want his information now, this day! I want indisputable proof of what's happening, one way or another, so that I may act decisively. This delay..." he looked disconsolately around the room, at the trappings of empire. "It's all rumours and hearsay, one man's voice against another," he stroked his beard once again, a habit of his in pensive mood.

"I know," said Turbo, "It takes so long to get word from Rome. But that distance works both ways. Those who fear or oppose you are equally in the dark about your plans, your movements. And by remaining here, we can increase our strength, choose our moment, and gather allies to us in decisive numbers."

"As always, friend, you are right," said Hadrian, somewhere between a sigh and a laugh. He picked up his goblet again.

Turbo raised his drink too, "Soon, all this will be over, and you will be happy again."

"Call no man happy till he is dead, as Aeschylus put it!" replied Hadrian with a grimace.

*

As Commodus passed through the portals of the Curia, a hand touched his sleeve, "Greetings, Ceionius!" said a voice.

Commodus smiled, "Greetings, old friend."

"We haven't seen you at the Senate House lately," said the ageing senator.

"No. I've been busy on other matters."

"And you've been somewhere hot, I see. Well, good to have you back. You may find it even hotter here in the Curia!" The elderly senator turned away, his eyes twinkling.

Commodus smiled again and looked around him. It was the first meeting of the Senate following the recess. Everyone seemed to have a freshly scrubbed air as the elders of Rome reconvened. Several other senators approached the entranceway, and suddenly Commodus was surrounded by friendly faces.

With skill and confidence he moved through the throng, greeting here, clasping hands there. He asked about wives and children and parents, about positions recently secured and sinecures granted. He was never wrong in the details, nor forgot anyone's name. Pleasure shone in their faces at his ready recognition of them. Others kept arriving, and it seemed as though the rejoicing at meeting again would continue forever.

At last, he and his fellow senators walked inside the majestic building. As Commodus progressed through the atrium he could see small groups of men standing around, half hidden by the huge pillars of the Curia, engaged in intense discussion and debate. Their voices were subdued but several times he caught the name Hadrian. He wanted to linger but time was pressing, so he made his way into the senate chamber and sat down. One or two latecomers hurried in quickly after him to do likewise.

Cremonus the Senate Consul looked around him, stood, and the ambient murmurs died away to silence. He turned to consult the Augur. Apparently the auspices were good for this day but the black look on the face of Cremonus seemed to doubt it; still, he made no demur. Commodus let his gaze wander around the Senate. He recognised some of the men who had accepted Attianus's hospitality at the Colosseum. Several of them had been those huddled in conversation as he walked through to the main chamber and now they sat together in a group like black sheep among the white.

Commodus forced his thoughts back to his surroundings. Cremonus was speaking, in a voice of distaste, "Our Emperor," he said, in a tone that seemed to undermine the divinity of that rank, "has decreed that the Senate should vote on whether I should continue in my current office or be replaced by my esteemed colleague Petronius Ovidius." He inclined his head briefly. Commodus looked in the direction and recognised an obscure yet trustworthy ex-military man. That made sense.

"As we have a quorum, that vote may now take place."

Commodus looked around the building. No doubt of that! It seemed as though all three hundred senators were present.

"Who stands for Ovidius?"

A number of senators rose at once: but surprisingly, by no means all. It was unusual for senators to vote against anything proposed by the emperor. But it was also unusual for the emperor not to be present in the Senate when the vote was called. Commodus looked over to the empty seat between the two consuls.

"Who stands for Cremonus?"

The supporters of Ovidius sat down and a considerable number of other senators rose. Cremonus, his gaze now less forbidding, motioned them all to sit, "We will count this vote by a show of hands. Tellers, get ready. All those for Ovidius, raise your hand." The tellers moved around the building counting the votes. The procedure was repeated for Cremonus. It was impossible to say what the outcome was. The tellers compared notes and the chief teller approached the Senate Consul. Cremonus took the parchment held out to him and spoke, in a voice drained of emotion, "By seven votes, I hereby declare that the will of this house is that Petronius Ovidius be the new Senate Consul. As always, a vote by the Senate is the unanimous will of the whole house. I thank the gods for their enlightenment, and my wish is that Fortuna favours my esteemed colleague." Cremonus vacated the seat of the Senate Consul.

Ovidius took his place. He looked beamingly around the assembly, "Senators of Rome," he began. "I thank you for the confidence which you have placed in me, and I shall do my utmost to merit it – and the honour that the Emperor has conferred upon me. My first..." But he got no further.

A senator rose from his seat and raised his hand. Commodus recognised the man as someone named Blandinus: a non-entity. He frowned with puzzlement. The Senate watched, rapt, hardly moving.

"What Emperor?" Blandinus asked. There was a hushed intake of breath.

"I crave your pardon, Senator, what do you mean?" said Ovidius.

Blandinus pointed to the empty seat between the two consuls, "I say again, what Emperor? Where is Hadrian? Why is he not here, in the Curia, as tradition and the respect due to this house demand? Why is he not even in Rome?"

Another senator rose several seats along from him. Commodus recognised him as one of Attianus's supporters, "He has not yet set foot in Rome, despite having taken office months ago. Is he sick? If so, what ails him?"

"His place is here," said Blandinus again. "Is it right that our Empire should have an absentee Emperor?" There were low mutterings throughout the assembly, quickly growing louder as Blandinus continued to speak, "Is he not strong enough to take his rightful place here? Is something preventing him? Is he afraid of something? If so, what does he fear?"

A third senator rose nearby, and the attention of the house fixed on him: "Perhaps he fears the just wrath of the Senate and the people of Rome!" There was an excited outcry from all around the assembly hall.

"Senator, please explain that –" began Ovidius ineffectually. Again he was shouted down.

"Four senators were killed – assassinated. Or should I say, put down like rabid dogs: no trial, no defence, no justice. Senators!"

The shouting was increasing to uproar. Not far from where Commodus was sitting, a senator leapt to his feet. He recognised Quintus Gario.

"I protest! There is no proof that Hadrian was behind those atrocities!"

"No proof? Who would dare to do such a thing if it were not the will of the Emperor?"

Sextus Scaevola stood, raising his hands as though to try and fend off the remorseless tide of sound, "Hadrian has expressly denied that this was his will."

"Denied it?" bayed the voice of Blandinus across the chamber, "Denied it? Let him come here and deny it to us!"

It was chaos. Senators were on their feet, shouting over each other in a direct flouting of time-honoured tradition. The Senate Guards at the door stood transfixed.

Commodus watched. In all this from the corner of his eye he could see many faces directed at him: all of them surprised he was not joining in to defend Hadrian but none of them sure what his silence meant. But he had no regard for them. He was watching the unaligned centre of the Senate slowly but surely going over to the side of Attianus. Tempers were running high and the mood was turning ugly. The Senatorial Guards watched nervously, pondering whether to intervene.

"Gentlemen! Gentlemen!" called Ovidius, "Gentlemen! This is most unseemly!"

But few, if any, had ears for the tool of the emperor.

*

That evening, his duties done, Marcus strolled about the fortress enclosure. It was a city in itself, spanning fifty acres of ground. But he was restless, his thoughts elsewhere. No doubt he was not the only one who was off in spirit with Juventius' troop. Unconsciously, his feet had led him to the entrance of the hospital area. The door of the main hospital block opened and an unusually lovely figure stepped through the doorway.

"Greetings, Cornelia," he said.

She looked up in surprise and smiled, "Greetings, Valerius Quietus."

"Are you finished for the day?"

"Yes – finally!" she laughed.

"Would you walk with me through Eboracum?"

She inclined her head and they walked out of the hospital grounds. Presently they passed out of the south gate of the fortress, heading towards the only bridge across the river. On their right hand, the clouds were flushing with a delicate pinkish grey.

Just last night Marcus had been striding this way to find the young man named Novantes, and soon afterwards, hurrying back to report to the legate. He had hardly been aware of crossing the bridge but he looked about him now. The river was tinged with mother of pearl and the settlement town looked thriving, prosperous, permanent. Once again, a doubt arose in his mind. Could it really be that Novantes had spoken the truth? Could such strength, such confidence, really be under threat?

"Pretty river," said Cornelia, interrupting his thoughts. "What is it called?"

"The Usa," he said. "I was talking to a couple of veterans about it earlier today. It's a Celtic name that means 'water'. So this is the River Water."

She laughed and he was struck by her intelligence, her understanding: many would have found nothing droll about this.

"Strange, is it not?" she said. "A Roman town and a Roman fortress, in the heart of a Roman province, and yet so many of the names of places and things are native."

They crossed over into the town. In front of them were public baths, temples, open air theatres, simple houses, luxurious houses, shops – everything expected of an important centre. The smell of cooked meat wafted towards them. Men and women were bustling about, in search of food, drink and entertainment.

"Can we walk along the river bank for a while?" he asked. She looked at him and acquiesced.

They turned off to the left and followed the path of the river, the town soon thinning out and the sounds of laughter and music fading. They walked in silence for a long time but the silence was itself a kind of sharing. Finally they came to a broken wall, low enough to serve as a seat. Marcus gestured to it and they sat down on the bricks. He glanced up at the stars beginning to appear. The sound of the tidal river came powerfully to them from below. To the north west, the lights and sounds of the legionary fortress dominated everything. From this distance, it was clear just how huge the fort was.

"I didn't really have time before," said Marcus, "to tell you how grateful I was for what you did for that young soldier last night – and how impressed I was. Many an army doctor would have lost him."

"Thank you," she said, her voice like the night breeze.

"How do you do it?"

"I seem to have a gift. I can sense pain, hurt."

"Ah. That is a great gift – and even greater is the power of healing it once you've found it."

She didn't immediately reply and they sat, feeling the cool winds playing on their faces.

"What I felt in the boy I sense in you too," she said at last. "A great pain, like a wound." The only sound was the motion of the river as it flowed past. "Will you not speak of it? I may be able to heal you as I healed that youth."

"I doubt it, despite all your skill," said Marcus.

And it seemed as though that would be the end of the conversation: but suddenly he found himself pouring out all the details of his loss: his father, cruelly murdered along with the three other senators, his family brutally wiped out merely because they happened to be there at the time. His whole life turned upside down. Cornelia sat in silence, taking it all in. She was no politician but what she heard had all the markings of Attianus. It was just the sort of thing that he would do: or if not him, someone equally bereft of humanity.

"I'm so sorry, Valerius Quietus," she said, her voice softer and more sincere than he'd ever heard it.

"Marcus," he said.

He felt her hand seeking out his and he returned the touch. Under the stars they sat hand in hand like little children, and for an endless moment nothing else mattered.

XIV Departures

Caelinus Juventius was unsatisfied, uncomfortable and
ill at ease. He sat on his horse at the head of his column
of cavalry, under grey skies and chill winds. Not much
more than two hours of movement before they'd arrive at
Brigantium. The first permanent fort with a fifty stationed
there. Now they were on the great road again, the Via
Domitiana but he was only too well aware of the distance
his small army still had to travel – and to find what? The
legate had tasked him to scout the terrain ahead and if
possible locate the enemy and acertain their strength
and position. Around Eboracum there was a persistent
word that something momentous had occurred to the
north of them: a rising of the barbarians, a sacking of the
watchtowers, perhaps even a fort or two razed. And if so,
he now had to find out where the Brigantes were hiding.
His brow puckered into a frown.

At the front of the column, a squadron of cavalry scouts
returned. Juventius saluted back. "Nothing to report Sir,
not even any traders on the road," said Juventius's second
in command.

"No," said Juventius automatically but then he paused.
Why was that? This road was a highway, a straight road,
cutting through all obstacles and kept free of trees and

other cover. Normally he would expect to pass traders on this causeway, or at least notice them in the distance but they had seen only a few isolated figures all day, and these had been crossing the road, not traversing its length.

"We keep heading north" then nodded Juventius.

Juventius smiled as he looked at the officers face covered in mud.

"Maybe the locals had good reason not to travel in the soaking rain. A few more hours and we will be at Brigantium. Hot food and a dry bed. Send out another squad to scout forward once more" smiled Juventius.

But the instincts of the old campaigner rose up in him like an ache in his bones. Part of him could not help but feel that the omens would not be good. The Brigantes were up to something.

*

"Secundus Blandinus!" announced the rodent-faced secretary of the Prefect of Rome.

Attianus made a regal gesture of admittance and the secretary bowed himself from the room, replaced by the portly figure of the senator, who inclined his head in obeisance. Although his features were composed, as etiquette dictated, it would have been obvious, to anyone with far less acute observational skills than Attianus, that he was brimming with self-satisfied importance.

"Senator," said Attianus. "You bring me good news?"

"I believe I can say that, Prefect," answered Blandinus. "And I think you will agree when I relate the recent happenings."

Attianus gestured to a chair. "Relate," he said.

As the senator described the events at the Senate house, Attianus began to smile. That smile continued to broaden, and he even allowed himself a rare laugh or two. Even the senator's attempts at self-aggrandisement failed to dampen his humour. What was he, after all, other than his tool, in this? And if a tool wanted to brag of himself, what did it matter?

"Excellent," he said at length. "Convey my appreciation to your esteemed colleagues."

"Your appreciation is always highly valued," said Blandinus, "although perhaps, if it could be accompanied by something more material...? I'm thinking of them, and of ensuring their continued loyalty. Not of myself, of course..." he spoke diffidently, but failed to entirely disguise the gleam in his eye as he lowered his head.

Attianus laughed again. He crossed the room, opened a chest, and hefted a hessian bag, the contents of which clinked, "Merit should be rewarded," said the Prefect of Rome.

The senator noted its satisfying weight, "Thank you, my lord. I really feel that our rhetoric won the day convincingly. The opposition simply faded away. As I said, Quintus Gario and Sextus Scaevola tried to defend Hadrian... one or two others perhaps, but they were simply overwhelmed by our side. Even Commodus did not dare to speak –"

"What! Commodus was in the senate!" Attianus shouted, looking the senator in the eye. All his poise and confidence vanished under the relentless stare. Attianus returned to his seat and sat down. He spoke in a normal voice but the quietness seemed to the senator no less menacing than his shout, "You did not tell me Commodus was there."

"Ah..." said Blandinus lamely.

But Attianus's eyes had left him and were looking at nothing, his mind elsewhere, "Commodus," he mused, more to himself than to Blandinus. "I did not know he had returned to Rome."

"Yes...er, yes. Quite recently. I believe."

"Very well. Continue to keep me informed of all developments. You may go."

"Thank you, Prefect. That is..."

"Well?" said Attianus, a touch of acerbity in his tone.

"The money for your supporters..."

Attianus tossed the bag over to him. "See that at least some of it reaches them, my friend. I will know if it does not."

Blandinus looked him briefly in the eye, a line of sweat running down his forehead, "Of course, my lord."

Attianus waved him away and he left the room with alacrity. For a while the City Prefect sat, musing on the formidable personage of Lucius Ceionius Commodus Verus. As a senator, he was naturally entitled to attend meetings of the senate whenever he wished. But he was also one of Hadrian's closest confidants. He would not have left Antioch on his own initiative, he felt sure of that. And yet, after further thought, his mood lightened again. What had Commodus done? Nothing! Commodus had seen the weight of opposition ranged against him, and his men had won the day. Of course, there would be another day; but would the outcome necessarily be any different? Hadrian was only a man, and his friends and advisers were only men too. Emperors had been deposed before: and men were even easier to take care of.

This was not Antioch, but Rome. He, Attianus, held the strings here. He was in charge: the most powerful man in the city. Hadrian might be the emperor – for now – but he was a thousand miles away in a distant province. His nomination of a new senate consul, which normally would have been accepted unanimously, had scraped through by the smallest handful of votes. Finally, his smile returned and he relaxed. The naivety of Hadrian, of Commodus, surprised and reassured him. To sit openly in the Senate house so that his presence was known to all! If it had been his move, he would avoided the assembly, waited in the shadows, building up his power until overwhelming force was at his disposal. And then he would have struck suddenly, decisively. But then, it had not been his move but theirs. And perhaps they didn't have his skills in this game.

He called for a servant, scribbled a note and sent him on his way. Fifteen minutes later the door opened tentatively and an auburn-haired vision stood in the doorway. It looked as though she had moved quickly to answer his summons, and the slight flush in her cheeks heightened her beauty even more.

He smiled, held out his hand, "Livia," he said.

"Publius," she said, with a slight hesitancy in using his name that charmed him even more than her appearance.

"Do you remember our conversation? About Neapolis?"

"Yes, my lord."

"I think the time has come to turn words into action. We should make the most of what's left of the autumn."

"You wish to go soon?" she said, startled.

"I wish to go *now* – this day."

"But I cannot explain it to –"

"Forget about your husband," he said, with a touch of impatience. "I will do all the explaining needed. And you should think not of the present but of the future – which is, I assure you, far richer and more interesting."

"Yes, Publius," she breathed.

"I had an urge to see Neapolis today, and one should always seize these moments. Besides, I have something to celebrate." She smiled, and for a moment her maidenly demureness vanished. "Can you be ready in an hour?"

"Yes," she said.

"Then go. I will make all the arrangements and call for you on the way to Ostia. We take ship for Neapolis this afternoon – and tonight we shall dine in my villa overlooking the justly famous bay."

She kissed him impulsively and hurried away. He stood gazing after her, glad that he was able to give her pleasure – and looking forward to her returning the compliment.

*

Commodus stepped out of his carriage. The street near the port of Ostia was little frequented – which was why he had chosen it. He saw his old friend leaning up against a wall, apparently lost in contemplation, and ambled over in his direction.

When they were close enough, Commodus spoke in a low voice. "Greetings, Ratho. How is the situation?"

With an air of unconcern, General Livianus replied in a similarly subdued tone, "All is well. As I said to you in my note: we have established that the port is being run by a Captain Paetus. All exports of grain, grapes, olives and every other basic commodity are being run in Paetus's docks there. His fleet is enormous and so is the quantity of foodstuffs. Not long ago the prices of most things started to rise. As we both know, they're still rising."

Commodus nodded imperceptibly, "Tampering with Rome's grain supply is a capital offence. I just have to establish who is protecting him – although we both have a good idea, I think."

Shading his eyes against the autumn sunshine, Livianus spoke again, "As you walk into the port his office is the first you come to. First floor, on the left. Two ex-Praetorians are guarding it."

"Await my signal before you move. It's important that I'm not implicated in this."

The general nodded. Commodus ambled away and walked through a maze of streets to the market. Even if he hadn't known the way, the smell of fish would have guided him, growing stronger as he approached. As ever, the market was bustling, shoppers seeking bargains by buying direct from the wholesalers before the goods were transported to the city centre. Commodus made his leisurely way through the crowd, stopping in front of a giant fish being weighed. The monster was still fresh, its silver scales glistening in the sunlight. A crowd had gathered, watching the shopkeeper add more weight to the scales. Commodus looked up at the office building. *Time to land my own fish*, he thought.

Two heavy set men stopped the senator at the bottom of the stairs. It was rare for Commodus to have to look up to people, but he had to with both of these.

"How can we help you?" asked one.

"I wish to see Captain Paetus."

"What is your business, sir?"

"That which cannot be spoken of in the street," smiled Commodus.

"Perhaps you could give me your name, then," said the second.

"Commodus Verus."

The two heavies looked at each other. After a cursory check for weapons concealed about his person, one of the sentries led him up the stairs. The door opened, releasing the comforting smell of freshly roasted almonds. A clerk appeared at the doorway and looked questioningly at the guard.

"This is Commodus Verus. He wants a word with the boss."

The clerk looked directly at the senator and smiled. "Captain Paetus is busy. May I assist you?"

"Unfortunately not," said Commodus: "I must speak privately with your master."

"Perhaps if you were to tell me the nature of –"

"As I said, it's a private matter. For his ears only."

The clerk seemed nonplussed. "And as I said, the Captain is busy. If you care to return later..."

"I will wait here, thank you – until he is no longer busy."

The clerk looked at Commodus again, unsure of how to proceed.

"What is it?" shouted a voice from inside the room.

Commodous moved forward at once. The clerk tried to block his path and found himself pushed unceremoniously aside. The guard grabbed Commodus from behind and a scuffle began. Paetus appeared, taking in the scene. He looked at Commodus and then at his clerk.

"This man insists on seeing you at once, sir. He says his name is Commodus Verus."

The captain's eyes returned to his visitor and stayed there for several seconds, "You checked him?" asked the captain. The heavy nodded.

"Very well, admit him," he said. Commodus was released and walked into the back of the office where the air was rich with the scent of almonds.

"Makes you hungry, that smell," observed the senator.

"How can I help you?" smiled Paetus.

"I have an opportunity for you to add to your wealth."

Paetus sat down in a superb leather-backed chair and motioned his visitor to a more ordinary one on the other side of his desk, "Indeed. What are you selling, then?"

"I'm not selling but buying. I am a businessman, Captain. I recognise a good business when I see it."

"Go on," said the captain.

"I can see that your ships are prospering you and that the gods have blessed you. To put it plain, your hard work deserves reward. An early retirement, perhaps, with a nice villa on the coast?"

"Perhaps you could it put it plainer still. What are you proposing exactly?"

"Why, to buy your business," said Commodus, "I will pay you a good price."

The captain smiled, "Thank you for the offer, but I must decline. I built up this business and wish to continue running it."

"Such industry, such application! Very well: how if I bought it from you but kept you on as the manager? I can make you a very rich man – and give you a good share of the business."

"When I'm ready to sell, I will give you first refusal. Now, if you'll excuse me –" he stood up, but Commodus remained seated.

"I see from the public record office that you now hold every contract for grain shipment, Captain. The company run by Captain Piso seems to have foundered. What happened to him?"

Paetus looked at him sharply, "Listen, old man," he said. "I won these contracts fair and square. I don't know what happened to Piso. Perhaps he got careless."

"Perhaps he did. It's always important to be careful... Yes, life is uncertain. Perhaps what happened to him could happen to you. That's another reason to listen to me. I have powerful protection and could extend that to you."

"I don't need you or your protection old man. Now, get out!" snarled Paetus.

Commodous did not move, "I don't think you know who you're dealing with."

"I don't think you know, who you are dealing with old man. I have the most powerful protection there is – the Emperor himself!" shouted Paetus.

"The Emperor?" said Commodus in amazement.

"His Praetorian Guard is always with me. If I wanted you flayed alive, I could command it and it would be done instantly. Now away with you before I give that order."

Commodus bowed and retreated towards the door. The clerk smiled at his departure, and the guard pushed him down the stairs. He hurried away, the laughter of the guards in his ears.

"We won't have any more trouble from that quarter," said one.

*

Marcus walked listlessly past the empty parade ground. His thoughts were off with Juventius' troop, so much so that he stood still for a while imagining it: sudden heroics, decisive action turning the advantage against the enemy. When his flight of fancy ended, it was almost a shock to find himself in the routine surroundings of the fortress. He glanced up at the sky: it was oppressively heavy with cloud, betokening the promise of rain. It suited his mood. A hand touched his shoulder behind him and he turned around, startled.

"Greetings, Marcus," said Cornelia, "You'd rather not be here!"

A smile interrupted his brooding," That had been my thought – until just now. But how could you know? My back was to you."

"I didn't need to see your face. Your feelings were clear from your posture."

They fell into step together beside the ground, which had been worn into fine dust by thousands of boots over decades of use.

"You are very perceptive," he said. "That could be a real benefit one day."

"And what of today? Nothing for the famous *Praefectus alae* to do?"

He laughed, "Actually, the famous prefect has a mission – and one I'm not looking forward to. The legate has charged me with tracking down a local tribal leader called Tobar, or some such name. It seems a far cry from leading a cavalry *ala* into battle."

She touched her finger to his crestfallen face, lightening his mood at once, "There are different kinds of battle – and many routes to adventure. Take me with you." His eyebrows rose, so she hurried on, "As you said, my perception may be useful, particularly on a mission such as this."

"Well," he said, "It is a military mission, at least in name. There might be danger."

"Looking for one man in the shadow of the Ninth's headquarters, with all the strength of Rome behind it, doesn't seem terribly dangerous." He stood for a moment, considering, so she continued, "There's nothing going on here. The hospital is almost empty, Diocles has kicked out all the malingerers in readiness for any casualties from the expedition. But that's not going to return for several days, is it?"

"No," he mused.

"And how long is your task likely to last?"

"A few hours, I presume."

"Well, then! Let's go. I can speak to Diocles. He won't mind. And I don't think your men will either."

Marcus stood for a few seconds longer, "Very well!" he said. "The decisive Prefect has made up his mind, and the word is given!"

Fifteen minutes later, they were astride the two horses Marcus' rank had procured for them: a proud stallion for him, an occasionally skittish mare for her. He reached a hand over the necks of the two steeds, extending a small canvas bag to her.

"What's this?"

"*Dulcia*. Take one. Keep your strength up for the journey!"

She took one of the exquisite pastries made with honey, and bit slowly into it. Marcus watched her mouth articulate,

"Mmmm. Have to be careful of these – I could lose my figure overnight."

"I don't think so," he grinned.

As the horses walked through the town of Eboracum, Marcus stopped frequently and made enquiries. Most people recognised the name of Tobar but were vague as to his whereabouts. They continued to walk, and finally the great town started to thin out. A droplet or two of rain dappled Marcus' arm, and he peered up at the clouds in mild exasperation.

"Something tells me that Fortuna is not smiling on this expedition," he said. "What do you say to turning back? I liked the look of that cook-house near the southern gate."

"Patience, impetuous one!" she laughed, "Perhaps if you asked to speak to an elder – a wise man?"

He nodded, smiled ruefully, and made enquiries. After a few words with a local, he pointed over to the left. They got into motion again.

The further they got from the fort, the less Roman the houses looked – and the less frequently spaced they were. Marcus pointed again, ahead of him, to a typical roundhouse hut, made of timber and thatched. They reached it, dismounted and stood for a moment in the grey surroundings, more countryside than town. The horses' breath clouded in the cool air. Marcus looked at Cornelia, and then several larger raindrops spattered on them. He took her hand and leaned in to the dark central opening.

"Anyone there?" he said.

In the shadows, something stirred, and a figure emerged: an old man, sprightly, with thinning white hair and a long white beard. He had a wand of yew stuck into a simple belt made of twine, and his clothes were rough fabric. There was something youthful still about the sparkle in his eyes.

"I'm looking for someone," Marcus said. "I thought you might be able to –"

The old man gave a wry smile, "My blame," he said, "little Latin."

"Ah," said Marcus. He thought for a moment. "I seek knowledge, I need your help..."

"Knowledge!" said the man, brightening up. "*Scientia.* That word I know. Come, enter please."

He lit a candle of tallow which gave off more smoke than light, and seated himself, gesturing for his guests to follow his example. Bemused, they did so. He took some wooden sticks and threw them on the floor. Marcus saw that they were marked with recurring symbols: trees and other images from nature. The man murmured words they didn't understand. Then his eyes opened, his vision refocused and he looked at them, nodding encouragingly. He moved to the lengths of wood and cut some into small sections, each marked with a picture from nature.

"*Ogham*," he said, but it was clear that the word meant nothing to them. He shook his head, "Watch. I cast the staves – learn from their fall. *Colebreni. Colebreni* with *Oghams.*"

Marcus nodded quizzically and gestured for him to proceed. With the sputtering candle and its noxious smoke for accompaniment, the old man threw the staves down with an unusual, jerky motion. The pieces of wood bounced, rattled and were still. He looked penetratingly at the mute pieces of wood, finally drawing breath with a gasp as though his study had led him to forget to breathe.

"Much upset," he said. "Alarms, disorder in the world. Great times for some – end times for other."

Marcus raised one eyebrow, thinking back to various charlatans he had met. The tiny gesture was caught by the old man, who seemed agitated.

A drumming of rain grew in intensity, and the two visitors became aware that the storm had broken in earnest. But no water penetrated the soundly made hut, crude though it looked.

The visionary looked at Cornelia as if a new idea had occurred to him, "I tell you about you – and your man. Yes?"

She nodded once, with a sympathy and an interest in her face that Marcus had not yet shown. The old man gently touched her wrist and turned her palm upwards. He did the same with Marcus, then breathed more incantations, entered his trance again, and emerged invigorated from it as before.

"This is *dichetal do chen naib*," he said. He frowned and then laughed at their incomprehension, "Hands, and... trees. Yes. The hands and the trees."

The phrase made no more sense to them in Latin than in Celtic, but his obvious integrity, his belief in what he was doing, drew them in. He looked at them both, and then moved over to Marcus first. He held his ancient hand over Marcus's young one. As he did so, the faded skin seemed to quiver with the tremor of old age. The faint shaking of the hand, the intensity of the old man's concentration, the choking smoke, the uncertain light, the incessant drumming of the rain: to Marcus it was as though the dark hut was stripped away, leaving only the three of them in the whole world.

A sharp cry of satisfaction slipped from the wise man's lips, and at the same instant, it seemed, something almost like pain entered Marcus' hand, right to the bone. He pulled it away and looked down, half expecting to see a wound running with blood. But there was nothing. The ancient composed himself, his agitation gone.

Then he spoke, "Much trouble. For you – much trouble. Past, and still to come. Much pain. Yes?"

"Yes," breathed Marcus.

"Sometimes pain helps. Sometimes destroys. You are young. You are strong. Be careful," he smiled at Marcus, and although his message was hardly cheering, the young man felt unaccountably encouraged. He smiled back.

The seer turned his gaze to Cornelia, and repeated the ritual. Then he looked up at her in surprise. She shrank from his gaze and would have pulled her hand away, but it no longer seemed possible. He continued to look, and at last, a peace came over his troubled face, the wrinkles that had stood out in sharp relief fading back into the leather of his skin. He nodded, the corners of his mouth turning up.

"You have had difficult path in world. Great pain for you. Your path is better now," She started to relax, but he leaned in towards her, "Keep to this path!" he said.

"I intend to," she answered.

*

The market place was crowded with an unusually large number of men: idlers and loungers, leaning against walls, chatting together in small groups, enjoying the late autumn sunshine. Then a signal was given and the men, fifty or so of them, began to move. They walked through the crowd, still seemingly unconcerned, pausing here and there to look at the market stalls as the selling and bartering continued. The air was heavy with the shouts of the traders, each trying to drown out his competitors.

One of Captain Paetus' men was looking around him in a desultory fashion, and then he fell backwards like a felled tree against a stall, his weight and momentum breaking through the wooden supports and showering fish everywhere. Puzzled traders gathered around. Then a woman screamed and pointed. Blood was pumping from a hole in the throat of the bodyguard, cascading like a scarlet river over the silver scales of the fish. The citizens backed away, shrieking, as the blood pooled towards them. One of the dead man's colleagues stepped forward, pushing people out of the way.

"Who did this?" he shouted, fear and outrage in his voice. And then another blade flashed behind him, and he fell across the body of his companion. More shouts, more screams – and then panic stampeded the citizens, one or two slipping on the slick red stones in their haste to be elsewhere. In a minute, the stalls that had been crowded earlier were standing untended like derelicts. Only Paetus's men stood, ashen-faced, unsure whether to fight or fly.

The fifty men arranged themselves into a formidable military-looking formation. An older man stepped forward and searched the faces of the men opposite. He spoke, in a loud but calm voice.

"My name is Ratho Livianus. Perhaps you have heard of me."

There was silence in the market place, the supporters of Paetus watching him.

"Captain Paetus is no longer in charge of this port. It has been sold to a new owner. He has no quarrel with any man who works here. Your jobs are safe. Lay down your arms, leave this place and report back here tomorrow."

All eyes suddenly turned round to the office on the first floor. The large golden bell outside the office was being rung frantically by one of the heavies. Captain Paetus looked up from his desk with a frown. Had a ship broken free? Was there a danger? He stepped outside the office and took in the surprising tableau. One of his men pointed at Ratho.

"He says there are new owners for the port, sir, and you no longer run it." There was uncertainty in his voice.

All eyes turned to Paetus standing at the top of the stairs. The bell had stopped. There was no sound.

Then Paetus spoke, in a strident, confident tone that reached across the market: "My friends, these men are trying to steal our business! Let's show them how we treat such vermin! Any man who stands with me today will be richly rewarded."

The captain looked back across the boats in the harbour and the men in the port. Already the men on cranes were climbing down their wooden ladders. The loaders had also abandoned their tasks and were following their colleagues. Sailors were walking over gangplanks towards them.

Paetus laughed, "You filth, whoever you are, have made the biggest mistake of your lives – and the last."

Over one hundred men who had just been working on the boats and docks had turned towards them. Everyone seemed to sense that a conflict was inevitable. The men closed in, brandishing improvised but still lethal weapons: poles, fish hooks, knives, swords. Captain Paetus smiled down at the general.

Livianus spoke again, "The new owner has no quarrel with any man who works here. Each of you will still have a job tomorrow. Go home and we can get this sorted out."

Something about the calm way he reiterated his message wiped the smile from Paetus's face. His eyes began scanning his forces, trying to estimate their numbers. The two groups of men were silent, still. Waiting for the next move.

The general turned to the man next to him. Although his voice was not loud, it carried across the market, "Any man with a weapon in his hand: cut him down."

His fifty men swept their cloaks aside. They wore old legionary body armour, with short swords at their sides. Paetus looked on, aghast. There were many small groups of men all over the market place now revealing their weapons.

"Get them!" yelled Paetus.

His men ran forward, but Livianus's troops stood their ground. Two heavies approached the general and his second in command. One of them flailed a wooden baton at the general, who stepped back out of its reach. He swiped again at the general's head and again the general stepped backward. Finally the heavy ran forward at the general, the baton raised above his head. Livianus stepped in and thrust his sword into and out of the man's chest with abrupt ferocious force. The giant man fell immediately at his feet as more blood flowed onto the stone pavement.

Fighting ranged all across the port; the sailors and Captain Paetus' heavies had no idea they were fighting the retired men of the Twenty fifth Legion. It had taken several minutes and a score of deaths on the sailors' side before they realised these men were trained. Their sword movements were comfortable and precise. There was minimum effort as they swung their swords round in killing arcs. Livianus had insisted that his men would fight together as pairs in order to help each other. They had drilled together, and even though they were slow they covered one another's weak points.

The sailors stepped forward slowly now and waited. Paetus gave a howl of rage and launched himself at the general and his second in command, backed by two huge men, one on either side. Three against two.

One of Paetus's men swirled a huge fishing net above his head and threw it forward, entangling the general's officer, who couldn't move his sword under the fibrous web. The general moved in front of his companion as the men circled around him looking for an opportunity – and then all three of them charged at once.

Livianus had seen the sword-stroke from the first man and avoided, it whilst equally parrying the captain's first stroke. Now both came lunging at him again. A bare arm flashed in front of the general, which he quickly cut across, and stabbed his short sword into more flesh, before sweeping his sword down again to meet Paetus's lunge. Both swords hit with force. Livianus overbalanced, and found himself slipping back on the spilled blood, as his feet moved uselessly beneath him. Captain Paetus recovered his stroke and quickly moved forward. Livianus struggled to gain his feet on the slippery ground.

As Captain Paetus closed in for the kill, Livianus scooped a handful of blood and threw it into his eyes. The captain staggered back, momentarily blinded. Livianus gave not a heartbeat's hesitation as he stepped forward under his defences and lunged into the captain's chest.

The sword dropped to the floor. General Livianus looked around. The man whose arm he'd cut was bleeding to death, spilling even more fresh blood onto the ground. The third man was down too, lying with the net tangled around his feet. His own officer next to him had no apparent wounds.

Livianus looked around the market place. The fighting was over. Perhaps ten of his men were wounded but those on the other side, who had been foolish enough to fight on, had suffered far worse. Some thirty men lay dead.

The general spoke again, "I repeat: the new owner of the port has no quarrel with any man who works here. Each of you will still have a job tomorrow. Go back to your homes and your families. Anyone who raised arms against us only followed their honour as they saw it. There will be no reprisals, no recriminations. So go home. Tomorrow is a new day."

The crowd broke up and quickly disappeared. The general looked around at Commodus walking towards him and saluted.

Commodus smiled and nodded, "General." They marched together towards the captain's office. Commodus ran up the stairs and found the clerk hiding in the back room. He inhaled the almond aroma with satisfaction. The clerk looked at Commodus and then back to General Livianus, who looked as if he had been through a slaughterhouse. Boots, tunic, face, and hair were all matted with fresh blood.

"My friend, General Livianus, formerly of the Twenty-fifth Legion," said Commodus. "And the old man you had thrown down the stairs not long ago."

The clerk's tunic rapidly became a yellow wetness soaking to the floor.

"You will provide me with the name of the owner and detail to me his books of accounts and receipts."

His voice shaking, the clerk replied, "It's Prefect Attianus, sir. I will tell you anything you want to know."

"A good start," smiled Commodus.

SPQR

Great empires are not maintained by timidity.

Tactius

XV   Daggers in the Dark

3.50pm, 26th November, 117AD: the Via Domitiana, Northern Britain

The fort at Coria lay in ruins. The wooden ramparts had been burnt down but the men of Legion Supply had fought a valiant defence. When Juventius' men had found the body of the camp centurion, a peaceful look was on his cold white face. Novantes had identified him as the man who had helped him to go south with the warning. They collected the bodies of their fallen comrades and burnt them in the traditional way.

Now they had found evidence he was looking for. The Brigantes had attacked this fort and killed every roman soldier within its walls. However they were long gone there was nothing left to do but return now.

Caelinus Juventius' mind was troubled. Half his troops stood guard while the other half built their new temporary camp in the ruins of the old one. He watched as the soldiers moved quickly into place, already laid out in outline by differently coloured flags planted by his advance troops. He watched as the tents were erected. For his men, there was comfort and camaraderie in this familiar work: the sense that the day's advance was over. A time to rest and to eat. Juventius had no such feelings of consolation, only his forebodings.

These tribes had been believed to have been 'romanized' or been a pacified territory.

Juventius knew as winter approached any plan to campaign against the Brigantes would need to be resolved quickly. Any delay by the Roman army to put down the rebellion would only be perceived by the tribes as weakness. The potential for unrest among the tribes would be even greater. Yet the campaigning season was at an end for this year. Normally the legate would order a resupply at Eboracum to begin planning operations for the following year. Faced with such a determined Brigiantian effort could he afford to let this insult go unnoticed over the winter months?

Rome's allied tribes to the south would be watching what the response would be. What would the Parisi and Cornovi tribes think if their larger neighbour had risen up now? A quick victory against the Brigantes was now required.

The path way north would be following the old Via Domitiana road. They would need to make a winter camp somewhere along the road north. Part of his mood was explained by the inhospitable nature of this country, which the gods had surely cursed. It was cold, and the wind-blown drizzle in his face made it seem colder still. All day the skies had been grey and heavy.

For four days now they had been advancing further north, into a territory that seemed turned against them. The scouts had failed to find any signs of the enemy. The traders, travellers and other elements of the native population had largely disappeared from the road.

His second in command reported, "Camp is secure, sir, and will be complete very shortly."

The commander sighed again, "Very well, I will take the first watch" he said.

"Ah, this country..."

"Sir?"

"So primitive. It's like the world in an earlier, earthier time. Sometimes it seems as if it's bewitched."

It would be a difficult campaign. The fate of the northern frontier lay in their hands.

*

Near the southern slopes of Mount Silpius in Syrian Antioch, Hadrian and Turbo were walking, with a bodyguard a discreet distance behind them. They entered one of the two long colonnades built by Tiberius. It was an especially beautiful autumn day, unseasonably warm, all blue skies and strong sunshine, as though Antioch were relishing the memories of summer and resisting the relentless onslaught of autumn. The smell of fruit was in the air. The sharpness of the late season's sun intensified the contrast of walking into the open areas and then back into shade. Shops dotted the colonnades, where passers-by walked, stood, conversed amiably. There was no hint of darkness in their world: it was peaceful and ordered. Hadrian envied them.

"You've made all the arrangements to receive the Parthian king?" asked Hadrian.

"Yes, Caesar. I thought an imperial barge, bedecked in finery, in the middle of the Orontes, and the king and his party will be rowed out to meet you, heralded by the majestic sound of horns drifting over the smooth waters."

A smile interrupted Hadrian's preoccupation for a moment, "You should have been a poet, Turbo."

Turbo nodded wryly, and they fell silent for a moment. They entered a gap between the colonnades, and the sun beat down fiercely. Hadrian shaded his eyes, not noticing that Turbo had fallen back to look at a shop selling curios, joking with the guards about some objects for sale. Hadrian's mind was wandering restlessly about his empire, which seemed to be in danger of fragmenting. It was as if he had to run from state to state, from region to region – as if only his will and his orders kept it from descending into chaos. Parthia, for example. He had abandoned Trajan's conquests in Mesopotamia in order to consolidate his empire but would the Parthian king see this as a sign of weakness, to exploit? And the growing revolt in Judea! It needed to be pinched off, severed like a diseased bud from a branch, before the disease infected the whole tree. Where would the next danger signal come from, he wondered, in all the vastness of the empire? Had Tiberius, who built these colonnades, faced the same pressures?

Hadrian entered the next colonnaded section and at once found himself in shadow, his vision restricted and his eyes half blinded. This was an area without shops, and with very few people. He realised he had walked ahead of his escort, and looked back over his shoulder. As he did so, a shape ran directly towards him out of the shadows. The light behind him flashed on an upheld blade. Hadrian's military skill made him duck instinctively to one side. A knife slashed through the space he had occupied less than a second before, and met empty air. Hadrian's awkward manoeuvre left him staggering, trying to catch his balance.

He knew he had to stay upright. His assailant rallied quickly from his lunge, sweeping his dagger in front of him in swift, deadly swipes. Only by movements borne of instinct did the Emperor evade the fanatical thrusts. Then the dagger was raised for a decisive stab down into his head. Hadrian wrapped both hands around the wrist of the assassin but he was strong: stronger than the Emperor. And meanwhile his other hand found Hadrian's throat and began to squeeze. The dagger inched towards Hadrian's eye, despite all his strength, and the grip around his throat made his vision grow red, while his life's breath was choked out of him. *No!* he thought. *It cannot be ending like this! I've done nothing yet!*

As that despairing thought ushered in blackness; as though from far away, he heard an insistent pounding: a man running faster than seemed possible. Bodies convulsed. Hot blood sprayed over Hadrian's neck and face. The grip on his throat was gone. He saw there, in the shadowy light, a body still holding a dagger, but writhing in death's agony, a sword rammed into his side. And there was Turbo, his true friend, his face aghast and pale, even in the wan light of the colonnades. He pressed against Hadrian, seeking to reassure himself, to repel the unthinkable thought, "Caesar –?"

Hadrian lay still for a moment, drawing in deep breaths, "Unharmed," he panted.

The Roman body guards had noticed Turbo's action and now sped towards their Emperor at full speed, their armour clattering along the colonnade. They made a circle around them both, with swords already drawn.

Turbo stood over the body on the ground and turned him over. His face was smeared with dust and mud, his eyes rolling up into his skull, "Who sent you?" he commanded. "Who is behind this outrage?" Turbo shock the man's robe, but not even the echo of his voice returned from Hades.

Turbo dropped the corpse and stood up, wiping blood from his hands down his tunic. He searched the man's robes and found a brown purse with five gold coins inside. He examined the dagger: a roman handle and design which was common.

"Forgive me, my lord," he said to Hadrian.

Hadrian looked him in the eye, his breath more steady now. He clasped his forearm.

"My good friend," he said. "But for you, that would be my body in the dust."

Hadrian took the long dagger and examined it. "Five gold coins, my friend. Is that the price of my life?"

The bodyguard who had followed Turbo's lead now stood, shamefaced. The captain of the guard approached and sank to his knees in the bloodied ground, "My life is yours, Caesar," he said, taking out his sword and offering it handle first, to the Emperor, his eyes averted, awaiting his doom.

Hadrian reversed the sword and handed it back to him, raising him gently to his feet with a touch of his hand, "I return it to you, Captain," he said. "The fault was as much mine as yours. Let us return to the palace."

"Have the body brought back and examined. I want to know who did this," motioned Turbo. The captain saluted.

Hadrian and Turbo turned and began to walk back, with the guards walking both in front and behind now. It was a subdued party that retraced its steps.

Inside the palace, they made their way to the emperor's quarters. Hadrian clapped his hands and called for wine. A silver pitcher and two flagons were brought in on an ornate tray. Hadrian strode over to the tray, but stood unmoving, the pitcher in his hand, "I was just thinking," said Hadrian, "Here am I, about to drink the finest wine this side of *Mare Nostrum*. I am Emperor of the world's greatest Empire, and men have to jump when I clap my hands, and yet I might have been cold clay by now."

"By the will of the gods, your assailant is, instead."

"Yes. He was alive an hour ago, and now he is gone. If it had been up to him, I would have been lying in the bloodstained dirt of the colonnades, and Rome would be about to appoint a new Emperor."

Turbo said, "From now on, Caesar I will make sure that your body guards are doubled and always march at both your front and back." He paused, and gazed in thought, "It is interesting that the man possessed a roman dagger".

"Who do you think is behind this?" asked Hadrian.

"Most likely a Jewish zealot or a disgruntled Parthian, my Lord."

"Possibly" nodded Hadrian. "Or a disgruntled Roman?"

"I'm sorry he didn't live long enough to tell us who sent him." Turbo spoke quietly.

"He had lived quite long enough, in my opinion!" laughed Hadrian "These things have a way of arranging themselves. We'll find out in due course, no doubt."

As they talked, Hadrian regained much of his habitual confidence. The conversation passed to the various trouble spots of the empire that were exercising their attention, which was business as usual for him, and it did him good.

After about half an hour, a servant entered, bowed and presented a scroll to Turbo.

"For the Chief of Staff," he said, and bowed himself from the room.

Hadrian looked quizzically as Turbo's brow furrowed as he broke the seal and unrolled the message, "What is it?"

"Disturbing news, Caesar. One of my sources in Judea reports that a new rebellion has broken out there. It's gaining ground rapidly. A new Jewish leader is organising hit-and-run tactics against the Seventh Legion: ambushes in their patrols, that kind of thing. They've sustained heavy losses."

Hadrian sat silent for a while, looking keenly down at the empty table in front of them. Turbo followed his gaze, sensing what his emperor saw – the pieces of a board game, moveable to meet this new threat.

"Yes," he said at last. "This needs immediate and forceful action – the only way to stamp out this sort of wildfire revolt. Send the Twenty Fifth Appollinaris from here to Judea."

Turbo reached for a stylus and a wax tablet, "Good plan. The Twenty Fifth Apollinaris are experienced in this sort of work."

"Yes and also, place all other units within a week's travel to Judea on heightened alert. Our legions are stretched so tight in the east. We seem to be in constant battle against new enemies. The Roman army cannot continue on different fronts in the east: so we must have peace with the Parthians. We must make it work!"

But then another servant entered, this time, with a scroll for Hadrian. Impatiently, he opened the message and read rapidly, "What?" he bellowed.

Then Hadrian was on his feet. He strode about the room, howling his anger and rage, wreaking havoc on innocent objects and furnishings.

Turbo caught his shoulders and looked into his eyes, "What is it, Lord?"

Hadrian made an explosive gesture, half sigh, half snort. He sank down into a couch and threw the scroll over, "Read it for yourself," he said.

Turbo did so, "So. The Senate itself."

Hadrian was on his feet again, "They tried to reject my direct appointment! Have you ever heard of such a thing? Who is this Blandinus, and these others?"

Turbo frowned, "Nonentities. Time servers in the Senate... At least, until now."

"Someone is pulling their strings, Turbo! I have dallied here in Antioch long enough! Make the preparations! Bring the Tenth to battle readiness! We march to the port tomorrow!"

Instead of jumping like one of Hadrian's servants, Turbo reacted like one of his true friends. With a smile that held sadness, he led Hadrian back to the couch, walked over to the table and poured them both another flagon of wine, "Your adversary in Rome, whoever he is, wants you to do exactly that." Hadrian looked up, raising his head from his hands. "Yes, Caesar; he wants you to rush precipitously there, unprepared, into ground that he has readied for you in ambush. And then you really would be lying in the dust, as that assassin intended – and your challenger might be the next Emperor."

Hadrian spoke, more quietly and calmly but with a brooding undertone. "I want to go to Rome, my friend. It is my place."

"You shall, Caesar. But on your terms, not on his. Who knows what plans have been made against you? Let's think this out and make the right decisions. You yourself said we must control this situation in Judea, and there is the Parthian king to placate. Leaving Antioch now would be seen, by many, as a sign of indecision. Let us sort out the Eastern front first, my lord. Then we march to Rome. And not with a single legion either, my lord, but in force."

Hadrian sipped wine, then looked up. He gave a grimace, through which a half-smile struggled to emerge, "As always, my friend, yours is the voice of reason. Your counsel has been good. We will prepare properly, and move at our pace. But when I arrive ..." And he picked up a piece of pottery and dashed it against the wall with a grim satisfaction.

*

The evening was cool and misty in northern Britannia, as the two horses bore their riders on at a gentle pace. Cornelia wrapped her cloak more tightly around her shoulders and rubbed her ears to warm them from the chill. Marcus's mind was back in the hut with the seer, taking out a coin, repeating the question: "I am looking for Tobar."

He remembered the way the old man's eyes lit up at the sight of the money, the way he almost snatched it from his hand, "Tobar...Fist... Tobar..Fist."

They looked at him quizzically, and he pointed impatiently to the north east. And he remembered looking back as they rode off and seeing the soothsayer biting into the coin with satisfaction. He returned to the present. "So, have you heard of the Fist?"

"No," she admitted.

"Me neither. I suppose all we can do is continue in this direction and see what turns up – if anything!"

"We really should head back to the Fort," said Marcus. "Let's give it another hour to see if we can find the Fist."

They fell silent again, and the horses continued to walk. There was something lulling about their constant rhythmical motion against the misty indistinct background; trees and sky blending together. A blackbird cawed loudly to its mate on the ground, then both took to the air as the horses came nearer. Indistinct rustlings suggested animals in the woods. In time, the mists began to lift and a fitful sunshine started to break up the cloud. Visibility soon improved.

"This is just a waste of time," said Marcus. "Looks like it goes on forever. Let's head back. "

"No, look: there's a house ahead," she pointed the way.

Marcus screwed up his eyes. Yes, he could just make out a large hut in the distance, almost merging into the countryside with its brown walls and roof. They approached to within an arrow' fire.

"Let me go first," said Marcus. ""Wait here for me."

He walked his horse onward. Two large tree trunks stood at the entrance to the hut. The trees bore Celtic markings carved on them and had strips of cloth tied to them. Marcus approached the house and shouted a greeting to anybody who was listening. A small boy came and looked out – quickly running back inside at the sight of a Roman officer. Marcus dismounted and walked up to the homestead. He called out again but no one else emerged.

Cautiously he raised the covering of animal hide over the front opening and looked inside. The furniture was of excellent quality. A large table in the centre of the room took up most of the space. His eyes were drawn to a big wooden chair by the fire, also decorated with intricate carving. After a last look around and another unanswered greeting, he walked back to his horse and rode back to Cornelia.

"What is it?" she asked.

"There was a child – a boy – but he's hiding somewhere. Otherwise, it's deserted. Looks like the home of someone important, though."

"Let me try," smiled Cornelia. "I have a way with males!"

Marcus grinned, nodded his assent.

As Cornelia approached the house she called softly to the boy, "Hello. Can you help me? Is Tobar here?"

She got down from her horse and took out the *dulcia* Marcus had given her. She unwrapped them, and the pleasant smell of apples and honey wafted into the air. She placed them just inside the hut. A pair of brown eyes appeared from below the table. Cornelia smiled and offered the boy the pastry. He looked hesitant.

"Roman solider gone," said Cornelia in broken Celtic, "He is bad. I need to find Tobar. Romans looking for him."

The boy nodded, "Mother at river getting water. Father at Fist."

"Your father is where?" said Cornelia gently. But the boy had his mouth full of pastry – and his face full of delight. Cornelia waited, "Where is your father?"

"Father at Fist."

"The Fist," said Cornelia. "Yes. I will go and tell him. Which way?"

The boy pointed north and settled down to finish the rest of his unaccustomed treat, and Cornelia smiled and rumpled his hair. She went back outside, jumped on her horse and waved Marcus over. They trotted their horses round to the back of the hut.

"The Fist is the place," she said, "Just like the old man said. North of here. But I don't know how far."

"Then let's ride!" cried Marcus, and he kicked his horse's sides with his heels. Soon they were galloping, hair flying in the wind. He looked back and noticed that Cornelia was keeping up well with a trained cavalry officer. He also noticed how the pace of the gallop gave her cheeks a rosy flush, heightening her beauty – if that were possible.

Their pounding hooves swept away the distance, and before long they saw a huge rock, the height of two houses, before them. It was like a giant hand punching out of the ground. On one side, against it, was a wooden hut structure covered with animal skins that matched the grey of the rock.

Inside the building, Tobar sat with his bodyguards and half a dozen tribal chiefs, grateful for the crackling fire that warmed their bones. Tobar looked about them, seeing disquiet and a sense of doubt in some of their faces.

"My brothers, let me speak plainly," he said. "The choice is simple: either we remain under the yoke of the Romans as a conquered people – or we rise up and push them out of our lands. Romans value strength, and their strength lies in their Ninth Legion, at Eborakon." He spoke its native name, the Place of the Yew Trees, and he saw something new in their looks at its restoration, "But we have seen this Ninth Legion, and it is at its weakest. Now is the time for us to attack – for, if we do not take that chance, it may never come again!"

"Three generations of our fathers failed to defeat them in open battle, even with superior numbers. But now we have surprise on our side. The Romans are going to get a shock so great, they will die with the look of disbelief on their faces!" There was appreciative laughter around the campfire. "My kinsman Arthmael is with our main force, led by Ortagorus," a murmur of respect at the greatness of the name, "And by Vordimus, a mighty warrior of his own people. He has lived among the Romans and knows their ways – and has turned those ways against them." Tobar smiled, "The Roman scouts cannot find our army. They are renowned trackers, but they are here. Here in Brigantia. And this is our country!" with fervour, "We know every hill and every glade – and the gods that look down and control our destiny are our gods, not these false Roman ones! Whatever power they may have in their own land, they are emasculated here." He paused, and saw that his words were getting through to them. There was a sterner, bolder look to their faces. Even their posture looked more confident.

"Ortagorus and his army are at this moment making ready for a great battle: a battle that, even if the Romans have the stomach for it, will drive them from our fatherland forever! So spread the word around each village and town. Every man who is able and willing to fight can join our battle and reap the rewards. Only this time it will be our victory! This time will be the time of the Brigantes!"

"You speak well, like a warrior," said one, a dour chief with a grizzled beard. "We know of the glorious attacks on the Roman forts to the north. But this Roman legion of the Ninth: it is not an isolated fort, but hundreds upon hundreds of men."

"My friends," smiled Tobar, "we will take those many hundreds, cut off their heads and make a new road with their skulls. Then they will have to negotiate a settlement with us – and the land will be ours again, forever!"

There was laughter, the fierce laughter of exultation and the promise of retribution long delayed. The chiefs stood up, shook hands with Tobar and promised they would gather their men and head north to join Ortagorus. Then they left, and only Tobar and his guards remained.

Outside, Cornelia and Marcus lay on a hillock overlooking the Fist. Marcus pointed. Just three horses were tied up outside the wooden structure. He pulled back down the slope and motioned to Cornelia, "I've got a plan," he whispered.

XVI Neapolis

7.40pm, 26th November, 117AD: Neapolis, Island of Sardinia

It had been a pleasant day – even for that most pleasant of Roman cities, Neapolis. Perhaps part of the pleasure derived from its long Greek history. It had been Parthenope for four hundred years before it became Neapolis. Even now, four centuries of Roman rule later, the inhabitants still referred to themselves as Parthenopeans and the city was still famous for its Greek culture, learning and even language. Even the climate seemed more Greek than Italian, lulled by balmy winds from the south. All this made it the most sophisticated of Italian cities.

Another part of the pleasure for Attianus had come from showing Livia around. Her naive delight at seeing the sights for the first time made Attianus glow with pride – the odeon, the theatre, the magnificent bay, which was one of the wonders of the natural world. Then he'd taken her back to his sumptuous villa overlooking the bay: and there, it seemed to him, the delicious prospect of the bay and the endless vista had merged into his own property. They were all his, to disburse as he wished. And he wished to disburse them to Livia, for today, anyway.

He sat in the open window of his villa, revelling in the gorgeous sunset above the bay's awe-inspiring expanse. Even that sunset seemed to have been orchestrated by him, to applaud his wisdom and perspicacity.

Visible to him in the next chamber, lay Livia, asleep on the bed, innocent as a child in slumber. He remembered how they had... pleasurably... toyed with the grapes and wine together, and smiled again.

The blush of the sunset mingled with her lustrous skin, darkening her complexion and soft cheeks. He admired the way the soft breeze fingered her hair, and thought about doing so again himself.

Careful, he thought. *Don't lose your heart when there's so much to gain.*

He was master of Rome, the world's greatest city, while the emperor sat skulking a thousand miles away, afraid to show his face. History showed that such emperors did not last long. So why shouldn't the master of the world indulge himself?

Yes, he reflected, beauty is fleeting. But there is a remedy for that – no shortage of younger girls. And power, fame and fortune, too are fleeting. And there was an answer to that too: immortality. Men would remember and revere the names of Caesars: like Augustus, and Tiberius... for hundreds of years to come; perhaps forever. Was it not probable that he, Attianus, could make such a mark? After all, history was written by the victors – and victory belonged to the bold.

He sat for some time enjoying the slowly changing view: the subtle gradations of the sunset, the deepening of the cloud colours, as the sun continued its descent; the clouds watching too like patient courtiers, acquiescent as slaves.

It was rare for him to be able to relax. He was the busiest man in Rome but today every part of his body was singing; it felt appropriate to become part of the moment.

A servant knocked at the door and entered, nervously, "Sorry to disturb you, my lord. A Nautius Rullus wishes to see you."

"And who exactly is Nautius Rullus?"

"Pardon, my lord. He says he is from Ostia."

"Ostia," said Attianus. He was silent for several seconds, while the servant waited, discomfited. "Admit him."

A man entered, by his gait and bearing, a sailor. But there was more: a dishevelled appearance, bruises, cuts, a black eye... Attianus took in all of this, at a glance.

"Well?"

"Forgive this intrusion, my lord. I am Nautius Rullus. I was the deputy to Captain Paetus."

Attianus looked him over again. "You say you *were*?"

"Captain Paetus is dead, sir – and many of your men with him. I was fortunate to escape with my life."

Attianus's voice was quiet, yet the steel within it was unmistakable: "What? What has happened? Who would dare?" This low tone was more intimidating than a shout.

"He called himself Ratho Livianus, master."

"Livianus. That old fox! I thought he was retired – or dead."

"He led a force of men into the warehouse square. He said that you were no longer in charge of the port – that it had a new owner."

Attianus was silent for a while, "But you resisted?" one look at Rullus told him that they had, but he needed to ask.

"To a man, lord. But they were well trained, skilled in the art of killing."

"Veterans."

"Yes, Prefect," Rullus described the fight in more detail, the killing of the guards, the rallying call of Paetus, the overwhelming force.

Attianus was scarcely listening. So his earlier concerns had been justified. And that withered goat Livianus would not have acted on his own initiative: he detected the hand of Commodus in this. He became aware that his visitor had finished speaking, and looked up again at the unhappy man.

"You have done well and acted with alacrity, Rullus." Attianus went to a bureau and drew out a clinking leather pouch and handed it to him, "I will be returning to Rome tomorrow. Come and visit me there. I can always use brave and resourceful men. You will be my replacement for the late lamented Paetus – and the inheritor of his fortune."

"Thank you, my lord. But –"

Attianus raised a finger and cut him off, "What happened at the port was an anomaly. It will be corrected and will not happen again."

"Yes, master. Thank you."

"Speak to my secretary as you go. He will arrange lodgings for you in the city for the night, and free passage back to Rome."

A weary smile flickered across the sailor's face, "Yes, lord." Rullus bowed himself from the room.

After a few moments, Attianus opened the door and spoke to the servant outside: "Send my secretary to me. I have instructions – and orders."

The servant scurried away and Attianus stepped back into the room. He stood for some minutes, lost in thought. Gradually the flush faded from his cheeks. He came to himself, walked softly into the chamber where Livia still slept, and lifted one tress of her perfect hair. Slowly he twisted the strands until they were taut. And then he laughed, let her hair drop back to the pillow, and roused her gently but insistently from sleep. It was time, he thought, for action.

*

"What weapon do you have?" asked Marcus.

Cornelia shrugged, "Nothing."

Marcus looked around him and pointed to a large flat stone, "Hit them on the head with that as they come out."

They left their horses at the side of the Fist and crept round to the wooden shack. Darkness was already falling, accelerated by the sunless winter sky.

"Three horses," whispered Marcus. "Hopefully one of them belongs to Tobar."

As they approached, one of the horses looked round at them and whinnied softly. Marcus rubbed its nose and it quietened. He untied the rough rope round its head and led it away. When he returned, one of the bodyguards lay unconscious outside the front door. Marcus stared at Cornelia, who mimed the way she had used the stone to knock the guard unconscious. He grinned but the door was opening again. They dived for cover. Who would come through first, and how would they identify Tobar?

A tall man with an animal-skin coat emerged, his eyes narrowing as the cold wind hit his face. Cornelia stepped around the door, lifted the stone and brought it crashing down on the man's head. He dropped like a felled oak.

Another companion was right behind him and leapt back, drawing his sword. Like lightning, Marcus swept his sword up, the steel cold against the warrior's chin. They looked into each other's eyes. Marcus gestured with his other hand. Its meaning was clear and the Brigantian dropped his sword to the ground. Marcus pushed him onto the floor while Cornelia stood over him with the stone lifted high. He tried to dodge the blow from the stone but it caught him across the side of the head. He fell flat with a yell.

As the man tried to move once more, "Again!" said Marcus. Cornelia brought the stone down. "Last time!" smiled Marcus

The stone cracked down onto the top of the prone man's head. Blood pooled from his skull onto the ground. The warrior moaned, and – almost incredibly – raised his head, looking at them both with horror. He started to plead with them not to hurt him any more and looked up with tearful eyes.

"I said knock him out, not stone him to death," laughed Marcus.

"You try, then."

Marcus took the stone from her hands, but looked into the bodyguard's eyes and let it fall to the ground: "He looks like he's had enough. Let's tie him."

They bound the man with strips torn from his coat. Marcus gave the unconscious one a shove with his foot and he rolled back into the shack.

"You know, if the legion ever runs out of torturers..." smiled Marcus.

"Is it my fault he wouldn't keep still?"

Marcus knelt and turned over the first unconscious body. A black animal pelt covered his shoulders and intricate blue markings decorated his face. He looked at the other men, but their dress was undistinguished and they had no tattoos.

"This must be Tobar," said Marcus.

Marcus untied the Brigantes horses, slapping their hindquarters to make them gallop off. He returned with their own mounts. They bound Tobar's hands quickly and efficiently and hefted him onto the front of Marcus's horse. The warrior moaned as the Roman mounted his horse and adjusted the weight of his body to balance it.

"Let's get back to Eboracum while we still have some light."

They kicked their steeds into a gallop, heading south in the gathering dusk. As they continued to ride, Tobar's groaning increased but Marcus ignored the sounds.

With the light fading fast, they at last reached the outskirts of Eboracum. Marcus slowed to a halt and signalled to Cornelia to do so too. The horses panted heavily, their exhalations frosting before them. Marcus could feel the sweat on the horse's side through his legs.

Marcus pulled back Tobar's head and whipped out his dagger, holding it to his neck, "Give me any trouble and I'll cut your throat. Understand?"

"Perfectly," replied Tobar in Latin.

Oaths and shouts of vengeance came to them from the north: and the sound of galloping horses.

"The bodyguards?"

"If so, these savages recover fast!" laughed Marcus.

"Or another troop?"

"Let's not stay to find out!" they pulled their horse's rope braces and kicked with their heels. The horses burst into reluctant motion, "Head for the road!" shouted Marcus.

The horses sped closer to Eboracum – and the protection of the garrison. The lights of houses came to them, comforting in the deepening gloom. Marcus motioned to Cornelia to follow him. The market square and the inn where he had met Cornelia were just a few hundred feet away. The horses were exhausted now and Marcus let them slow to a trot. Great beads of sweat were dripping off their side and their nostrils flared with every breath.

"Not long now," whispered Marcus, pointing to the lights on the fortress battlements.

He pictured the Legate smiling at him. *Excellent, Prefect. This more than makes up for everything. You have proved yourself a worthy cavalry commander...*

He grinned at the thought, and as he did so, two voices, shockingly near, shouted a challenge. Two warrior savages were charging at them at full speed.

"Ride!" he called, jabbing his heels into his horse's flank.

*

As the autumn wind blew briskly, Commodus emerged from his nondescript house and made his way through the milling throng of the ordinary citizenry of Rome, the slaves, and the poor. The crowds dispersed as he headed towards the Caelian Hill. The houses grew larger and more splendid as he advanced and now he was clearly in the district of the wealthy and the well-heeled. The clamouring crowds had given way to the occasional passer-by, sober, well dressed, intent on his business.

The senator stopped outside a large house, its opulence reflected in its pristine cream- coloured facings and ornate timbering. A bell-pull hung down below the arch of the gate and Commodus rang it. The sound was delicate and elegant, redolent of the neighbourhood. A servant appeared and looked enquiringly at him.

"Senator Commodus Verus – to see Tullius Gracchus."

The servant unlocked the gate and admitted him, leading him into an ante-chamber. He signalled politely for the senator to wait, then left him. Commodus looked around at the collection of expensive paintings on the wall. A scene of Antony and Cleopatra on a ship covered most of one wall; on another, Jupiter himself was handing down his sword to mortal man. *But who is man enough to take it?* he wondered.

A short, energetic figure entered the room; grey was fingering through his temples, but most of his hair was brown. The lines around his eyes wrinkled into a smile of recognition, and he extended his arms in welcome. "Lucius!" he cried.

"Vibius, my old friend," said Commodus, returning the embrace.

"It's been far too long. How are you?"

"I am well," smiled Commodus, "and I see the gods have blessed you even more."

"From what I hear, they have blessed us both," laughed Gracchus. "Come, let's have a drink. What have you been up to?"

They moved through to a cooler and even more impressive room, and a servant poured two cups of wine. Commodus took his and sat down on the luxurious couch.

He glanced up at the servant, and Gracchus gestured him from the room.

"My friend," said Commodus. He sipped from the wine, savouring the vintage. "I had thought my days in the senate were drawing to an end. However, I've been given a great commission." He unrolled a letter and passed it over.

Gracchus's eyes opened wider as he saw the imperial seal and read the letter: "From Hadrian himself. So. How can I help you?"

Commodus paused, "A somewhat delicate subject, my friend. Your business covers all the important lending accounts in Rome."

"Yes," smiled Gracchus. "Most of the older senators do their banking business with me. I flatter myself that I've built up something of a reputation."

"Undoubtedly. But I see from senate records that your business has recently increased the borrowing rate for most of the city."

"True. It was not my idea. But I was visited by Attianus, our City Prefect, and Senator Blandinus. They said that, due to the difficult trading conditions, it was necessary to increase the borrowing rate to all citizens. Attianus was most insistent. He told me the order came from the Emperor himself: money was needed for the imperial treasury. I had no option but to comply."

Commodus smiled wryly, "I understand, Vibius my friend. But I have come direct from our Emperor Hadrian. He is concerned that food prices and other basics are rising out of control – yet why? Rome is well supplied by cheap grain, we had an excellent summer with a good harvest. There were no costly punitive war expeditions. On the contrary, the Parthians have recently rewarded us with great gifts of gold. So he now orders the rate to go back to its old level."

There was a twinkle in Gracchus's eye, "I am happy to obey." He clapped his hands, called for a secretary and dictated orders.

"Come my friend, have some more wine. Stay awhile and tell me what's afoot."

Commodus allowed his cup to be refilled. "What's afoot is a struggle for Rome – for the Empire itself."

Gracchus lowered his voice, "The Praetorian Guard are formidable, and not easily swayed."

Commodus shrugged, "They are indeed formidable, but history suggests they will turn the way the wind blows. If it blows against the Prefect, I don't believe he can count on their loyalty. You and I, and people like us, can help turn that breeze into a whirlwind."

Gracchus laughed. The two men stood and shook hands.

"One more thing," said the senator. "I need a substantial loan."

"How much? A thousand denarii? That would pay for a nice holiday!" Gracchus laughed.

Commodus shook his head. "A bit more, Vibius."

"Five thousand? Ten thousand, even?"

"A million would be nearer the mark."

Gracchus's face turned white, "You're not serious!"

"I am. Or rather, our Emperor is. For funds to run his campaign – and to guard against problems until he returns to Rome."

The moneylender's hands shook as he sat down, "A million denarii. It can be done, but it will take a few days."

"My own properties will be security for the loan, if that suits you," said Commodus.

Gracchus nodded with gratitude. As Commodus moved to go, Gracchus caught him by the arm: "I hope we're on the winning side."

"So do I. I'd hate to be without a roof over my head!" smiled Commodus.

SPQR

Armed forces abroad are of little value unless there is prudent counsel at home.

Cicero

XVII Gathering Storm

4.05pm, 30th November, 117AD: outside
Fortress Eboracum, Northern Britain

Marcus pounded his heels repeatedly against his horse's belly, and knew that Cornelia was doing the same. Their horses had their necks extended and their ears flattened back against their heads. Sweat flicked into the faces of the riders, tossed on the headlong charge. Part of him wondered how the *Brittunculi* had got so close so quickly. Had they known a short cut? It was their territory... but there was no time to think of that. There was only time to seek safety before he felt a barbarian javelin in his back.

The body lying across his horse suddenly burst into life. Tobar kicked out at Marcus and hit his stomach. Marcus just managed to keep his seat, regaining the saddle and punching the chieftain in the back of the head.

"Cornelia, keep up!" he shouted, the thunderous hooves and the wind drowning out his words.

She was too far behind anyway – at least ten feet. The two bodyguards were gaining fast. He had to do something now. Peering into the twilight gloom, he saw the lights of the fortress braziers on the ramparts. With one hand pressing down on the neck of the squirming and struggling Tobar, Marcus shouted at the top of his voice: "Enemy approaching! Stand to! Stand to!" But there was no reaction, no movement ahead. "Stand to! Stand to!" he bellowed.

Still shouting the alarm, Marcus slowed his pace and Cornelia drew level. The bodyguards were just a few feet behind them now. The leading warrior drew his sword. Marcus urged Cornelia's horse past so that he could draw his own.

As he reached across, Tobar's bound hands grabbed Marcus' sword arm, restraining his movement. He heard and felt the whistle of the enemy sword through the air, inches from his back, and shock thrilled through his body. He cracked his knee into Tobar's face with all his force, and the chieftain's body hung limp again. Marcus drew his sword and looked behind him. A furious face, mud-spattered and bloodied, was bearing down on him. Marcus recognised one of the men they'd felled at the shack. The warrior leaned forward in the saddle and aimed a scything stroke at Marcus's head. It was deflected by Marcus's sword, the blades ringing in the gathering darkness. A cry of defiance came to him from behind – just as an arrow shaft shot from the fort whizzed past his head. Although it had missed him by scant inches, Marcus was glad of what it meant.

"Stand to, stand to! Enemy approaching!" he cried.

Torches and more braziers added to the illumination, and the bowmen picked out their target. More arrows flew past Marcus, now clearly aimed at his pursuers. One buried itself in the lead warrior's left forearm and he gasped with pain and shock. He reined back his horse, and his companion also pulled his mount to a standstill. They hurled shouts of abuse at Marcus and Cornelia, who galloped onward to safety. More arrows were loosed, and the two men turned their horses and retreated.

Marcus laughed, slowed down from the mad gallop, and put his arm round Cornelia. "Well done!"

"Well done to you," she smiled back at him gratefully.

Then they were under the battlements. Shouts came down for them to identify themselves.

"*Praefectus Alae* Quietus reporting, with Cornelia and a prisoner. Password: Jupiter."

Faces appeared, looking down over the wooden battlements. The door swung open and Cornelia and Marcus fell inside, exhausted. He helped her dismount and took her hand.

"Thanks for your help... couldn't have done it without you," he panted. Their eyes met and stayed locked for a few seconds. Marcus smiled, "Get yourself washed and rested. I must report to the Legate, and he may want to talk to you too."

He leaned over and kissed her on the cheek. There was a raucous cheer from the battlements at this lapse in military protocol. As she walked wearily in the direction of the infirmary, he stood watching after her. Then he wiped the smile from his face and called over an officer, "Centurion! Have an escort lead this prisoner to the cells."

He stretched, wiped his brow and his mouth, "Do you know where the Legate is?"

"I believe, in his quarters, Prefect."

"Thank you, Centurion."

Marcus would have liked to have washed and changed clothes himself, but he knew his priorities. Minutes later, he stood in front of the legate in his quarters. He remembered the last time he had done so, after reporting what Novantes had told him. The legate looked in no better mood now.

"Where have you been? Is this a time to be gallivanting around the countryside? These are momentous times. I expect Juventius to return any day with good news, but he may need reinforcements. You should have been here awaiting my orders."

"Legate –"

"And look at you! Is this any way for a Cavalry Prefect to appear ? I expect you to set an example to your men, not be a laughing stock. Well, why did you leave the fort?"

"You ordered me to, Legate."

"*I* did?"

"A few days ago. You told me to seek out a man named Tobar, to confirm that there was no truth in the story I brought to you. You described him as a 'docile old dog', if I recall."

"Did you find Tobar?"

"I ran him to earth. He may be a dog, but he's far from docile. Rabid, more like. I found him plotting with his clan chiefs to rise up against the Empire."

"Nonsense!" cried the legate. "Impossible!"

"I have him brought in, Legate," said Marcus. "Let him deny it to your face."

The legate frowned and was about to make a dismissive reply: but he stared into Marcus's eyes, and seemed to change his mind. He barked an order to the guard outside, and strode about his quarters.

Presently, a body of guards knocked, entered and placed the still bound and battered body of the chieftain into a chair.

"My dear Tobar," said the legate, then broke off. He saw the Brigante's look of hatred towards Marcus, took in his wild, dishevelled appearance, and noticed the necklace of animal teeth around his neck, "*Praefectus Alae* Quietus here has come to me with an extraordinary story," the legate began again. "About you formenting insurrection among your people. I wanted to hear you deny the accusation."

Tobar looked at Marcus as if the commander of Eboracum had never spoken. One eye was half closed and his cheekbone below was blackened with bruising, but the other glared steadily ahead at the young man.

"Well?" cried the legate impatiently.

Tobar glared round, "There is no need to taunt me, Legate," he said, "I do not deny it."

"What?"

"I am proud to admit it. The Brigantes have risen! We have thrown down your forts and your outposts, and killed hundreds of you Romans. I myself led the men that destroyed your fort at Vindolanda."

"Vindolanda destroyed!" gasped the legate.

"How many are you?" asked Marcus.

"More join us every day, and no man can number them. Many hundreds. Many thousands. Proud warriors, eager for war."

"How dare you! You traitor!" screamed the legate.

Tobar raised himself with difficulty onto his feet, "Traitor!" he yelled. "I am no traitor, nor are my comrades. We are patriots – and we shall have our vengeance on our slave masters!"

"What you'll have is death – every one of you. And you shall lead the way!" the legate turned to the escort in a towering rage, "Bring the *Praefectus castrorum* to me – at once!"

In short order, the Camp Prefect arrived, glancing with surprise at the strange tableau in the room.

"*Prefectectus castrorum,* have this man tied to a stake in the parade ground and form a flogging party. Immediately!"

"What level of punishment, Legate?" asked the taciturn officer.

"To the death."

"What! This is an outrage! I am a clan chieftain!" still struggling and shouting defiance, the Brigantine warrior was bundled from the room.

The *Prefectectus castrorum* saluted and was gone. The legate sat down heavily, his hand pulling at his already wispy hair, evidence of his anxiety. Marcus coughed, and the legate looked up as if surprised to see him still there.

He spoke without bluster, "You have done well, Quietus. I should not have doubted you. I will not do so again."

"Thank you, Legate. But ..." The legate frowned, and Marcus pressed on, "Is execution really necessary? I thought perhaps a severe flogging..."

"No," he said. "I put my faith in this man. I trusted him – and this is how he repays me. Let these savages learn how Romans handle uprisings – and traitors. His body will be flung outside the fortress walls, for all to see and for vermin to feast on."

"Yes, sir," Marcus saluted, turned and left the office of his commander with a heavy heart.

*

Ratho Livianus, retired general, head of the *frumentarii* and the man who had cleansed the port of Ostia, strolled about the quayside, watching the dock workers labour at their mid-morning tasks. Many of these men were survivors from the battle, who had taken him at his word that their jobs would be secure under the new management. Some of them avoided his gaze, others seemed happy to meet it. Perhaps they were relieved that order had been restored. Still others darted looks of hatred at him, maybe thinking of fallen comrades, nursing wounds that pained, wondering whether their career plans still held good. Ratho was unconcerned by those glances; enough of his veterans were in evidence to see off any possible threat that sailors and dock workers might present.

Ratho was concerned, however, that Paetus' secretary had named Attianus as the controlling agent. Commodous had written to Hadrian immediately detailing the information. And now that Commodous had reined in the moneylenders and other corruption, Attianus seemed to be on the back foot. But personally, Ratho wouldn't trust the likes of him – while he still lived.

A cool breeze blew in from the sea, and the general turned to walk back the way he had come, heading for his office. The market place had been scrubbed clean, all traces of spilt blood removed, the stalls in their accustomed places, the stallholders crying their wares. But there was something subdued about the people there, doing their business under the watchful eyes of Ratho's veterans. Only the squabbling of the seabirds as they fought over fish heads and guts was truly normal.

A disturbance made him look up. A body of men, several hundred strong, were moving into the great market square. They wore the black cloaks of the Guard. There was no pretence here, no subterfuge: the men clearly bore the uniform and insignia of the Praetorian Guard. Buyers and sellers quickly made themselves scarce, leaving the field to the combatants.

For a moment, Ratho was shocked. The Praetorians were answerable only to the Emperor. For them to desert their guard duties at the imperial palace and buildings and to move about Rome in military formation was treasonable – without direct orders from Hadrian! But then he reflected. With Hadrian a thousand miles away, there was another controlling force in Rome...

Ratho Livianus ordered his men into formation. The Praetorian Guard were an elite body, representing the finest in the Roman army but his veterans were battle-scarred, seasoned and well used to the tricks of war. He rubbed his hands with satisfaction at the prospect. The veterans were now in position, adopting their formation almost instinctively after their years in the field. And was there indecision in the face of the Praetorian commander?

Captain Drusus of the Praetorian Guard stood before General Ratho Livianus.

"General Ratho Livianus, it is a surprise to see you sir. However I have orders to arrest you and your men."

"Upon whose authority?" asked General Livianus.

"The Emperor of Rome of course," replied Captain Drusus.

The general walked forward and lowering his voice to a whisper spoke directly to Captain Drusus.

"My dear Captain, I am under direct orders from Hadrian himself. It is Attianus who has exercised his powers beyond his charge."

Captain Drusus, looked into the eyes of Ratho. He knew, before his retirement Ratho had been one of Trajans most trusted Generals: a man who had served in the inner circle of Trajan's military command for over 30 years. A veteran who had campaigned against almost every known tribe and whom Drusus himself had served under in the Sixteenth Legion before joining the Guard.

However Attianus orders were specific. Kill the Roman veterans in the port of Ostia and restore control. Bring their leader back to him.

"I am sorry sir. Will you allow us to arrest you and your men without any unnecessary fighting?" asked Captain Drusus.

He knew the answer before Ratho even spoke a word. The tired eyes and wariness of the general answered.

"One day Captain, you will make a decision that affects both your future and that of the Empire. Our highly ambitious prefect of Rome knows no limit to his treason. I cannot stand by and let my loyalty for Rome be bought so cheaply."

But then the ranks of Guards moved aside and two *turmae* of Praetorian cavalry thundered into the square, *spathae* out as they charged the veterans. Ratho sighed. It was typical of Attianus to have left nothing to chance. Well, better to die like this than in a bed somewhere in his dotage...

Ratho glared at Captain Drusus once more.

And then the market place was full of movement, swords clanging against swords and clashing against body armour, shearing through body parts, the cavalry backed up by the Praetorian infantry coming on at a run. Soon the fight was over, as quickly as it had begun. The paving stones were once again slick with bright blood, corpses lay slumped on the floor and heaped over one another, opened bodies steaming in the cold, the groans and screams of the wounded tearing the air.

The Praetorian commander looked around at the carnage with grim satisfaction. Several of his Guards moved forward holding Ratho Livianus captive. He nodded and gave orders to have him taken to the rear; then he gestured a man forward from the edge of the market. Nautius Rullus stepped over the blood and the bodies and joined the officer.

"They gave a good account of themselves," said the sailor.

"Yes," observed the Captain Drusus. "They fought bravely and well, as I expected. But the outcome was never in doubt."

Captain Drusus strode about, issuing orders, calling for doctors to attend to his wounded, stationing guards throughout the market, docks and port. He looked back again at Natuius Rullus and waved him forward, a couple of his soldiers joining him.

Captain Drusus was still thinking about what Ratho had said to him and would continue to do so.

I cannot stand by and let my loyalty for Rome be bought so cheaply he had remembered. Drusus looked down at the blood on the ground before him.

This was Roman blood, a soldier's blood. These veterans believed themselves to be protecting Rome now. What had he done?

*

Around twenty-four hours later and a thousand miles to the west, a lookout on the ramparts of fortress Eboracum saw something in the distance. He looked again, shading his eyes with his hand, then he called the alert. The column was returning.

The regulation challenge rang out, and from below the battlements, the answering shout returned.

"*Praefectus Equitatus* Juventius, two turmae of cavalry. Password Jupiter."

The gate swung open and the column entered. Juventius reported to the officer at the gate and headed to his quarters for a much-needed wash and change of clothes. The officer headed in the opposite direction, to the quarters of the legate.

At that moment, Marcus was one of the few who had failed to notice the return. He was in the infirmary, watching Diocles prepare his staff, having them sharpen and burnish the saws and other medical instruments, instructing orderlies in a dozen other tasks. There had been no official word from the legate, no dispatch from Juventius' column to say how it was faring or when it was expected back, but camp rumour had a way of interpreting reality. And while Marcus watched the bustle and hubbub in the hospital, he found time to see Cornelia after the stress of their recent adventure.

A *decurio* entered, flushed from running, "Excuse me, sir, the column has returned. The Legate requests your presence in his quarters at once."

He smiled at Cornelia, and their fingers, which had been touching, moved apart. He left the infirmary and walked out into the tenuous sunshine of the fort. The legate's sentry ushered him in to the presence of the Praetorium, and he entered, saluting.

The legate addressed the two officers present.

"What report do you bring?" said the legate neutrally.

Juventius began to speak, "Sir we have been unable to find any trace of the enemy or locate their position and strength. However I have seen the fort at Coria which the Brigantes have attacked. There were no survivors".

The legate remained quiet. Finally, the report came to an end. Silence filled the room until it was shattered by the legate slamming his hand down onto his desk.

The legate stood, glaring at Juventius, considering his words, "I am disappointed, Prefect. I was hoping for more. As you know the campaigning season is coming to an end. I was hoping we could wait until summer to plan our next move. However we cannot let this incident go unanswered.

Juventius added, "Sir we could not conduct a protracted campaign in this weather. The roads are passable but the fields have turned into a glutinous mud that would be hard enough for the infantry and calvary but impossible to the wheeled transport."

"I understand your concerns" nodded the legate. "My plan would be to push north up the Via Domitiana and camp at Trimontium."

Juventius remembered the name of the fort at the three hills near the river. The site had been used by General Agricola as a camp some 20 years before.

"We shall establish our forward command base there and seek to deny these barbarians any further hit and run attacks. We shall plan our operations from there to engage the enemy and destroy them where we find them."

The legate paused, stroking his chin.

"Pass the word to the other officers. We will have a military counsel tomorrow. We shall hunt down and destroy this enemy and return this region to our control. I will not have it said that the northern Frontier is an uncontrolled outpost."

The legate looked at them, and then glanced away. "Dismissed men".

The two officers saluted and left the legate's quarters.

Juventius shook his head at Marcus, "this is not going to be easy, the campaigning season is over. The weather and the Brigantes will both be against us."

Chapter XVIII: The Politics of Discontent

There was a buzz of expectation in the Curia. Once again, the chamber was filled nearly to capacity. By now, everyone had heard of the activities in the port area – and the almost unprecedented action of the Praetorian Guard in the streets of Rome itself. Under normal circumstances, reflected Commodus, there would be anger, raised voices, a sense of outrage. But there was no such thing, only a sort of subdued anticipation of the next move in the game.

Senate Consul Petronius Ovidius entered. The usual rituals were observed, the Augur consulted. Then he faced the senators.

"Gentlemen," he said. "Everyone here knows what happened at Ostia four days ago. I have invited Publius Acilius Attianus, Prefect of Rome, to address you and explain the situation."

The tension increased to fever pitch. Everyone craned forward as the prefect entered the chamber. He showed no sign of discomfiture as he walked forward at a ceremonial pace. He stood, looking around him. Whenever he entered the Senate, he experienced a feeling of irritation. Here was a place, the most important in Rome, that he did not control – that he did not even have a right to enter without an invitation or a summons. And yet that could change. The emperor could attend the Senate meetings whenever he wished. His eyes rested briefly on the empty chair between the two consuls. He looked up, and found himself meeting the gaze of Commodus.

"Senators of Rome," he said. "You will know what took place earlier this week. I need not say that I deployed the Praetorian Guard only after the most serious consideration. But in the end, I felt I had no choice. Once I explain the situation, I am sure that you will agree. Rogue factions had taken over the port and were artificially raising the prices of everyday commodities. As you know, that is the one sure way to get the populace to complain and perhaps, to revolt."

There were murmurs of agreement, of recognition that prices had been rising rapidly.

"Corruption was rife. There was bribery, intimidation of ordinary citizens – and increasingly, of patricians. It was a disease in the body of the Empire – and it had to be excised, before the limb itself perished."

Blandinus stood, "I am sure that this House is grateful for your prompt and effective actions, Prefect," he said, to a groundswell of approval. To Commodus, the sound was strangely like the bleating of sheep.

Another senator, seated on the other side of the chamber, rose, "May I speak?"

"The Senate recognises Quintus Gario," said Ovidius.

"No one here would oppose the suppression of bribery and corruption," said Gario, "but as the Prefect well knows, the deployment of an army within the City of Rome is prohibited, from time immemorial. When Julius Caesar himself crossed the Rubicon with his army over one hundred and sixty years ago, it precipitated the *Senatus consultum ultimum,* and plunged Rome into civil war."

A wave of noise broke as the senators considered those words and that history. It was as if many of them were remembering powers they had almost forgotten.

"My dear Gario," said Attianus smoothly, "there is no cause for alarm. No army has entered the City. Indeed, if you consult your senatorial constitution, I believe you will find that the Praetorian Guard is in fact stationed here in Rome." There was laughter in the Curia at that remark. "Nor was an army deployed, or anything like it. It was less than a century of infantry, and a mere two *turmae* of cavalry. Just enough to guarantee that the threat could be dispelled – and with the minimum loss of life. Those traitors merited swift retribution."

Cheers of approval greeted this. Attianus flushed with pleasure.

"I would like to say on behalf of the Senate that we are fortunate indeed to have an authority in the City we can rely on; especially in these uncertain times," said a senator near to Blandinus.

A surge of approbation filled the hall. Another senator rose.

"The Senate recognises Sextus Scaevola."

"And what of the future?" asked Scaevola. "Will the Praetorian Guard remain on the streets indefinitely – to guard against some future unspecified threat?"

"Not at all, Senator," said Attianus blithely. "They remain on guard in the port area, to prevent any further demonstrations by traitors. As soon as the area is fully secure and Rome is once more under complete control, the

Guard will be ordered back to its barracks. As everyone in this House would expect. They will not take to the streets again unless there is a threat of equal or greater magnitude to this City."

There was more of the same, approval on one side, questions and uncertainty on the other; but the longer the debate continued, the more secure the Prefect was.

"May I add that I have ordered a full investigation of this incident," said Attianus. "If there are any other perpetrators of this revolt still in hiding, they will be rooted out and the evidence laid before this House."

There was widespread approval; senator after senator rose to give thanks and appreciation for the City Prefect's actions.

Finally, Attianus looked steadily around the Curia, "If that is all, Senators, I will leave you to your deliberations."

Attianus looked at Commodous Verus and smiled faintly. "I leave you with my pledge of assurance that, should any danger threaten the Senators and the People of Rome, I will not flinch from meeting it – with all the force my authority gives me."

He bowed to the assembly and left the building, shouts of acclamation ringing in his ears. Commodus watched him as he walked away, a spring in his step.

*

Hundreds of miles to the east, the Emperor of Rome waited in a barge in the middle of the Orontes River, the water reflecting back the late autumn sunshine.

Everything about the scene reflected the full panoply of state: the ship bedecked with pennants and flags, the imperial bodyguard in gleaming and burnished armour, unit after unit of the Praetorian Guard lined up on the shore. Despite the sunshine, the breeze off the river was cool.

"I suppose we can trust them?" asked Hadrian, with a gesture at the ranks of Praetorian Guards.

"These men with us, I can vouch for their loyalty myself," said Turbo. "Have you any reason to be concerned?"

Hadrian smiled wanly. "No," he said; "but the Praetorians have often been a law unto themselves. And these are uncertain times."

Trumpets blew a fanfare from the shore, and a magnificent ship of state began putting out into the Orontes.

"There he is," said Hadrian.

"The renowned Parthian punctuality."

They watched as the ship was rowed out at ceremonial pace, the bank of oars rising and falling as one.

"An impressive setting," said Turbo.

"Yes. And meeting on the river like this gives it an air of neutrality. We're meeting as equals, not as king and vassal. That's important in their eyes."

After what seemed a long wait, the ship lay alongside the imperial barge and their hulls were lashed together. The Parthian king, accompanied by his chief ministers and advisers, stepped aboard to another fanfare of trumpets.

The formal greetings and salutations over, Hadrian and the king sat down together. He looked at him: a strong man, in his prime, with a full, black beard. Hadrian could see pride in his eyes, a respect for his own place in history as the representative of the Arsacid dynasty.

The emperor waved a servant over, and fine wine was served in golden goblets.

"And now to business," began Hadrian. "I now formally confirm that I will support Parthia as a client kingdom – and you as its king."

"Thank you, Emperor," said the king, stroking his beard. "There is still some disorder in some of the provinces, but I will put it down."

"I will leave a small garrison of troops at your disposal."

They discussed the details, and finally the king seemed to be almost content with the arrangements.

"You have my word as Emperor of Rome that I will not overturn today's agreement or interfere with your governance – as long as you remember who put you on your throne."

The king bowed, and the conversation turned to other matters: the tribute from the king, advantageous trading terms for foodstuffs, gold and other commodities.

Finally, the conference was at an end and the Parthian King gathered his advisers and returned to his own vessel. A final trumpet fanfare came to them from the shore.

Turbo rejoined his friend, and found him mopping his brow.

"Warm work?" he grinned, pouring out some more wine and handing a goblet to Hadrian.

"Diplomacy always is," he grimaced. "Give me an army to lead, and I'm your man – not all this dancing around the subject!"

"You are Rome's man, sire."

Hadrian sipped his wine. "The king wasn't so sure. I could see it in his eyes: the merest hint that he might have someone else to deal with, before the year's out."

Turbo poured himself a goblet. "Well, it doesn't matter what he thinks."

"No – unless he turns out to be right!"

Back on land and in the imperial palace in Antioch, they gathered around a large map of the empire. Hadrian spanned it quickly with his hands.

"For now, we will keep the Empire's boundaries in place. I want no further expansion; the army is already overstretched."

Turbo lifted several dispatches, "The Judean situation is worsening, Caesar."

Hadrian frowned. "Yes – at any sign of uncertainty, there are jackals out there willing to take their chance. When will the Twenty fifth Appollinaris leave here?"

"They're being mustered now. I have the report here."

"Good. It can't be soon enough for me, " Hadrian affirmed, "Judea needs an iron fist – and the *Twenty Fifth* is just the legion to wield it!

A secretary knocked, entered, handed Hadrian a report and bowed himself out.

"Ha!"

"Caesar?"

"It's from Commodus. He's had Ratho clear the port of Ostia of these rebels and installed our own men there. He's also...yes, he's gained control of the moneylenders... taking measures to bring the prices of commodities down. Excellent! There are more detailed reports on the Senate meetings; I'll read those tonight."

"It all sounds encouraging," said Turbo.

"It does, old friend. Perhaps the Gods are finally smiling on us!

*

Although this prison was clean and free of other inmates, its purpose was unmistakable. The face of the Prefect of Rome was dark – but darker still was the bruised and bloodied visage of the general, his beaten and damaged frame suspended by ropes. His breathing came heavily as he hung by his wrists, waiting for Attianus to speak.

At length, Attianus did: "Do you wish now that you died at Ostia, Ratho Livianus?"

"All must die, " the general gasped, through broken teeth and bloodied lips, " The time and place are of no importance."

Attianus drew an ornamental dagger from his belt and moved its blade gently over Ratho's cheek, "Perhaps so. And yet, and yet...was not dying on the field of battle more fitting for a man of arms? Where is the honour in this situation?"

Ratho breathed stertorously for a moment, as if summoning enough breath to spit out his next words: "There is honour enough in resisting a tyrant."

Attianus laughed, "A tyrant? Hardly. There is no more reasonable man than I."

Ratho snorted in reply.

"Yes, you may scoff, General. But all I want is a quiet life, to go about my business and tend to my concerns. It is you, and those whom you represent, who are – unreasonable."

Attianus walked over to the barred window high up in the wall. The setting sun had stained the sky a delicate warm orange-pink, and some birds sang to each other in a tree nearby.

"Such beauty, and so fleeting. For you. Unless you tell me what I want to know. I have prepared a series of questions, and if you prefer that this evening is not your last on this earth, you will answer them."

Ratho lowered his head as though to rest it, "You may put aside your questions. I have nothing to say to any of them. All I will say is that the treatment I have received is illegal. I am a Roman citizen. I have rights: the right to a trial, the right to be questioned without..."

"Rights!" roared Attianus. "You have *no* rights save those that I grant you. *I* am in command in this city." He moved back to his chair and sat down, "So you refuse to be reasonable. Well, it's a pity, but I know what I need to know anyway. You are in the pay of Commodus, and he is under the rule of Hadrian – the absentee Emperor!"

"He will not always be absent."

"Hadrian is like me, I think. We both understand power and the balance of force. And as for you underlings, you need to be taught these things. Ratho Livianus, by leading a force against the rightfully appointed authorities in the port, you are guilty of treason. And there is but one penalty for treason."

"My guilt or innocence will be determined at my trial."

Attianus gave a bitter smile, "Trial? You have had your trial, General. Verdict has been given. Have you any last words?"

The general raised his head at that, and looked steadily at the prefect: "Yes. Your time is coming fast."

Attianus made a motion to the guards. One grabbed a fistful of Ratho's hair and jerked his head back. The guard in front of the general drew his sword and held it against Ratho's neck.

"And your time has come," said Attianus, gesturing for the kill.

The guard slashed his blade through Ratho's neck and blood fountained out into the prison floor. Attianus stepped back quickly, but not quickly enough. He looked down at his blood-spattered tunic. The guard stared at him with undisguised fear. Attianus stood for a moment, watching the spirit flow out of the general's body. Then his corpse hung limply from the ropes.

He spoke to a servant, "Bring me a cloth."

The servant leapt to comply and the prefect took the cloth and wiped his face. He looked down at the former general's lifeblood on his hands, then tossed the cloth from him.

"Bring me a bowl of fresh water." He turned to the servant again. "We'll return to my palace. Give orders to send the captain of the Praetorian Guard to me there."

*

At the palace, Attianus spent longer than usual bathing. It had somehow been difficult to remove all traces of blood from his neck and arms – almost as if that minion of Hadrian's had reached out to him, and marked him... He dismissed the thought with impatience. That was the whole thing about blood, at least other people's blood: it wasn't permanent.

Dressed in finery again, he awaited the arrival of the Captain Drusus of the Praetorian Guard, gazing out into the courtyard, where a pleasant breeze wafted through the open door like the last sigh of autumn.

"Vitruvius Drusus," announced his secretary.

A big, burly man entered the room, almost crowding it. The City Prefect looked at him, at his shrewd eyes. *Yes*, he thought, *There is a man who would betray me, if it was worth his while. But while the money is right, there is no one more loyal.*

And if he acted precipitately, this man knew what would come to him, from those whose loyalty to Attianus was unimpeachable.

"Greetings, Drusus."

"Hail, Prefect."

"How is the general ?" asked Drusus.

"The rat is dead" smiled Attianus.

Nothing more was said on the matter.

Attianus gave the man his orders and knew there was no need to task informants with reporting that they were being carried out. He could see in his mind's eye the well-drilled Guards patrolling the port, enforcing the curfew, cordoning off certain areas of the City.

At length, Drusus saluted, bowed and left the chamber. He still thought of Ratho's last words.

*

Over the port of Ostia, a fug of unease hung like an oppressive heat of summer, suffocating the life-breath of the city as the day went on, until, shimmering like haze on a dusty road, it played tricks and deceived the eye. The dockworkers and sailors worked under a cloud of tension and suspicion, unnerved by the presence of the Praetorian troops, fully armed, now stationed at the port to oversee developments. The workers kept their heads down, moving like wraiths through the dockyards, wary of being seen, and shot reptilian glances at one another under the steely glares of the guards.

The other citizens and slaves of Rome were also uneasy at the unaccustomed visible presence of the Praetorian Guard, still mobilised on the streets. Only the most elderly people could recall these troops appearing in such strength in the streets of Rome. There were mutterings amongst the people of the oppression of living in a military state. To the average person on the street, unaware of the political nuances, such visible force was a sign of the Emperor Hadrian's personal oppression of the people. Since they were the imperial guard whose primary purpose was the protection of the Emperor's person – who else could have ordered them here? That Hadrian... what a tyrant!

*

Hadrian, preoccupied, paced the room, and then turned his acute attention to Turbo, "Turbo, I cannot wait for Commodus and Ratho to respond to my requests for information on affairs in Rome. I am eager to return."

"But is that wise, under current circumstances?"

"Once this Parthian situation has settled down, it is time to return to Rome."

"With such unrest still at the Judean borders?" Turbo frowned.

"And, also, in Rome," Hadrian added, "We shall return with several legions. Then we'll see who has the stomach for a fight in the capital – if anyone!" he grinned, "But we must be sure of the Praetorians. Their action – one way or the other – could decide history."

"And Attianus is the head of the Praetorian Guard," Turbo shook his head.

"He is, but I've ordered Commodus to raise sufficient funds to give them cause to consider whose side they are on." He threw over a scroll.

Turbo unrolled it, then whistled, "A million denari!"

"Yes. Should give them – and whoever is behind all this – something to think about."

*

Gracchus the moneylender wiped the sweat from his brow in the stuffy anteroom of Attianus' grand home, and noticed that his hand was trembling. He had been summoned by a servant of the City Prefect, who had demanded that he accompany him at once to his master. He had been peremptorily marched through the streets, left here to bake, and had hardly had time to catch his breath before the Prefect himself swept open the chamber door.

"Gracchus – enter!" Attianus' tone was clipped and authoritative.

Inside the room, Attianus wasted no time with petty formalities.

"Did I not expressly ask you to raise the interest rate on lending?"

"Yes, you did, Sir, but..."

"And why, then, have you done exactly the opposite?" Attianus queried, tight-lipped.

"Senator Commodus..."

"What? Commodus? What has he to do with it?" Attianus' eyes flashed.

Taken aback by this uncharacteristic outburst from a man who always kept his emotions in check, Gracchus found himself gabbling out words, 'The Emperor sent orders that we should reduce borrowing rates to facilitate spending amongst the people of Rome, Sir.'

Attianus turned away, his mind quickly calculating meaning, implications and response. After a second, he turned around so quietly now, that Gracchus was more unnerved by this calm, than by any fury.

"The Emperor is not here... but I am. He is far away in the provinces, and far too busy to know the fine detail of the local economic situation in Rome. His news travels slowly and is greatly out of date. He does not understand the situation. As Prefect of Rome, my duty is to run the province and oversee the economy in the Emperor's name and – de facto – my word is law."

Gracchus swallowed, his mouth dry, "You wish for me to go against the Emperor's decision."

"Come, come, Gracchus – you have a mind of your own – surely?"

Gracchus stood unable to answer.

Attianus took a step closer to Gracchus and whispered in his ear: "Choose which side you are on," he stepped back. "And choose fast."

He smiled benignly, chilling Gracchus to the bone.

*

Attianus clapped his hands and his rat-like secretary appeared again, "My lord?"

Attianus laughed softly, "bring me some fruit: some grapes, perhaps. There is a taste in my mouth I seem unable to rid myself of."

The grapes were quickly brought, ripe and purple from the hothouses. He picked up a small bunch and fingered their taut skins, then raised them to his mouth. Cool sweetness filled his senses. His chief thought was of the house of Lucius Ceionius Commodus Verus, as stately and imposing as befitted an elder statesman and a confidant of the emperor. That lavish home was about to become a prison cell.

*

When Commodus' servant, Cato, opened the front door, he was horrified to see four huge Praetorian guards standing in the entrance, blocking out the sun.

"We are here to see Senator Lucius Ceionius Commodus Verus."

"I'm sorry, but my master..." began the servant, only to be flung back against the wall by a leathery arm, as the first of the guards strode through the door and towards Commodus' private chambers, followed by his burly colleagues.

The first thing Commodus knew, seated on a couch, dictating to his secretary, was the rush of air and slam of his door being flung open, and the four Praetorian guards bursting through, fully armoured; although thankfully, their weapons were sheathed.

"How dare you? What rudeness brings you forth?" cried Commodus, aghast at the intrusion. His secretary stood pale and quaking at his side.

"Senator Lucius Ceionius Commodus Verus," spoke the first guard, unfurling a parchment, from which he announced, "By the imperial authority..."

"By Hadrian?" cried Commodus, in surprise.

Captain Drusus glared, "By the imperial authority of the Prefect Publius Acilius Attianus, for the safety and security of Rome, it is hereby pronounced that Senator Lucius Ceionius Commodus Verus be held under house arrest until further notice."

"What?" Commodus' quick mind flew through several emotions, "This is an outrage! Upon what charge am I to be held prisoner in my own home?"

Captain Drusus presented Commodus with the parchment, "On suspicion of treason."

The secretary gasped and clutched his robes to his chest. Treason meant certain death.

"Ridiculous!" Commodus burst out. He considered the irony of this accusation by the initiator of this act – Attianus – but dared not speak aloud, adding slander to his alleged crime. *If ever there was a traitor against the Empire – it is the Prefect himself!*

"Is it not usual," began Commodus, narrowing his eyes, "That a suspect of such a serious crime as treason should be arrested and immediately brought before a court for public trial?"

"Our instructions are to hold you under house arrest until further notice," the Captain stated firmly.

The guards stood silent, in attendance. Commodus appraised the situation and decided on his approach. He looked from one to the other, scrutinising their steely glares for any sign of empathy or humanity. He saw a flicker in one, which might be useful.

"So be it," Commodus sighed, in resignation. "Although I cannot accept the crime, I accept my situation."

"Wisely done, Sir," nodded Drusus.

"So how does this work?" smiled Commodus, amiably. "Do you need to shackle me by the neck to my couch like a slave? Or do we take wine together, as civilised human beings?"

"Sir, you are subject to our protection and oversight, but otherwise our instructions are to keep you within these walls and allow you to live your domestic life as you wish. Within reason," said Drusus.

"It is only your political life that is curtailed!" sneered another guard. The Captain gave him a sharp look that wiped the snigger from his face.

Commodus snapped his fingers to attract the attention of the concerned servant hovering in the doorway; Cato was winded by the guards' harsh entry, but recovered enough to support his master. He entered and poured wine quickly into the goblets on the sideboard, and stood attentively with the wine on a tray.

"Come, gentlemen," Commodus cheered, suddenly, "If you are to be guests in my home, at least let me show you some hospitality!"

One guard raised an eyebrow to the Captain, who answered, "Well, lads. We may be here some time."

Commodus raised a cup in a toast, "To the Empire!"

The guards could not refuse such a commendation and joined him in raising their goblets. In fact, Commodus' hospitality was such that after he had called for food, and more wine, the Praetorian guards settled in comfortably for the night, well-pleased with their duties on this occasion.

And so it was, that when Commodus excused himself to use the *fornicae*, the privy in the kitchen, one of the guards accompanied him but was distracted by the rosemary-scented sight of a hot roasted chicken on the table, fresh from the oven.

The guard's mouth was already watering, and since the servant Cato was occupied, filling a bucket with water ready to flush Commodus' toilet waste, the guard needed no extra coaxing to serve himself, and commenced to tear at the best of the succulent meat, its crisp skin gleaming.

His back turned for a moment, while Commodus squatted, it gave him time to write the few words of a hasty note with his bronze dyptichon on the small wax sheet of the folded wooden writing tablet he had secreted about his robes.

When Cato came over with the bucket to flush the waste, Commodus urgently pressed the wooden tablet into the servant's hand, and hissed beneath his breath, "Senate Consul Petronius Ovidius!"

Cato nodded discreetly, and slipped the tablet beneath his tunic with one deft hand, whilst swilling the water through the privy to the cess pool below.

The guard turned his oily face to the pair, grease running down his chin, as he waved a chicken leg, "I prefer to stand here with the scent of cooking than over there! Senator sewage will quite put me off my eating!"

"Nothing puts you off eating!" the gruff voice of Drusus announced his entrance into the kitchen.

Commodus stepped forward, "You fellows have terrific appetites! I am embarrassed that my humble home has not been set up this day to cater for such guests. I must send out for more food and wine. Please tell my servant if there is anything you most desire, and he will go most swiftly about this business." He caught Cato's eye in understanding.

The guards gave their elaborate wish-list, taking advantage to the full of this old senator's disadvantaged state and generosity, although the Drusus cast him a look of suspicion.

"Do not be mistaken. We serve the Prefect of Rome and cannot be bought by sweetmeats and fine wine."

Commodus nodded graciously, "I would not have it any other way, Captain."

Cato slipped easily outside: a shopping list in his head, the folded tablet in his tunic.

*

As soon as Attianus strode into the Senate chamber, he surveyed the bustling individuals on the benches with satisfaction. There appeared to be several empty seats, and most notably those of Commodus and Gario. Attianus smiled graciously at the senators still present, who watched him warily but silent. No-one questioned his presence, and when he spoke, no-one dared debate.

Attianus gave a beaming smile as he addressed the cowed senators, "We have witnessed that since the Praetorian Guard have been on the streets of Rome, there is no longer unrest and bloodshed, and peace reigns at last."

Murmurs from some of the senators, but no individual was distinct enough to draw the attention of the Prefect, preoccupied with declaring his control of the situation.

"Since the Emperor absents himself..." Much jeering and castigation from his audience, "...to make friendship with our enemies on the borders..." A greater roar of disapproval from the senators... "It behoves us to secure Rome until treachery is wiped out and Roman people can live their lives without fear again!"

An acknowledgement repeated from the senators moved by his speech.

Even the Senate Consul Petronius Ovidius composed himself and contained his dissatisfaction, allowing Attianus his head. For Ovidius knew that it might be six days before his message about Commodus, Ratho and the affairs of Rome reached Hadrian, with the gods' speed. It could be another week before any response was to be expected from that direction: ideally, Hadrian's return. It would be worth Ovidius biding his time, since he had seen the fate of those who openly questioned Attianus' authority. He did not wish to share that fate. His loyalty to the Roman Empire would manifest itself in other ways.

*

The beds in the hospital's central room were unoccupied, yet the doctor's face lacked his accustomed smile at this situation.

"You seem dissatisfied," said Cornelia.

The leathery face of the doctor creased into a smile: "No, Cornelia," he said, "It's wonderful to have nothing to do – and I know that much of the credit for that situation is yours." His smile faded away, "But an old campaigner like me can already see those beds full of wounded men – indeed, three times as many beds crowded into this hospital, and still more, maimed and mutilated soldiers lying on the floor, or up against the walls."

"There has been no official word, has there?" said the dark-haired nurse.

"Yes all troops are leaving tomorrow at first light. We are to stay here along with some of the auxiliaries troops and the Third Cohort. The legion will march north, and set up a winter camp. This will be no easy march and no easy task in this weather."

"You are a soothsayer, then?" There was a teasing hint in her voice. He smiled again, wryly. "No, Nurse. Not a fortune teller – just someone who has seen this sort of thing too many times.But either way, this hospital will be full to overflowing before the end."

He looked around the well-kept chamber, noting its especially spruce and smart appearance as a result of Cornelia's ministrations.

"We should make use of this lull before the storm to build up our supplies. You mentioned that unusually efficacious maggots were to be had from the market in Eboracum. And lime as well, I think, for its purifying qualities."

"Yes, Doctor."

"Go and purchase some. And here is a list of herbs that need replenishing. Let me give you some money from the medical chest." He drew out of a bureau a bag of money, handing it to her with the list.

She nodded, "I pray to Fortuna that these will not be needed."

He sighed. "I pray so too, Cornelia. But I fear that our petitions will end up in the court of Mars."

She nodded, pulled on a cloak and left the hospital. He stood in the middle of the room, distracted for a moment; and then moved over to sort through his stores of medicines.

*

In Rome, the Praetorians continued to patrol certain streets, and even the most illustrious citizens of Rome were under curfew. No-one but soldiers were allowed on the streets after nightfall, under Attianus' decree, and rumblings of discontent were bubbling up from a façade of submission. Evidence of Attianus ruling under a state of oppression was becoming clear for all to see, and there was only so much the people could take. Yet it had only been Commodus who managed to send word to Hadrian of the dire current affairs in Rome.

Gradually, even the political corruption and bribery of the senate and governing officials at the ports and in the city were obvious not only to certain loyal senators and the higher echelons of citizenry alone – but to the proletariat themselves, and to any slaves who had mind to give it a thought. Rome was sick. Something must be done.

*

Since Hadrian had already begun to plan his return to Rome, and was fixed in his determination, Turbo advised, "It is likely that there will be armed rebellion,Caesar. Better to take two legions with you, at least – depending on which way the wind has blown the Praetorian Guard. We have made the preparations for marching into the city for battle if need be."

"The Tenth Legion – the favourites of Julius Caesar, and loyal to the core – were ever-ready to fight for the Emperor's cause. They were issued orders to leave Antioch this night" affirmed Turbo.

"I have also called the Eighth Augusta from Gallia to supplement the force marching upon Rome" added Turbo.

Hadrian nodded. Two Legions marching to take back Rome from Attianus.

Would it be enough? Would the guard fight against their own Emperor?

"Let us hope that a million denarii say the wind blows favourably for us!" Hadrian said, grimly.

"Rest assured, Caesar, that we will leave nothing to chance. We must be prepared for all circumstances" warned Turbo.

They set off from Antioch to the port of Seleucia. Six triremes were waiting to take them on the two week journey back to Rome.

Hadrian looked out over the figure head of Egeria,the water godess carved on the prow of the boat.Turbo and Hadrian nodded at each other. Attianus's fate is coming to him thought Hadrian.

*

About the noonday hour, Marcus entered the hospital and surveyed the empty beds.

"Something amiss?" asked Diocles, appearing from an inner room and breaking in on his thoughts. "Any sprains, twinges or aches? I'll put you right for the battle ahead!"

Marcus grinned. "No, Doctor, I am well."

"There can be only one reason for a well man to visit the infirmary – and I'm sure it isn't to talk to me!"

Marcus laughed, "Where is she?"

"I sent her to the market to buy herbs and other necessaries."

"Very well, I'll look for her there. I hope that my men and I won't need your services in the coming days, Doctor."

Diocles bowed his head in acquiescence as the cavalry commander left the room.

Marcus strode back to the officer's quarters and called for a horse. Two of his officers appeared with information about the mustering of the cavalry, but his thoughts were elsewhere. When the mount was brought over to him he saluted his officers, leapt into the saddle and rode over to the main gate.

*

When word reached Attianus that Hadrian and his legions were marching upon Rome, he smirked with satisfaction. Whether they expected to face the Praetorian Guard or not, he was confident that Hadrian's men would be hacked down by his elite force, still under his pay and command, leaving the absentee emperor as vulnerable as a slave. Public and political opinion was now on Attianus' side. The people favoured a leader who was present in the city, wielding his strength – rather than a faceless man who spent all his time abroad, ignoring his own country's affairs. Attianus had already planned his coronation speech – revealing his plans to extend the Empire again – always a popular proposition to the citizenry. The Roman Empire would advance once more, and Attianus' glorious name would go down in the annals of history!

SPQR

*Self control is the chief element in self respect, and
self respect is the chief element in courage.*

Thucydides

Chapter XIX: The North Wind

8.15am, 16ᵗʰ December, 117AD: outside Fortress Eboracum, Northern Britain

The fleeting sunshine of the morning had disappeared as the clouds massed over Eboracum, and a cold wind buffeted Marcus's face. He searched in the usual places he might have expected to find Cornelia, the market stalls, and even the inn, but without success. He continued to look, exploring streets he'd never even known had existed, but still with nothing to show for his efforts. A frown began to appear on his brow.

Part of his mind was concerned with the action to come. At first light tomorrow, virtually the whole legion would be starting north to take the adventure that the gods had prepared for them. He was aware that matters of great portent hung on the next few days, with the legion representing a bulwark against barbarism in this remote country. Perhaps, too, there would be a chance to distinguish himself in battle, win renown and put some of the horrors of the last months behind him... but it was no good. His mind refused to focus on the past or on the future. It was the present that preoccupied him, and Cornelia.

He was distracted by some commotion ahead. Two men, shopkeepers by their appearance, were running towards him. One had blood on his clothing.

"Soldier, come!" said the uninjured one, in the imperfect Latin of the townspeople. The shopkeeper seized Marcus' horse's bridle and pulled it from his hand impatiently.

"Let me go. I have urgent business. Find guards from the fort."

"But soldier, barbarians from north – they came, stole woman –"

"A woman?" Marcus' stomach turned over in dread.

"She buy herbs at my shop. They take her, threw her on horse."

"What was her appearance?" Marcus cursed the blank looks that his question threw back at him, "Was she tall or short? Fair or dark hair?"

"Tall, dark."

"Where?" Nausea further rose in Marcus' throat, but he had to be sure.

They led the mounted prefect into a warren of small streets and shops. He dismounted, tied his horse and followed them on foot, urging them on faster.

They entered a shop that was greatly disordered, the door broken and products strewn around the floor.

"She fight," explained the first man.

"I try help," the second looked down ruefully at his bloodied clothing.

Marcus knelt and glanced about him. The straw covering the floor was spattered with drops of blood. He dabbed one finger in it and held it up, horrified.

"Was she harmed?" he cried in alarm.

'Me, blood,' said the injured man, holding up his gashed arm. Marcus found himself able to breathe again.

Then something glittering caught his eye. He picked it up and turned it in the light. There might be many dark-haired women in Eboracum, but surely only one decorative pin like this one. The last time he had seen it, it had fastened Cornelia's cloak to her neck... He stood up quickly and walked outside, his face clouded with concern and determination. The two shopkeepers followed him.

"I help," said the second man once more, dolefully.

Marcus clapped him on the back, "Which direction did they go? Which way?"

The first man pointed to the north. Marcus thanked them, ran back to his horse and leapt astride the saddle. He pulled the reins to turn the horse's head in the direction Cornelia had been taken – and galloped his horse hard to the north.

*

Hadrian and Turbo had not needed the message from Ovidius, having already set off on the long journey from Antioch. However, the arrival of news of Commodus' incarceration and absence from the Senate added further fuel to the fire, which burned for vengeance.

"What!" roared Hadrian, opening another urgent dispatch from senators, this one more detailed, and from Ovidius: "Attianus is once again controlling the port, after much bloody battle – Ratho killed – and Commodus imprisoned and barred from senate! Attianus is filled with hubris enough to challenge the gods! But his overweening pride has gone too far! I warned you, Turbo."

"Did Commodus fully manage the financial transfer to buy the Praetorian Guard, before his demise?" Turbo asked.

"I hope and trust so, Turbo," Hadrian growled, "Else our fate truly lies in the gods' hands, and not our own."

"If he should not stand down before the Emperor of Rome, then he shall suffer our extreme wrath – Guardian and advisor or not!" vowed Hadrian.

Hadrian, Turbo and ten thousand men, all grimly determined to take back Rome, were on their way to march upon the city, prepared for whatever it might take to resume control and to reassert the Emperor Hadrian's power.

*

Cornelia scowled and bit into the leather belt that gagged her into silence, ridiculous that this should be necessary since they were far from the fortress at Eboracum now. She had stopped struggling long before, resigned to her impotence, and with her wrists bound behind her, she relied on the arms of the rough horseman behind her to protect her against falling from the horse and breaking her neck.

She squinted her eyes against the weakening sun and turned her head southwards, from whence she had been captured by the two barbarian outriders. That was the direction from which the legion would advance. There was nothing to be seen of the hundreds of men and horses she expected, no sign of them or anything to suggest that they might even have set off. Did Marcus know she was missing? Somewhere, miles behind, amongst his fellow soldiers he would be busy with battle preparations. Was he giving her a second thought? She hoped so. Cornelia longed for him to be here, like before.

*

At the outer edge of Eboracum, having ridden his steed hard, Marcus came to a panting halt. He looked north again, in the direction the shopkeeper had pointed. There were no signs, no trail to follow. There was nothing on the horizon but a distant forest that he would have to pass through to stand any chance of picking up a trail. All his instincts as a man urged him to follow. All his instincts as a soldier urged him to go back to the fort. He sat still in the saddle, pondering his dilemma.

The wind blew even stronger from the north, whipping his hair about his face. A real winter wind. Boreas, the Greeks called the North Wind. Boreas, the Devouring One. He looked to the north as the wind whistled about him. He could well believe that the howl of the gale was a bad-tempered, vindictive roar.

He had no doubt that the woman who had been carried off was Cornelia — and that her captors were Tobar's men. They would be taking her north, to the bleak lands of Boreas. Whoever had taken Cornelia wanted her alive, otherwise they could have killed her instantly in the herbalist's shop.

If he deserted his post at this critical time, his army career would be over. More importantly, so would his part in this war. And if there was any chance of successfully finding and freeing Cornelia, it would have to be through working as part of the Ninth Legion. His mind made up despite his reluctant heart, he tugged on the reins and turned his horse's head again, but this time to the south — and to Fortress Eboracum.

*

Vordimus cleaned beneath his nails with the point of his dagger, and smiled at Cornelia.

"A firebrand, eh! Just my kind of woman" he said, in perfect Latin.

Cornelia frowned, pretending not to understand.

"Come now, Lady. I know a Roman when I see one. I spent enough time in their company, learning their... ways.

"What is your name?" Vordimus asked.

Cornelia did not reply.

"I ve always wanted a Roman woman – someone to share my enjoyment of life with," he grinned. "Take her further north behind our lines. I will see you later, my pretty one" he smiled.

Cornelia's head whirled around.

"Vordimus, is my name... in case you are wondering."

Cornelia could only wonder.

*

Standing in the legate's offices with the other officers, Marcus' mind was whirling with possibilities. They were to march north upon the enemy. Here was a great opportunity for him to further prove himself in the field. Hadn't he already taken on three men and captured a clan chieftain, only the night before? But with Cornelia's help. And Cornelia – where was she now? Would he be able to rescue her? Two goals ahead, and the process was the same to different ends – find Cornelia, and defeat the barbarians.

"Gentlemen" called the legate to open the war counsel.

The centurions of the Ninth Legion stood to attention in the Praetorium and saluted the legate.

The legate returned the salute and started the briefing.

All officers eyes fell upon the map pinned against the front wall. "As you know our job here in Eboracum is not conquer northern Britannia but to reinforce the status quo. It is to re assure the local tribes here, both Brigantes and Selgovae that their loyalty to Rome is in no way misplaced. We must show that these tribes who rebel against Rome, will be beaten by us once more."

The legate paused. The centurions had expected such an announcement but did not want it.

"Our plan is simple. We will march north up the Via Domitiana, past Coria and the northern outposts beyond the frontier. We will make camp at Trimontium once more and use this as a base for an immediate attack against the tribes as soon as possible. If the barbarians are not forthwith to attack us we shall have the advantage of an early start to the campaigning season next year."

Silence filled the room.

"I shall take three cohorts and a small baggage train with us. The third cohort and two auxiliary units will remain here in Eboracum."

"Legate – we should be careful not to over extend our supply lines", questioned Juventius. "Trimontium is one hundred and fifty miles away and in the immediate centre of the Selgovae and Votadini tribes."

A murmur of agreement revolved around the room of centurions.

"I am well aware of your concerns,' smirked the legate. That is why we are taking a *small* baggage train north. We will not be repairing any forts that have been damaged. We will march north directly and make winter camp there."

Juventious continued "Sir the roads are passable for the horses however the fields are a sea of glutinous mud. We may not even be able to find the enemy."

The legate flew into a rage.

"We shall not delay here any longer. We will make a winter camp at Trimontium. The greater the delay the greater the potential for unrest. Let us get this over with, and march north before the snows of winter approach. Who knows we may meet the enemy on the march north and resolve this uprising."

The legate smirked once again at the thought, "Yes, four weeks from now we may even return back to Eboracum, without annoyance."

Juventius raised one eyebrow, but said nothing.

"Any further questions?" offered the legate.

"We leave at first light tomorrow morning" ordered the legate.

"Dismissed."

The Praefectus Castrorum nodded his head at the other centurions. Rome's prestige was now at stake. Marcus looked at Juventius and understood.

*

The legate had instructed his senior officers to direct all troops to pass through the north gate in preparation for his address. Smoothly, every soldier had silently packed and prepared to leave; first, each infantryman had marched through the open gates, the deafening sound of thousands of boots crunching, in time, on the gravelly roadway to reach the field outside the fortress, where they now stood assembled in serried rows.

There could be no greater sight than a legion fully prepared to march upon its enemies for battle. Every helmet shone, every breastplate gleamed over a valiant heart, and uniformly, every shield was held in the perfect position, ready to form an impenetrable barrier. The great powerful Roman military machine was oiled, primed, and already under operation, with well-timed precision. The cavalrymen then walked their powerful, fresh warhorses through the gates and took up position behind. Banners and flags were whipped up by the northerly wind, but the men stood strong, still and silent. The Ninth Legion was fully assembled before him outside the fortress of Eboracum, all standing to attention, in perfect formation and providing a stirring vista as far as the eye could see. The golden Eagle of the Ninth held proud by the standard bearer was ready to swoop down upon its prey, and its attack would be relentless.

Marcus' thoughts turned to Cornelia and his own guilt. After all, he was responsible for drawing her into his plan to capture the chieftain, and rattling the barbarians' cages. He wondered how long it might be before he saw her again and how she fared this morning. Would she be all right after her ordeal? Was she even alive, still? He only hoped her resourcefulness and strength would see her through her kidnapping and whatever fate awaited her thereafter. His knuckles whitened as he gripped the reins.

As the legate looked down and surveyed the expanse of highly trained men, well-disciplined and fully equipped, in glittering formation, even his stony pebble of a heart swelled with pride.

"Men, our job is to march north and suppress this rebellion, and to take back Roman land in glorious victory."

The men of the Ninth Legion cheered as one.

Leaving the third cohort and two auxiliary units of soldiers at Eboracum under the command of the camp Prefect, the legate had committed himself and his men wholeheartedly to battle against the northern tribesmen. The Ninth Legion was on the march.

Chapter XX: Caesar returns

8.55 am, 17th December, 117AD: outside the walls of Rome, capital of the Empire

It felt good to be back on land again as Hadrian looked around his Tenth Legion. The Tenth legion had been the personal favourites of Julius Caesar and now they were proving themselves to be his, too.

They had sailed from Antioch and landed in Rome after two weeks at sea. When they set foot on Roman soil they had marched north to the start of the Via Flamina, the main road leading right into the heart of Rome. Hadrian had insisted upon this show of pride, power and strength. He would not return to Rome by some minor road.

Now outside the walls of Rome, arrayed in full armour, with the helmet and scarlet cloak of a general, there was no longer any need for Hadrian to disguise himself. The first of his reinforcements, the men of the Eighth Legion, were only a few days' march away and any other general would have waited for them to arrive so that his force would have the maximum number of soldiers.

The Via Flamina led straight to the Porto de Popolo – the People's Gateway – the main gate in the north of the city, which would be heavily defended. Hadrian had not given it a single thought. The Guard were his men; he was their Emperor, and more than that, he had served beside them in the thirty years he had been in the army.

A number of deeds of daring had won him a certain reputation in military service, although had they been performed by a common soldier they might have gone unnoticed. However, he was obviously now of great renown in the army. The favourite story passed from soldier to soldier, and into the annals of history was the tale of when the Danube was swollen by floods. It was on an autumn day, as Hadrian crossed the river on horseback wearing heavy armour and under fire. The Bavarian soldiers beside Hadrian were stuck in the middle of the river, unable to move either forward or back. Hadrian had struggled to cross the raging floods himself and felt the rush of water against his war horse's strong legs. No-one realised the horse's need to escape the river was even stronger than Hadrian's, until it panicked and bolted across the swollen river bed at full speed. Upon seeing their commander charge bravely across, with no thought for his own life, his men's courage was redoubled and they also drove themselves forward with mad recklessness, to win the day.

The story had been told a thousand times and was now apocryphal – as if carved in stone. Hadrian's name was one to be remembered, and his reputation and standing went before him. He knew the Praetorian Guard would stand with him when he entered the city, and turn against their commander, Attianus.

It was fitting, since they were the Emperor's guard. Besides, Hadrian had arranged for Commodus to give them all handsome bounties from the public purse, if they would return their loyalties to him.

Whereas Attianus, confident in his own position of self-created power, had never imagined Hadrian would be audacious enough to go to war within his own country. Attianus had already declared Hadrian as unfit to rule as emperor and had bribed the entire Praetorian Guard to oppose the Emperor Hadrian, and maintain their allegiance to Attianus himself.

The Legion of the Tenth came to a halt just beyond missile range outside the Popolo Gate of Rome. The great Obelisk of Popolo, stolen from Egypt's Ramses the Second was in the centre of the square, and the Tenth legion took up formation around it.

Hadrian swiftly dismounted his horse, grabbed a shield from a legionary soldier and barged his way through his troops, with grim determination. He turned to Turbo and his staff officers around him, and declared firmly, "If we fail here, this will be the end of my life – and your careers."

He drew his sword and strode towards the great gate.

A junior officer on the gate yelled an order, and the Praetorian Guard within range loosed off a volley of missiles in his direction. The range was long, the target small, but the Praetorians prided themselves on being the best soldiers for a reason. A dozen javelins flew singingly through the air, toward the lone exposed figure of Hadrian. Turbo, the chiefs of staff and the men of the Tenth held their breath.

No one could live through a volley like that. Not even the famously brave Hadrian.

*

They had marched north with mud on their boots for seven days now, covering one hundred miles on the old roman road. Cold wet rain fell everyday from the grey skies.

Marcus's cloak was soaking wet still from the previous day. Now he knew why the Romans resupplied at winter time in Britannia. In accordance with standard procedure half of the Cavalry went first as a vanguard to scout ahead of the main body and give advance warning of any problems that might be encountered, whilst the remaining ala of cavalry followed the rear cohort. They were no longer in Roman territory.

They finally arrived at the burnt out Fort of Bremenium. It was just as Novantes remembered, although the smouldering had long stopped. The memories of his riding south on horseback, searching for aid or even shelter, came flooding back into his head, with sadness for his lost colleagues. Now, he was here again, and still looking for the same people. Except this time, they had not seen a single Brigantian. He didn't like it at all.

The Roman Legions had quickly set up a temporary camp once again and that night around the briefing table, Novantes heard the legate gives his orders to the officers, marvelling at his optimism.

"Men, we must push forward and gain this victory! Our leader, General Falco, awaits great news from us. Our scouts saw Brigantes just five miles north of here. We have made great progress and tomorrow we will make our march north again in readiness for battle. His beady eyes gleamed, "This will be a glorious victory for the Ninth Legion!"

The legate had assured them, and therefore it would be so. Novantes had caught Marcus' eye across the room and given a grim smile. Marcus' eyebrows had shot up in wry response. After the meeting they had spoken together.

"Prefect, do you truly believe that we can defeat these savages?" Novantes asked.

Marcus smiled, "These men are the best soldiers in the world. They are professional soldiers. They have the best equipment, the best training and of course – the best officers!"

Novantes laughed his agreement, as Marcus continued, "Tomorrow and from then on, you stay right at my side. You know this land better than any of us."

Novantes had nodded. A horse had got him out of trouble before. Maybe it would be useful to be seated on one again.

*

At first light, the Roman army had packed up and resumed their march north. The first of the columns had passed over the bridge north of Bremenium. The endless clatter of Roman sandals upon the wooden structure had long ago alerted the watching Brigantians.

An arrow shot straight up into the air from where Mar's Field watchtower had once stood upon the hill. Vordimus nodded to Ortagorus in satisfaction at the signal. Now the Romans must take the bait.

Vordimus gripped his brother's arm, "I am going to make sure that the trap is fully set," he smiled, and rode off to his awaiting cavalry.

*

The despatch rider pulled up his horse in front of the legate and saluted, "Sir, Decurion Juventius has seen a group of some thirty horsemen and wishes to engage."

"Very well," nodded the legate, gravely, "Tell Juventius to get after them and destroy them. Take all of his calvary alae with him."

"Yes sir," the messenger saluted and left quickly.

"It is a historic moment men" spoke the legate.

"Our cavalry, full of spirit, have found the enemy. We must strike a heavy blow against them."

The junior staff officers nodded in agreement.

"My only fear is that the Brigantes will continue to avoid us. First blood to us as soon as Juventius engages them. Inform Prefect Quitetus to bring forward his alae of calvary to the front now. We expect contact."

"Yes sir", nodded a messenger and sped off to the rear of the column.

Juventius had been tired of chasing shadows and now was the time to give some payback, he thought. With their tight formations and long swords they would run this rabble down. They sped quickly away from the column in chase.

*

Vordimus looked forward and saw the Roman cavalry again, "Right men. Fall back," he ordered. "Follow me."

Their light ponies quickly covered the ground. There was no way the heavy Roman horses would catch them.

*

To the south, the rest of the Roman column had passed over the bridge now, too. Arthmael passed the brew around the men. Several large bowlfuls of mushrooms had been mixed with the strong beer and left to ferment. The smell upon opening the pot was overwhelming. However, better still were its effects. Arthmael knew that these mushrooms were regarded by the druids as magical, and they would make the warriors *invincible.*

Each man drank deeply from the cups of beer, wiping their mouths of the scummy froth, and wincing from the sour taste. These men were some of the best warriors in the Brigantian army, highly courageous in hand-to-hand combat. Their pagan beliefs in the afterlife made them fearless of death, and they would charge recklessly into danger even without the powerful psychotropic drugs. Several had been bodyguards for Vordimus himself. Animal skins over their back, a large axe or sword were their primary weapons. No skill was required, for their brute force and persistence against all odds were legendary.

Arthmael knew that it would start soon, with the chattering of their teeth. Then their faces would swell and redden, indicating the rise in blood pressure and rush of adrenalin. Arthmael knew that they had to get within range of the Romans before the madness took complete hold of them, or they would start to kill mindlessly, even attacking each other. Soon they would believe they were indestructible monsters, immortal and unbeatable. They would lose all human reason and hack down everything they came across in their path.

Speed was of the essence, and they made their way towards the Roman army, as yet unseen. Once they had moved around behind the column, Arthmael pointed out the Romans, still mere dots in the distance.

Arthmael spoke quietly, addressing his tribesmen with the full knowledge that his words would be the catalyst for chaos: "Those men say they have come to take our lands and our women. I say – we stop them. They must all die!"

By now, each man was recognisable as a berserker, in the first flush of entrancement. The forty warriors around him were all red faced and fazed. Some stared obliquely into the sky. One warrior was hacking at a fallen tree stump with his sword. There was a roar from those who took in the sense of Arthmael's words.

"Attack!" the leader of the group pointed towards the distant troops.

They drove forward and a few minutes later Arthmael heard the first howl. He smiled and turned to catch a glimpse of them moving north in pursuit of the Romans. Whomsoever these men met would be slaughtered without a second's thought.

SPQR

The proper acts of a general are judgement and prudence.

Tactius

Chapter XXI: Deeper into the unknown

9.50am, 17th December, 117AD: Via Domitiana, Northern Britain

Marcus and his cavalry approached the front of the column and saluted the legate.

"Reporting as ordered sir."

The legate nodded at Marcus, "Quietus, are those sheep I see on the hillside?"

"Yes, sir, it appears so," agreed Marcus.

"Take ten of your men and go and bring them down here."

"Sir, we are in hostile country. We should be cautious that it may be trap."

The legate laughed scornfully, "Not unless shepherd boys pose too much of a threat to you, Quietus!"

Marcus blushed, but the legate continued in his greed, "Besides, I don't fancy hard tack for the next week on the march. I am sure each legionnaire will thank you for their supper tonight! We shall feast well!"

Marcus said no more, but saluted and rode off to his alae of cavalry.

"Right. first ten men with me," he motioned to his German cavalry, struggling to keep the sarcasm out of his voice, "Let's ride up the hill and get the Legate's dinner down here. Novantes, you stay here."

They rode off at pace. *Bloody waste of military resources*, thought Marcus to himself. *Still, if it keeps the old man happy...*

*

The legate had raised his hand and shouted the order to advance, but with over six miles of troops from beginning to end, it took fifteen minutes for an order issued at the front to be fulfilled at the rear. They would catch on soon enough and follow the rest.

At the rear of the column, still waiting for the order, stood Metellus and the Fifth Cohort. Metellus' ears pricked up as he heard a wild howling now from behind them and glanced back to see the shapes of men advancing in the distance.

"Eyes forward, ladies! There is nothing to see."

Metellus called over a despatch rider, "Tell the First Spear we have spotted some filth behind us and we are turning to face them."

"Yes sir," nodded the messenger and shot off to the front of the column which had started to move forward now.

"Fifth Cohort will About Face!" ordered Metellus, and the men turned in unison.

"First and Second century, step five paces forward!" commanded Metellus.

Both centuries split their formation across the road, ten men in each century, eight ranks deep. Their formation was tight between the hill on one side and the drop to the valley on the other. Metellus was certain that one would squeeze past them.

*

The column snaked forward. Six men wide, they marched north up the Via Domitiana built by Roman troops some forty years before. They moved forward with the cavalry and legate at the front, followed by the cohorts in line. The First cohort contained the best and most experienced troops: hardened veterans who had fought many battles.

The Second cohort came next, followed by the baggage train in the middle: stores of wood and supplies for rebuilding a camp, a small paychest containing the Legion's money, food and water as well as tents.

The Fourth cohort marched behind them and assisted the wagons to move in the mud when necessary. The Fifth cohort came at the rear and had now taken position across the road.

*

Marcus and his ten horsemen approached the sheep cautiously. There were three shepherd boys who waved at them in the distance. Marcus thought it strange that they waved, but waved back. Perhaps they hadn't considered that they might take their sheep. But as Marcus drew closer and his men circled the sheep, the boys drew back now, intimidated and afraid.

Marcus stopped and looked back down the valley. He could see the Roman army glittering in the pale sunlight of the winter's day. A cold breeze swept across him. It was quiet and beautiful.

Suddenly his horse sprang back without command. Marcus smoothed its side and kept his hands on the reins but he could not control it. The horse reared up and suddenly Marcus saw that the ground beneath the horse was moving.

A man wriggled free from a piece of loose turf and wrenched his sword out from beneath him. Within a second he had risen and swung his sword, hacking Marcus' horse's leg wide open, forcing him to fall from its back.

"In the name of the gods!" swore Marcus, gathering himself up as the Brigantian charged at him with sword raised high. Marcus missed the first attack as he stepped back out of range and as the sword passed by, he plunged his own blade into the warrior's side. The man cried out and fell. Marcus quickly stabbed him in the chest as he lay. He looked round and saw that his fellow cavalrymen had been attacked too.

None of his ten troopers had survived and a dozen Brigante's were now moving towards him on foot. Marcus knew that his own horse was mortally wounded and of no use, but he ran towards another loose cavalry horse pawing the ground nervously nearby and mounted it swiftly. The Brigantes came towards him, still thirsting for blood. He turned the horse around and headed down the slope. The enemy jeers echoed in his ears.

"Enemy sighted from behind, sir!" saluted the *first spear*. "The Fifth cohort has turned to face them just in case of any surprises".

"Excellent," nodded the legate." This is all going to plan. Our cavalry have engaged the enemies and our Fifth Cohort have found some sport too. Let me know enemy strength and numbers. Halt the column."

The *first spear* was the senior centurion of the Legion and shouted out the order to halt the column again.

The legate laughed and turned to the *first spear*, "Maybe they have finally realised that they cannot keep running and hiding," he smiled.

The *first spear* replied, "Sir our old camp is just a few miles away from here. Just past the hills, and across the river. It would be an ideal battlefield to engage them."

"Yes, yes," nodded the legate, "Plenty of space for a full battle. Let's hope Juventius can entice them out."

*

Juventius was frustrated. His heavy horses were always just reaching the Brigantes' light ponies when they seemed to effortlessly slip away. The Roman horses were tired after the elusive charge north, and the Brigantes clearly knew the ground well, thought Juventius. Still, that would not matter when they finally met. He knew that his heavy cavalry would cut through them without any difficulty.

He raised his hand once again and the two groups of thirty men slowed to a halt.

Juventius looked up the hillside at the group of warriors once again. He considered that maybe he could confront their leader by himself, and save the others. He trotted his horse forward, testing the air. The Brigantes didn't move. So, he trotted his horse further up the hill and stopped again. They still hadn't moved. This was curious but he wasn't about to let an opportunity pass.

He signalled back to the German Cavalry and they slowly urged up their horses beside him. Juventius looked up in expectation as the Brigantes slowly took up formation in a straight line on the brow of the hill. They had not run away but perhaps now they would charge down at them after all. They would soon all be dead if they did.

Juventius trotted his horse forward again up the gentle slope. Second by second, he edged closer to them. The warriors stood perfectly still. But their leader, Vordimus raised his sword once and cried an order.

"Charge!" Juventius shouted. He couldn't fail to get them now.

The Trumpter sounded 'Charge' again and the notes sounded out in loud sucession.

The Brigantes' horses turned quickly on their heels and fell back down the other side of the hill. Juventius couldn't believe they still had not reached them. But as they browed the hill, he observed that the tribesmen had paused again below them, and this time he had the higher ground. He felt sure this was it. Juventius swept his sword down once more to signal the advance, and the heavy cavalry raced down.

He had them now. He could see the legate's smiling face and thought of the Brigantians' imminent destruction. The barbarians raced for their lives down the hill and into the valley, hooves thundering. Any delay and the Romans would be upon them.

Juventius knew he was merely a few seconds behind them now. Nothing would stop him. He heard the trumpter sound the two tones of 'charge' again and again behind him and smiled. He shouted the battle cry to the German troops around him and in earnest they dug their heels once more into their horses' flanks and sped them forward. He looked ahead as he saw the Brigantes race into the swollen waters of a river ahead. He smiled and saw them floundering.

"Kill them all!" he shouted as he looked around and watched his soldiers in full attack.

Juventius was within a sword's reach of the enemy. He had raced down the hill into the valley with only one thought in mind – to pursue and attack the enemy ahead.

He had been blinkered in his approach. The coldness of the water around his feet made him come to his senses now, and he looked around wildly.

Ortagorus, meanwhile, from his vantage point on the hillside to the far left of the road had watched the Roman cavalry sweep past them. He dropped his sword to start the charge. Now this flank of troops had the opportunity to launch a sidelong attack upon the spent Roman horses.

Juventius looked around – too late – at the closing barbarian troops. He glanced back along the way he had come, and noticed that the decurion of the other thirty Roman cavalry had charged after the first troop of enemies, too. Their peripheral vision and excitement at success in sight had not allowed them to see the danger beside and behind them. They were surrounded, completely sandwiched by enclosing barbarians.

A great melee erupted. On one side more Brigantian infantrymen were trying to get into the water to join the horsemen, and attack the Roman cavalrymen. On the other side, Brigantian troops were hacking at everything that moved. In the middle, what was left of sixty Roman cavalry fought on the banks of the ford, trying to escape.

The water was high and slowed down the horses on both sides but the push from the Brigantian infantry was winning. Juventius quickly realised that as soon as he killed one man, that enemy was being replaced by another. He looked out over the swarming enemy troops. There were hundreds of them on both sides of the river. He had less than sixty men.

*

The legate was frustrated, "Any messages brought from Juventius yet?"

"Nothing sir."

"Very well, send out a messenger to see where he is. I know Juventius will have shown them that Roman Calvary is the best in the world."

He smiled and cast his gaze across in the far distance, as if he could see the three miles.

"*First spear*, if Juventius does not sight the enemy we will get round the hill and establish the camp immediately."

Yes, sir, acknowledged the *first spear*.

"Lets us hope that Juventius can tempt the enemy to those killing fields, where the rest of our troops can cut them down. Until then the Fifth Cohort can deal with the skirmish at the back."

The legate was certain that they would manage to stave off these ruffians.

*

Metellus laughed out loud at the approaching Brigante warriors, wavering their way towards them, unkempt and unmilitary. Vagabonds all of them.

"Right, ladies. No matter what happens, we are going to kill these bastards!" he roared, "First man to kill five gets promoted!"

A laugh went up around the cohort. Metellus stood on the front rank and glared at the howling barbarian troops making their way towards them. Their trotting speed quickly changed to a charge as the leader shouted something to encourage them forward. Metellus noticed that each man wore a large animal skin on his back. A great giant ran forward towards them.

Metellus shouted, "First Rank! Prepare to release Javelins. Choose your target."

The men in the front rank steadied their arms, taking a mental note of their targets. They kept their heads level, arm taut, eyes forward, fixing on the target. The wild men approached, and at two hundred yards distance, Metellus' voice rang out.

"Release!" Twenty javelins shot forward, arcing gracefully in the air.

All eyes on the Roman side looked upwards, hoping and praying they would hit a target. One barbarian was hit in the chest and flung backwards. He was pinned to the ground but continued to struggle to get up, even with the javelin buried in his chest.

He continued to shout and cry oaths at the Romans. He was dead, but just hadn't realised it yet. None of the other injured Brigantes stopped the charge, but just pressed on, relentless.

Metellus and the rest of the cohort looked on in disbelief. They had never seen men like this before.

"First rank, Second Javelin. Prepare!"

Their eyes stared forwards at the men, still running without reason.

"Release!" shouted Metellus. He could not believe their fearlessness as the second volley of deathly spears hit them.

A dozen men were hit. Javelins pierced through shields were disregarded. Some men stopped momentarily to pull javelins out their arms or legs, and resumed the charge as best they could. The rest ran on without hesitation.

The giant at the front had a javelin in his shield and gave it no heed whatsoever. He approached, wild-eyed, just yards away now

Metellus drew his sword and pointed it at him, "Oy, you bastard! Over here!"

The giant veered to his left, following the sound like a wild beast, rather than making a thoughtful decision, and made his way straight towards Metellus.

"Shield wall up!" shouted Metellus and the thud of wooden shields went all along the front rank.

A great axe hacked heavily at Metellus' shield with a mighty blow. The force of it on his left arm made Metellus fall backwards.

The giant stood visible before him now, swinging the axe high once more.

Metellus stepped forward and lunged at him with his sword. With unlikely swiftness, considering his size, the giant stepped sideways and attacked again as his axe whirled past. Metellus felt the rush of air as the weapon swept by him. The other soldiers around him still had their shields up and were not aware of how personal this fight had become.

Suddenly the axe swept vertically down at the soldier beside Metellus, who immediately let go of his shield. The massive man howled like a werewolf at the two Romans who now stood in front of him.

Metellus knew exactly what to do. He just had to get the timing right. Once the huge man had started to swing the axe, exposing his torso, it was simply a matter of stepping into the circle he swung and killing him with a thrust from his sword.

The man swung the axe round again in a great arc above his head. Metellus stepped in quickly, and jabbed hard with the point of the sword entering the man's stomach and then ripped it back, stepping swiftly out of reach. To Metellus' horror, the giant never flinched.

The monstrous axe caught the legionary standing beside Metellus and took his arm cleanly off. The stroke of the man's powerful arm hit Metellus on the way back and knocked him unconscious to the ground. The giant howled his own war cry, and continued to swing his axe, despite the savage wound he bore.

The men of the First century, Fifth cohort shrank back. They had never seen men behaving like crazed animals before. These men were not human.

*

Cornelia motioned to the guard standing beside her to take off her gag. He eyed her suspiciously.

"I need the toilet," she muttered in Celtic.

The guard shook his head, "Vordimus said I must watch you. Just you wet yourself."

Cornelia looked at him, "How is it going to look when he wants me later and I am covered in my own dirt? Who will he blame?"

The solider glared at her hard, considering his options, then sighed, "Make it quick. Over there in the trees. Make sure I can see you."

He untied her bonds and kept the spear close.

The guard watched her head into the trees and suddenly she disappeared. With a roar, he ran in to follow her and was greeted by a large stone on the head, knocking him out.

Marcus would be proud of that, she smiled.

She dragged the body further into the trees and stripped him of his clothes, removing her own. She had to act quickly before the other guards noticed, and she dressed in the brigand's tunic, leggings, boots and sheepskin.

*

Marcus rode down to the column as the men still stood in marching formation but nobody was moving.

A look of frustration was set across the legates face.

"Sir, we were ambushed whilst trying to bring back the sheep" reported Marcus.

The legate looked at him questioningly.

"Prefect Quietus, you are a professional soldier so please keep your voice calm in battle. These Brigantes are nothing more than Vermin. Right. Let's advance the column, First Spear. I am not waiting here any longer. Once we join battle with these barbarians we will soon see who has the stomach for it."

The legate, resplendent in his red cloak and white crested helmet, rode forward. The *first spear* shouted the order to advance when an arrow ripped across the front. The legate was down.

Marcus dismounted and quickly ran over with the *first spear* to the legate's side. The *first spear* ordered shields up and the first century ran forward around their officer. The men raised their shields around the outside in Testudo formation.

Blood oozed out his armour. The arrow had gone straight through it at the side. The legates face was white.

"You're in command Quietus. Finish the job. "

As the legate tried to speak, he coughed ugly mouthfuls of blood. Marcus nodded as the legate's eyes closed and his head rolled to the side. The body was lifted upon a shield back to the baggage train.

"Over there" motioned Marcus. "Bowmen. First century up the hill and get them. Spread out."

The *first spear* ordered the first century forward. The rest of the column stayed shields up.

"Novantes", called Marcus. "What's at the top of this hill?

"This is Hades End, sir. The most northern outpost. Over that hill you can see right across the river below and all around."

"Well, let's go. Better than sitting here. First Spear, you're in charge. Fall in behind the first century climbing up", Marcus ordered Novantes."

The legionnaires of the two centuries had quickly identified two bowmen hiding in the grass. The bowman had been told specifically to shoot Roman officers and now up close against the legionnaries they had no chance in close combat. More arrows hit shields but the Roman legionnaires closed the distance quickly and with their Spanish short swords finished them off.

Marcus ordered the soldiers to remain here while he and Novates climbed further up the hill.

Within the Ninth Legion word had quickly spread. The legate was dead. Quietus and Novantes were climbing the hill to get a view of where Juventious was.

The *optio* of the Fifth cohort poured the cold truth of water from his bottle on Metellus' face.

"Sir, the Legate is dead. Quietus is in charge."

Metellus woke up, startled.

"The Legate is dead" the *optio* repeated emphatically. "Novantes and Quietus have climbed the hill to find out where our cavalry are."

Metellus' face looked up at the hill.

"Sir. Those Brigantes fought to the last man. We have twenty dead and another twelve wounded".

The numbers didn't register in Metellus head. "Stay here", he ordered. Metellus grabbed the nearest horse and jumped on.

Libo looked around and saw Metellus take off.

"Where do you think you're going" demanded the *optio* as Libo dropped his shield and raced after Metellus. "You're on a charge!" he shouted after Libo. But both men were gone.

"Sir, where is the new Legate?" asked Metellus as he pulled the horse over to the *first spear*.

"He's gone up Hades End to get a view, Centurion. What's your report?"

Metellus jumped off the horse and looked up at the hill again. "Urgent report for the Legate sir", he spoke quickly.

"What's your report, Centurion?!" ordered the *first spear*. But Metellus was already gone, tearing up the hill.

Chapter XXII: The Praetorian Guard

Advancing upon the Popolo Gate alone, Hadrian took several of the slim javelins on his shield and evaded the remaining missiles aimed at him. Standing before the gate, he swept off his helmet and threw down his shield. In a commanding tone, loud enough for all to hear, he called to the guards on the gate.

"Soldiers of the Guard, do you not recognise me? General of our Legions, Son of Trajan!"

The soldiers stood silent, looking to Captain Dresus. Hadrian stepped closer to the gate.

"I have come back. To make Rome greater than before!"

The troops and officers of the Tenth gave a great roar behind him.

"By the blood of the Gods!" shouted Captain Dresus, from the fortifications of the Gate, "The Emperor is back!"

Captain Dresus was forty two years old and had served in the army since he was eighteen, an amicable man but not very imaginative. Long service in the army could make a man like that.

He had been rewarded for his service in a way that was rare among Romans. He was a peasant by birth, not highly educated, starting as an ordinary conscript but being promoted from the ranks to Captain simply because he was an excellent soldier. In his twenty years he had fought in dozens of major battles and more skirmishes than he could remember. He had marched continuously, month after month, summer and winter, thousands of miles all over the Empire for the glory of Rome. He always felt honoured to serve the emperor, and privileged to share in the glory of his victories. Captain Dresus might have hesitated to say that he worshipped the emperor, but there was no other word for it. The emperor had been his god on earth, more present than Jupiter in heaven. In his eyes the emperor was wiser, more powerful and altogether far more than any mere human could be. In the six months of aimless misery since Attianus had taken over, he had longed for the emperor to return.

Captain Dresus took off his own helmet and placed it on the point of his sword. He raised it high above his head and waved it for all to see.

"Our Emperor has returned! Long live the Emperor!" The shouts reverberated around the gateway and soon shook the very walls of Rome.

"The Emperor has returned!" echoed the soldiers of the Guard.

The great gate of Popolo was opened and Captain Dresus humbly went out and bowed before Hadrian, "We are your soldiers, Caesar."

The drums beat and the trumpets of the Tenth sounded behind Hadrian in celebration, adding to the cacophony of cheers within the gates.

Hadrian shouted to his men of the Praetorian Guard, "I knew I had to fight for Rome, but not for my very life!"

The men of the Tenth Legion and Praetorian Guard laughed from their separate directions, together.

Hadrian shook the arm of Captain Dresus, "I am your Emperor Dresus. And you are my Guard".

Captain Dresus smiled. "It is my honour, Caesar."

The Tenth legion quickly formed up and readied themselves for marching through the gate, as if on a parade ground, with helmets' crests and standards to the front.

Shouts of approval rang around Rome as the citizens emerged from their houses and into the streets. They saw the way the Guard had welcomed Hadrian home and now they joined in with them. Once more they would be free to walk down the streets and go about their daily duties.

The men of the Praetorian Guard walked with purpose at the side of their emperor. In front of them a cohort of the Tenth legion marched in serried rows.

Technically, it was illegal for the emperor to enter Rome with a legion; however, Attianus had certainly been irregular in his dealings with the law, and Hadrian would deal with that later.

Hadrian travelled up the Via del Corso whilst the Praetorian Guard marched in front. An atmosphere of joy filled the city. The crowds had not seen their new emperor since his inauguration several months ago, and they eagerly took to the streets. Hadrian ordered a proportion of the public coin to be distributed as they marched through Rome, similar to a first inauguration.

He tossed a new coin to Turbo as he rode behind him.

Turbo laughed as he saw the image of Hadrian with full beard on one side, and the crest of Rome on the other, "It does make you look younger."

Hadrian grinned, "But I am much more handsome".

"Many will welcome you back, for such gifts, Caesar".

"People are fickle enough. I know that the ale houses of Rome will be bursting tonight, Turbo," he smiled back. "It is merely a gesture to Rome's citizens, to show them that I have returned".

Upon the news of Hadrian's arrival, the crowd swelled the streets to bursting point. The Praetorian Guard could barely march without bumping into onlookers as they made way for Hadrian on his horse.

*

Novantes and Marcus had climbed Hades End for half an hour. The slope was now becoming steep and the grass slippery below their feet. Novantes pushed ahead.As they neared the top, Novantes and Marcus stopped. The Roman legionnaires looked like toy soldiers from their elevated position.

As they rested near the summit Marcus could hear chatter in Celtic tongue coming from the other side. Marcus quietly drew his sword and with a cutting motion across his neck indicated the job to Novantes. Both men edged up closer and quickly jumped on the flat surface of the top. The four Brigantes looked astonished to see any Romans and jumped back. Marcus stabbed at the nearest warrior with his sword as he didn't move fast enough. He fell off the edge on the other side, clutching his stomach.

Now Marcus and Novantes were both attacking the Brigantes. Attack,feint, block – these men seemed to know how to fight with their swords. Eventually Novantes caught the leg of another warrior and as he tumbled to the ground stabbed him in the chest.

Both sides backed off now, two versus two, each edging close to the outside of the hilltop, careful not to fall off. Marcus judged the warrior nearest to him and looked for an opening.

They were eyeing each other warily when suddenly a huge body came flying across the top of the hill and struck the nearest Brigantian. Marcus smiled and guessed it would be one of the legionnaires from below. Novates and Marcus closed on the other warrior. A quick dispatch was easy with the two of them against one. But he hadn't fancied his chances and threw himself off the hill top, down the steep slope to his own troops far below.

They turned and watched the massive legionnaire choke the life from the final warriors throat.

Relinquishing his death grip, Metellus grinned and turned round to them both.

"Centurion Metellus, thanks for your help", spoke Marcus.

Metellus stood up and knocked Novantes straight from the hilltop with one punch. He looked at Marcus and lifted his sword. He took a swipe and Marcus blocked it.

"Look, Centurion. The problem we have right now is bigger than anything between you and I."

"*You* are my problem", explained Metellus, swinging his sword across Marcus's face. Marcus dodged the blow and looked around for space.

"Whatever it is, we can fix it!" acknowledged Marcus.

Metellus swung his sword again and again against Marcus as he tried to block the heavy strikes.

"Centurion! We are surrounded by thousands of Brigantes. We need each other!"

"You need only die. Like your father", Metellus spat out.

"What?! You know nothing of my father", Marcus replied, angered.

"I know he was a coward who tried to kill our Emperor", smirked Metellus.

"No, he did not!"

Marcus attacked Metellus now with renewed fury. The swords clashed again and again. Attacking, blocking, neither side willing to back down.

Metellus sneered. "It's nothing personal, you know. It's just my job. To *kill* you".

Marcus didn't understand. "What are you talking about?"

Both men were edging close around the hilltop. Marcus could feel his arm getting tired. He considered his options. It would be better to just jump off the hill now and slide back down to the rest of the Legion but he couldn't as Metellus kept attacking his every move. Metellus lunged again and as his sword struck the pommel of Marcus' weapon, he let it go instinctively. The sword flew through the air and off the hill top.

Metellus smiled. He closed towards Marcus.

Suddenly another body shot across the gap between them. Metellus looked around in astonishment as another legionnaire attacked him with sword drawn. Metellus fell to the ground as the legionnaire landed on top. With a quick stroke Metellus stuck his sword into the body of the legionnaire and pushed him off. The legionnaire fell back with the sword impaled in his stomach and both men watched his face. Marcus screamed in anger as his cousin Libo rolled back dead.

"Nooo!" screamed Marcus, jumping forward onto Metellus.

Metellus sunk to his knees to retrieve his sword but Marcus was quicker, drawing his own dagger. He jabbed Metellus in the throat. Blood spurted out of his neck and coated Marcus' armour.

"You bastard!" cried Marcus. "He is the only family I had left. Who sent you? Who?!"

Furiously he shook Metellus inert bulk. But his adversary was already with the Gods. Marcus kicked Metellus out the way and lay crouched beside his cousin, gently lifting his cousin's body up. But he was already gone. Marcus' anger rose up again and he cursed the Gods.

Why had Libo to die! Surely fate had given him enough bad news in his life. He thought of his family murdered by Hadrian and now his only cousin had been killed. He lay for a few moments beside his body. Shouts from below brought him back to the present.

Marcus looked out over the position of Hades End. The sight took his breath away. Vast numbers of Brigantes were moving towards the legion from both north and south. Marcus tried to gauge the number. Maybe five to six thousand. He could see dead horses below to the north. That was where Juventius must have fought them. He had to get back quickly to the rest of the legion.

Sliding back down the hill he picked up Novantes and his sword.

"What happened, Sir?" the younger soldier stammered.

"Explain later", motioned Marcus. "We have to get back."

*

Vordimus and Ortagerous had met in the middle of the Roman cavalry slaughter. Not a single Roman horseman was alive.

"Well done, my brother", shouted Vordimus. "We have destroyed their best troops now."

Both men smiled and grasped arms in friendship again. The warriors around them cheered and yelled in delight.

"Now a full attack in the front. Let's see what these Romans are made off."

"This is so easy", smiled Ortagerous. "Within a few hours we shall clear the field of these invaders."

"These troops fight like viscous dogs in the field", cautioned Vordimus. "This victory will not be easy."

Ortaegous was already calling the clan chiefs to be heard. "Prepare for attack again."

The last glimmers of winter sun shine shown upon the armour and helmets of the Roman troops. The valley ahead of them flooded with Brigantes.

"Keep the Votadini tribe back, out of sight", ordered Vordimus, "until we can taste victory."

"I am not sure they can wait, brother".

"They must be ordered too. This is what the Romans do. They are called reserves. If we need them at a difficult time they will plunge in without hesitation. These men may hold the battle", explained Vordimus.

"Very well", replied Ortagerous. "I will send another message to their chief to stay where they are."

The remaining Brigantes cheered and shouted their arrival on the battlefield.

Both armies could see one another clearly. By comparison the Roman troops stood silently. The small square of Roman soldiers was all that stood in the valley.

The standards of the Cohorts fluttered in the wind and the Eagle of the Ninth Legion stood at the centre, guarded by the bravest men on the northern frontier of Rome's Empire.

*

In a private chamber just off the main senate floor, Attianus had heard the shouts of jubilation. He immediately dispatched a messenger to Captain Drusus. Grimly he awaited the news he suspected must come and stood stormy-faced at the window, considering his options whilst listening to the cheering and shouts, his jaw tightening in anger. The messenger had promptly returned with the dreaded news: Hadrian had returned and was inside Rome.

Attianus acted swiftly. He addressed the messenger again, "Go to Mehus," he said, directing the messenger to his paid assassin, "He is waiting outside. Tell him to get together as many men as he can and that I offer fifty thousand denarii for the man who kills Hadrian! Then go to the ale house and tell Delano I offer his brigands the same deal. You understand?"

The servant bowed and hurried through the side door.

*

Commodus stood at the entrance to the front of the Senate house. The sun was warm and his eyes squinted in its brilliant light but it was good to be free from his house at last. Gazing around, growing accustomed to the air again, his eyes were drawn to a furtive man, moving with determination. He recognised Attianus' messenger and watched as the servant pushed through the crowd.

Commodus motioned to a few of the *frumentarii* soldiers left, and made his intention clear. They all followed the messenger.

Attianus' servant wasted no time in speaking to a group of known disreputable hired men. These men had quickly split up and moved into the crowd towards Hadrian's retinue.

In a quiet side street a few hundred yards away, Commodus' men caught up with the messenger, one placing his hand over the servant's mouth while the others dragged him backwards to the wall. With the servant's arms pinned against the wall, they realised his mouth.

"What is your message?" the soldiers asked him.

When he did not answer, a dagger was swiftly thrust into his stomach. The servant's eyes widened in agony but still he refused to speak. One of them leant on the dagger, pushing it in a downward motion. The servant's scream was muffled into the hand over his mouth.

"What is your message?" they demanded. "Last time."

"To kill Hadrian," the servant dribbled blood from his mouth. The dagger was quickly pulled from the stomach and drawn across his throat.

"That's for Ratho," one of them said as he kicked him backwards into the gutter. They turned and ran back to the main street. They had to warn Hadrian.

*

The Via del Corso was considered one of the widest and grandest streets in Rome and ran to the base of the Capitoline Hill. The crowd surged into their thousands as more and more people came out to see their new Emperors arrival. The Tenth Legion marched forward down the Via del Corso keeping the crowd back as Hadrian rode behind them surrounded by the Praetorian guard. Their formation made a rectangular box of bodies surrounding Hadrian's mount, on the march.

Suddenly one soldier of the guard fell back and two men from the crowd moved forward, inside the rectangle. The guard behind stepped forward into the space, believing them to be over enthusiastic citizens wishing to greet the emperor, and placed his enormous arm across their path. Not realising the true intent of these men, he was pushed back by their brutal force.

Hadrian looked down at the two approaching his horse and smiled at them, until he saw the sun glinting off their drawn daggers.

The first man's head rolled slightly and fell forwards, blood pouring from the sword wound in the back of his neck. The second man paused for a fraction of a second before a sword swung across his throat from the same direction. Captain Drusus' blade sprayed a fine shower of blood into the air. Hadrian's horse continued to step forward as both bodies fell to the ground.

"Draw swords!" Drusus commanded, "There are assassin's here."

The Praetorian Guard drew their swords and marched on. The crowd around them continued to cheer, unaware of what had happened. The remaining assassins, fully aware, stood back now, drifting into the crowds.

Hadrian arrived on the steps of the Senate house to a packed forum of citizens, applauding and cheering. He looked at Turbo and smiled. This was a better return than either of them had expected. Hadrian raised his hands to silence the crowd.

"I have come back!" There was a tumultuous roar, "I have come back to make Rome great!" He paused, to permit the uproarious audience response to die down before he declaimed, "I am Rome and Rome is me."

The crowd cheered in delight. He raised his hands again, and the audience quietened.

"I have travelled across the length and breadth of our Empire to make Rome safe. Our legions at this moment are fighting in various corners of the Empire to maintain our glorious lands and to keep us free!" The audience broke again into spontaneous applause.

Hadrian raised his hands now to quiet the crowd.

"Whilst I have been away, I have received reports that my plans for Rome have not been fulfilled. I am disappointed. But listen hard, for I am a just man – I grant an amnesty to all those who raised arms against me. To those who disagreed with my ideas – I forgive them, since they were only following their duty and honour as they saw fit. I have still greater dreams for Rome and we will begin afresh today!"

The crowd whistled, cheered and clapped their approbation. With this, Hadrian walked into the Senate house with the crowd cheering his name behind him. The Senate hall was packed to capacity, as Hadrian had expected.

The Senate Consul Petronius Ovidius bowed and called the meeting to order. Hadrian walked to centre and started to speak. Hadrian addressed the Senate authoritatively, and they attended, rapt, as if they were children listening to their much beloved and respected father, who laid out new rules and gifts.

"...And there will be new reforms for granaries which will be to the benefit of all!" He had the audience already in the palm of his hand, "New buildings will be built to honour my great father Trajan! And there will be help for senatorial families who have fallen on hard times..."

As Hadrian rattled through many social changes, the Senate sat in stunned silence. The scribes who had been writing furiously to keep up with his impassioned outpouring of words, rulings, concessions, plans, laws, taxes, had been aching for Hadrian to finish after an hour of his continuous speech.

And still there was more: "I promise to remake Rome, with great temples, new roads, more gold coin and a monument reflecting my father's glory. Rome is great – and will be greater and more glorious still!

Commodus and his supporters rose and applauded Hadrian loudly, as he finally sat down. The rest of the Senate stood and clapped slowly in appreciation and some bewilderment. Senator Blandinus made no movement.

Hadrian had the backing of the people outside, clearly. It seemed that some of the Senate still needed to be convinced. Attianus had balanced the scales in his favour. Now Hadrian had to remove them.

The great bronze doors of the Senate creaked open. Who would dare enter the Senate house when they were in session?

Attianus walked forward, with two of the Praetorian Guard at either side of him, their swords drawn.

Silence filled the room as every eye watched the two great men – Hadrian and his 'guardian' Attianus – greet each other.

Hadrian smiled and turned back to the Senate, "I have asked my guardian and Prefect of the City to appear before us today."

The senators held their breath, wondering what punishment Hadrian would deliver. It had not gone unnoticed that Attianus had overstepped his position, and tension was taut in the air.

Hadrian went on: "Attianus has been City Prefect for some twenty years, for which we thank him for his most loyal service," Every man swallowed at the unspoken irony which belied the words, "And he will now be retiring to his villa in Capri." Hadrian stepped over the Senate floor to where Attianus stood stiffly before him and kissed him on both cheeks.

Quietly Hadrian whispered in his ear, as he kissed one cheek, "You will leave Rome today and not come back." And to the next kissed cheek he muttered, "If you do, I will kill you without trial. Just like you did to those senators."

He stepped back and smiled publicly, then turned to the Praetorian Guards, and announced, "Walk him to the gates!" More privately, he added, "And make sure he leaves."

Attianus looked stunned. He gazed over at Blandinus and their eyes met, as they shared an impassive look.

The soldiers motioned for Attianus to move. He took one more steady glance around the room, perhaps searching for some allegiance, unfound, before turning on his heel.

Hadrian turned back to the Senate, still smiling, "Let us adjourn early this day, my friends! I have given you much to think upon. We have just started to renew our glorious city. Together we shall make it stronger than ever!"

The Senate broke out into spontaneous applause, and Hadrian allowed himself to be greeted and congratulated by the senators who crowded to offer their support.

SPQR

The Spartans do not ask how many but where they are.

Agis 2nd of Sparta

Chapter XXIII: Open War

12.05pm, 17th December, 117AD: Hades End hill, Northern Britain

Sliding back down Hades End hill, Marcus immediately re-joined the Legion.

"*First Spear*. Form a square. Have four centuries of the First cohort facing north up this way. Make them four lines deep for reinforcement. Second cohort facing east, down the hill, Fourth cohort facing west up Hades end and the Fifth cohort facing south."

"Yes, sir", replied the *first spear* and the orders were relayed by the Centurions of each cohort.

"Form Square, form square!" bellowed the *first spear*.

The remaining cohorts marched double time up the Roman Road and took position.

The baggage train and remaining fifty troopers of cavalry were brought into the middle. Marcus knew he might need them later.

"They are coming," Marcus pointed. "Right up this road."

"We will be ready for them", acknowledged the *first spear*.

"Did Centurion Metellus speak to you sir?".

Marcus spoke quietly to him. "Metellus is dead. As is Juventius and the cavalry. We are on our own. Our fate is coming right around the corner now. We must stand fast and encourage the men."

The howling Brigantes closed upon them.

In his loudest centurion voice, the *first spear* walked along the First Cohort. "Right, men. This is what we trained for. Hours of practice throwing wooden javelins. Days and weeks you've carried them on your back. Now you have a chance to use the bloody things, let's make them count."

The men's backs stiffened.

The *first spear* ordered: "At two hundred yards, first rank step forward. Pick your targets. Release. First rank, second javelin, pick your target. Release."

No pause between commands. The Brigantes were moving fast. The sky was black with javelins. The front lines of warriors crumpled as they hit their targets. All along the line the centurions barked out new commands.

"Draw swords and reform line."

The cohort's front rank snapped their shields back into place creating an unbroken wall to the Brigantes. A messenger appeared in front of Marcus, "Sir, enemy sighted to the rear, also."

"These barbarians are no amateurs", nodded Marcus. "First Spear, you take command of the First cohort and direct our defence against the northern attack. I will take the Fifth cohort and direct our forces against the southern attack to the rear. They will try to use their numbers against us. Jupiter, greatest and best, protect this legion".

"And you, sir", repeated the *first spear*, touching the pommel of his sword.

The *first spear* spoke again. "Right lads, this isn't going to be pretty but it will be efficient. Concentrate on the same old drill. Shield and sword. Get your shield up and parry their attack. When you see an opening thrust your gladius into the bluenose's guts and get back behind your shield double quick. Don't stand and laugh at him or his mate will get you. And remember lads. We stand together."

Marcus looked at the *first spear* and smiled. The leading wave of Brigantes had slowed now, fighting their way between the bodies of their fallen comrades. The Romans stood in silence, as the distance between them and the screaming warriors shortened.

At running speed, the lightly armed Brigantes crashed into the front line of the legionnaires. The Roman infantry repeatedly punched the metal bosses of their shields into the oncoming men, parrying their attack and then stabbing their short swords into their chosen targets.

Blood splattered across the gap between the two lines as men fell back dying or trying to hold their stomachs in. The ground was a mixture of blood and bodies.

As the minutes passed, Marcus realised that most of the dying was being done on the other side. Still they threw themselves upon the Roman line, trying to break the shield wall and again and again the Roman troops stood firm.

Marcus moved to the other side of the square. The Fifth cohort faced south, shields up. Marcus looked back down the road which they had walked up from the bridge. All he could see now were thousands of tribesmen heading this way: so many there was no daylight between their massed ranks. They formed a solid body of men, hundreds of bodies thick, massing towards them, bellowing like wild animals. The men of the Fifth cohort looked at Marcus.

Marcus addressed everyone within earshot. " A Roman square might not look much, but it is the safest means to defend oneself. Hold your positions and you will hold the square."

Men nodded in acknowledgement. A general feeling of acceptance grew around the Fifth cohort.

"Your arms will be aching tonight, you've killed so many" laughed Marcus. "A civic crown to the man I see kill the most barbarians."

The men pricked up their ears. The civic crown was presented to any soldier who had saved the life of another Roman soldier in battle or had displayed an unusual act of valour. It was made of three different types of oak. Soldiers conferred with this great honour had a place reserved next to the senators at all the public spectacles. Gatherings of people would always stand as a mark of respect to such a soldier. He and the closest male members of his family were even freed from all public burdens.

They knew he was serious now. No legate would offer such a decoration without meaning it. The men were stunned.

Marcus rode his horse over to the other side of the square and repeated his offer to the men of the First cohort, "The man who kills the most of our enemies today will receive the civic crown for his actions".

"One civic crown might now be enough!" shouted a centurion. Marcus smiled and laughed.

The enemy were approaching the Fifth cohort now.

"At two hundred yards", shouted Marcus, "front rank step forward. Eyes front and pick your targets. Release. Next javelin. Prepare. Pick your target. Release".

The sky turned momentarily black with the dense rain of missiles.

None of these javelins missed. It was impossible not to strike a man's head or body as steel rain hit the Brigantes running forward.

"Second row!" shouted Marcus, "prepare to release javelins. Pick your targets, release. Second javelin, prepare. Pick your target, release. "Front row back into position. Shield wall up!" And the sound of wooden shields snapped back together.

Dozens more of men fell under the barrage of javelins with no defence.

Marcus watched as the screaming tide of men hit the Fifth cohort. The front rank sheltered behind their shields as the Brigantes hit and swung their swords. A young legionnaire dropped his shield slightly to observe what was happening and was instantly hacked to shreds by the warriors in front of him. The Roman soldier in the rank behind him swiftly stepped over his body and took his place.

Marcus bellowed, "you must not drop your shields!"

Now more and more of the enemy pushed forward. Hundreds more behind them tried to do the same. The gap which had existed between the opposing lines had gone and the leading Brigantes were pushed against the Roman shields by their advancing comrades behind.

The Fifth cohort were beginning to be pushed back. Marcus ordered his cavalry to dismount and help push back to support them. In the slippery mud underfoot the legionnaires could barely keep their balance. Now, as thousands of warriors pushed into the fifth cohort, each rank was ordered to support the one behind it.

The Roman troops now stood behind their wooden shields, pressing them into the face or the body of the Brigantian in front. It was impossible to move the shield or get a chance to use their swords. Marcus noted that even when a legionnaire near him had stabbed an enemy the body rarely fell right over, remaining propped upright by the force from all sides.

There was no opportunity to rotate the men to the front lines and give the tired troops on the front line a rest. It had grown into a stalemate. After half an hour's intense combat, neither side could make progress. Marcus looked over at the First Cohort. They were being pushed back in the mud too. The Brigantes were using their numbers against them.

As more and more warriors pushed forward in the hope of killing a Roman, the crush at the front became unbearable.

Marcus could see that even with his men supporting them they could not keep this up. He had to come up with a plan. He turned to the nearest soldier. "Pass the word down the ranks. We charge at my command."

The men on the front rank were exhausted beyond belief now. It was simply a matter of trying to maintain their balance without losing their shield.

"Soldiers", shouted Marcus loudly enough to be heard by the entire cohort. "This day will be decided by you the legionnaires and centurions of the Ninth Legion. Our loyalty is to each other and our cause is to protect the ones we love. For them we will hurl these savages into the abyss of Hades."

A roar began among the silent Roman troops like a great swelling. Then the Fifth and First cohort charged.

Never before had soldiers of Rome fought as hard for the Ninth Legion as that day. Calling on some mysterious inner reserves, the front rank began pushing the Brigantes back. Just when they forced them back far enough, the Romans jumped back and stabbed and slashed at everything before them with their swords.

Marcus knew some of his men would be unable to lift their shields or wield their weapons due to their exhaustion. But he knew their skill at killing would show through.

Fifty yards away he watched the men of the front rank do what they did best. Kill.

The man closest to Marcus parried and blocked a warriors attack overhead with a sword. The legionnaire rammed his shield against his adversary's face, bursting his nose, before stabbing him in the stomach. He thrust his sword into the face of another moving forward and parried another attack with the rim of his shield. With another attack he had his sword into the stomach of another barbarian and watched as yellow intestines spilled outwards, steaming against the cold ground. The man swung and cut and parried non-stop, killing numerous savages in the space of thirty seconds.

"This man here", pointed Marcus, "has just killed a dozen. He is the first for the civic crown!"

The Fifth cohort cheered and reached within themselves for a strength they did not know. They tore into the Brigantes. Although hundreds had died within minutes, still they came on.

Marcus nodded with satisfaction. In leading this unexpected charge he had certainly seized the initiative and had the element of surprise on his side. Now he ordered the back ranks of cohorts to step back two paces. Rank by rank they discharged their javelins over their fellow soldiers' heads.

Hundreds of javelins of Roman steel flew through the air and split barbarian heads open or pierced their limbs. The Brigantes at the back of the column could do nothing as the javelins fell down upon them. Hemmed in from the front and the back by their own troops, they fell in vast numbers, like the scything of wheat.

The enemy warriors who had been pushing forward had no cover from the Roman missiles. They tried to take cover but it was useless. Wave after wave of javelins maimed and killed hundreds in seconds. Some froze and edged backwards. Hesitation suddenly crept into their minds, spreading like an infectious disease across the remaining troops. With their front line being pushed back and hundreds of javelins raining on their heads they broke. The barbarians to the north and south turned and ran.

Some dropped shields or swords. But most just ran for their lives, frantic to escape the constant pitiless thumping of Roman spears into bodies.

The Romans in the Ninth Legion cheered and cheered again. They were too tired to kill any more.

"Maniple the lines", ordered Marcus so that the fresh troops at the back now moved to the front line. The exhausted troops who had been on the front line for almost an hour, their relentless defence broken only by their desperate charge, now lay on the ground, exhausted. Marcus moved amongst them and went over to congratulate the nearest legionnaire he had watched single-handedly dispatch a dozen shrieking enemy warriors.

The soldier removed his helmet and Marcus found himself face to face with Novantes. Marcus laughed. "Not bad for an auxiliary troop", he announced, grinning widely.

"The gods are still protecting you, I see!" They clasped hands and embraced. "Remind me always to be on your side in a fight!" he added.

Marcus moved amongst the rest of the shattered soldiers, speaking to each group and encouraging them all.

"Tonight the Ninth Legion will celebrate. We have honoured our dead and brought great distinction for the Legion.

"Well done, *first spear*", said Marcus. "Get the men some rest and bring food for them from the baggage train."

The two men looked at the stack of corpses and the seriously wounded around the carts.

"Find out the casualty figure, too", nodded Marcus.

"Yes, sir. There are probably several thousand barbarians still out there. I expect them to take to the hills at some point", smiled the *first spear*.

"Hopefully now we can head back south to Eboracum. Get resupplied and re-equipped", concluded Marcus.

Marcus sense of victory was brought to an abrupt end as the *first spear* re appeared some twenty minutes later. "I have the overall casualty figure, sir. Forty eight dead. One hundred and five wounded of whom at least half will die. I also have three officers dead".

"Thank you", said Marcus. "It's not a pretty scene but at least we can still fight."

Marcus gazed out over the battlefield, still amazed at the slaughter they had inflicted. Several hundred barbarians lay dead, dying or brutally injured in the field surrounding the Roman's defensive square. Overhead, crows were already congregating, their greedy cries adding to the anguished wails of the wounded to create an unearthly choir.

"Catch your breath lads, before they come back" ordered the *first spear*.

All along the Roman lines, centurions ordered their men to stand easy, with men resting their shields on the ground and telling each other of how they had killed their enemies.

Marcus rode along the first cohort. "Well done, men. Good work. You showed them not to mess with us." The men looked up at their legate and smiled.

"We don't have to kill them all" spoke Marcus loudly enough to the First cohort, "just enough to demoralise them and they will lose heart. I think they now realise that."

"After this is all over, *First Spear*, I intend to retire to a nice civil job where people don't hit you with swords!"

The soldiers of the First cohort and *first spear* laughed. "I don't blame you, sir. Once this is all over for me, I can see me settling down on a nice piece of land and doing a bit of farming in peace."

Both men smiled and thought about their wishful future. It was much better than their bloody present.

*

To the north, six men in dark robes appeared in front of the First cohort of Roman troops, just out of javelin range. Marcus listened as they called for their Gods to wipe these Romans off the face of the earth. They cursed the Romans with their own Gods and promised that they would be victorious.

Ortagerous was furious. He held up his hands at the retreating men. "One more time and we will have them beaten. I myself will lead our cavalry". He gave orders to the Votadini clan chiefs who had been waiting behind. "Now brother, I understand why Romans keep troops hidden away. *Reserves* they call them, you say?"

Vordimus nodded. "Yes, my brother, this is our final chance to beat them. You see our warriors flow around them like water flows around a rock? Yet still they are in the valley. We charge them on all sides again."

The fresh troops with Ortagerous in the north now split across the battle field. Desperate for a Roman head or kill of their own, a thousand of them had been kept back in case of defeat. Now they charged headlong towards the Roman First cohort without hesitation.

At the front a mass of cavalry swerved down the valley. Vordimus guided them by himself. He knew they must use every man to attack this small Roman square.

*

Cornelia heard a noise behind her: voices were moving this way. Had she been discovered? She moved quickly away from the trees until she found a path and followed it towards a river. The noise from the warrior troops was getting quieter now. Just before the river she saw a horse rider approach. She pulled up her hood and raised her sword.

"Help!" she cried out.

The man rode up and pulled over, addressing her in quick Celtic. She wasn't listening too intently, speedily stabbing him with her sword. He cried out but Cornelia pulled him by his leg from the horse, swiftly slicing across his throat. She didn't want further noise alerting any one. She had to head south and warn Marcus – if it wasn't too late already.

Armthal and the clan leaders stood with their hands raised and turned back the Brigantes in the south, "We can beat the Romans. I know we can." Their cries of vengeance and retribution had rallied the men now. Armthal led them himself.

*

"Listen?" said the *first spear*.

Dark clouds filled the sky and the first drops of rain had come on. A distant thunder rolled across the valley.

"Thunderstorm? "moaned the *first spear*, glowering up at the sky.

"No", replied Marcus. "That's not thunder. It's horsemen".

Marcus shouted the command to the trumpeter who blew a single note. Every soldier knew their rest was over and resumed their defensive stance with their shields. Death was racing towards them.

"This is it!" called out Marcus. "They have come back to be beaten again "

"Long live the Ninth Legion!" echoed around the square as the men knew they could beat these savages.

*

Marcus knew now he had no choice. He had been holding his cavalry in the centre of the square in case they were needed. Now was their time. He called the German auxiliaries to get ready. The First cohort opened their lines and the fifty horsemen rode out to meet the enemy calvary.

Marcus made to ride with them as they formed a neat line across the road and down the hill but their German decurion insisted he return to the square.

Marcus watched as the two sides sped towards one another with swords outstretched. Equal in numbers, yes, but the Roman horses were heaver. The sides smashed into each other at enormous force. Hands, arms and even legs were hacked off as the men on horses rushed past their opponents, flaying at everything that moved.

Vordimus rode directly in the front of the cavalry charge. "Throw your spears first into the Romans and then attack them with your swords" he screamed.

Vordimus threw his spear at an approaching Roman, pushing him back off the horse as it landed in his chest. The next one he cut with his sword as the soldier passed. Swords clashed as men cut men. Horses stuck in mud could not move as the battle became a sea of sticky heavy slime. The heavier armed Romans appeared to be winning. But not for much longer. Vordimus looked around him. Just twenty feet away came the fresh troops of the Votadini tribe. A thousand men screaming their war cries swept over the Roman calvary, hauling them from their horses, then bludgeoning them. The Brigante's leader rallied his troops for a moment and the Roman swords were prised from death grips to be re used.

"Follow me!" shouted Vordimus, wheeling around his horse. Up the hill of Hades End they struggled before stopping and turning. Vordimus knew the momentum of a horse charge down the slope could not be stopped.

"Charge!" he shouted and let his sword fall. Thirty men on horses were all that was left and they followed his path down.

The Fourth cohort, who had never been blooded so far, were four lines deep facing up the hill at Hades End. They had seen the horse turn and face them. Expecting their charge Marcus ordered them to keep their shields up and javelins pointed outward.

Down the barbarians came, thundering louder and louder. Screams of pain were heard as the Brigantes cavalry hit the Roman troops. The momentum of the horses meant there was no way to avoid the Roman javelins. Down went the horse under Vordimus as he tried to control it. However, it was mortally wounded, with two javelins thrusts piercing its front. The fatally injured horse continued thrashing as it tumbled over and without Vordimus realising it had suddenly crushed two men while the others around it had fallen backwards. A huge gap had been created in the line and the other Brigitian cavalry saw their opportunity. Into the opening they poured, jumping over Vordimus horse, others trying to make the breach wider. Brigantes swords flashed at Roman shields.

The *first spear* turned and saw that gap opening, too. He ran forward with his sword drawn and slayed the first rider after cutting down the horse. More horses were charging down the hill into the Fourth cohort, most being killed outright or falling back from the Roman soldiers jabbing them with their javelins.

Vordimus tried desperately to extricate himself. One leg was still trapped beneath the horse but his free hand was lunging at the Romans around him. A further horse plunged into the gap and the soldiers around him threw their javelins at it. The horse fell and rolled to the opposite side. The gap had got wider still. Yet another horse jumped over both and suddenly it was inside the square. The *first spear* moved forward again and swung his sword, the barbarian parried it back with his own. The horse reared up now and kicked the *first spear* full in the face. He flew through the air and crashed to the ground.

*

Cornelia had rode the horse down the side of the river. In front of her were a great number of dead Roman horses and riders. She looked out over the sea of bodies, hoping Marcus was not amongst them.

In the distance she noticed tribesmen moving down the valley. Further into the valley she could make out the standards of the Legion still camped in the middle. She hoped Marcus was still alive. But what could she do on her own?

An idea came to her. She remembered the Roman standard she had seen lying at the river crossing. She went back to retrieve it at once.

*

Centurions barked orders to face forward but it was too late. The men of the Fourth cohort started to turn inwards to face the threat behind them. As they did so, more horses charged down the slope and into the unprepared troops.

Marcus moved quickly to the Second cohort on the other side and ordered half of them to about face and run over with their javelins. A massive melee broke out in the centre of the square. Panicked horses jostled in the tight space, some with riders, some crushing and stamping as Roman soldiers tried to kill them. More horses charged freely into the square as there was nothing to stop them. Centurions caught in the crush were cursing and bellowing orders.Half the Fourth cohort had turned to face the horses inside now. There was no one listening to the screams of centurions any more.

Armthal could hear the commotion and see the Roman soldiers in the Fifth cohort glance backwards. "We have them now!" he shouted, "Charge!" The men around him attacked with renewed frenzy.

Marcus watched as half the Second cohort now stood with their shield wall up, trying to drive the horses out. But it was of little use. Their targets had far greater weight and were freely stamping the men inside. Armthal ordered his troops to push the Roman shields again. His men closed the gap and a thousand Brigantes pushed into the shield wall of the Fifth cohort.

It was as if the entire Brigantes nation had launched itself in one final assault against the Ninth Legion. The Roman line was bending, the Fourth cohort was now a commotion of horses and Romans, the First cohort turning to face the new horses entering, while the Fifth cohort were being pushed back again. The Second cohort were the only ones facing the horses in line. Marcus ordered all legionnaires to discharge all javelins at the nearest enemy and a satisfying swish of iron swept through the air once more. The Roman line could not hold out much longer. The entire battle rested on this moment. The fate of the Ninth Legion, of the northern frontier of Rome, lay open. If they did not win this battle there would be no legion to stop the Brigantes marching on through central Britannia.

At that moment a great chariot appeared charging down the hill, two ponies pulling it, an elaborate gold design flashing against the sunlight.

Ortagerous, standing behind his driver, had thrown his spear into a Roman soldier and killed him up close. As they headed for the gap in the First cohort, another javelin took the life of his driver. Ortagerous grabbed the reigns of the chariot as it veered off course and plunged into the Roman soldiers of the First cohort. The men fell like reeds as the two horses threw them aside. Ortagerous drew his sword along the Roman line and killed three of them as they sought to get out his way. The men of the First cohort had been taught to believe in their own invincibility. They had not expected determined opposition like this. Attacked on the front by the fresh troops and the side by horses and chariots, they recoiled backwards to protect themselves. There was no officer or *first spear* to correct them now. Soldiers caught in the crush were cursing and shouting orders to halt.

Marcus called the entire Second cohort to stand in line facing the enemy. The trumpeter beside him called the retire. Four notes sounded out. The legionnaires looked around and took a step back. A fighting retreat was all they could do now. Shields up and still facing the enemy, the Romans soldiers disengaged.

A few centurions barked orders, retiring behind the Second cohort, as the soldiers spilled around the sides. The enemy attacked with even greater frenzy as Arthmal and his men saw the Roman line falling back.

He laughed and cried, "we have them beaten my brothers, onwards, kill them all!"

As the Romans retreated only the First cohort kept good order. The Brigantes killed hundreds of their adversaries who broke ranks.

Marcus stood beside the trumpeter and the Eagle standard. "Fall back to the bottom of this hill", he ordered. "Second cohort stay here in line". Marcus stood by as he ordered another centurion with the trumpeter and Eagle to the foot of the hill. "Where are all the other officers?" he asked.

"They are dead, sir", came a breathless reply.

The First cohort enacted a fighting retreat as best possible. Down the hill they retired, backwards, step by step, down the slippery grass. Any who stumbled were swiftly engulfed by barbarians hovering around them like wolves trailing weaker prey. A centurion barked orders to redress lines and form shield walls. They retired until they were level with the Second cohort.

The First and Fourth cohorts held the line. In danger of being outflanked, Marcus also ordered men down either side. They slowly fell back. Marcus looked behind to see the rest of the legion forming up.

Even with the shield wall in place, legionnaires would succumb to exhaustion and fall over. Fatigue had crept in.

"We have to climb this hill behind us", motioned Marcus. "This will be where we make our stand. We can beat their infantry and retreat down the other side".

The Romans climbed the hill as darkness was falling. They had been marching for six hours and battling some three more on the battlefield. Every legionnaire was exhausted and felt the tiredness creeping into their very bones.

"Halt. Form a line!" was shouted when they made it to the top. Some men had already looked over their shoulders and saw the barbarians chasing after them and broke rank. Overcome by uncustomary panic, legionnaires dropped weapons and shields and fled from the hilltop.

Marcus tried to stop them. "Halt! Dress ranks. There is no disgrace in dying here for the legion. If you run, you are a coward!"

The hundreds of men remaining around him formed another square around the crest of the hill. The dead bodies of their comrades lay heaped at the bottom, the wounded amongst them. Now only the baggage train was left.

The Brigantes warriors had a free rein to loot both the wounded legionnaires and ransack the baggage train. Injured men were robbed of valuables then summarily executed. Marcus and his comrades rested at the summit, witnessing their enemies plundering everything they could get their blood-stained hands on.

Eventually Ortagerous and Armthal managed to get the men organised again. "The Romans are still here. We must destroy them", they cried.

*

Marcus looked around at the exhausted and wounded men on the hilltop who still held their discipline. "When everything else is lost, the army has a last few shreds of diginity and pride. We are the Ninth Legion and we know how to fight".

Marcus knew his job above all else was to maintain their ranks.

"At best these men who leave us disgrace the Legion. They will be killed or wounded trying to escape for nothing.

I pride myself that I can keep my oath for this Legion and its fallen dead."

All this was common knowledge to the men. And there was one other thing so deeply embedded in their consciousness that it was never forgotten: their reverence for their Eagle standard. Standards were originally simple rally points for troops lost in the heat of battle. However for Romans, the Eagle standard had evolved from a mere flag to the physical manifestation of what they believed they were fighting for.

Their Eagle was presented by Caesar himself hundreds of years before and had become a precious token of their parades. Their Eagle had been touched by every emperor and blessed by priests from Rome, such was its Godly significance. To lose it was a disgrace which could haunt a legion for ever. To defend it, men cast away their lives.

"When they come up here, try to keep the square. Then fight in pairs with your partner. If he falls, find another, or fight in a group. Watch each other's back."

Marcus watched the Brigantes reforming below. With great cries from their leaders they climbed the hill towards them. Beyond them, Marcus glimpsed the darkening fields below, where friends and mortal enemies were reduced to broken corpses, ignominiously strewn around, mixed together.

The outcome of the battle seemed largely to rest on his shoulders. He knew precisely what he had to do.

He turned to the men. "By every rule of military code there is only one thing we can do. Defend the Eagle. My death will not be usless if I can do this before the gods."

The men nodded as one.

"Stand up and prepare to receive them."

The enemy infantry were climbing the slopes, inching closer. The remnants of the Ninth waited as their enemies progressed nearer the summit. With both sides exhausted, the battle seemed to have regressed to slow motion, the sword blows and parries almost lethargic in execution, the dull clunk of metal against metal betraying that vitality had long seeped from tired limbs. If anything, the tide appeared to have turned again as the Romans fought for their very lives. And, crucially, their Eagle.

A large barbarian appeared early in front of Marcus. He feigned a thrust and then smashed his sword across Marcus' arm, the blow severing flesh. Falling back, Marcus propped himself up on the grass and, as the giant moved clumsily closer, delivered the fatal blow. The barbarian stumbled backwards, striking the men behind. More took his place and Marcus could see nowhere to manoeuvre. The whole Roman line was engaged in hand to hand combat now.

Romans troops disciplined in killing still took more lives than the Brigantes. However, the numbers piling up the bloody slopes were just so many. Marcus parried another attack from the front, while thrusting into the groin of another. An unseen hand lunged at his already bloody arm, cutting it further. Marcus knew he had to hold onto his sword.

More and more Romans were being overwhelmed. Marcus looked around as he saw Novantes striking and killing in a circle around him. Like a cornered animal, he struck and dodged and struck again, killing at least five men before going down to a spear thrust. The Standard bearer gripped the Eagle and swung the great symbol around as a weapon, knocking two barbarians to the ground, using the sharp point to despatch them with thrusts into their guts. A barbarian stabbed him in the back just as he regained his grip.

Marcus moved and gripped the Eagle standard as it slipped from the bearer's hand and he forced it into the ground. A command was shouted from behind the warriors. Adversaries ceased their desperate final struggles. Nobody moved. Then a great barbarian leader moved forward. The circle around Marcus slowly parted to allow him passage. Marcus waited, breathing harshly, the standard in one hand, his dripping sword in the other.

The barbarian laughed at him scornfully.

"Come on, you bastards! Get it over with!" screamed Marcus. "At least I will take one of you with me".

Vordimus scolded him. "You may be a great Roman officer and very brave. But your head will adorn my homestead well tonight."

As Vordimus lurched forward to take the prized Eagle, Marcus tried to stab him quickly with his sword. Vordimus jumped out the way and another warrior swung a huge sword across his torso. Marcus felt a pain in his side and fell over. He tried to hold onto the Eagle while Vordimus prised it from his hand.

Vordimus stood on his Roman sword as blood poured out from Marcus' multiple wounds. Marcus felt the world around him dissolving, as if his entire pain-wracked body was sinking into the blood-drenched battlefield.

Vaguely, he thought he heard a sound. It was hard to identify. But as he latched onto this through his failing consciousness he identified it. It was a cavalry trumpet, somewhere in the valley far below. He brought his other arm round to keep hold of the Eagle but Vordimus was pulling it out the ground.

The trumpet blast sounded again, more forcefully this time and the chieftain looked up. Vordimus swore under his breath. "I thought we had finished the cavalry?"

He hacked at the Eagle with an axe until its wooden pole broke. Vordimus lifted the Eagle standard high and a cheer went up.

"Come, my friends. We have what we wanted. Let's us leave this place of death."

Marcus was mildly aware of receding voices, until he sank into the comfort of defeat and death, and his broken body submitted to the welcome blackness and calm of the void.

Chapter XXIV: Aftermath

10.05am, 21st December, 117AD: The Infirmary, Eboracum

Through the blackness of death, Marcus opened his eyes. He lay looking upwards. White light filled his eyes and he could feel his chest rise and fall with his breath.

"Am I in Elysium?" he asked anybody.

The metallic tang of blood was still in the air, or maybe still in Marcus' nasal passages. He didn't know. He had no idea where he was and had no desire to wonder. He simply accepted.

Diocles face appeared over him.

"Ah. You're awake. No you're here with me. Now drink this water, Prefect."

Diocles lifted his head up slightly and Marcus drank the cold clear water.

"You're lucky to be alive. If it hadn't been for Cornelia, you would most certainly not be here."

Marcus eyes opened wide. "She's alive?"

"Yes. You can thank her for your life. Quite remarkable. Never seen such medical skills. She used your neck scarf as a tourniquet to stop the bleeding and applied some lime plants to prevent infection in the wounds. Wrapped your leg in your cloak and brought you here. Quite remarkable, Prefect. Couldn't have done a better job myself. She persuaded some other soldiers to bring back Novantes, too." He paused. "Although he is in a worse condition."

"Orderly" shouted Diocles to the nearest attendant.

"Novantes is here too? How in the name of Jupiter did she manage that? "

"Well, you can ask her. She should be here within the hour, " smiled Diocles. "If you would excuse me, Sir, I have other patients to attend to, now. I will come back in an hour or so."

Diocles passed a jar of water over to an orderly. "Keep him drinking this."

And left the room.

Marcus finally realised that he was in the infirmary at Eboracum. Alive. He smiled in wonderment.

*

Hadrian stood on the steps of the Senate steps as the crowd continued to chant his name.

" Caesar, Caesar, Caesar" was shouted from the rooftops. Hadrian looked around and smiled at Turbo at his side.

Senator Commodus approached them both and Hadrian embraced his old friend.

"Senator, you have done well. Without your help I would not have been able to enter the city."

"Yes", said Commodus. "Did you get my letter about being under house arrest?"

Hadrian shook his head. "No, I was not aware, old friend. Are you hurt?"

"No, no, it's fine. It's just that I was not able to distribute the money we spoke off to the Praetorian Guards, as you asked me".

Hadrian's head swung round. "You *didn't* distribute the money? I walked up to the Gate of Polopo with javelins being thrown at me."

"That would probably explain why, Caesar", said Commodus weakly.

Hadrian laughed. "If I had known that before, my actions would have certainly been different!"

Turbo smiled. "Then you have the loyalty of the Guard, even without the money, Caesar".

Hadrian, Turbo and Commodus walked through the crowded streets once more. With the Tenth Legion lining the route back to the Regia and the Praetorian Guard around him, the sight of one hundred thousand citizens of Rome thronging the streets was a memory to cherish. It was good to be back.

*

The next time Marcus opened his eyes, he thought he was imagining the face of Cornelia, leaning over him. His bewildered look made her smile.

"Hello," she said, "Bet you didn't expect to see me here!"

Marcus was speechless, and could only summon a quizzical look in response.

"What happened on the battlefield?" Marcus struggled to recall the events.

Cornelia smiled, one eyebrow raised in irony, "Lucky for you, I blew a Roman cavalry trumpet I had found. The Brigantes thought I was the reinforcements arriving!" she grinned now, "Which, indeed, I was!"

"What?" frowned Marcus, bewildered, still not quite fully awake.

"I managed to escape my captors and discovered the area of riverbank where our cavalry had been beaten," Cornelia explained gently, "I picked up one of their standards and a discarded bugle from the scene, rode towards the battlefield, and blew as hard as I could," explained Cornelia, with a twinkle in her eye. "The Brigantes had obviously had their fill of fighting. And they're terrified of Roman cavalry. They made do with grabbing what booty they could and turned tail."

Marcus' brow wrinkled, half in disbelief that the barbarians had been so easily deceived, and half in amazement that this woman would do something so audacious to save his life.

Cornelia, chattered on, delighted to see Marcus more conscious after a feverish few days, "Then we were able to save the few men left, and bring you back."

"What happened to the rest of my Legion?" he asked, wearily lifting his head.

Cornelia looked at him seriously. She shook her head. "Everyone was killed Marcus. Only a few survived, all wounded."

"Our Eagle?" Marcus enquired raising his head.

"They took it." Cornelia murmured.

The hair on Marcus neck stood on end. They had lost the Eagle. His head dropped back onto the bed.

"It would have been better I had died" he said. "Death before dishonour."

He lay back and thought of the consequences.

"No, it's not. You're still here for a reason. The gods are watching over you."

She took his hand. "You're here for a reason", she repeated. There is no dishonour in defending your Eagle. That's what you did. They took it but it cost them dearly. Hundreds of Brigantes died in that final assault."

Marcus looked away. She was right. They had defended it with all their might. There was nothing more he could have done. He searched his head. What could he have done differently? Maybe if they had left it until the new campaigning season, maybe if they had scouted the land ahead better. Maybe, maybe...

Cornelia made to leave.

Marcus called after her. "Thank you Cornelia, for saving my life. It is a debt I cannot repay."

Marcus lay back. As soon as he was better they would recover the Eagle again. He would recover the Ninth Legion's honour. It was not finished just yet.

*

Hadrian had just settled into the Regia. Its surroundings were small but comfortable. He sat in the sunshine of the garden and drank in the view of Rome before him.

A messenger appeared in the state room. Turbo took the message bearing the Imperial seal. "Caesar is not be disturbed."

He opened it and read.

News from Governor Quintus Pompeius Falco of Britannia. The tribes in northern Britannia have risen and defeated the Ninth Legion in Eboracum. The northern Frontier has fallen.

Turbo approached Hadrian.

"Caesar. I have grave news for you. The Ninth Eagle has fallen."

*

Around a briefing room an hour later stood Hadrian, Turbo, and General Patois Nepos, with maps strewn across the table.

"Based on the limited intelligence, we have we must react as appropriate. We must move the Second Augusta based at Caerlon up immediately. Move the Twentieth Valeria Victrix from Chester up. Also bring over the Sixth Legion from Gallia," motioned Hadrian. "Order conscription of further auxiliary troops throughout Britannia."

"Caesar, this is a huge amount of men for such an uprising" questioned General Nepos.

"I understand, my friend. However, my plan is not destruction but construction." Hadrian said grimly. "We leave tomorrow. I shall assess the situation when I am there.

"Turbo,you are here by promoted to City Prefect. I need someone who will attend to affairs in Rome in my absence. It is imperative that... certain parties are kept in order," Hadrian stated.

Turbo knew exactly whom he meant. He nodded sharply, with determination. He would ensure that everything in Rome was kept in order, and that Attianus was kept strictly out of harm's way – although Turbo would gladly have dispensed with him more radically than that. However, killing Attianus would not be politic, and Hadrian could suffer the backlash of such a rash deed perpetrated by his right-hand man.

"General Nepos, you are promoted to Governor of Brittania with immediate effect. I need a man who can quell this uprising."

"Yes, Caesar", nodded Nepos.

Hadrian had made his decision that the northern reaches of the empire now needed his attention if the Roman Empire was to be retained. Although Hadrian had no desire to further expand the empire, or vanquish more countries, he wanted to retain and consolidate the imperial lands he was ruling over. He had his staff quickly pack up and headed for the far northern frontier. Britannia could not be lost, and the defeat of the Ninth meant radical intervention was necessary.

He had long pondered upon how to keep the northern tribes out of Roman Britain. There was only one thing for it, and the sooner the better.

*

Hadrian had travelled for many days, stopping off in Londinium to berate General Falco for the dire situation in the north. The Roman legions were highly trained, proficient soldiers. Yes the Brigantes were a warlike tribe but they had been pacified some forty years earlier. Eboracum had been placed in the centre of their land and the tribe won over. How had they failed this?

It was outrageous that the tribes from the north had been permitted to beat the glorious forces of the empire!

"Caesar, it is unthinkable, I know," Falco lowered his head in shame.

"Unthinkable, yet true!" Hadrian roared, "Ye gods! I had hoped that the news I heard was unfounded rumour. And yet, I arrive and the story is worse than I feared! Our outposts burned out, many thousands dead, and the enemy warriors loose in the countryside!"

He paced the room angrily, his eyes flashing, and his fists clenched so tightly that Falco feared that he himself might be punched to the ground. "There will be changes here," Hadrian seethed. "I shall begin with new appointments in the army. How many of the Ninth remain?"

"No officers, Caesar, but one: Marcus Valerius Quietus. And few men. We are talking merely handfuls, and then mostly wounded."

Hadrian cursed, and smashed his fist against a table top.

"Falco, you are hereby dismissed of your post. Your retirement will be announced with immediate effect. You have brought a great shame upon our Empire."

Falco stood, dry-mouthed, unable to speak.

Both men thought of General Varus some hundred years before them who had lost three legions in the Tuttenberg forest in Germani. These legions had lost their Eagle standards and with it their name and title. Caesar Augustus had ordered the removal of the three legion numbers from the Roman army list, never to be used again.

Hadrian thought of the alternatives. There were none. At this stage in his reign the public outcry would damage not only himself as their commander-in-chief but more so his standing with the Senate. It would be a public disgrace upon him.

No, he would not allow Rome's confidence in him to be destroyed. This uprising would be dealt with in a new way.

*

Northern Britannia had never seen such a military build-up of men and equipment. Boat after boat arrived at Pons Aelius. The Second Augusta, Sixth Victrix and Twentieth

Valeria Victrix Legions were all moved up into the area. The Sixth Victrix now took over the barracks at Eboracum.

Along with Hadrian's advisors and travelling court, some eighteen thousand soldiers filled the area.

*

Marcus was by now almost fully recovered from his wounds, when he was summoned for an audience with the emperor at Eboracum.

Hadrian looked at him keenly, with a twist to his mouth that Marcus found difficult to read. Was it approval or disappointment? Marcus was ever aware that this man was his enemy, as well as his Emperor. He had ordered the death of his family, and Marcus would never forgive him that. Marcus' loyalties as a soldier lay with the Roman Empire, not with this callous, inscrutable man before him, who seemed half amused to see his only surviving officer standing before him, still alive.

"Quietus," Hadrian stroked his beard thoughtfully, and Marcus braced himself for the worst. If Hadrian wanted Quietus dead or out of the way forever, the defeat of the Ninth was his very excuse to do his worst.

"I hear that your valour and persistence was second to none in the recent... incidents," Hadrian said, his eyes never moving from pinioning Marcus' own gaze, "And for that, I thank you on behalf of the Roman Empire, the Senate, its citizens. We appreciate the bravery, courage and fortitude you displayed in the face of relentless onslaught and insurmountable odds.

As you are aware, the Eagle standard of the legion was lost. Therefore I have no alternative but to disband the Legion."

Marcus's head fell.

"It is not a reflection upon you, Prefect. The remaining men of the Ninth Legion will be distributed among other legions. If your injuries do not allow you to fulfil your enlistment, you will be honourably discharged from the army with immediate effect. If you make a full recovery and you wish to return, then I need good officers like you."

Hadrian missed nothing.

"You did your best, Prefect. Your record will reflect that."

Marcus said nothing.

"Quietus, I understand your disappointment. Your face is an open scroll, and it reads of bad news. You may speak freely."

Marcus' mouth twitched but he could not keep the truth of his feelings from Hadrian any longer.

"Caesar.I have to ask you a question. My father was senator Lucius Quietus who was killed on your orders. I cannot hide my feelings for the man who killed my family."

Hadrian had never forgotten the four senators who had been executed on his orders.

"Ah,Quietus. I understand then that you think I ordered their execution. Believe me – this was none of my doing. Attianus gave the command, as head of Praetorian Guard."

"On your behalf, Sir. I cannot blame the sword, but he who wields it."

Hadrian's face darkened with anger, "I knew *nothing* of this matter. He worked alone, and took action of which I had no knowledge. This has been too much his trouble in many recent incidents. Quietus, I asked the City Prefect to retire, several months ago after the execution of your family. However, he refused. I had spies in Rome who told me how he sought to undermine me. When I arrived in Rome I forced him to retire publicly.Politically, he is yet a powerful man, so it was all I could do as yet.

I cannot further express my extreme regret at the loss of your parents and sister. Still yet, I regret that a murderer should allege that such a deed be done in *my* name."

Hadrian paused.

"Quietus, I swear by my family's name to you that I did not order their deaths."

Marcus scrutinised the dark eyes, and saw only a gentle empathy. In Hadrian's lips, a shape of sorrow.

"I fear we are both victims of an arrogant man's overweening pride, Quietus," Hadrian added, softly.

Attianus. That made sense. Marcus nodded, "Then I accept your word Caesar."

Hadrian extended his hands, "And if there is anything else I can do..."

"Yes," Marcus said quickly, "As a matter of fact, there is. I need transport to Rome Caesar"

*

Fortified by purpose and fully recovered, Marcus made plans to travel back to Rome and shared his intention with Cornelia.

"But why go to Rome?" Cornelia cried, uncomfortable at the thought of returning within her Master's reach.

"I have a duty," Marcus said grimly, "To the memory of my family, and to the honour of my family name. Hadrian told me he has retired Attianus but did not say where. If I have to knock every door in Rome to find out where he is I shall find out!

Cornelia, you told me the Gods have saved me for a reason. My reason is to revenge the death of my father and family. I believe our Emperor to be true to his word."

Corneilla nodded." I may be able to tell you *exactly* where he is", she offered.

Marcus looked at her questioningly.

"But before I do, I have something to tell you. You trust me, Marcus?"

"Of course", he said.

Cornelia held his eyes and nodded, blushing guiltily at the same time. He did not know the whole truth, for sure. But those days were over.

"I knew you had been posted to Eboracum and to the Ninth Legion. Attianus posted you here to get you out the way and then sent myself to kill you."

Marcus laughed. "Are you joking?"

"How do you think I got a job in the busiest ale house in Eboracum? I knew soldiers in garrisons would eventually spend their money there. It was my way to find you. One day I came upon Metellus walking down the street and recognised him to be an assassin of Attianus, too."

Marcus couldn't believe what he was hearing. "Now that makes sense!" he recalled all of the times that Metellus had put him in danger, nearly drowning. He hadn't just been an overweening bully. And on the hill top? "He said it was his job to kill me! He was a hired assassin."

He paused. "And yet you saved my life on the battle field?"

"Because I knew that you were an honourable man. A man I could trust."

Marcus had stepped back. "How did you learn your medical skills?" he asked. Cornelia had slumped to the floor.

"I learned how to kill a man with poisons and I also know how to make them better", Cornelia carried on. "However I *hate* Attianus now! While he had power, he had control over me! I don't want to be that person anymore, Marcus. I fear for my own life. Attianus is a powerful man in Rome. But here I felt free of his grip. I don't want to go back there now."

Marcus looked deep into her eyes, acknowledging the logic of her argument and the intensity of her emotion, with his anger dissipating. Marcus understood. "Then we both have a vested interest in finding him as soon as possible."

Marcus' brows knitted together, compounding his decision.

Marcus held her close. "I have to do this and so do you. The gods have spared us for this very reason, I know it."

Cornelia smiled weakly as Marcus planned it out.

"Besides now that Novantes is better, let us take him with us. An extra sword hand would be useful."

"I know exactly where he is." Cornelia spoke quietly, "but I am scared Marcus."

*

The Mediterranean Sea was still a glorious turquoise although the afternoon had long slipped into evening. The sky was a swirl of blues, oranges, reds and lilac as the sun began dipping its burning sphere into the sea's horizon.

Attianus stood on his balcony and sighed in relaxation and relief. He always felt at his best in Capri. Safe. Whether it was the island itself, or the fact that he was secure in his own home, a day's distance from the bustle and cut-throat politicking of Rome, he didn't know, but it was his haven. This was only respite, after all, and he needed this time to regain his energies and rally support before his next great strike upon Hadrian's governance.

Livia, Attianus' latest concubine, was somewhere in the house, but he frankly could not be bothered with her or entertainment at the moment. He would call for her when he wanted her. For now, he wanted to be left to his own devices, and to think.

Attianus stood with his hands on the marble parapet surrounding his balcony terrace, and smiled out at the beautiful sunset before him. Hadrian might think he had bettered him this time, but the fool had let him live. And while Attianus was alive, he vowed to become Emperor. But for now, he would lie low for a while and take advantage of this 'banishment' to consider his next foray for the imperial purple. Ha! Did he not already have the robes? Let Hadrian's simmering resentment die down, let him forget all this, and when Hadrian's guard had slipped, Attianus would be prepared to strike. He almost laughed.

Suddenly, the door of his chamber opened, and he turned, abruptly torn from his musings.

Cornelia stood before him.

Attianus' eyes widened in shock, "Vulpecula! My Little Fox! I had no idea you were returned!"

Cornelia smiled, and stood demurely where she was.

"Have you... er..." he cleared his throat, "I expect you may have met Livia, Senator Quillius' wife, who visits me here?"

"Yes," Cornelia smiled, "But she will not be joining us this evening."

Attianus' lip flickered with a nervous tic. He struggled to make out Cornelia's intention, to arrive unannounced in Capri like this. He had had no word of her for months, and presumed her dead.

"The woman is... a mere diversion, Vulpecula," he waved his hand dismissively, "I am so pleased to see you alive and well! You know I have missed you, of course."

"Of course," Cornelia said, sweetly. She did not move from the door, but Attianus felt compelled to step towards her.

"You were successful?" he queried, trying to bluster his way through his surprise, "In your mission?"

"Oh, yes," she smiled, and Attianus approached her to embrace her.

Marcus stepped out of the doorway shadows, his sword drawn. Attianus' smile dropped from his face.

"I'm afraid I brought my work with me," Cornelia said, stepping next to Marcus, united against Attianus.

"Marcus Valerius Quietus," Marcus introduced himself, "Son of Lucius Quietus. You must remember him – and his wife? And daughter? You had them killed, remember? You were the one who ordered their deaths."

Attianus laughed scornfully, as if the idea was ridiculous, "Ha ha! Where do you hear such lies?"

"The truth that I hear is from the Emperor Hadrian himself."

Attianus raised an eyebrow, "The Emperor has a good sense of humour! And of course, he has every reason to protect his own guilt by blaming me. But, sadly, your family's assassination was all his doing."

Marcus laughed, "It was *you* that posted me to the northern frontier to get me out the way.Then *you* sent Cornelia here and Metellus to kill me. You didn't want any loose ends to come back to get you. Well I am back ex-Prefect."

"Now, now – what is this talk of 'ex'?" Attianus stepped backwards, eyeing Marcus' sword, "You may have the advantage of me, unarmed as I am, but I still have power here. I tell you, the absent Emperor cares for no-one and is ruthless against opposition. Look me in the eye while I tell you – I did not effect your family's death!" Attianus smirked.

"I asked Hadrian the same question and looked into his eyes," Marcus remarked steadily, stepping forward and pointing his sword. "The Emperor's eyes bore honesty, empathy and trust. Unlike your malevolence and deception. I accuse you, Attianus, and sentence you!"

"Guards!" yelled Attianus, backing away, "Guards! I warn you, my personal bodyguards are trained killers."

"They won't be joining you " said Novantes as he stepped forward out the shadows wiping his sword of blood.

Horrified, Attianus backed onto the balcony, Marcus and Cornelia stepping forward to follow him.

"I see you are unswayed," spoke Atttianus, struggling to maintain his dignity and arrogance, beset by nervous fear, "All right. One million denarii! "

"I want nothing for myself," Marcus said.

Attianus took one more pace backwards, closer to the marble palisade overlooking the cliffs above the Mediterranean Sea. Dusk had fallen, but the colours of the sunset were still evident, creating a spectacular backdrop to the drama on the terrace.

Marcus still approached. Sword drawn pointing at the neck.

"Two million denarii!" cried Attianus desperately, but Marcus continued his steady step towards him.

Marcus said, "Money is no recompense for my father, my mother and my sister's lives."

Marcus raised his sword again, "I am going to kill you. And when you're dead I shall throw your body into Potters Field on the Equiline Hill. Where the paupers and dead animals are thrown. Where the plague inflected bodies and filth lie. You shall have no funeral rites or burial chamber. Your soul will not rest as your body will not be laid to rest. Your carcass shall be left to the beasts of prey to feed upon."

Marcus moved forward again.

Attianus, shocked by the determined venom of the young man, wriggled his sandals to get his footing, holding his shoulders far back over the balustrade to avoid Marcus' advancing sword.

"You would not..." was all Attianus could utter, before he mistook the weight of his upper body leaning into the air behind him. He overbalanced, his feet scrabbling for stability, his hips leveraging themselves over the broad top of the marble balustrade by his head and shoulders tipping behind him, and he toppled over backwards, screaming. His last political speech and bartering for his life went unsaid.

Headfirst, all his hopes of returning triumphant to Rome in the purple robes of imperial office went hurtling through thin air and crashing on the sharp steep stairway of rocks below.

Cornelia ran forward, and she and Marcus peered over the terrace to the cliff bottom far below. Attianus' broken and bloody body was still bouncing off jagged promontories from the rock wall and into the seawashed rubble far down.

Cornelia held her trembling hand to her face.

"It's all right, Cornelia," Marcus dropped his sword and embraced her.

"Is he dead? Is he really dead?" she sobbed.

Marcus had seen for himself the flopping, loose head, obviously broken at the neck, the smashed limbs flailing like a rag doll.

"He is," he soothed.

"I'm only afraid he's not! Is he really dead?" Cornelia's teeth chattered with shock, then she wiped her tears.

"He truly is." said Novantes.

Marcus, Novantes and Cornelia looked out over the bay of Naples, their eyes far beyond the bloody mess of broken death below, turning to the glory of last remains of the sunset, and the deepening of night.

"Thank you both," whispered Cornelia, "I feel free again."

"Tonight, we celebrate," he announced. "My family were dead but now they have been avenged."

"I have reason to celebrate, too", smiled Novantes. You promised me a civic crown for killing more barbarians than anybody else". He added, "But after all he's been responsible for, the sight of that human weasel down there fills me with far more satisfaction than all the Brigantes we left lying in Britannia".

Marcus grasped his arm and they shook firmly. Then he turned to Cornelia, taking her hand with an altogether more delicate touch.

"I feel we've reached the end of a long, often fraught journey", he said to them. "Time to move on".

SPQR

Varus, give me back my legions!

Augustus Caesar after the defeat and annihilation
of Varus's column in teutoberg Forest.

Epilogue

10.05am, 18th July, 118 AD: Eboracum

Hadrian stood with the plans of the wall before him and smiled. General Nepos had overseen the start of work.

The architectural drawings indicated a great wall, 73 miles long, snaking across the northern limits of the Empire from coast to coast. Ten feet thick and constructed from solid stone, this impregnable barrier would be reinforced with regular towers. Strategically positioned forts placed along its length would be connected by a road.

Never again would the Roman Empire allow the unruly northern tribes to rampage freely across its territory. Britannia could never lose another Legion of Rome.

"History shall be kind to me", mused Hadrian. "For I intend to write it as such."

Appendix

The Roman legions

Until 31 B.C. legions had a number, or a name, but never both. Caesar Augustus (63 B.C. – 14 A.D.) reformed the Roman army, reducing the legions to a total of 28, giving each a number between 1 and 28. He also bestowed titles on the legions as rewards, or to celebrate their land of honour. These new legions were transformed into permanent units staffed by professional soldiers.

The new numbering system worked well up until a military disaster in 9 A.D, when three legions were completely annihilated by Germanic tribes during the Battle of Teutoburg Forest. Augustus retired their numbers – the Seventeenth, Eighteenth, Nineteenth – and these numbers were never incorporated again, a step respected by every subsequent Roman Emperor.

The Ninth Legion, known as "Hispania", were one of the oldest legions of Rome. Raised by Pompey the Great in 65 B.C. around Cordoba in Spain, they distinguished themselves in several major battles with Julius Caesar as their leader. For its emblem, the Ninth took the bull, a popular Spanish symbol. The bull emblem would appear on its standards and upon every soldier's shield.

The senior officer in charge of a legion was its Legate, usually around 30 years old and a member of the Senate. The Legate has six tribunes as his aides. The senior Tribune was invariably a young man from the Senate who, by virtue of his class, was the Legate's theoretical second in command. However, his main remit was to watch and learn. The five other tribunes served as staff officers. These young men were recruited from respectable Roman families, with experience of commanding auxiliary cohorts prior to this position.

The real officer of importance below the Legate was the Camp Prefect. His role was to oversee the running of the camp, particularly in terms of training and logistics. The Camp Prefect was an experienced career soldier who had spent his entire life in the army.

Attached to each legion were also was a small cavalry force of some 120 men, commanded by three Decurion officers. One Decurion would act as squadron commander and the other two as his deputies. Cavalry was primarily used for scouting, guarding and escorting the legion. Their offensive weapon included the cavalry sword which was much longer than the infantry *gladius* to provide greater reach.

However, as far as the Romans were concerned, the centurions were the backbone of the army. If the centurions performed well, the legion performed well and if the legion performed well, their General's reputation improved. Centurions were hand-picked men who would obey orders without hesitation. They were professional soldiers who led from the front.

Each legion consisted of 1 Legate, 6 Tribunes, 1 Camp Prefect, 120 cavalry, 60 centurions and around 5,000 Legionnaires. Roman Legionnaires were fighting fit young men, recruited at the age of 18 to serve for 25 years. They were capable of marching 25 miles a day with a pack on their back and expected to build their own fort when they arrived at their destination. Right from the start, these men were drilled in fighting formations and hand-to-hand combat. Later, the men were given a trade and became blacksmiths, carpenters, cobblers, clerks and builders within the army too. If you didn't have a skill, you were given one.

Ninth Legion

In 43 A.D. the Ninth Legion, along with three others, participated in the Roman invasion of Britain led by Emperor Claudius and General Aulus Plautius. In 50 A.D., the Ninth was one of two legions that defeated the forces of Caratacus at Caer Caradoc in Shropshire. Under the command of Caesius Nasica they put down the first revolt of Venutius between 52 and 57 A.D., who fought against the client Queen Cartimandua of the Brigantes. The client Queen caused a great deal of upset by divorcing her husband and marrying a Roman soldier. Later on when a second revolt broke out the Ninth returned to help her once again.

In 61 A.D. Boudica, the Queen of the Iceni, in Norfolk, almost destroyed the Ninth Legion when she fought them in Colchester. It is estimated that over 80% of the legion had been killed fighting. They had then been quickly reinforced in later months and helped pacify the remaining tribes. However, it should be **noted** that, based on a retirement period of 25 years, by 117 A.D. two generations of soldiers had retired and the soldiers of Ninth were now young recruits, with *six years' service, or less.*

The edge of civilization

In 117 A.D. the northern frontier of the Roman Empire lay across the Cheviot Hills between southern Scotland and northern England. Prior to the building of Hadrian's Wall defences relied on watchtowers that flashed signals between stations to the small isolated forts.

A simple road called the Stanegate ran between the larger forts of Carlisle in the west and Corbridge in the east, allowing Roman troops to patrol the region. The Ninth Legion themselves had created a permanent fort in the area occupied by the largest and most hostile British tribes much further south, in York.

The Brigantes were so numerous their territories stretched from southern Scotland all the way down to North Derbyshire. This single tribe had caused more problems for the Roman army in Britannia than any other. With time, the Brigantes began to appreciate there were more benefits to living alongside the Romans, trading with them, as opposed to violent confrontations that would provoke punitive retribution. Nevertheless, the threat that relations might once again deteriorate was never far from the minds of the legionnaires of the Ninth.

Two sources tell us about Hadrian's problems in Britannia upon his inheritance of the Imperial throne.

"The Britons could not be held under Roman control". Historia August, Hadrian V2.

"As many Roman soldiers were killed by the Britons at the beginning of Hadrian's rule, as by the Jews". Letter written to Emperor Lucius Verus by Marcus Fronto in 162 A.D.

Evidence of war with the Britons

Three tombstones which are worth mentioning identify officers who were stationed in Britannia. A tombstone in Frentium in Italy of Titus Sabinus as *first spear* of an 'Expedition Brittanica' – he fought around the time of Hadrian's succession. Further evidence of a conflict under Hadrian was found on the tombstone of Titus Annius, a centurion serving as acting commander of an auxiliary cavalry unit at Vindolanda. This suggests that the fighting with hostile Britons actually took place well north of Eboracum, almost where Hadrian was to later establish the wall.

Finally, in 1997 archaeologists discovered another fragmentary tombstone in Vindolanda of a centurion in a unit there around the time of Hadrian's succession. Unfortunately, the war is not named; however, the fact that so many officers died within that single area provokes several interesting theories.

The *first spear* of an auxiliary cavalry unit and two centurions were clearly leaders of men and as such would have been in the very thick of any battle. These men were hardened veterans and would have been supported by hundreds, if not thousands of other men. For officers and centurions to fight and die in such proximity would clearly suggest they were involved in a large scale battle.

There is one other particularly surprising historic detail from this period.

After 120 AD the Ninth Legion is never mentioned in any further campaigns, later service, archaeological finds,historical documents or by Roman historians anywhere in the Empire. In fact the Ninth Legion were later removed from the Roman army list of available legions. No other legions were given the 'Hispania' title or re-used the Ninth number again.

Roman artefacts and the fate of the Ninth

Pottery was produced in enormous quantities in Ancient Rome. It was used to transport and store liquids like olive oil or wine; it was fashioned into cooking pots, lamps, tiles or even bricks. These objects of trade are easily identifiable today because they were stamped with each potter's mark.

Yorkshire Museum is rich in pottery, with the potter's stamps clearly pinpointing the place where and date when items were made. Based on the evidence collated, it can be demonstrated that there was sharp drop in pottery production and use in York, in the period leading up to 120 A.D. In fact, the pottery created in York by their own potters leading up to 120 A.D. is similar in number to objects produced after the Romans had left Britain in 200 A.D.

In assessing the proportion of pottery, and therefore population, it is apparent that there was a large reduction in the occupation of York in the period leading up to 120 A.D. This would be consistent with the Ninth Legion leaving Eboracum at this time. After 130 A.D. it appears that York was once again fully garrisoned, as the pottery found dating from that period increases dramatically.

There are four Roman inscribed stones in York Museum which date to the presence of the Ninth Legion being garrisoned there, the most famous being the Tombstone of Lucius Rufinus, the standard Bearer of the Ninth Legion who died at 28 years old. All these inscriptions have been dated to around 108 A.D., when the Legion were last recorded. Further evidence of legionary tiles found at both Nijmegen in Holland and Carlisle do indicate that task forces of the Ninth Legion appeared to have been stationed at both locations.

Eminent Dutch archaeologist Professor JE Bogaers had suggested that the IX Hispania were transferred to Nijmegen in Holland having sustained heavy casualties, with the VI Victrix sent to replace it in Britain. Examination of the tiles at both Nijmegen and Carlisle were stamped LEG VIIII HIS, in contrast to the legion's tiles from York which were stamped LEG IX HIS.

However, these attest to the presence of Vexillations or sub units, in particular at Nijmegen, where it was believed a task force of many different units formed the garrison for a short period of time. Other tiles found from other Legions there indicated Vex(illation) Brit (annica). In fact it was common military practice that small units were transferred to other garrisons to complete specific tasks and then return.

There is no evidence to suggest that the whole legion was removed from York prior to 117 A.D. Infact I find it difficult to believe that Trajan would have felt it safe to remove one legion from Britain and even if one legion did have to leave, the Ninth would have been the least likely in a period when archaeological evidence indicates that there was constant trouble brewing. It seems more likely that Platorius Nepos, the new governor of Britain, brought with him the VI Victrix Legion to enlarge the number of troops required to build the wall. In any case, Hadrian now had a few legions to spare since Trajan's provinces in the east had been given up.

Finally, as Hadrian's Wall was being built from 122-128 A.D., there is not a single mile that was dedicated to the Ninth Legion. We can identify the legions responsible for constructing each section because the tradition of the time was to leave inscriptions. The Second, Sixth and Twentieth Legions have all left their mark in the stone. It is apparent that by the time the wall was being built, the Ninth Legion had ceased to exist.

Hadrian's succession

The Emperor Trajan died on 8th August 117 A.D. at Selinus in Cilicia in modern-day Turkey. He was returning to Rome from a campaign against the Parthians. Aged almost 65, he and his wife Plotina had no children.

On August 9th, Plotina announced that they had adopted as their son Publius Aelius Hadrian, commander of the army of Syria. Hadrian was related to Trajan on his father's side. Hadrian's father had died when he was nine years old; Acilius Attianus was appointed as his guardian.

Cassius Dio, who was a consul as well as a historian, claimed he heard that the news of Trajan's death was deliberately suppressed by Plotina so that Hadrian's adoption might be announced first. At the time Attianus held the influential position of commander of the Praetorian Guard, in which capacity he represented the Emperor. Attianus had been present at Trajan's death and helped the Empress secure the succession of Hadrian and forge Trajan's will.

Hadrian travelled from Antioch to Selinus in order to attend Trajan's cremation, returning to Antioch afterwards.

Meanwhile, upon arrival in Rome, Attianus immediately uncovered a plot to assassinate Hadrian by four high-ranking senators: Lucius Quietus, Avidis Nigrinus, Cornelius Palma and Publilius Celsus. Who actually ordered the death of four senators remains a mystery. However, all four men were prominent politicians who could have been considered as successors. The Senate remained furious that they had not been consulted by Trajan upon his appointment of Hadrian and the execution of the four prominent officials.

Lucius Quietus was a Roman General and Governor of Judea in 117AD. He served as an auxiliary officer in the Roman Cavalry and was elevated to the position of Senator after the successful conquest of Dacia.

Quietus was murdered in 118AD on the orders of Attianus.

Hadrian always denied that he had anything to do with the deaths; however, the Senate regarded him with suspicion for the rest of his life. This contributed to him spending over half his years as Emperor away from Rome, travelling the frontiers and provinces of the Empire.

Hadrian also never forgot the lesson he had learned at the start of his succession and around this time the *Frumentarii* were set up to watch over what was happening across the Imperial Borders. The Emperor had originally depended upon the Military Governors of each country for their intelligence on the security situation of their provinces. Hadrian decided this was not enough and a central military intelligence would be employed. These men were originally couriers charged with the conveyance of military dispatches. Many of them became attached to the Imperial Service as a secret police. This network had exclusive powers and reported back to Hadrian everything that was happening. Roman historian Aurelius Victor quotes their duties were to 'Investigate and report of potential rebellions in all provinces'.

Hadrian eventually left Antioch, almost a year after he had been crowned Emperor, leaving Catilius Severus as Governor of Syria. He travelled back to Rome where he was received very coldly by the senate. Hadrian resented Attianus' power over Rome and asked him to retire with immediate effect. Due to the politics of the situation, not least Attianus being head of the Praetorian Guard, it proved difficult to persuade him to stand down.

Attianus eventually retired in 119 A.D. and he was still a powerful figure. Nothing was ever heard of him again. Hadrian, of course, visited Britain in 121 A.D., where the construction of the wall that would bear his name had already started. The design of the wall had started several years before around 119 AD and its possible that Hadrian had visited as coins were issued. General Falco was dismissed by Hadrian and General Nepos installed as the new Governor of Britannia.

A massive troop redeployment swung into action bringing the Northern frontier back under control with the II Augusta, VI Vitrix and the XX Valeria Victrix being moved north.

Marcius Turbo had a long and distinguished career in the Roman army. He established military control over Egypt and eventually Cyprus and was a close friend, advisor and confidante of Hadrian. Hadrian elevated Turbo to the position Praetorian Prefect, the leader of the Praetorian Guard, after returning to Rome in 125 A.D.

Hadrian would have been well aware of the public outcry at the loss of a Roman Legion in Britannia. It remains unknown if Hadrian ordered the removal of the Legion number IX from the army list. However, it would seem on the surface that since this had happened to Caesar Augustus some 100 years before, it was following the same precedent. The public disgrace of the defeated legion could be seen as a condemnation of having failed their duty to Rome. The cohort left behind at Eboracum and the remaining survivors would be simply re-distributed amongst the new units being deployed.

Hadrian's Wall remains the largest and most impressive building project ever completed by the Romans in Britain. A wall, 73 miles long and nearly 10 feet thick. It was a clear declaration of what the empire was and where its limit reached. During his life time Hadrian consolidated the boundaries of the empire, which stretched from Britain to Africa, Spain to Asia and which contained some 60 million people.

It is now possible to walk the wall and stay in guest houses as your luggage is taken ahead of you. This is an easy way to travel as you take in the awe-inspiring views and visit the forts and museums to see what it was like at the time.

Tribal uprising and present-day locations

Based upon the historical quotes, evidence of wars with Britons, Roman pottery in York, tiles found in Nijmegen, tombstones found in Vindolanda and Hadrians own personal circumstances of politics, the conditions existed that the legion was annihilated and its fate covered up for sake of public morale.

The steps which Hadrian took to repair the damage suggest that the seat of disturbance lay just north of the present day Hadrians Wall.

This was a huge uprising of the tribes in northern England and southern Scotland and it would have been the Ninth Legion's responsibility to quell this revolt. Marching north up Dere Street (Via Domitiana) and using the old Roman road, they would have easily marched over their old ground. Looking at the map north of York, there is only one area around the borders containing enough hills to allow an ambush orchestrated by large numbers of rebellious tribesmen. Just after crossing the Pennine Way in the Cheviot Hills and then heading into Scotland, the Roman road becomes confusingly hilly.

These hills were the very ones the Romans had signal stations on and to this day outline defences still survive.

Wooden Law (Hades End) is the highest hill in the area and provides a clear vantage point over southern Scotland. Brownheart Law (Last Hope) has already been proven to be a Roman signal station for the area. Having walked the landscape myself, I have discovered it to be the only route surrounded by enough hills to allow any Roman column to be constricted and stopped. The area would be well known to the Roman officers – as it is near their old marching camp at Pennymuir. After almost a full day's march they would be concentrating on getting across the Kale water ford and building their camp once again.

After studying the entire vicinity at ground level, I became aware that the hill the Romans withdraw up is actually called Standard Knowe. A coincidence? It is an enjoyable walk from the outline marching camps at Chew Green to Pennymuir and back again; the journey takes a whole day. For further walking information I would recommend *The Legacy of Rome* by Lawrence Keppie (John Donald Publishers, 2004).

It took almost 2,000 years before a British amateur archaeologist discovered the site where the Romans lost three legions in Germany in 9 A.D. The location of the last stand of the Ninth Legion remains waiting to be discovered.

Brian Young